*Redway Acres
Helena*

*By
Trish Henry Green*

This book is a work of fiction.
Names, characters, places and events are products of
the author's imagination or used fictitiously.
Any resemblance to actual events, locales or persons
is entirely coincidental.

Copyright © 2016 by Trish Henry Green
All Rights Reserved

ISBN: 979-8-8781-0991-8

Cover design and interior illustrations
by Adriana Tonello

For

Emily

Redway Acres

The Redway Acres saga chronicles the lives of several dynamic women, beginning with Helena, the granddaughter of Redway's owner. Each title character in the series confronts a challenge women faced in the early 19th century, including forced marriage, domestic abuse, property rights, and the impediments to owning a business or pursuing a profession.

Redway Acres' stable in Lincolnshire, near Grantham in England, is the common ground for the six families portrayed in the saga: the Stocktons who own Redway Acres, the Harkers from the neighbouring estate of Eastease, the ennobled Ackleys, the beleaguered Wyndhams, the well-connected Bainbridges, and the notable but unwealthy Hopwoods.

Although each story is standalone, the series should be read in the suggested order to avoid spoilers, as the timelines of the families intertwine throughout.

The Redway companion books explore the lives of minor characters in the series whose behind-the-scenes stories begged the author to pick up her pen again.

Become immersed in the lives, loves, and hardships of the women and men destined to cross paths at Redway Acres.

Praise for the Redway Acres Saga

"Once you meet these characters, you will not be able to put the books down."

"I love Redway's strong female characters."

Helena (he-LAY-nah)
Shining light/The bright one

~

Coverture

By marriage, the husband and wife are one person in law: that is, the very being or legal existence of the woman is suspended during the marriage, or at least is incorporated and consolidated into that of the husband: under whose wing, protection, and cover, she performs every thing; and is therefore called in our law-French a feme-covert; is said to be covert-baron, or under the protection and influence of her husband, her baron, or lord; and her condition during her marriage is called her coverture.

From William Blackstone's Commentaries on the Laws of England (1765)

~

It is a truth universally acknowledged, that a widow in possession of property, must be in want of a husband.

Variation of the opening line of Pride and Prejudice by Jane Austen (1813)

~

He's more myself than I am. Whatever our souls are made out of, his and mine are the same.

Wuthering Heights ~ Emily Brontë (1847)

~

www.trishhenrygreen.com

Redway Acres books in order
Redway Acres – Helena
Redway Acres – Maria
Redway Acres – Martha
Redway Acres – Harriet
A Redway Companion - Charlie
Redway Acres – Amelia
Redway Acres – Emmalee

Note

The first six Redway Acres books and 'A Redway Companion ~ Charlie' were previously released under the author name 'Trish Butler'. The main stories remain; however, some scenes have been deleted and may return in future books.

WARNING

This book is not suitable for readers under 18 years of age. It contains detailed sex scenes, and elements of violence and sexual abuse.

Map

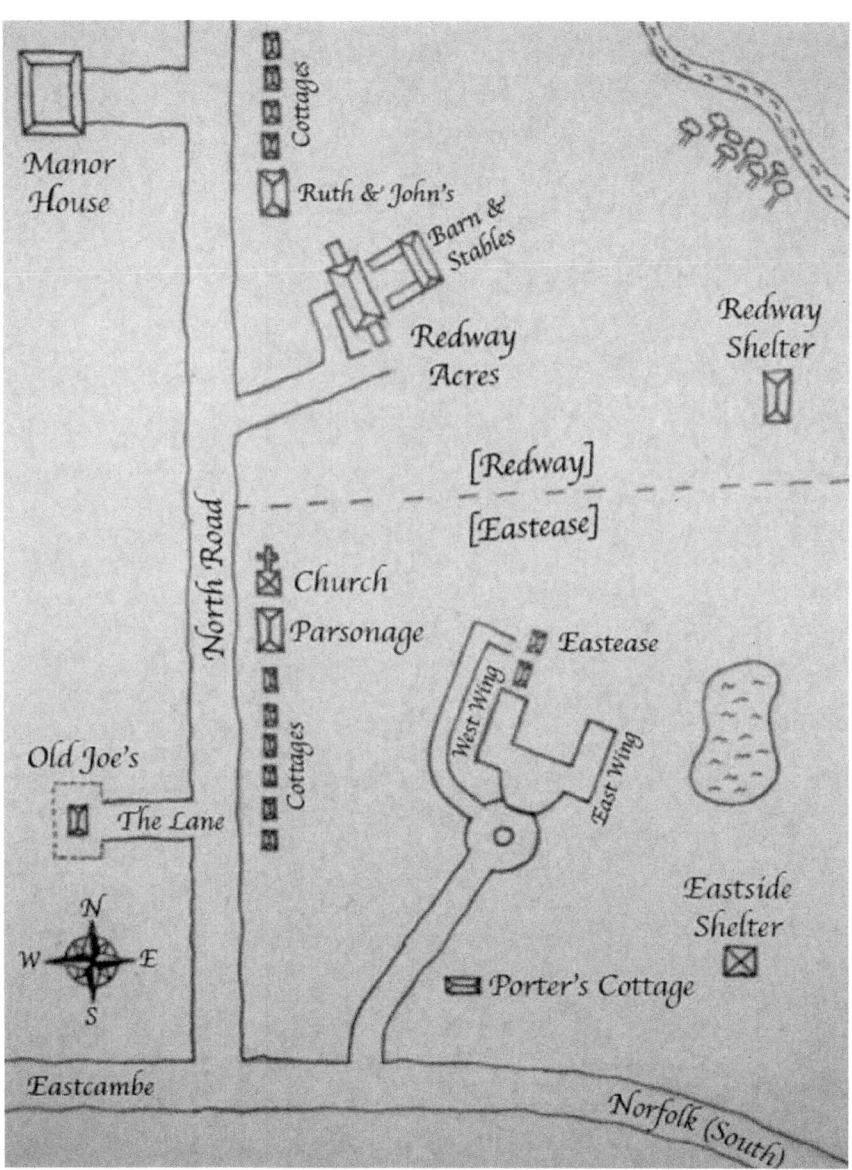

Prologue

Always the cuckoo in the Billings family nest, it was time for Helena to fly.

She studied her mother within the fussy parlour for any acknowledgement, but the woman stared resolutely out a window from her position in an ornate, uncomfortable armchair. Her hair cinched into a tight, ordered bun, and her expression forbidding.

Helena's travelling cloak draped from her shoulders, curtaining the growing mound of her abdomen while she deliberately resisted straightening her bonnet that sat slightly askew upon her head—red hair escaping in unruly ringlets tickling her face and back of her neck. The disarray would annoy her mother.

With a baby on the way and no husband to support her, Helena expected no help from those she had called family for nearly one-and-twenty years. Still, the sting of her mother blaming Helena and refusing to acknowledge her hurt less than her father not standing up to his wife. So Helena's only recourse had been to write to her beloved grandfather in Lincolnshire. She would be eternally grateful to George

Stockton of Redway Acres stable for welcoming her with open arms.

Helena spoke sadly, "Goodbye, Mother."

Two figures shuffled in the hallway to Helena's left, pulling at her attention. Her father's appearance was rather haggard—the hair at his temples greyer than ever, his dark hair now more salt than pepper. No doubt his wife's complaints about their daughter exacting their toll. Helena's younger brother's hair was as dark as their father's had once been, and he filled the space with a midriff almost as large as her own. They nodded goodbye, then followed their father outside to the coach their grandfather had sent for her.

"Am I to write, Papa?" Helena asked, searing every line of his face to memory lest she never see him again.

"No, it will only cause her, and therefore me, more angst. Ask George to advise me of your safe arrival. That is all."

The tension in her father's voice caused hope to flicker that perhaps he, more than anyone else, felt the pain of her leaving. If that was the case, he chose not to show it. She kept her tears and fears in check.

"Goodbye, Papa."

~oOo~

Two days later, the countryside became more familiar, and Helena rubbed her rounded stomach with relief. The prolonged days of travel caused an ache in her back, and she longed to stretch her legs.

Ruth Robertson, the Billings' cook, and Ruth's two young children accompanied her. Following behind, driving a cart heavy with their belongings, Helena occasionally spied Ruth's husband, John; her greater concern was the large, grey stallion hitched to the cart tail. Thankfully, Perseus maintained the leisurely pace with ease and equanimity. Helena, who shared her grandfather's love of horses and had spent much of her time in her family's stable helping John, held a fondness in her heart for the couple.

"Baby should be 'ere in October, ma'am," Ruth spoke kindly to her new mistress.

"It sounds strange when you call me ma'am."

"Am I to call you Mrs Andrews, then?" Ruth smiled.

Helena's left thumb toyed with the ring on that hand. "Yes, but call me Helena when it's just us. Grandfather is not a stickler about society's rules. Neither was my grandmother. It is a mystery to me where my mother acquired her airs."

"Did Mr Stockton say much about the house we get?"

Helena smiled gently. "No, just that it will be large enough for a family. I suspect it is bigger than the one you had before. You will find out soon enough. The entrance to Eastease is coming up, and Redway is but five miles from there by road."

"And I'm to be the housekeeper? A'yer certain? He 'as not met me yet."

"You are more than capable, Ruth, which I told him. He takes my word seriously."

As they passed the entrance to the grand estate of Eastease, the children clambered over their mother for a glimpse of the large house. Neither would spot even a chimney-pot. Before they reached the village of Eastcambe, they turned down the North Road. Ruth peered anxiously out of the coach window to be sure her husband had managed the turn of the cart and continued to follow them.

Satisfied, she leaned back and pressed Helena again, "And John is to be the stable manager?"

"Grandfather met John as a young boy when my father first set foot at Redway. John is more than capable, too," Helena confirmed.

"Of course he is," Ruth said quickly, not doubting her husband for a moment.

Resigned, Helena shook her head. "You should have as much faith in your capabilities as in his, Ruth."

"Will we stay another night at an inn, Ma?" Ruth's daughter asked.

"We are nearly there," Helena cut across Ruth, who was undoubtedly weary of the children's constant questions about their destination. "All these properties to this side belong to Eastease. Including the church and parsonage coming up. After the church, it is all Redway land."

"Is Eastease a big 'ouse, then?" Ruth's son asked, his gaze fixed on the passing greenery. "I can't see it from 'ere; it can't be tha' big."

Helena confirmed. "I was only fifteen when I last visited Redway, so I did not go inside it. But, it is enormous even from a distance."

"Who lives there?" The children resumed their seats, waiting for Helena's answer. She resigned herself to keeping them occupied for the remaining miles. It would take her mind off her aching back. Helena considered what her grandmother told her about that house's occupants.

"Mr Harker, who is a very wealthy man, owns Eastease. My grandmother told me tales of him and his three friends who were always into mischief when they were younger."

"Who were 'is friends?" the young boy asked, and Helena aimed to satisfy his curiosity with the details she could remember from her grandmother's stories.

The coach turned into the welcoming gates of Redway and pulled to a stop beside an ox of a man with green eyes and a head of thick, red hair. Helena inherited the latter two traits from him.

"Grandfather!" Helena called from within the vehicle. She had not been allowed to visit him in almost six years, but to her, he had not changed one bit. Perhaps a slight sadness around his eyes due to the loss of his wife.

Heedless of her condition, she jumped from the coach and into her grandfather's strong arms. Although she was tall, her head barely reached his broad chest. She sobbed, her long ordeal prior to arriving on this day finally over.

Four Years Later

One

Helena breathed a contented sigh as she led her grey mare, Missy, into the mating paddock behind Redway's southeast row of stalls. The August day promised to be warm, with a blue, cloudless sky into which the mid-morning sun steadily climbed. Life at Redway Acres had been a dream come true for her and her daughter, Isabella, named for Helena's grandmother. She fed the mare a treat with an absent pat to her nose as she considered the irony that her mother's rejection directly caused her happiness.

"What do you think, Missy?" Helena consulted the horse her grandfather had gifted to her after she gave birth to his great-granddaughter. "Is it a good day to make a foal? The filly you and Perseus made for us fetched a fine price from the Cuthbertsons this year."

Her grandfather rounded the barn corner, holding a pulling and prancing Perseus in check. The temperamental stallion baulked at having anyone other than Helena handle him. But her grandfather insisted on managing him today, claiming that once the horse got a whiff of the mare in heat, his struggles would rip the lead rope through Helena's hands, slicing her gloves and flesh like butter.

"He's in a fiery mood," he grunted.

"You can't catch me!" Issie's voice teasing an unseen pursuer tore Helena's eyes away from Perseus as her daughter ran to her from the opposite direction.

"Issie, no!" Helena cried. "Go back to the house." But her determined three-year-old ran on, searing the next moments into Helena's memory.

Scenting the mare, Perseus bolted; the gloves ripped from her grandfather's hands as he tried to restrain the stallion, but even his power was no match for the amorous beast with only one purpose in mind.

He leapt in front of the grey to save his great-granddaughter from being trampled, causing the horse to rear up and lash out with sharp, deadly hooves. Helena scooped up Issie, carrying her to safety as man and beast lurched towards them, locked in a contest of strength and will. A scream came from Issie's nanny, who stood frozen at the stable corner.

Then Helena's grandfather braced against a sturdy fence post, still struggling to control upwards of a thousand pounds of horseflesh. Perseus wheeled his massive body, crushing him against the post before lunging away to get at his prize. The loud crack of bone reached Helena's ears and chilled her heart.

"Grandfather!" Setting Issie down, she ran to his prone form, calling for help as she sank to her knees beside him. His gurgling breaths wheezed, each shallower than the last. Tears welled and streamed down Helena's face as a frail, shaking hand clasped her wrist. Their eyes, so alike, met and held.

"Aw now, Gal," he rasped. "If you are crying, I must be dying."

"No, Grandfather—"

"Not his fault." As he spoke, his eyes rolled in Perseus' direction, then at Issie. "Nor hers."

"G-G-Papa?" Issie's small voice sounded in Helena's ear as she spoke from behind her shoulder.

"I love you, Grandfather."

"Me—an' all—Gal," the words came harder to him. "Don't worry—I've taken care—care of you."

When Helena returned to the kitchen, John was leaning against a cupboard, loading the shotgun, his face a mask of determination.

"He might as well enjoy 'is last moments out there wi' Missy," John said tersely.

"Put it away, John. You are not shooting Perseus." Helena put as much command into her voice as she could muster. Then, overwhelmed with shock and grief, she collapsed into a chair at the kitchen table. "Where have you put my grandfather?"

"Master George is bein' laid out on the dinin' room table," Ruth replied as she brought over a tea tray and poured them each a cup. She sat on one side of Helena, John moving to the other, flanking her as constant pillars of support. Ruth's eyes were tear-filled while John's gaze glinted with cold intent.

John spoke quietly but firmly, "Yer 'ave a soft spot where that 'orse is concerned, Helena. He 'as killed twice. Yer must let me shoot him."

"Where is Dom?" she asked instead. Dom had been her grandfather's friend for decades.

"Out by the paddock, watchin' o'er that brute of an animal."

"Please bring him in here. He is the only other person who knows what happened with Perseus before. I have something to say about it, and with all of you together, I need to explain only once."

After John left, Ruth retrieved two large teacups for the men. "How is Issie?" she asked tentatively.

In tears, Helena buried her face in folded arms while her shoulders shook. With her world collapsing, she must somehow find the strength to be calm for her child and help her endure this ordeal, but for now, the loss overpowered her. Ruth put her arm around her, resting her head on Helena's shoulder, her own tears gathering as she spoke, "Your grandfather wer the best master I 'ave ever known. Best man, aside from my John."

When John and Dom returned, the two women composed themselves again, and Ruth poured the tea. Silence descended as

Helena surveyed their grim faces.

"His last words were that it was neither Perseus' fault nor Issie's. He is right in that. It is as natural as breathing for a stallion to be single-minded with a mare in heat." Pausing, she eyed the men with unwavering resolve. "I forbid you to shoot him."

John shook his head, but Dom nodded in understanding. "Ha'way now, John, the lass is reet. George wouldnae ha blamed thee 'orse."

Helena nodded thanks to Dom, his thick northern accent as understandable to her as any of the local country accents. Then she cleared her throat and steeled herself to say more. "No one is to speak of Issie's part in this. She only needs to know that her G-G-Papa saved her from a wild horse. Grandfather did not blame her; she must not grow up blaming herself. She is but three, and if we are to continue living and working here, she must not be afraid of horses."

Everyone at the table nodded.

"Anyone o' us would ha done the same fah Miss Issie, Missus," Dom said. "I would ha gladly tacken George's place, yae nar. All he did fah me."

Helena scanned his lined face; his kind grey eyes glistened with tears. "Thank you, Dom."

Ruth frowned. "What *is* to become of us, Helena? Will we continue ter live and work here as you say?"

Hearing these words reminded Helena that her mother's rejection had brought about her living at Redway Acres. Now, she was back at square one and might again find herself without a home. Perseus might be hers, but he and Missy were all the property she owned. Even the dowry that her father had given to her grandfather for her care was part of the Redway estate and, therefore, would return to him as the husband of George Stockton's only heir.

Helena stared back at Redway's housekeeper. "Ruth, I have no idea."

~oOo~

Helena stood in Redway's small family cemetery to one side of the gaping hole where they had lowered her grandfather's coffin.

Dressed in black—back straight, head held high, as was her natural posture—the respect and love for George Stockton from the Redway workers a few steps behind her bolstered her.

Joining the mourners at the graveside, the clergyman read from his bible, but Helena barely heard his words. Instead, her gaze roamed the adjacent headstone beneath which her grandmother lay. They would be together, George and Isabella, along with the four children the couple had buried. How different life might have been for them all had any of those children survived. Her mother might have been kinder with siblings to influence her.

Helena did not truly believe in God but hoped there was something after death where souls could exist happily together forever.

"...till thou return unto the ground; for out of it wast thou taken: for dust thou art, and unto dust shalt thou return."

Helena and her parents attended Mr Thorpe in Redway's study. The solicitor set his leather document case on the desk and took up the position behind it—a small man with dark, thinning hair and a kind face. He waited for them to sit before following suit.

Methodically, he opened his case and spread out some pages in front of him, reviewing each one before he spoke. He began with the usual declarations of sound mind, witnesses and the date, which was only months ago. Helena's attention became rapt upon the man behind the desk. *Why did Grandfather change his will such a short time ago?* He had said he had taken care of her, but could he have left a cottage where she and Issie could live?

"To Mrs Helena Andrews, I leave Redway Acres house, stable and barn, one thousand acres of land and all the livestock. I leave the remaining properties, including the five-hundred-acre farm on a long-term lease with Alfred Cranshaw, to Mrs Joy Billings."

Helena could scarcely believe her ears as she held her hands to her chest. *Grandfather has come to our rescue once again, sweet girl,* she thought to her child.

"That cannot be right." Her mother's voice raised considerably in her shock.

"Please allow me to finish, Mrs Billings," Mr Thorpe asked politely, her rude interjection not troubling him. He continued, "*All cash monies are to be divided equally between Mrs Billings and Mrs Andrews, with the exception of the sum Mr Gregory Billings provided me for Mrs Andrews' care. That sum, I wish to be passed to Mrs Andrews in its entirety.*"

"No. I do not accept this will. You—" her mother jabbed a finger in Helena's direction, "—you have schemed and cajoled your way into your grandfather's favour and made the addled old man change his will."

"I am as shocked as you, Mama." Was it possible they could stay at their beloved Redway Acres? This past week of grief and worry melted away from Helena's burden. How wonderful her grandfather had been. She would remember all the goodness he had shown her, all the lessons she had learned from him, and lock them away in a part of her heart reserved solely for George Stockton.

"Mr Thorpe," her mother turned to the man, with a tone that made Helena flinch, "though it pains me to say, I must inform you that this will is null and void. There is no such person as *Mrs Andrews*."

"Mama!" What justification could her mother have for revealing her secrets to this man?

"My dear, I must insist that you say no more. I had been considering Helena's suggestion of her having Redway as her inheritance anyway." For once, her father's tone was firm, but there was no thwarting her mother where Helena was concerned.

"No. She is not going to deprive Isaac of what is rightfully his." Helena's mother turned again to Mr Thorpe. "My daughter never married the father of that child, and now he is dead. She has taken up the name *Mrs Andrews*, but it is not legal. Does she care one jot? Care that anyone could discover her secret and ruin our family name? No, she does not. Until she is respectably married, she is no daughter of mine. As there is no *Mrs Andrews*, she cannot legally inherit."

"Mama, you seem to be the only one willing to reveal this secret."

"Ah, I see." Unperturbed, possibly even amused, Mr Thorpe put away the pages from which he had read and produced a second set. "Mrs Billings, I agree with your assessment. That will is null and void."

Helena's heart sank. She had been so close to independence and providing for her daughter. "What have I done to you to make you wish the worst for me, Mother?"

"What is right is right." Helena's mother seemed satisfied.

"This is the second will Mr George Stockton arranged with me on the same date. All the standard particulars at the beginning of a will are the same. I will continue from the date. *In the event of Mrs Joy Billings revealing my granddaughter's unfortunate circumstances to secure all of my wealth and properties for herself, I hereby declare my first will null and void. This will should be considered its replacement. To my granddaughter, currently known as Mrs Helena Andrews, I leave all my worldly possessions, including Redway Acres, all properties, the Cranshaw farm and all cash monies.*"

"Well, Mother, what is right is right." Helena stood. "Please excuse me; I must attend to my guests. Mr Thorpe, please join us in celebrating the life of my grandfather. I know he will be happy that Redway Acres will continue to thrive and stay within his family."

The man smiled. "Your grandfather was a true gentleman. He trusted me with all his business, and I hope to speak to you often in the same capacity should you wish to retain my services. George asked me to give you this."

Helena took the proffered letter. "Thank you. Of course, I wish to retain you. Mother, Father, the time has come to say goodbye. I hope you have a safe journey back to Norfolk." Helena turned on her heel and walked calmly out of the room. Once she had closed the door on her mother's shrieks, she leaned against it momentarily. "Thank you, Grandfather."

Then she ran to tell Ruth and John the news.

Helena sat in the kitchen of Redway Acres as people milled in and back out into the courtyard. A few neighbours looked in to pay their respects, and Helena had greeted those who expected it in Redway's parlour. Of course, those who knew George Stockton best happily rubbed elbows with the stablemen and their families. But mostly, her horses fared the best as people fed them treats when their heads appeared over the half-stable doors seeking attention. People rubbed their noses and patted their necks, and Helena smiled each time as if her grandfather stood beside her. *There is nothing like the feel of a horse to put your world to rights and ease your soul.*

When there was a lull in proceedings, Helena read the letter Mr Thorpe had given her, smiling, crying and shaking her head throughout the missive.

Helena,

If you are reading this, then I am dead and buried. I hope it has been a long time coming after I've written this note and you have settled. Perhaps you are married with more children? Issie could be grown up with children of her own. Might I even be a great-great-grandfather? Now, that would be something.

Please know I'm not afraid to die. My body will lie in the ground with my Isabella and our children, but my heart and soul will be wherever they are in the afterlife.

I will be content with the knowledge I have provided for you and Issie. Undoubtedly, you will have possession over everything I owned, for surely I understood my daughter well enough to know she would try and take everything from you. I hope she will have learned a lesson from it, but I find it doubtful. My wish was that Joy, or at least your father, would effect a reconciliation with you.

Redway will survive without me. It has you, and I have yet to meet a better horse trainer. I am so proud of you. Still, you do not have a head for business. The basics, yes, but Redway will need to grow, and you will need a husband to guide it.

If you have not already found one, get out there and meet the right people. Despite your mother's failings, she has prepared you to rub elbows with the 'toffs', as Dom would call them. Find a husband who will work with you to make Redway all it can be. Choose wisely, and I do not doubt that you and Redway will thrive, for he will see the benefit of you working beside him.

However, many years bestowed upon me, having you here has got me through. If that old blaggard Joe Baxter has outlived me, take care of him.

I love you, my delightful granddaughter, and there isn't a soul alive who could not love our Issie.

Your Grandfather and proud G-G-Papa

Helena looked up from the letter into the kind face of Ruth, who had always been more like a mother to her than her own.

"Old Joe didn't make it to see Grandfather off?"

Ruth smiled a little. "Yer didn't expect him to, did yer? Too many people fer his taste. He'll be along in his own good time."

Helena nodded. "Ready a basket for him, would you please? I'll have John harness the gig and will see him now. Further guests are unlikely today."

~oOo~

Helena drove the gig easily down the North Road, taking the right turn into The Lane that led to Old Joe's cottage. After tethering the horse out front, she knocked on the door before opening it and calling, "Joe, it is Helena. Are you here?"

"Where else wud Oi be?" Joe croaked from the parlour.

Helena stopped in the small kitchen to put the basket of wares on the table before picking up two glasses and the stoppered bottle she had brought with her. Then, entering the parlour, she placed the glasses on the table flanked by two armchairs, one of them occupied by a wizened man of dark skin and grey hair—Old Joe, as frail as her grandfather had been robust though only a year separated them. After pouring two glasses of whisky, she passed one to Joe, picked up the second, and sat in the empty armchair.

"T' George," Joe said and raised his glass. "Gawd bless yer. Oi'll miss yer."

"To Grandfather." Helena toasted before knocking back the amber liquid.

Joe picked up the bottle and poured himself a second. He lifted his eyes to Helena, but she shook her head.

"Just the one for me, Old Joe."

"How'd yer ma take the will readin'?" Joe said with a chuckle

"You knew? Of course you did. There was a lot of shrieking and name-calling. On her part, not mine. I said goodbye and left the room."

"D'yer get the lot?"

"Yes, everything. I'd rather have him back, though."

"O'course yer wud, Gal. We all wud, but na one can live fa'ever. Not ev'n George." Joe lifted his second glass and drank deeply.

"He wrote me a letter. The solicitor gave it to me."

"Wha'd he say?"

"That, while I could run Redway as it stands, I would need a man to make it more successful—to marry."

"Tha's funny. I found a letter from my Bertha t'other day, said much the same. I'd go ter wrack an' ruin if I din' find someone ter take care o' me."

"You found a letter? Where was it? She died twenty years ago, Joe."

"T'was inside Bertha's remedy book. Ah, Gawd bless 'er."

"I'm so glad you found it, Joe." Helena's eyes filled with tears as she patted his arm. "You did not want to marry again. Now you have Issie and me to look after you, and if ever you tire of living alone, you need only ask. We have room for you at Redway."

"There's a'nuff a tha'," he said gruffly, briefly putting a hand over hers. "We wer talkin' of yer marryin'."

Helena sighed. "I do not want to marry. Grandfather knew that. I have John—"

"John canna move in the circles George cud. Fer all 'is rolled-up sleeves an' muckin' in wi' the men, George wer a gen'leman. 'E wer a rare breed tha' cud mix in both circles. Same as yer. Mebbe, yer'll find a man like tha'?"

"Only today, I have become an independent woman. Why would I give that up? Why would I marry and give myself and everything I have to a husband?"

"I din't say yer 'ad ter marry 'im. Yer cud employ 'im as a manager o' sorts?"

She smiled. "I could do that, and then I need not get myself out and about as Grandfather said."

"I don' see as tha' wud hurt none fer yer business. And yer're a yung 'un. 'Ave some fun. Yer still 'ave ter find this man. Yer gon' ter have ter mix."

"I will think about it, but first, I must mourn Grandfather."

Joe picked up the third glass of whisky he had poured and tipped it towards her in a salute once again. "Here's ter yer, Gal. Find yerself a man, either ter marry yer or ter manage yer. If he be brave a'nuff, p'haps both, an' Gawd bless 'im—'e'll need it."

Two

Clouds of smoke drifted across the battlefield as Colonel Nathaniel Ackley wiped gore from his sword blade. He sat astride his chestnut stallion, Thor, surveying the carnage spread over the shell-torn landscape. What had begun as a sunny, late June day had deteriorated into a bloodbath. The lull in the fighting enabled Nathaniel to assess a battleground littered with the bodies of his comrades and their French foes. Those of the enemy who had not fled lay dead or dying in the bloodstained grass. Many British uniforms adorned the casualties, too, and Nathaniel swallowed down his remorse. Today was not the first time he had witnessed such a sight, and against all hope, it would not be the last. They had not defeated Napoleon Bonaparte, and until they did, the horrific battles would continue, keeping Nathaniel on foreign soil.

As the smoke from the cannon fire cleared, a dark figure rose from the maze of strewn bodies. Nathaniel tensed, sword at the ready, then relaxed again—British uniform. The soldier stood awkwardly and hobbled as he tried to walk. Focusing upon the man's face,

Nathaniel recognised Tommy Smithson, an army stableman who enjoyed working with the sometimes-temperamental Thor. Sheathing his weapon, Nathaniel started the stallion at a slow trot towards the injured man.

"Colonel!" Tommy called out in acknowledgement.

Movement on the field behind Tommy caught Nathaniel's attention—another rider galloping full speed towards the soldier, his drawn sword aimed at Tommy's heart.

"Tommy, beware!" Nathaniel shouted, pointing at the Frenchman while urging Thor to move faster, confident he could reach Tommy first. Seeing another bearing down on his quarry, the French soldier shifted to pass Tommy on the opposite side and avoid a collision.

Halting Thor, Nathaniel reached down for Tommy, but they were not quick enough to escape the charging threat. The air rushed around Nathaniel as the French horseman swept past.

Instinctively shielding Tommy with his body, the Frenchman's bright steel flashed towards Nathaniel. The movement of the horse carrying the sword upwards as it whipped across his torso, the razor-sharp edge searing his flesh as the blade parted his heavy coat as easily as his skin. The strike carved a deep wound from his ribs to his shoulder.

With pain overwhelming him, Nathaniel battled his fear to breathe evenly as the danger was not over. After Tommy pushed him upright, he scanned the area within a narrowing field of vision to find the Frenchman. Hunched over his horse's neck, he would not remain conscious much longer. "Tommy, where is he?"

The Frenchman came out of nowhere, hurtling towards them at the gallop. Nathaniel tried to reach his sword, but the slightest movement caused blood to gush from his wound onto Thor's neck and withers, making his head swim with nausea. From the periphery of his vision, he saw Tommy pull a knife from his boot. Taking careful aim, Tommy threw it as straight as an arrow. Nathaniel heard the horse's hooves slow and then stop, followed by the dull thud of a body striking the ground.

"Tommy?"

"He's dead, sir."

"Thank God. Come—mount up behind me." Nathaniel did what he could with his remaining strength to help Tommy aboard Thor. Warmth spread across his chest as blood continued to flow from him; everywhere else, he felt cold.

Cradled against Tommy's chest, Nathaniel was vaguely aware of him taking control of the reins. Under Tommy's guidance, Thor cantered towards the relative safety of the British encampment. Nathaniel fought to remain conscious, to make the journey easier for both passenger and horse, but the light diminished to a mere pinpoint in his vision.

"Take me home, Tommy," he murmured, his last thought a hope that his body, at least, would reach England for interment in the family tomb.

Tommy's reply, "Yes, Colonel," faded in Nathaniel's ears as he succumbed to oblivion.

~oOo~

At Eastease in Lincolnshire, unaware of his friend's peril, Alexander Harker surveyed the flowering gardens out the French doors of his study. Nearly a year had passed since his marriage, and Genevieve grew larger every day with their first child. Life was peaceful and good, yet one problem troubled him—Harriet Wyndham, for whom he and Nathaniel were guardians.

Alexander's consternation involved a recent connection between Harriet and their widowed neighbour. Mrs Andrews, the young widow of a captain who died fighting in France and the granddaughter of George Stockton, had inherited Redway Acres stable from her grandfather after his death in a tragic accident. Since making Mrs Andrews' acquaintance, Harriet had become outspoken about a woman's role in marriage and decision-making. After each visit to Redway, she talked endlessly of its female owner, so much so that Alexander had seriously considered forbidding Harriet from seeing the woman until Genevieve mentioned that banning anything might make it more enticing.

But today had been the final straw. Harriet returned to Eastease, asking to be allowed to wear breeches beneath her skirts and ride astride a horse rather than side-saddle. Recalling his reaction, Alexander shook his head and sighed.

There was a gentle knock at the door.

"Come," he ordered and turned from the view when Genevieve entered, her soft brown hair framing her face in ringlets, her pale blue eyes filled with concern.

"How is she? Is she still angry with me?" he asked, grateful Genevieve put out her hands to comfort him.

When Harriet had made her request, he was so shocked he had brooked no argument from her after his refusal. She had been upset, saying she only wished to ride astride at Eastease. *I am not planning to ride through the village of Eastcambe naked, like Lady Godiva through Coventry!* she had shouted before storming out of the room. An action reminiscent of her absent twin.

"Yes, she is, but it will pass," Genevieve consoled him.

"She wants to ride astride her horse." He shook his head again, still aghast.

"I know," Genevieve answered with a small smile.

Alexander returned her smile ruefully. "Since she made friends with Mrs Andrews, she is all we hear of, and her influence may not be the best thing for Harriet."

Genevieve nodded in understanding. "Well, you wanted Harriet to become more outspoken and express her opinions. Unfortunately, those opinions would never mesh entirely with yours, and this outburst is the price we pay."

Alexander harrumphed. His wife was an expert negotiator—her skills honed, no doubt, from soothing the friction between her parents.

"Mrs Andrews is a widow, and with her grandfather dying so suddenly last year, I am afraid she does not have a male influence in her household. George asked my opinion on leaving the stable to her rather than his son-in-law, who has no passion for horses. He had hoped it would encourage her to marry, which would certainly put to rest some of the rumours around the village."

Genevieve sat down on a loveseat and rubbed the mound of her stomach. "Since when have you listened to village news? All I hear of Mrs Andrews is that she does a lot of good for people in the area."

Alexander did not usually take heed of such talk, but he could not be too cautious where Harriet was concerned. Though he had been close to George Stockton, he knew little of the man's granddaughter as she had kept mainly to Redway since her arrival. He had seen her out visiting those in need, but there had been no opportunity for an introduction between them. "People wonder why she does not have family visit her. Then again, they rarely visited her Grandfather either. She keeps to herself, and anyone interested in horses buys from her because she breeds and trains the best in the county. Should I forbid the acquaintance? Whether or not she is a good influence, poor Harriet has had little in the way of friendship in the year since Maria married."

Genevieve's kind eyes held sympathy as she made her suggestion. "It was so sad that her grandfather died so close to our wedding day. Then she was in mourning, but I should have visited her. I will do so."

He sat beside her and placed his hand on her stomach. "You could go in the new coach to visit her. That would be most comfortable. I think that might be the best course of action. How on earth did I manage to do anything without you?" He smiled.

"I am sure I have no idea." She giggled as he manoeuvred her onto his lap.

~oOo~

When Nathaniel regained consciousness, he was surprised, yet very grateful, to be alive. Tommy had single-handedly brought him back from Spain to the south coast of England, and they convalesced together at a convent hospital. Seeing the big man without his lower leg and foot was disconcerting and guilt-provoking. Tommy had avoided treatment for his broken leg to take care of Nathaniel.

Weeks later, Nathaniel came out of the building entrance to greet his mother standing nearby an Aysthill carriage. "Mother, I am surprised to see you. I had planned to make my own way north."

Lady Aysthill was shocked. "I doubt you are well enough. Gather what you have, and we will be on our way. This is no place for you, and your attire is atrocious."

"This place saved my life, Mother. As did a young man named Tommy Smithson, whom I would like to ride with us. His family lives in Sheffield. A carriage can take him home after we stop at Aysthill."

His mother's face blanched. "Sheffield? Who is his family?"

Nathaniel refrained from rolling his eyes at her words, hoping to be as tactful as possible, but there was no covering the truth. "There is only his mother and father. Unfortunately, his father is ill and can no longer work in the mine."

"The son of a mine worker! This is the man you want to ride in our coach?"

"I insist. You would be here collecting my body were it not for Tommy."

Lady Aystill looked up at her son with an exasperated expression. "He can ride with the driver."

"But he has lost a leg."

"He can still sit; can he not?"

The carriage pulled away from the convent hospital within the hour—with Tommy sitting alongside the driver and Thor tethered behind. Nathaniel, now formally dressed, sat inside the vehicle. Uncomfortable within the hot confines, he was less sorry for Tommy than expected. When his mother began to regale Nathaniel with news of their family, he closed his eyes and rested his head against the window. The droning of her voice faded in and out while he sought the oblivion of sleep.

"Your cousin, Grace, has written to me often to find out how you are faring. She is very concerned. When you are fully recovered, you should visit her. Perhaps you can consider selling your commission? You are thirty, after all. You should be taking a wife and making a family of your own. You could not do any better than Grace..."

~oOo~

Helena rode Perseus side-saddle to keep Harriet company. They rode over green fields, allowing their horses free rein to race across the grass. Helena led them to a favoured spot by a small stream. A willow hung low over the water, and several trees grew in a little copse, perfect for hide-and-seek or chase with Issie. They dismounted and walked the horses over to the stream to drink.

"Is everything well, Harriet?" Helena asked with a glance at the young woman's concerned face. With her cheeks warm from the exertion of riding, Helena sorely wished to join the horses dipping their faces in the cool babbling stream.

Harriet still looked perfectly groomed from head to toe, though her eyes were red and puffy. *Does anything make this young woman look unpolished?* Helena wondered. Her own hair was escaping its confines; her bonnet had fallen and was held on only by the ribbons tight at her neck.

Helena recalled submitting to her mother's ministrations every five minutes due to some hair being out of place or a ribbon being untied. Then she shook off the contemplation of her parents, with whom she had no contact since the day of her grandfather's burial. To distract her thoughts, she encouraged Harriet to confide in her. "Please tell me what is upsetting you."

"As you know, Alexander is not my only guardian," Harriet began firmly, her voice only faltering as she spoke of her cousin, Colonel Ackley. "We had word last week that the colonel sustained an injury in a battle in Spain. He has been brought back to England and is recovering near the south coast. Lady Aysthill went to collect him. She should be there by now."

"So it is good that he is recovering and will return to his home soon?" Helena asked gently, placing a hand on Harriet's arm.

"Yes, but I wanted to go and see him for myself. He has cared for my sister and me over the years, and I should be caring for him." Harriet looked forlorn, which raised an affectionate smile from Helena. Sometimes, the girl still showed herself through the woman.

"You must be excited at seeing him again," Helena suggested, hoping to lighten her mood. Harriet clearly felt concerned about her other guardian.

"But he will be at Aysthill. Alexander will visit him, but Genevieve will not want to go, and I can't leave her alone. I will not be allowed to go alone. I must wait until he is strong enough to visit us."

"Issie and I will visit you shortly. That will be fun, will it not?" Helena was unsure whether she was trying to convince Harriet or herself, but she had no choice but to agree to the invitation to return Genevieve Harker's visit to Redway.

"It will, of course. Do you think Alexander will forbid me to visit here?"

"I hope not. Issie and I love your visits, and so do the horses. I will do all I can to show that I hope only to open your mind. I would never force my views upon you but encourage you to think for yourself. You are intelligent enough to listen to a friend and your guardian and make your own decisions. Neither of us should be upset with you if you agree with the other."

"You would not be angry with me if I did not agree with you?"

"Of course not."

Upon these words, a more carefree attitude came over Harriet, and she broadly smiled as she asked after Helena's dams, which would be foaling soon.

"In another month or so, we will have two new foals," Helena confirmed.

"It is so exciting. Not long after, there will also be a baby at Eastease."

As the women continued to walk and enjoy the day, they talked more of the two dams.

~oOo~

Luncheon at Eastease had been a pleasant distraction to Helena's concerns over what Mr Harker might have to say about her relationship with his ward. Harriet had been showing Issie the pianoforte when the tall man entered the room, praising her daughter's efforts to emulate Harriet and kindly insisting upon Harriet's suggestion of lessons for Issie.

When the group made their way to the stairs to view the new nursery, which was ready for the birth of the couple's first child, Mr Harker asked Helena for a quick word in his study, assuring her they would rejoin everyone else shortly. With a glance first at Genevieve, Helena followed Mr Harker towards a dark oak door across the hallway after receiving her friend's encouraging nod.

As she entered his study, Helena took in the rich sights and smells of old polished wood, well-loved leather upholstery and expensive lamp oil approvingly. She imagined he worked hard at the broad mahogany desk he moved naturally to stand behind. The room was very functional, but with views out to the luscious gardens of Eastease, it was restful, too.

Her comfortable surroundings did little to calm Helena's sensibilities. She sat in the chair Mr Harker had indicated, her back straight as was her habit.

"Mrs Andrews, I would like to apologise for being remiss in expressing my condolences for the loss of your grandfather in person. He and I often discussed business, and I miss him. He was an admirable man, and I am sure he is dearly remembered."

"Thank you, Mr Harker." She did not move as he clearly had more to say.

"During one of our many conversations, George spoke of his decision to bequeath Redway Acres to you. He appealed to me to assist you if ever the need arose. I want to encourage you to make use of my knowledge of business. I would be happy to serve you and fulfil his wishes."

"Thank you again. How very generous of you to offer your time." Still, she waited.

"My pleasure, Mrs Andrews. And now, I would like to make a request of you." Mr Harker leaned forward. Resting his elbows on his desk, he joined his fingertips to form an arch. His intense, brown eyes gazed over them at her. "I am delighted that Harriet and my wife have found a friend in you. However, I would like to request that you refrain from imposing your, let us call them, independent opinions on Harriet, who is at an impressionable age."

Interesting that he only mentioned his ward in that request, she thought. Before he could take her silence for acquiescence, in the way that most men would, Helena replied, "Mr Harker, let me ask you this. Should I require your business opinion, as you have generously offered, would you inform me of a course of action I must take, or would we discuss the merits of various approaches from which I would be free to choose?"

"The latter, of course," he exclaimed with surprise.

"Then please be assured, when Harriet has sought my opinion on any matter, we have always discussed the merits of varying viewpoints. I have given her my thoughts with reasoned arguments, and she has been free to make her own decisions. You have no need to make this request, as your ward is an elegant, intelligent, caring, and charming young woman, Mr Harker. She is also a first-rate horsewoman. You have raised her very well, and I value her friendship."

"On Harriet's finer points, we certainly agree, Mrs Andrews." Alexander nodded with a wry smile. He recalled Genevieve warning him that this woman was quick-witted. Mrs Andrews had outsmarted him quite calmly, and he looked forward to discussing business with her in the future. "Let us rejoin the others."

~oOo~

In the weeks since Nathaniel returned to Aysthill, his mother's instructions to staff saw him regress to childhood. Once again, he had to fight to find his way in the world. Her insistence on knowing his every move was as stifling as the heat from the fire constantly built up in every room. For the first week, Nathaniel's only escape was at night, sneaking out to the stable just as he had done as a child.

After a while, his mother stopped fussing whenever he left his bed, although she continued to talk of him giving up the life of a soldier and a bachelor. She also had an idea as to whom he should marry. Nathaniel subjected himself to her demanding care only because she had been so upset over his brush with death. And, if he were honest, he was rather weak.

More recently, his stamina had significantly improved, and a visit to his long-time friend was in order before he behaved very badly towards his well-meaning but intrusive mother. With this in mind, he put pen to paper.

Harker,

I hope this finds you, Mrs Harker and my dear Harriet in good health. After my previous letter from the convent hospital, I am pleased to confirm I am much recovered.

The final step in my recuperation should be a trip to Eastease, lively conversations and superb music. All of which, I am sure your wife and my cousin could provide.

What say you, Harker? Can you endure me for a few weeks before Mother drives Father and me completely mad? She has every fire roaring and talks of nothing but when I will sell my commission and marry.

I think that she may wish to see me in situ before she rests at ease at home. Perhaps a dinner invitation would not be too much of an imposition? Include William and Phoebe, as my brother is visiting at present. I promise to remove myself once the heir to Eastease is born, if not before.

Confirm as soon as you can. I am already packing. Yours,

Ackers

~oOo~

Upon reading his friend's letter, Alexander smiled. He had worried about Ackers, but so much of the colonel's humour shone through in the short note his concern subsided. After dashing off his reply, he went to find his wife and Harriet.

Fortuitously, he found them in a meeting with Eastease's housekeeper, making arrangements for Genevieve's aunt and uncle, who were to visit before Genevieve's confinement. Alexander informed the ladies of their impending visitor and requested dinner.

Harriet spoke quickly, "Is he really well enough to visit?"

"Yes," Alexander assured her. "He says that Lady Aysthill will not leave him alone."

Gennie laughed. "He will not be happy with that."

"Neither is Lord Aysthill, as his wife insists upon a blazing fire in whatever room Ackers is in." Alexander joined in with the laughter.

"Knowing Nathaniel," Harriet said through her giggles, "he is probably following his father around the house just to annoy him."

Alexander agreed, "At least until he notices how unfair that is on the servants. His mother talks of him giving up life as a soldier and getting married."

Gennie gave him a knowing smile. "Does he mention how often the countess has suggested Lady Grace as a good wife?"

"He does not say. I am simply relieved he is much recovered and would like to visit Eastease. He says he needs some lively conversation and superb music."

"Oh yes, he must come here," Gennie agreed. "I am sure Aunt and Uncle would love to reacquaint themselves with him. Should we invite Mr Brooks, our new clergyman, to dinner? But then, who to make an even number?"

"How about Mrs Andrews?" Harriet suggested.

"Alexander, did you not say she had refused to sell a horse to Lord Aysthill the other day?" Genevieve's voice held concern.

Alexander considered. The woman could not avoid the earl forever, and their meeting again might as well take place under Eastease's roof, where he could oversee any unpleasantness. He owed George Stockton that, at least.

"She did. Just be sure you do not sit Mrs Andrews next to him. I will keep an eye on the proceedings to ensure everything remains cordial."

Harriet rose. "I will take the invitation personally. You know Helena is not one for social gatherings. However, I have an idea for some entertainment. I hope to talk her into it."

Three

"Colonel Ackley, welcome to Eastease," Genevieve Harker greeted him with a curtsey, as gracious as always. Marriage and impending motherhood served her well, for she looked radiant.

He bowed. "Thank you, Mrs Harker. And I thank you for the invitation to stay awhile." In response to her raised eyebrows and slight glance behind him, he explained, "I rode ahead of the rest of my family. So we have but a few minutes respite before they descend."

"How are you, Nathaniel?" she asked. Last Christmas, he requested a brother's privilege and allowed her to use his given name. "Are you fully recovered?"

"I am well, I assure you."

The noise of Harker striding into the room prevented the need for him to provide further detail. He turned to greet Harker and quickly found himself in his friend's hearty embrace.

"It is good to be at Eastease again, Harker. Thank you for inviting me, or should I say for accepting my invitation to myself. My word, I must say that marriage suits you."

Harker's frown did not directly disappear. Instead, he studied Nathaniel intently, clearly concerned about his physical well-being. Put in mind of their long-time friend, Mark Wyndham, who had died in battle many years prior, Nathaniel smiled to allay Harker's worry. For possibly the first time since being wounded, a genuine smile stretched across his face, crinkling the corners of his eyes. Coming here had been the right thing to do.

"I am good, my friend. I am well, I swear to you. A good dose of Eastease and escape from Mother is what I need."

Harker's anxious expression dissolved into a grin. "Then you are welcome, Ackers."

"Cousin!" This exclamation came from Harriet, who forgot all her training and wrapped her arms around his neck. Nathaniel supposed he was the closest relation she had to a father now that her stepfather had passed away.

"Harriet," he murmured as he returned the embrace, "You have not lost any youthful exuberance. That was my best welcome since setting foot back in England."

The noise of the rest of the Ackley family's arrival filtered into the sitting room. Eastease's butler announced from the doorway, "The Earl and Countess of Aystill, sir. And the Viscount and Viscountess."

Harker welcomed them all to his home.

"So, you see for yourself, Alexander, Nathaniel is recovering superbly," said Lady Aysthill.

"Indeed, I do, My Lady. Your ministrations have worked wonders."

Nathaniel smiled gratefully when Genevieve, always astute to others' distress, directed the discussion to another path. "My aunt and uncle arrive this afternoon. I know they will gladly reacquaint themselves with you, Colonel."

"And I, them," he replied, asking after all her family.

The awkward moment forgotten, Genevieve addressed the whole group, advising them that the final members of their party for dinner would be Mr Eliot Brooks, their new local clergyman, and Mrs Helena Andrews of Redway Acres stable.

"Harriet and I recently became friends with Mrs Andrews,"

Genevieve explained to Nathaniel as her husband engaged the rest of the Ackleys in conversation. "Of course, they have horses in common, which I understand is a failing of mine."

"Quite so," added Harriet. "Alexander's two Yorkshire Coach Horses that you hanker after come from her stable, Cousin."

"And does she also share your love of music, Harriet," Nathaniel asked, "or do you only talk of horses?" To his enjoyment, Harriet was no longer reluctant to join in a conversation. *Did this, Mrs Andrews, have something to do with that?*

"She does not play an instrument," Harriet replied. "Says she has neither the time nor the patience for it. Claims that she would rather spend her time with a living, breathing thing, preferably a horse."

Enjoying everyone's laughter, Harriet continued, "She does, however, have a wonderful singing voice. So we have been practising a surprise for you tonight, providing neither of us loses our nerve."

"Then I cannot wait to meet her, Harriet." Nathaniel smiled, pleased that his ward was moving in social circles beyond the familiar environment of Eastease.

~oOo~

While the Harkers greeted their guests that afternoon, a nervous Helena sought refuge in Redway Acres' stable. Being in the company of horses had always calmed her, but today, not even her beloved beasts could achieve that.

"Oh, why did I acquiesce to this dinner party?" she muttered for the hundredth time. "Why did I say I would sing that ridiculous aria?"

Going to the dinner party was in honour of her grandfather's memory. It had, after all, been his wish that Helena move in more social circles. Then, the charming sight of Harriet enthralled by the romance of the music, such that none of the usual qualms about performing marred the young woman's face, caused Helena to agree to sing. Harriet had spoken of Leonore's love for her husband and how she posed as a guard to free him from unjust imprisonment. Such a strong woman, willing to serve her husband so daringly, certainly appealed.

At first, Helena understood the audience to be the Harkers and their friend. Now, there would be an audience of ten, including Lord Aysthill, with whom she'd had a heated disagreement about selling her horses. She could not back down.

Helena left the stable with renewed determination to arrange Issie's care with Ruth. After spending time with her daughter, she swallowed her misgivings and headed to Eastease for dinner. She rode Perseus so she could wake early in the morning and return to Redway without much assistance.

~oOo~

Nathaniel visited Thor and discussed the horse's care with a young stableman named Adam, who was good at handling the beast. After Adam departed, Nathaniel fed Thor a piece of carrot, speaking to him as he might a human friend. "It is good to be back, is it not, boy? Harriet looks happy. We will go out riding with her, I am sure."

Thor whinnied his displeasure as Nathaniel approached the opposite stalls and fed carrot pieces to the two Yorkshire Coach horses stationed there. They were handsome and strong yet temperate, and Nathaniel envied Harker's possession of them. Stroking their pale grey noses, he continued to speak, "She has a new friend, albeit an old widow. Let us hope the woman is willing to converse in horses, at least."

All thoughts of potential conversations with old widows fled from Nathaniel's mind when he glimpsed a large grey stallion's face appearing over a far stall door. The sight triggered a six-year-old memory, but he must be wrong. How could that horse be here at Eastease? Had the animal recognised his voice? Nathaniel had a carrot left in his pocket, which was this beast's favourite treat if he recalled correctly. With the carrot in his open palm, he approached the stall.

"Hey, big fellow. You remind me of—but no, you cannot be him, yet your markings are the same, and so is your face. Yes, I know you."

A voice behind him warned, "Watch out for that horse, sir. He has a dark reputation."

Nathaniel glanced over his shoulder at the stable manager. "If he remembers me, I will be fine. Thank you." Then, in a gentle voice, he asked the stallion, "Do you remember me, old man? Remember your friend? Have a good sniff."

The horse caught the scent of Nathaniel's extended hand and then accepted the carrot. While the animal chewed, Nathaniel stroked his neck and a muscular shoulder, murmuring reassuring words. The horse then put his head over Nathaniel's back and rubbed none too gently in greeting. At the edge of his vision, the stable manager stood frozen. Amused by the man's astonishment, Nathaniel opened the stall door and entered.

"You do remember me then, boy," Nathaniel crooned. "It is you; here are the scars. No new ones, though; thank goodness for that." He ran his skilled hands over the horse's back and haunches, feeling the ridges of old whip lashings. As the horse nuzzled into his shoulder again, Nathaniel flattered himself that this response stemmed from the pleasure of seeing him. But, on a practical level, the stallion only wanted another treat.

"I have a few scars, including a good, new one. It is not quite as well-healed as these." The stallion appeared healthy, and the scars were many years old. *Where the devil did Harker get him?* This remarkable specimen was supposed to be dead. Nathaniel experienced a sense of peace that had eluded him for quite some time as he rested his forehead on the horse's neck,

"Sorry, old fellow, I have no more treats on me, but it is good to see you." Nathaniel patted him once more and exited the stall. Had the stable manager remained, he would have asked him how this particular horse came to be in Harker's stable, but blast it, the man had disappeared.

~oOo~

After dressing for dinner, Nathaniel found his father and brother with Harker in the study. The topic of discussion was the very one he had talked of to Thor—the old widow, Mrs Andrews.

Harker reasoned, "She is opinionated, My Lord, but not overbearing. However, we do not see it as a problem to expose Harriet to others' views, and Mrs Andrews encourages discourse, not acquiescence. As a result, Harriet is coming out of her shell and expressing herself admirably."

"How is she supposed to get a husband if she is too opinionated? No man worth his salt will endure her," countered Lord Aysthill. As Harriet was his great-niece, the earl clearly felt entitled to have a say in her future despite not being her guardian.

"I agree, Father. Phoebe would never disagree with me," said William.

"Are you sure that is why you object to Mrs Andrews?" Harker asked with a whisper of a smile on his lips.

To what is Harker alluding? Nathaniel raised an eyebrow in his friend's direction.

The face of the earl quickly turned puce as Nathaniel's brother answered, "You would think that someone in the business of selling horses should not be so particular about who purchases them. Why does it matter to her what becomes of a horse once she reaps her profits?"

So, the widow refused to sell horses to his father. Given his treatment of his more temperamental animals, Nathaniel's admiration for this woman doubled instantly.

"With respect, Father," Nathaniel joined the conversation, but his tone held no deference, "neither you nor William is Harriet's guardian. That honour falls to Harker and me. I have not met the lady yet, but I trust Harker's judgment. We have met enough old widows to know they can be opinionated. I am sure Genevieve can help Harriet determine what is useful or not from the information she learns from Mrs Andrews."

Nathaniel narrowed his eyes with suspicion at Harker's smirk that he attempted to cover with a scratch to his nose. A glance at his father confirmed that the man was hiding his own small smile. *Have I said something amusing?*

Mr Ridgefield entered the room. "Gentlemen, I understand that the ladies are waiting for us."

Upon entering the sitting room adjoining the dining room, Nathaniel scanned all those present for Mrs Andrews. *Does the old widow have a daughter?* was his first thought upon taking in a younger face than he expected. He had never asked if she had children. If so, then where was the widow?

Nathaniel glanced at Harker, whose eyes sparkled with mirth at Nathaniel's reaction to the woman. *Damn the man; he tricked me.* It was his fault for assuming that a widow should be an older woman. As a soldier, he had seen enough young men die to know there must be a lot of young widows—Nathaniel thought Mrs Andrews a particularly attractive one.

She was not coiffed and powdered like the ladies of the ton he had met with his brother or Harker prior to their marriages. Her thick, red hair was loosely tied up, with only slight curling. Her skin was pale, as befitted her overall colouring, but freckles fought with the minimal powder on her face. She obviously spent a lot of time outdoors.

As the introductions began, Helena made her assessment of Colonel Ackley. He was almost as tall and lean as Mr Harker. In the same way she judged a horse's muscles beneath its coat, she took stock of the man's build. He appeared stronger than his friend, both in his arms and across his chest. She was startled to find his gaze upon her.

Genevieve was making the introduction. "Nathaniel, please allow me to introduce Mrs Helena Andrews of Redway Acres. Helena, my husband's dear friend, and Lord and Lady Aysthill's son, Colonel Nathaniel Ackley."

Marching forward, the colonel bowed smartly. "Mrs Andrews, I am pleased to make your acquaintance." Surprise flitted across his face when he straightened to note she drew back a pace. He flashed a disarming smile. "I have long admired my friend's Yorkshire Coach horses and understand he obtained them from your stable."

Helena curtseyed, recovering from her involuntary retreat, and began to spout trivialities about the horses. "I am pleased to meet you, Colonel. Those were my grandfather's horses. Cleveland Bays bred to thoroughbreds. It gives them a longer-legged stride with unmatched ability for speed, style, and power. They make a striking scene on the roads here and, I am sure, on the streets of London."

In response, the man nodded politely and then turned his attention to his mother, who called him over to introduce Mr Brooks.

Helena's cheeks warmed as he left. Her perusal of his body and startled step backwards had not gone unnoticed. Helena had covered her embarrassment with shallow talk about horses. *Stupid, stupid,* she admonished herself. Not being in society much, she had learned some general, conversational and hopefully witty things to say. But unfortunately, none had come to mind under the stare of those blue eyes. That horses did not interest him was evident, as he was eager to leave her presence. However, he had ridden while in the army. She had seen his magnificent mount in the stable. Perhaps the horse was a means to an end for him, the same as his father. She hoped that was not the case but prepared to be disappointed.

~oOo~

Nathaniel thoroughly enjoyed dinner, though he doubted all those present could say the same. Happily, Genevieve did not sit Mrs Andrews next to his father or brother, clearly mindful of her disagreement with them. Therefore, Nathaniel found himself sitting across from her, with Harriet and Phoebe on either side of him.

As Nathaniel spoke to Harriet on his right during the first course, he lent half an ear to the conversation opposite him. Mrs Andrews had little to say to Mr Brooks, even though the man tried eagerly to draw her into a conversation. Nathaniel cringed inside at Brooks' babbling—mundane subjects such as the weather, the meal, and the Eastease décor. *No wonder the young woman is so reluctant to speak.*

Too soon, the servants cleared their plates. Nathaniel had hoped to question Harriet about the mysterious Mrs Andrews. Instead, he turned his attention to Phoebe during the second course. After several inane exchanges about the weather and upcoming London social events, boredom prompted him to poke at a hornet's nest. He said quietly, "I heard from Harker that Mrs Andrews refused to sell horses to Father."

"Dreadful woman," she exclaimed under her breath. "What is it to her to whom she sells her horses? Then she had the insolence to suggest she buy Moses."

Nathaniel smiled. Moses was his father's prize stallion. "What were her reasons?"

"For not selling? She said she had not loved and trained these beautiful animals to be beaten because they had lost father a bet. As for buying Moses, she said she wished to save him from more of the same."

Nathaniel nodded in agreement, musing, "I have often wished I could save Moses." He glanced at Mrs Andrews. She was engaged in a spirited conversation with Mr Ridgefield about—fishing. *Did they mention fishing?* She mimed a technique using her hands. Nathaniel looked pointedly back at Phoebe, who opened and closed her mouth several times like one of those fish, unsure how to react.

Mrs Andrews may be cut from a different cloth, but should that not make life more interesting? He smiled as she laughed at one of Mr Ridgefield's stories.

By the time Nathaniel attacked a delicious dessert, Brooks had seised upon a topic less banal than his previous attempts to impress Mrs Andrews. Confidence rang in the clergyman's voice, but given Mrs Andrews' narrowing gaze, Nathaniel doubted the man could sustain it.

"Mrs Andrews, I have not yet had the pleasure of seeing you at Sunday service."

"The sauce served with this pudding tastes as fresh as if they picked the fruit only this morning," she replied, pointedly changing the subject.

"Quite," he conceded, but undeterred, he continued, "Do you not think it prudent for the owner of a residence such as Redway to set a good example in godliness by attending church regularly?"

Brooks should have heeded her annoyed expression, stemming from the pursuit of the touchy subject or the thinly veiled implication of her imprudence. But Nathaniel sensed danger stirring beneath her courteous veneer.

"Is being a churchgoer the only requirement to prove godliness, Mr Brooks?" she inquired politely.

"Well, no," he stammered. "Attending church is not the *only* proof of godliness or its close neighbour, goodliness."

"Exactly!" she exclaimed, catching the attention of Mr Ridgefield to her right and Harriet beside Nathaniel, to whom he was supposed to be paying more attention. However, Mrs Andrews was eyeing the preacher, and Nathaniel was transfixed as she continued, "Pray tell me, how has the church behaved goodly recently? Perhaps in aiding a local family by purchasing shoes for its children?"

Brooks smiled confidently, believing himself on solid ground, while Nathaniel shook his head. She was leading the preacher by the nose. He imagined a bridle snugged around Brooks' head and smiled broadly.

"Mrs Andrews, you have found me—I mean the church—out. A mother did ask for some assistance the other week. After consulting the church coffers, I was able to give the money to her husband when I saw him in the village on Saturday. He attended church on Sunday and thanked me—nay, the church."

"Mrs Miller had gathered all her courage to ask you for that money. It caused much shame, but she did so anyway for the good of her children. Did so despite knowing she would face Mr Miller's wrath. And you gave the money to him?"

"Of course I did. As the man of the house, it is his responsibility to manage money matters."

"If Mr Miller could manage money, Mr Brooks, his family would all have serviceable shoes. So tell me: How well-shod are the Miller children these days?"

Nathaniel marked the anger in her demeanour. Although she remained poised, her green eyes sparked with ire. It was a miracle the clergyman did not combust in his chair under that scorching gaze.

"I do not know the answer to that," Brooks blustered, that he had made a mistake now clear, but uncertainty remained as to what it might be.

"Unhappily, I can tell you they still wear the same tattered shoes. After meeting you last Saturday, Mr Miller proceeded to the village tavern, where he got well into his cups. Upon returning home, he felt within his rights to beat Mrs Miller for daring to ask for the money he had happily squandered on ale. He then showed his *godliness* by attending church the following day and thanking you."

To Nathaniel's mind, the chastised Mr Brooks must either cut his losses or go up in flames. Mrs Andrews held an ace up her sleeve; he had not prospered at the card table merely through luck. Unwisely, Brooks chose the latter course.

"As unfortunate a situation as that may be, I do not see what that has to do with me or why it means you should not attend church yourself."

Nathaniel shook his head. *Poor fool. A lamb to the slaughter.*

"Firstly, you should have given the money to the person who requested it."

"How was I to know he would spend it on ale?" Brooks' defence was poor, his face red.

"You must get to know your parishioners, Mr Brooks." The voice came from the end of the table, where Genevieve sat listening intently to the exchange.

Brooks nodded politely in the direction of his hostess. The matter was closed, and everyone turned back to their own conversations.

Dissatisfied with not hearing Mrs Andrews' hidden 'ace', Nathaniel leant forwards in amusement to ask, "—And secondly?"

Her startled green eyes delved his mischievous gaze without reciprocating his mirth. Hard jade were words that came to his mind as he leaned back in his chair to a respectful distance. Apparently, she had overcome her earlier timidity in her passion to highlight an injustice.

"Secondly," she said, "I spent my churchgoing time last Sunday attending Mrs Miller's cuts and bruises, and measuring her children's feet. They will have new shoes within a week."

Delighted with her response, Nathaniel picked up his wine glass, raised it towards her and drank deeply while watching her over the rim. She was magnificent. Passionate, eloquent, and as fiery as her glorious red hair. His stay at Eastease took an upward turn, and his spirits rose higher than they had in all this abysmal year.

Four

After the ladies withdrew, the subject of the men's conversation was once again the widow, Mrs Andrews. Nathaniel allowed Harker a chuckle at his mistaken conclusion that the widow was an older woman.

"Ackers, your face when you clapped eyes upon her."

"She is a handsome piece, that is certain." His father guffawed, causing Nathaniel to scowl. Mrs Andrews was not a woman he cared to see suffer under his father's hands.

Ignoring the earl, he spoke to Harker. "I assumed the widow you referred to had been the old man's wife."

"Stockton? His wife died a few years before him. He left everything to Mrs Andrews. She is his granddaughter," Harker confirmed.

"Not to her father?"

"Mighty unusual, isn't it, Son?" his father said. "It's a nice parcel of land, though."

Nathaniel frowned again. He wouldn't put it past his father to compromise the woman and take over Redway Acres himself.

Harker continued, "Her mother was Stockton's daughter, apparently not one for horses and doesn't visit."

Curious to know more, Nathaniel pressed Harker. "And what of Mrs Andrews' husband?"

"Captain Andrews died in battle about five years ago. Have you heard of him?"

"Captain Andrews? No, I have not."

"She has a daughter by him. Robertson, her stable manager, travelled with Mrs Andrews from Norfolk when she came to live at Redway. She is lucky to have him, and his wife is the housekeeper."

Her comments on Harker's Yorkshire Coach horses came to mind. "She seems to know her horses."

"She certainly does. She visits here, and we talk business. I find her very intelligent and logical."

Lord Aysthill harrumphed. "Not the two words I would use to describe the woman or any woman, come to that."

"I believe all the ladies dining with us tonight deserve those descriptors, David," Mr Ridgefield said, aiming to keep the peace as was his want. Knowing Nathaniel's father of old, he used his given name, but Nathaniel still found hearing it odd.

Aiming to lighten the conversation, he turned to Genevieve's uncle. "Mr Ridgefield, I believe I overheard the mention of fishing in your conversation at dinner."

"Indeed you did, Colonel." He laughed loudly. "She claims she tickled trout out of the stream on Redway property as a young woman."

An image of Mrs Andrews with her skirts hiked up, standing knee-deep in a stream, entered Nathaniel's consciousness. How odd that he could visualise it with the clarity of a fond memory.

"She spoke affectionately of her grandfather," Mr Ridgefield offered. "Did you say his name was Stockton? It must have been his daughter, Mrs Andrews' mother, who married Gregory Billings. What happened to George Stockton?"

Harker grew sober, taking a mouthful from his wineglass before answering. "George met an unfortunate end. Crushed by one of his horses just a few days before my marriage."

Nathaniel listened carefully to the tale, surprised to find the man's funeral was held right after Harker's wedding. At the same time, he had been enjoying his friend's nuptials and the company of Genevieve's sisters; Mrs Andrews had been grieving for her grandfather. He felt a pang of sorrow that he had not known her then and could have offered some comfort.

There were murmurings amongst the men. *How unfortunate. Wouldn't any man worth his salt do the same for a grandchild? Such a shame that it put a blight on the Harker wedding.*

All at once, Nathaniel broke from his thoughts and looked at Harker. "Was it a grey stallion? The one I saw in your stable this afternoon?"

"That is Mrs Andrews' horse, Perscus, but I doubt he was the one who killed her grandfather. She would have disposed of the animal, wouldn't she?" Harker reasoned.

His father laughed. "Of course she would have, boy."

Nathaniel was doubtful. Mrs Andrews spoke lovingly of horses before dinner, showing her soft spot for the beasts. If his suspicion that the same grey stallion currently in Harker's stable killed George Stockton proved right, then the horse had taken two lives. The fact that she called him Perseus was telling. While Nathaniel wouldn't necessarily condone shooting the horse if there were extenuating circumstances, her riding that animal from Redway did not sit well in his gut.

He resolved to say nothing further in front of his father, but intended to find out more when he could. Perhaps Redway's stable manager, Robertson, could tell him? Then, he would write to his army contacts about Captain Andrews. It would interest him to know something of the man who had captured her heart and hand in marriage. And why did her family not visit their daughter and granddaughter? Should the opportunity arise, he would ask Mr Ridgefield where their property was in Norfolk, as he seemed to know Mr Billings.

~oOo~

When the men entered the drawing room, Genevieve was laughing with Aunt Miriam and Helena, who had been regaling them with one of her stories. If pressed, Gennie's friend was sure to say she did not know where her daughter got her storytelling abilities from, but to Gennie's mind, that answer was clear.

Aunt Miriam rose from the comfortable couch with Helena to approach Gennie's uncle. He enjoyed Helena's story as his round belly jiggled when he laughed. Mr Brooks stood on the periphery of this group, close to Helena, and attempted to join in the laughter. Nathaniel's father and brother joined their wives while Harriet, who had been talking to those ladies, moved to stand near Helena.

Nathaniel observed them all before sitting down on a chair close to Gennie's couch with an expression of much satisfaction. Alexander, who had taken Aunt Miriam's seat, doted upon her, asking if she had enough to eat, whether she needed rest, and whether was she comfortable. Then, smiling at him, Gennie patted his cheek before turning to Nathaniel.

He spoke indulgently, "Genevieve, I would like to thank you for allowing me to escape to Eastease for a time and for this welcoming dinner party. I have enjoyed myself immensely this evening."

"Do not think I missed your mischievousness at the dinner table, Ackers," she exclaimed, admonishing him with the nickname her husband used. "If you continue misbehaving, we might return you to your mother."

"Gennie, please do not spoil all my fun. It is, after all, part of my recovery," he jibed, his eyes shifting away from her momentarily as they caught the swish of a green skirt when Helena moved around Gennie's uncle, only to rejoin the same group.

Mr Brooks, who had been edging ever closer to her, seemed about to make the same manoeuvre when Gennie's all-seeing aunt stayed him with a hand on his forearm. She asked firmly, "Mr Brooks, please give me your opinion on—"

Nathaniel's attention upon this grouping consumed him so much that he missed hearing the comment Gennie directed his way. She felt she could see the cogs turning as he smiled at her, then gave her a general response in an attempt to save face.

"Yes, I am sure that would be wonderful," he replied.

Gennie would not let him off the hook that easily and gave him a pointed look. He spoke loudly to the group, "Is it time for some entertainment? Harriet, I believe you and Mrs Andrews have prepared something for us?"

Gennie studied him intently, aware of the source of his preoccupation. It had been an inspired guess about the entertainment. Nevertheless, a vital someone had galvanised his thoughts, which made her smile.

As was often the case with a happily married woman, she wished for the same for her widowed friend. She had considered that Helena might pique the interest of either Mr Brooks or Nathaniel. However, she felt the colonel was the better match as Mr Brooks lacked Nathaniel's knowledge of horses and might not have enough confidence for the headstrong Helena.

Socially, Nathaniel could work a room better than anyone in Gennie's acquaintance. He could be faultlessly formal in the presence of nobility and rank, join in the laughter of men playing cards and drinking, or flatter every woman in his company, young and old alike. But tonight was different. She had never seen him as distracted as he was by Helena, watching her every move, yet more or less still holding a conversation. She believed Helena would benefit if he were to court her, no matter where it led, and she suspected he might find it advantageous, too.

Gennie watched as Helena and Harriet walked towards the pianoforte to a light smattering of applause. Harriet settled on the stool while Helena stood beside her, ready to sing. The two women looked at one another, each waiting for the other to speak. In a series of nods and squeaks, they seemed to be communicating. The colonel appeared to find this amusing as he smothered his snorting laugh with his hand, pretending to rub his chin. Gennie reached over and pinched his upper arm and could not keep from smiling when his surprised *ouch* drew all eyes to him.

The diversion allowed Helena to compose herself and find her voice. "This is Leonore's aria and will be sung in German. It is from Beethoven's opera, Leonore. She dresses as a man to pose as a guard and rescue her wrongfully imprisoned husband."

As Gennie anticipated, her friend looked mainly at her as she spoke. Earlier that evening, Helena had explained that she thought it might help her nerves to look at a friendly face, but her gaze moved slightly as she began to sing. Helena stared at the colonel, who seemed enraptured to Gennie's mind, staring right back. Gennie thought him fortunate that everyone was focused on the performers and did not notice his dazed expression. Gennie fondly recalled her first dinner at Eastease, when she had played and sung for Alexander in this room. His look had been remarkably similar to the one she now saw on the colonel's face.

Just as Nathaniel began to appreciate his cousin's improved talent, Mrs Andrews raised her voice in song. He stared at her, utterly mesmerised, for she looked directly at him. My God, the woman's voice was glorious, her range incredible, and she seemed lost in the character of Leonore, who was rescuing her husband. Being fluent in German, he appreciated how Mrs Andrews showed nervousness over what Leonore was doing, the love she expressed for the man she hoped to save and the duty she felt in rescuing him. As she sang, he translated:

Abominable one!
Where are you going?
What will you do?
What will you do in wild anger?
The call of sympathy,
The voice of humanity,
Does nothing move your tiger sense?
Like turbulent seas,
Anger and hatred rage in your soul,
So appears to me a rainbow,
That bright on dark clouds rests.
A quiet gaze,

Redway Acres - Helena

So peaceful,
That mirrors old times,
And new appeased my blood flows.
Please, hope, let the last star, the last star,
From fatigue not fade!
Please, illuminate, illuminate my destiny, even if it's far,
Love will reach it. Love will reach it. Love will reach it.
O please, hope, let the last star,
From fatigue not fade!
Illuminate, illuminate my destiny, even if it's far, even if it's far,
Love, love will reach it. Love, love will reach it.
I follow an inner drive,
I will not waver,
My duty strengthens me,
My duty of true marital love.
I will not waver,
My duty strengthens me,
My duty of true marital love.
O you, for whom I bore everything,
If only I could be at your side,
Where evil has you bound,
And bring you sweet comfort!
O you, for whom I bore everything,
If only I could be at your side,
Where evil has you bound,
And bring you sweet comfort!
I follow an inner drive
I will not waver
My duty strengthens me
My duty of true marital love.
I follow an inner drive,
I will not waver,
I follow an inner drive,
I will not waver,
My duty strengthens me,
My duty of true marital love.

Swept away by Mrs Andrews' words and talent, Nathaniel held her gaze through the entire piece. Then, all too soon, the music ended, and she glanced away as the ensemble applauded. He felt suddenly bereft, as though he had lost an intimate connection. On the periphery of his consciousness, Harker was standing and loudly applauding Harriet, Brooks was overdoing it trying to catch Mrs Andrews' attention, and Mr Ridgefield was, as always, enthusiastic. But Nathaniel could only sit there transfixed.

"Would you like me to pinch you again, Colonel?"

Genevieve's soft inquiry brought him out of his stupor. He started to clap as everyone else stopped. Discussions were breaking out about Harriet playing some more, and with renewed confidence, she found another piece.

Nathaniel heard his father's loud voice before he noticed the earl approaching Mrs Andrews. "What a surprise, my dear, what a surprise."

"You had better get over there, Ackers," said Harker. "He has had several glasses of wine."

Nathaniel sprang to his feet to intercede for Mrs Andrews, who was trying to extricate her hand from his father's.

"Thank you, My Lord. I think your wife requires you." So saying, she all but dragged him over to Nathaniel's mother.

As Nathaniel reached them, Mrs Andrews was accepting Lady Aysthill's praise more graciously than it had been given. He grimaced as his mother said, "My cousin's daughter, Lady Grace Bainbridge, sings superbly, too. Had she been here, she would have been considered the best singer in the room."

Mrs Andrews smiled with what Nathaniel thought might have been a pitying look. He had not thought her aware of his close presence, but she deliberately turned away from him towards Mr and Mrs Ridgefield. Nathaniel moved to the back of the room to pour himself a drink and observe her more.

"Marvellous, Mrs Andrews. I do not think we have heard better," Mr Ridgefield complimented her effortlessly.

"It was so moving, my dear," his wife agreed.

Mrs Andrews smiled graciously. "Thank you both, though you are too kind. It was all Harriet's talent."

Nathaniel appreciated that Mrs Andrews deferred the compliments to Harriet, proud of his cousin. The woman seemed tricky for a man to engage in conversation, earlier with Brooks and now with his father. He wondered if that was by coincidence or design. The only exceptions seemed to be Mr Ridgefield and Harker.

As he watched, Brooks stepped up and complimented her, too. Nathaniel muttered, "He is standing a little too close again. I see you think so too, madam." Mrs Andrews turned, but the Ridgefields looked the other way to Harriet, whose second piece ended. "Oh, that was a mistake," Nathaniel murmured, seeing the manoeuvre left her alone with the clergyman.

His observation continued as Mrs Andrews walked beside Brooks as he talked, bringing him closer to Genevieve and depositing him into the chair Nathaniel had vacated. Then, with a well-aimed question to Genevieve, the two became engaged in conversation, leaving her free again. "Very clever, madam."

Nathaniel wondered about Brooks' intentions towards Mrs Andrews. Whatever the man had in mind, she had no interest in him, much to Nathaniel's delight. Of course, Brooks would need to challenge him, too, and he never bet against himself.

Surprised by that thought, he barely noticed when Harriet had graciously allowed Phoebe to take over at the pianoforte. William took his opportunity to seek out Mrs Andrews and compliment her singing. Nathaniel wondered what would become of his brother. The woman had just escaped from Genevieve and Brooks and stood close to Harker. She asked him a question that set him into a heated discussion with William, leaving Mrs Andrews alone again.

Nathaniel watched all of this from his vantage point with much amusement. It was as if watching a dance. The principal was Mrs Andrews, and each time she was alone for a moment, a new partner arrived that she managed to deposit elsewhere. Nathaniel considered that he would undoubtedly receive the same treatment if he approached her. He wondered what her motives were. She was not allowing a man to speak with her alone or stand too close.

Nathaniel considered his strategy. He would need another

woman with him. While keeping his distance, he would engage Mrs Andrews in a subject sure to hold her interest—horses, and it was close to foaling season. She must have mares ready to foal. *Excellent.* Harriet was speaking with her, which was fortuitous timing. *I will do you a good turn soon, Harriet.*

He arrived as his cousin tried to persuade Mrs Andrews to sing again.

"Oh, Helena, please do."

"I would rather not, Harriet. They are all making such a fuss."

"But your voice is so lovely that I must insist."

"No need to browbeat her, Harriet," Nathaniel said as he strode over to them, keeping a step further back than usual. "Although you sing beautifully, Mrs Andrews, if I may say so. You played incredibly, too, Harriet, as always."

"Thank you," they said in unison.

"Tell me, Mrs Andrews, do you have any mares ready to foal? I am right in thinking it is almost foaling season, am I not?"

"This season, we have two. We did plan for more, but after my grandfather's death, I didn't have the heart for it, and with the delay, the mares, for the most part, were beyond their mating time. These will be the first foals born without him there. They will truly be my responsibility."

Nathaniel spoke in a kindly tone. "I was sorry to hear of his passing. I know Harker held him in great esteem and wish I had made time to meet him myself. I am sure he would be proud of you."

"Thank you. It is kind of you to say. Grandfather and John have taught me everything. I have been so lucky."

It was clear to Nathaniel that she loved what she did. To his delight, when Harriet left them to go to the pianoforte again, he found himself alone with her.

"Harker mentioned that your stable manager is very competent. So that is John, I take it? He said you are lucky to have him."

"He and Ruth have been my rocks," she confirmed, relaxing sufficiently not to notice Harriet had returned to her playing, and she was standing by herself in discussion with him.

Their conversation lasted but a moment more before her

realisation that she stood only with him became evident to Nathaniel. Mrs Andrews stiffened, and her eyes widened almost imperceptibly. To avoid being rejected, he spoke before she could. "I wonder if you are rested sufficiently to sing? Harriet is looking annoyed with me for monopolising you. She is probably worried that someone will insist that *she* sing."

Nathaniel gestured towards the instrument, and she nodded. He moved to offer his arm, but again she stiffened. Nathaniel reminded himself to be cautious or risk losing her good favour. So, clasping his hands behind his back, he accompanied her the short distance to the pianoforte.

Delighted that Helena would sing again, Harriet picked a well-known, lively song of summer days. "Cousin, please sit by me and turn the pages?"

Unable to deny Harriet anything, Nathaniel dutifully positioned a chair beside her stool and set to his task. Once or twice, he felt her elbow nudge his side as she neared the end of a page. He could not take his eyes off the talented Mrs Andrews.

Once the song finished and the applause ebbed, Harriet quickly launched into a familiar melody of love and loss. Mrs Andrews continued to sing. One page into it, Nathaniel felt another sharp elbow and tore his eyes away from his enchantress to see Harriet indicate that he should take over the playing. He gave her a wry look but obliged her. Moving stealthily, they switched places, fingers replacing fingers seamlessly on the keys.

As Harriet stood to move behind him and take the seat he had vacated, Mrs Andrews turned slightly. Singing of the love that had left her, she looked straight into Nathaniel's eyes as he played. It provided contact with the bewitching redhead that he had not yet been able to attain. To her credit, though she blushed, she did not falter in her singing, rising to the challenge.

"Thank you, Colonel," she said when the song ended. "Your playing is very good."

"Not as good as my dear Harriet's, but your splendid singing allowed me to get away with it."

"You are rusty; that is all," exclaimed Harriet. "He is modest. He is an exceptional player."

The applause was dying down, and Genevieve was getting to her feet. "I apologise for being a poor hostess, but I must get to bed, or I will be asleep on this couch within minutes." Harker had been helping her to stand, and she leaned upon him heavily. Mrs Andrews and Harriet were soon by her side, exclaiming about their own tiredness and Mrs Andrews planning an early start in the morning. Everyone exchanged goodnights, and the two women escorted Genevieve to bed.

Nathaniel, who had walked over with the performers, stood beside Harker, feeling the loss of the retreating forms until his father's loud voice stirred him.

"Cards?"

Five

Helena's sensibilities returned to her when she entered the tranquillity of her bedchamber, which adjoined Harriet's via a connecting sitting area. She allowed Rebecca to serve her, but only with unbuttoning her gown and unpinning her hair. She then dismissed the maid.

"Thank you, Rebecca. I can brush it myself. Get off to your bed. It will be no good if you have dark circles around your eyes next time you see Jacky Robertson."

Rebecca blushed and then bobbed a curtsey. "Thank you, ma'am."

Helena wandered to a window, dressed in her nightgown and brushing her hair. Setting the last lit candle on a nearby side table, she opened the curtains and sat on the narrow window seat, peering out into the darkness. Her rooms faced southeast, which meant the early rising sun should slant through the window and wake her. By the faint light of a moonless sky, Helena made out the shape of the east wing, with the bedchambers above, including the one where she and Harriet had left Genevieve. Those windows were dark, or the servants had drawn the curtains.

Candlelight illuminated the rooms below. The east wing contained the dining and drawing rooms where Helena had just been, but those windows faced out to the gardens on the other side. So, which room was she looking into?

She made out a billiards table through the farthest window, so it must be the game room. She could also see two tables of card players. Near another window were four men. The stout figure, with his back to her, was Lord Aysthill. She closed one eye and made a pinching motion with her thumb and forefinger, pretending to squash him, and then giggled. It was a game she and Issie sometimes played.

The tall, dark-haired men that flanked the earl were the viscount and Mr Harker, which meant the lean figure reclining back in his chair and facing the window was that of Colonel Ackley. Helena watched his languid movements. Mostly, he stayed lounging, except to lean forward and occasionally sip his drink or collect his winnings, something he did more often than the others at the table.

"Oh, I see you are good at cards, Colonel," she mused.

Helena was not tired, and the cushions on the window seat were comfortable, so she draped a cream, woollen coverlet over her legs to deflect the draught and thought of this man who attracted her. Helena had seised the opportunity to leave his company when Genevieve stood because she worried about her oh-so-new feelings. Never before had she reacted so to a man. The way he had looked at her as she sang the aria and how singing while he played the pianoforte felt intimate in a way it did not with Harriet.

It had not escaped her notice that he watched her while she spoke with various dinner guests. However, he kept his distance when he finally approached her, unlike Mr Brooks or Lord Aysthill. His behaviour was confusing, yet somehow comforting, and she had felt relaxed talking to him of her mares.

During their introduction, he met her nervous talk of horses with indifference, so Helena assumed he would be as stiff and formal with her as with his family. However, she was astonished to discover Colonel Ackley's interest in horses when he talked as warmly with her as with the Harkers and Harriet. A pleasant feeling spread within

Helena and relaxed her usual wariness, so she had not noticed Harriet returning to her pianoforte.

In the game room below, the people at the second table were departing. Rising from his chair, Mr Harker turned, bowed to Lord Aysthill and left. Helena watched as the colonel swiftly went to the sideboard and procured a decanter, three large cigars, and three brandy snifters before returning to the table. He poured their drinks, and Lord Aysthill and his older son, who had already removed their topcoats, lit their cigars.

"So this is what men get up to without ladies present. Oh!" Distracted by the colonel unbuttoning his waistcoat and untying his cravat, Helena did not quickly register his glance up to her window. In shock at being caught observing him, Helena sat up and blew out the candle.

She did not move from the window seat, confident the candle no longer silhouetted her. Instead, she remained still so she could continue her observation. Colonel Ackley undid the top button of his shirt and then rolled up his sleeves before rubbing his hands together.

At first, he lost a few hands.

"Have I unsettled you too? Turnabout is fair play, they say," she murmured.

Shortly, his familiar lounging and winning took over. Amused, Helena savoured the sight of him until her eyelids drifted down as she fell asleep on the cushions.

~oOo~

After another hour of card playing, little remained of Nathaniel's cigar, the decanter of brandy was nearly empty, and his winnings on the table were more than that of his brother and father combined. Delighted—it would serve him well over the coming months.

When the light in a top window had caught Nathaniel's attention earlier, he had stopped for only a second at the vision in a white nightgown before glancing back quickly and paying attention to dealing the cards. He had surreptitiously peeked at the darkened window often during the past hour, carefully avoiding his companions' notice. The pale shape he detected might be cushions or the intriguing Mrs Andrews, but would she have watched them for over an hour? If she was still at the window, perhaps she had fallen asleep.

His father's voice broke into his thoughts. "My boys, we have drunk enough to dent Harker's brandy, and I have lost enough money to keep you for the rest of the year. So, I am off to bed. I wonder if your mother is still awake?"

His leering gaze sickened Nathaniel, who glared back at him.

William smirked, too. "The advantages of having a wife are few, but that is one of them, Father. Poor Nathaniel having to warm his own bed."

Nathaniel followed them up the east wing staircase and said goodnight before entering his rooms. *A warm woman waiting in my bed*, he thought, as the image of Mrs Andrews in a white nightgown drifted into his mind. Shaking his head clear, Nathaniel removed his cravat, tossed it and his coat onto a nearby chair, and then frowned at his bed. It seemed less welcoming than he thought when he had left the game room.

His valet came in from the dressing room. "Can I serve you, Colonel?"

"Good lord, James, are you still up? My apologies. I am used to taking care of myself. You did not need to wait up for me; I should have said so earlier. Go to bed, man, and do not get up early for my sake, either."

The grateful valet hurried from the room, closing the door behind him. Less than two minutes later, the man was back.

"Begging your pardon, sir. Your father, I mean Lord Aysthill, is heading towards the west wing, but his rooms are two doors down from yours. He seems a little unsteady, and I thought I had better advise you."

What is Father thinking? Nathaniel wondered. *Surely he is not going to 'teach her a lesson'?* He had heard the earl say that of many a woman he considered impertinent.

"Helena."

"I beg your pardon, sir? Is there any assistance I can give you?"

James' concerned eyes searched Nathaniel's.

"No, but thank you for informing me. I expect Father is a little too merry and forgot where he is. I will lead him back to his rooms."

~oOo~

The valet left, and Nathaniel marched down the west wing. He saw his father attempting to open a bedchamber door that appeared to be locked. *Thank heavens the woman has good sense.*

"Father, what the devil are you doing?" For an instant, something crossed the earl's face that Nathaniel had never seen there before—fear. No longer was his father the formidable Lord Aysthill but a frightened old man. Nathaniel's anger seethed as he spoke through clenched teeth, "How dare you try to force your way into Mrs Andrews' rooms? And in the home of the man I consider a brother. Did you think I would not stop you?"

In response to this challenge, the powerful personage of the Earl of Aysthill returned, bolstering his demeanour as his body seemed to overcome its intoxication. Nathaniel made a conscious effort not to step back, subduing a childhood instinct born of the many beatings he had received at this man's hand.

"You never have been able to stop me. So why would you try now?" his father taunted him. "Could it be that you want to have at her instead?"

"Have at her? Listen to yourself. You are speaking of a person, a lady, not a joint of meat on your dining table. Shame on me for not having stopped you before." Nathaniel felt sick to his stomach to have been sired by this pathetic excuse for a man. He had seen ordinary but courageous men cut down on the battlefield who stood head and shoulders above his father.

"What could you have done?" the earl sneered, swaying as the effects of alcohol consumed him once again. "What is it that you think you can do? No matter what you say or do, you cannot stop me where your mother is concerned, and that bothers you most of all, doesn't it—*boy?*"

Had his father's eyes not rolled out of focus just then, Nathaniel might have thrashed him, but this was neither the time nor the place to vent his rage. Instead, he seised his father's arm to steady him. He wanted him stone-cold sober when he took him in hand, as revenge was a dish best served cold. But, for now, his priority had to be his mother, to whom his father would shortly return.

Releasing a sigh, he assumed an amiable countenance to diffuse the situation, but his words seemed to stick in his throat. "Steady there, Father. Have you really had that much to drink?"

Laughing, Lord Aysthill muttered, "Must have, me boy. Must have." Then the earl, no doubt believing Nathaniel would forget the whole incident, wove his way back to the east wing and the rooms he shared with his wife. Nathaniel sorely hoped she would not bear the brunt of the older man's frustration.

Unfortunately, he could not be sure his father would not return. Glancing around the wide corridor, he decided he had better sleep on the ornate couch situated against the opposite wall. Although his *bed* did not look comfortable, Nathaniel doubted he would sleep much back in his rooms anyway. Sinking onto the couch, he rubbed his hands over his face as the shame of his father's actions overwhelmed him. He would have to do something about it, but for the life of him could not think what could possibly deter the pigheaded man.

A soft footfall pulled Nathaniel's attention back to the corridor, where a pale hand held a pillow in front of him—haunting green eyes that studied him carefully above it. He hastily rose. The lady was a vision in white, her red hair cascading around her face. She wore a white silk wrapper over the nightgown he had seen from the game room window. It was a minimal barrier, and it took all his self-control not to scoop her up, march back into her bedchamber, deposit her on the bed and—*And what?* he chided himself. *Have at her, as father says?* That thought dampened his ardour. Unlike his father, he preferred a willing woman in his arms, in his bed. Mrs Andrews' eyes were wary, not willing.

Accepting the pillow, he spoke softly, "Thank you. I am very sorry. You must have been frightened. I doubt he will return, but I will sleep here tonight—just in case."

"I nearly fell off the window seat."

He laughed at her acknowledgement and brushed a wayward strand of red hair behind her ear. To his delight, she did not shy from his touch. Had he proved himself trustworthy by dealing with his father? Her gaze lowered to glance at his exposed neck. Biting her lower lip, she offered a cream-coloured coverlet from behind her back, thus diffusing the tension between them.

"I found this suitable coverage on a summer night. Perhaps you will find it so."

The coverlet felt warm in his hands from being wrapped around her body.

"How did you know he would come here?" she asked.

"The Eastease manservant who attends me, James, saw him staggering this way. He informed me at once."

"And you came after him because you knew his intentions?"

"Yes."

"Because it is something he has done before?"

"Yes," he confirmed again, "but he went too far this time. A guest at Eastease, no less."

"I am afraid we do not agree, Colonel. I would say that too far was the first time he forced himself on a woman. Evil will always succeed when a good man does nothing to face it down."

As Nathaniel searched her inscrutable face, the truth of her remarks galvanised in his mind. He knew he was dead wrong for not stopping the earl before tonight. His complicity in the continual cover-ups of his father's depravity had led to this moment. Spending an uncomfortable night on a hard couch barely seemed an appropriate penance for his inaction, and his hope that she might view this office of protection as admirable crumbled away.

"Mrs Andrews, I—"

"You could summon a servant to take your place on the couch—" she waved a hand towards an adjoining room "—or I could share Harriet's bed. That would spare you a night out here."

"Well, yes, but—"

"But, I suppose that would require explanations you would rather not give if we are to forget this matter. I'm sure Mr Harker would not want Eastease's good name sullied."

He hesitated, realising then that the plan he had been trying to share with her might not suit Harker's wishes. He must speak with his friend before deciding what action to take.

"Quite right," he agreed and then indicated the pillow and coverlet he held to his chest. "But thank you for these."

"Thank you," she replied, "for doing something." She walked to her bedchamber door and paused to look back at him. "Goodnight, Colonel Ackley."

"Goodnight, Mrs Andrews."

After she disappeared into her bedchamber, Nathaniel sank onto the hard couch. As he put the pillow at one end, he listened for the turn of the lock, but it didn't come. She trusted him. Almost nothing else at that moment could have made him happier. He lay on the couch, still clutching the throw to his chest. The soft material wafted the scent of her rosewater perfume around him. Nestling his cheek into the coverlet, he closed his eyes and gradually drifted off.

~oOo~

Bright sunbeams slanted through the open curtains in Helena's room, awakening her from a pleasant dream she had experienced several times before. The first was after witnessing John and Ruth share an intimate kiss in her kitchen. Unaware of her watching them, they displayed a tenderness that caught her by surprise. In her dreams that followed, she had encountered a featureless man in shirtsleeves. Standing close to her, he held her face in his hands and kissed her gently. This night, the man had Colonel Ackley's features, and she woke with a throbbing and frustration through her body as she had never known before.

Tiredness from rousing several times during her few hours of slumber, coupled with this frustration, brought her anger to the fore, and many ideas went through her mind as she dressed. When the colonel confronted his father, she felt gratified a man in this society was prepared to protect her. She had not felt this secure since before her grandfather's death. That the colonel decried his father's conduct and made it clear he considered her as a person warmed her heart. Once his anger subsided, however, and he jovially sent his father on his way, she understood the incident would be swept out of sight as countless others must have been. How many more occurrences would there be in the future?

Sitting in front of the mirror, loosely pinning up her hair, Helena discussed the matter with her reflection.

"What right does he have to make me feel this way?" she asked, her hands in her hair and pins in her teeth.

Her reflection smiled as she removed the pins to speak. "None. None whatsoever. But Grandfather did say you should find someone to help run Redway."

"I do not need a man in my life. I manage Redway well enough without one, thank you," she chided.

The Helena in the mirror sighed. "You could manage even better with one. Why not this man when you find him so appealing? You simply do not wish to marry and give up your independence."

"Why are you talking of marriage? I do not know the first thing about him," she argued with herself.

Her reflection counted on her fingers. "He is handsome, certainly, charming, gallant and honourable. He is also thoughtful and handsome."

She pointed a hairpin towards the mirror and admonished, "You already said handsome. It will not do. I will leave this house and not return until the entire Ackley family has left. He will probably die in France fighting Bonaparte, and I will never have to see him again."

With a gasp, she clamped her hand over her mouth and stared wide-eyed, mortified with herself. Her tired, glassy eyes filled with tears as her reflection shook her head.

"That is shameful. Poor Harriet has already lost her stepfather to war. She would be distraught if the same happened to her cousin."

With a last abashed look into the mirror, Helena picked up her bonnet, leaving her things for the maid to pack and return with Issie. Then, cautiously, she opened the door.

Colonel Ackley lay on the couch. His eyes were closed, and he hugged the bunched coverlet tight to his chest, which she thought odd. Surely, he would have gained more warmth from it by draping it over himself. Helena contemplated not waking him, but it would not do for a servant to find him thus. She imagined the colonel had spent a miserable night on that uncomfortable couch, and guilt felt heavy in her belly. What might have happened had he not confronted his father? She did not want to think of it.

"Colonel Ackley," she said softly, then a bit louder, "Colonel."

"What the blazes!" he almost shouted, and her hand came down over his mouth in reflex to stop him from waking Harriet in the next room. Horrified that she should do such a thing, she quickly took her hand away.

"Sorry," she whispered, "but you were loud. I wanted to let you know you can return to your rooms before the servants come, and I wished to thank you." With that, she hurried down the hall and dared not look back.

Nathaniel shook off the fog of sleep, the effects of a late night, and the feel of her fingers on his lips. Gathering his wits, he rose and strode after her.

"Mrs Andrews," he called out as loudly as he dared, but she seemed to walk faster. *What is she wearing?* It had looked like a riding habit, but as she walked away, he could see separate material surrounding each of her legs—voluminous, skirt-like trousers. Not willing to wake the entire household, he did not catch up to her until she had exited the house and reached the stable. Damn the woman, why was she leaving so early?

He stopped her from closing the door and stepped into the short corridor that led to the stable proper.

"Wait," was all he managed as her retreating form disappeared around the corner.

She stepped back into view. "Why are you following me?"

"I wondered why you were leaving so early and without a hint of grace after I had a very uncomfortable night. Also, if I might add—what on earth are you wearing?"

She looked affronted, then glanced down at her attire. "It is a riding habit, not that it is any concern of yours. I said thank you quite gracefully more than once, and your uncomfortable night was not my fault. I am, however, annoyed at myself for feeling guilt over it. Leaving at this time was always my plan. As you can see, my horse is ready for me." She gestured for him to look around the corner.

The mysterious grey stallion stood there fully tacked but not with a side-saddle.

"Astride?"

"Yes."

"Like a man?"

"Yes."

"On this beast?" he blurted out.

"Absolutely, yes."

She took the reins from Adam, who was patiently holding the grey and led the horse out of the larger barn doors at the rear of the stable. When Adam made to follow, presumably to assist her in mounting the horse, Nathaniel held up his hand to stay him and followed her outside himself.

"Where did you get this animal?" he demanded.

"I fail to see what business that is of yours."

"I knew his previous owner," he responded quickly, keeping his eyes on her face and seeing fear. Not much could escape his detection when he had a mind to read a person, and he wondered again how she came by the horse.

"I think you must be mistaken. Will you help me mount, as you have sent the stableman away?"

"No." He folded his arms across his chest. "You should not be riding this horse." He refused to help her break her neck.

To his astonishment, she led the horse to a water trough and stood on its wooden edge. Then, resting her hands on the horse's withers, she hoisted herself up and swung a leg expertly over the saddle. She was much stronger than her womanly form led one to believe.

Holding the stallion steady, she turned in the saddle to look back at him. "I suggest that you and your father stop trying to tell me what to do and stay away from me, Colonel." With that, she legged the horse into a canter towards the green fields of Eastease, beyond which lay Redway.

Nathaniel watched her for a moment before turning back towards the stable.

Adam, leaning casually on the doorframe, asked in amusement, "Would you like me to saddle Thor so you can go after her, sir?"

"Yes, saddle him, please. As I am here, I will take him for a ride, but no hurry. I do not stand a chance of catching up to her. She is a most capable horsewoman," Nathaniel spoke with some surprise.

Adam straightened up and gave him a look that brooked no argument. "She's a better rider than any man or woman I've seen."

Nathaniel harrumphed, unable to resist another glimpse of Mrs Andrews and her magnificent horse speeding across the green fields. He would never admit it to Adam, but she was a better rider than any man he had met and had the full respect of that stallion.

"Well, I have seen more riders than you."

"I've seen you ride," Adam smirked before being cowed by Nathaniel's glare. "Sir."

Six

Thor's hooves thudded softly into the damp grass, sending the morning mist swirling in all directions as Nathaniel rode across the fields. He kept to the right of the various cottages and the church lining the North Road, not stopping until he spotted the stone pillar marking the boundary between Eastease and Redway Acres. As Eastease's magnificent house fell far behind him, the buildings of Redway Acres became visible in the distance.

He had set out in quite a temper, and the fresh morning air had not improved his mood. As Nathaniel paced Thor along the invisible property line he did not have her permission to cross, he wondered if she watched him from the house or stable.

His stallion, happy to have been given free rein, continued to run effortlessly beneath him as he turned his back on Redway, heading across Eastease's fields. It was the first time in Nathaniel's convalescence that he had pushed his body with such rigorous exercise. Nevertheless, he found that he felt energised despite a lack of sleep and the excesses of the previous evening.

Nathaniel held Thor to a loping canter and then reined him to a trot, allowing them both to cool down as they approached Eastease again. He decided to ride along Redway Acres' boundary during his stay to see how far her property extended.

For today, he planned to return Thor to the stable, clean himself up, and, after breakfast, inform Harker about the events of last night. He also intended to write a few letters to see if he could learn more of Captain Andrews. Despite Mrs Andrews' insistence, he had no intention of staying away from her.

His father had behaved abominably, though he doubted the earl would agree. Facing him down would require great fortitude, but Nathaniel had never felt more prepared to stand his ground. If Mrs Andrews was vulnerable here at Eastease, she might also be vulnerable at Redway Acres. Considering her remarks from last night, he decided to consult Harker to devise a plan that would redress, at least in part, his inaction in the past.

~oOo~

Helena had ridden Perseus as if the wind itself chased them. At first, she feared Colonel Ackley would leap onto a horse to chase her down, but then she realised that even if a horse were readily available, it would be unlikely to catch Perseus.

Despite the enormity of Eastease, Helena had felt cloistered in the stifling atmosphere, or perhaps it had just been the company? She had not meant to be so cruel in comparing the colonel to his father, an assessment she knew he resented. But, on the other hand, neither should she lead him to believe there might be any future with her. While Helena did not think he would behave like his father, she hoped her parting words would keep him at bay. Both father and son had tried to dictate what she should and should not do, though neither man had any authority over her.

When the colonel had appeared in Eastease's stable, the glorious sight of him dishevelled from sleep and in a state of undress made her breath rush out in a sigh. It had been as well that in the morning light, the softly spoken, concerned and considerate man who protected her from the earl the night before had disappeared. The colonel had been annoyed by her riding habit and offensive about her ability to ride Perseus. If she were a man, he would have given her the benefit of the doubt before commenting. Surprisingly, her stallion had been calm in his presence, even upon hearing his raised voice.

As Perseus crossed onto Redway land, Helena breathed in her freedom and blew out the tension in her shoulders and neck. Then, leaving the horse with John to rub down, she entered the house through the door at the back and wearily wound her way up to her rooms.

At the top of the stairs, a window looked out towards Eastease. Peering into the distance, she spied a figure in a red coat riding an enormous chestnut. The rider reined in his mount as they approached Redway's border just past the church. The chestnut paced as the man fixed his gaze on her house, craning his neck as the horse circled. To all appearances, an invisible barrier prevented their crossing onto Redway land, and Helena could not decide whether she wanted the man to defy her or turn back defeated.

Helena watched him for a while until he reined his horse towards Eastease. As he rode off without looking back, she did not experience the relief she had expected and wondered if she would have been happier had he not.

~oOo~

After refreshing himself in his rooms, Nathaniel headed downstairs for breakfast. His bed had looked inviting, but he did not want to miss his opportunity to speak with Harker before his father left. On his way to the breakfast room, he ran into an agitated Mrs Hopkins.

"Oh, Colonel Ackley, how are you this morning, sir?"

"Well, I thank you. Can I assist you, Mrs Hopkins? You seem a little perturbed."

"Oh, sir, I don't know what to think. One of the maids found a pillow and a coverlet from Mrs Andrews' rooms on the couch in that corridor this morning. It seems someone slept there, but what an odd thing to do. Unfortunately, I can't ask her of it as she has left."

Oh lord, in his haste to catch up to Mrs Andrews, he had forgotten about the pillow and coverlet. "Allow me to explain, Mrs Hopkins." Nathaniel gestured to a small sitting room. "I plan to talk to Harker as soon as he has finished his breakfast. He will speak to you of the matter later. However, please let me put your mind at ease. I slept there."

"You, Colonel? Surely not," she spoke a little harshly, and he felt somewhat abashed at the words from the woman who had known him for most of his life. "What on earth were you thinking, sleeping outside the two young ladies' rooms?"

"I am ashamed to say that my father drank too much brandy last night and roamed the corridors. He was confused, thinking he was at Aysthill House instead of Eastease. James rightly informed me of the matter, and I directed the earl back to the east wing. I thought it might be wise to stay and ensure he did not return. Mrs Andrews overheard our voices, and seeing my intention, she kindly gave me the pillow and coverlet from her rooms. I left them there after seeing her safely to the stable this morning. So, you see, all quite innocent. But given the conclusions people can mistakenly draw, I would appreciate you ensuring the Eastease staff's discretion."

Mathilda Hopkins' eyes narrowed.

I should have known I couldn't fool her, Nathaniel thought. She knew several Aysthill House servants and would understand his father's intentions. This loyal servant, who exemplified discretion, would not expect him to explain further.

"Of course." She placed her hand on his arm with a reassuring air. "May I say thank you for taking the trouble, sir? Mrs Andrews is a favourite of ours ever since that business with Adam's poor sister."

Nathaniel stared at her, his mouth slack as his sleep-deprived mind struggled to make sense of her words. As she turned to leave, he asked, "What business, Mrs Hopkins?"

"Two years back, Adam's sister, Rachel, was walking to Eastease to see him on her day off. They only have each other left. She worked for one of those families who come up from town and have a country house hereabouts. Ah, bless her, she was only fourteen then, but these two scoundrels set upon her. After they left her at the side of the road bloodied and beaten, John Robertson's boy, Jacky, happened by and took her straight to Redway. Mrs Andrews tended the poor girl while Jacky came here to fetch Adam."

Envisioning the scene, Nathaniel yearned to lay his hands on the blaggards who had violated the girl. "What happened to Rachel?"

"Oh, Mrs Andrews helped her get through her misery. Rachel knows her words and numbers and has an aptitude for learning, so once she recovered and they were sure there were no consequences, Mrs Andrews employed her as Miss Issie's first governess. Mrs Andrews intends to keep her when Miss Issie's learning outstrips Rachel's capabilities. She says Rachel can learn at the same time and then find a good position elsewhere, with references from Redway. From what I gather from Adam, Mrs Andrews has given the girl a small dowry, just enough to overcome the stigma should she want to marry."

"How considerate of her," Nathaniel said, an idea shaping in his mind. "That goes above and beyond a helping hand."

"That's Mrs Andrews for you. She thinks everything through."

"Indeed. Tell me, Mrs Hopkins, has she assisted others as generously?" His interest earned a shrewd smile that made warmth suffuse his face.

"Well now, let me think." She tapped her finger against her pursed lips. "She isn't one to make a big fuss and bother of what she does. I hear she was goaded into mentioning Mrs Miller at dinner last night, so you already know about that. Then there's Old Joe, who lives in that ramshackle place down the lane a ways. He's a widower and doesn't care for himself as he should. So she goes down there with Miss Issie of a Sunday with a basket of vegetables her housekeeper grows. Gives him a bit of coin, too, but he spends that on ale. Ruth says Mrs Andrews knows it, but she just shrugs and says at this point in his life, having a spot of ale might be all he has to look forward to. Another poor soul she helped is young Lilly Stubbins. Her husband got himself imprisoned a while back. Lilly had nothing to pay her rent, and she and her three children were evicted. So now she works in Redway's kitchen and lives with her brood in one of their cottages. Oh, and I know a couple of widows around here that Mrs Andrews took under her wing. Got them on their feet before they moved on with references. That's all I can think of offhand, but I wouldn't be surprised if there were more."

Impressed and humbled, Nathaniel could only shake his head. Mrs Andrews' selfless gestures of kindness and caring must mean the world to her beneficiaries. Small wonder that so many people in this village admired her. He thought of the many women his father had harmed over the years. Were they in dreadful situations through no fault of their own? Did they have the good fortune of a *Mrs Andrews* to help them?

He drew in a breath, his head suddenly clear, his purpose settled. "Thank you, Mrs Hopkins. You have inspired me, or should I say Mrs Andrews has? Please be sure to reward James' vigilance somehow."

~oOo~

When Nathaniel entered the study, Alexander did not immediately register his friend's severe demeanour. He sat behind his desk and indicated the facing chair for Nathaniel. Finally noting his unhappy countenance, he inquired, "What's troubling you?"

"Mrs Hopkins wanted to ask you about a pillow and coverlet left on the couch outside Mrs Andrews' rooms this morning. She said it seemed as if someone had slept there."

Alexander blinked in surprise. "Good God! Who on earth would do such a thing?"

"I would, on account of my father's refusal to control himself." Nathaniel then related the evening events that led to him spending the night in the hallway. "I'm sorry that this occurred in your home and for what *could* have happened. This time, I must take action. I cannot allow this to be covered up for him again. What if he were to go to Redway Acres?"

Fury burned in Alexander's chest. "How dare that man defile the sanctity of my home? How dare he disrespect one of my guests? I am sorry to talk of your father this way, Nathaniel, but I don't care about his rank—I will not have it." As he searched the grim face across from him, he feared Nathaniel was right. Lord Aysthill might contrive to make mischief at Redway Acres. He rose with single-minded intent, but Nathaniel's insistent plea stopped him.

"Harker, wait. Help me work out a plan. I have one in mind, but it will take both of us to convince him."

Curious, Alexander sat back down. "What is it?"

"Mrs Andrews said something that shamed me to my core. She rightly guessed that I knew what Father meant to do because he had done it before. In so many words, Mrs Andrews pointed out that the first time should have been the last. She was right. Had I acted sooner, it would not have come to this."

"If *we* had acted sooner, my friend. Knowing she had refused to sell horses to your father, I invited her, but I thought she would be protected here—I am grateful to you that she was. Unfortunately, none of us is innocent in this." Alexander reached out and gripped Nathaniel's arm. "I say it's high time we remedy that."

~oOo~

"Lord Aysthill is here, sir," Watkins announced, then stepped aside to let David enter Harker's study.

"Little formal there, Harker," David quipped and begrudgingly took a seat. Having slept late, he did not appreciate Harker's summons before breakfast. Moreover, Harker's slight bow seemed less deferential than David felt his title required.

"Sir, I wish to address your behaviour towards Mrs Andrews last night." Although Harker's voice was calm, anger blazed in his dark eyes.

David shifted in his chair. For the first time in his acquaintance with Harker, he felt uncomfortable under his gaze. How much did the man know? David decided to bluff.

"I do not know what you mean nor appreciate your tone. You forget yourself, boy."

"It is you who have forgotten yourself, Father."

A chill shivered down David's spine. Turning, he saw Nathaniel leaning against the end of a large bookcase, his arms folded across his chest, menace in his eyes. He wore his full regimentals, including the sword sheathed at his side. Hidden in the shadows, he had kept so still that David had not noticed him—*had he even breathed?*

Now David distinguished something else that gave him pause. Nathaniel had become a man. David had never regarded his sons in that way, despite their ages. And this man was a soldier. Struck, David realised Nathaniel had killed more than a few enemies. Shot them or cut them down with that razor-edged sword. True, he had done so for King and Country, a noble reason, but one could not mete out death without acquiring a dark side. It was there in his son's face and, most certainly, had revealed itself in that dark corridor last night.

"My boy," David began in a conciliatory tone. "Must we talk of this? I had hoped to keep it between ourselves. I confess to being a bit drunk, but as you know, nothing untoward occurred. Let bygones be bygones. You know I shall make it worth your while."

With a flex of his shoulder, the soldier straightened, his arms still folded. "You keep your money," he said in a soft but penetrating voice. When he stepped forwards, David instinctively recoiled.

"Harker will decide what must be done," Nathaniel continued, "since you chose to dishonour his home."

In the pause, David could see his son trembling with the effort to control his temper, yet his tone, like his eyes, remained rock hard.

"I told him all of the particulars. You will listen while he has his say. Then I will have mine."

David craned his neck as Nathaniel moved to stand directly behind him, assuming a martial stance. He managed not to squirm in his chair, but the hair rose on his neck as he waited for Harker to address him.

Ignoring David's glare, the young man began, "Lord Aysthill, to secure my discretion over what occurred here last night, I require the following from you. You must locate all the women that you have violated in the past and make restitution. By restitution, I mean you must ensure their health and that of their immediate relations; that they and their family members have gainful employment and suitable living arrangements. Restitution will be made to their families if they are no longer living. If there was issue from these assignations, you must establish a trust to supply their needs for the rest of their lives. You may do all of this anonymously, but I expect to see evidence regularly in the form of a ledger. At my own expense, I will secure the services of a discreet man who will find these women for you and make any arrangements necessary to help fulfil your obligations. As your memory may not serve you as well as it should, your son will ask Lady Aysthill to assist you in recalling the names and circumstances of your victims. Genevieve assures me that your wife has not forgotten the particulars."

"I will do no such thing," David blustered in astonishment. Why, he had not even entered the woman's rooms. She probably did not even know that he had been there.

Harker shot a glance past David before fixing again on his face. "You will do it, sir. If you do not, the colonel and I will ensure that all your acquaintances here and in London know that you attempted to"—he paused, seeking the right word—"fornicate with an unwilling young widow. A guest in my home whose husband died honourably in battle and who is much beloved in this community. No one will invite you to their house again for fear of what might happen to their guests or families. You will not be able to show your face in society and will live out your days in seclusion at Aysthill. Do I have your agreement, sir?"

"You leave me little choice in the matter. Send me your man, and I will get him started. Although I must say that I am not happy."

David made to stand, but heavy hands gripped his shoulders and pressed him back down. My goodness, he had no idea his son was so strong. Why had his mother been fussing over him these past weeks? He was no invalid.

"Just a moment, Father."

David held still, warned by the steel in Nathaniel's voice. His youngest son, so amiable and full of laughter, hid this side of himself from his family and, from the look on Harker's face, his friends.

"You have not heard me out, so listen closely if you hope to ensure my secrecy. You will never again force yourself on a woman. And you had better hope to God that I never hear of you taking out your frustrations on my mother. Drunkenness is no longer an excuse for your behaviour. Lastly, though of equal import, you will not set foot on Redway Acres property. If you harm one hair on Mrs Andrews' head, I will run you through. Do you understand me, *old man?*"

With a roar of indignance, David roughly pushed his chair away as he turned to his son. But, unlike the child of days gone by, the man David faced did not flinch or cower. They stood nose to nose at almost the same height, but the battle-hardened soldier remained still and unfaltering.

David hesitated for only a moment, but the insolence of his son's behaviour was not to be borne.

"Kill me?"

"Yes."

"In cold blood?"

"Yes."

"You think you could?"

"Absolutely, yes," came the swift response.

"Mark my words; I'll see you hang," David shouted. The froth of his spittle landed on the face that was so close to his, but the man did not move.

"No," Nathaniel ground out the words. "You—will—be—dead."

David swallowed the lump of fear in his throat, his words coming out in a rasp, "You—you wouldn't dare."

His son's bristled face brushed up against his own as David felt a harsh, threat-laden whisper in his ear, "Test me, Father, and we meet next in hell."

David slumped back into his chair, rubbing his face with his hand.

Nathaniel strode to the door and paused. "Those are my terms. Take them or leave them." Then the door slammed behind him

Seven

In church on Sunday, Nathaniel scanned the congregation for a familiar head of red hair without luck. Masking his disappointment, he smiled and nodded to acquaintances. *What excuse might Mrs Andrews offer Brooks should he dare to inquire about her absence?* When the singing of the first hymn concluded, the clergyman stepped up to the pulpit and surveyed his flock. From his fervent gaze, Nathaniel imagined he was looking for her, too.

"The LORD is good to all; He has compassion on all He has made. Psalm one hundred and forty-five, verse nine." Brooks brought his flock to attention with a commanding voice. "God said, *Let Us make man in Our image, according to Our likeness; and let them rule over the fish of the sea and over the birds of the sky and over the cattle and over all the earth, and over every creeping thing that creeps on the earth.* Genesis chapter one, verse twenty-seven."

Nathaniel's ears pricked up. The Brooks in front of him was more confident than two nights ago. He had not heard the man's sermons before, but in his experience, preachers tended to drone on about sin or read long bible passages. He listened more attentively.

"The Psalm," Brooks continued, "is simple enough. God is good, and He has compassion for everything because He created everything. He has compassion for man and woman, animals, trees and flowers, and the earth and sky." He paused, gauging the congregation with a commanding air. "God is good. God is compassionate." A murmur arose from the pews as many parishioners echoed his affirmations.

"The Verse: God made man in His image. As God is good and compassionate, so must we be, must we not? We know some of us are not good or compassionate, so it is a choice. God wants us to choose Him and choose goodness and compassion as He does. You may tell me, *Mr Brooks, we are good and compassionate. We are here, attending church.* Yes, you are, and I thank you, and God is pleased, but is attending church Godly or goodly?" At this point, the clergyman caught Nathaniel's eye and bestowed a small smile. Recalling Mrs Andrews' comments at dinner, Nathaniel nodded and smiled in return. As the man seemed to want an answer, Nathaniel complied.

"Godly, I believe, Mr Brooks." Nathaniel's deep voice carried to every corner of the church.

"Colonel Ackley, who is attending with his friends from Eastease, is correct. We are being Godly today, respecting and praising God together on His day, as we should. But when were you last good? When were you a good neighbour, a good friend or a good master? When and to whom have you shown compassion?"

Nathaniel thought Brooks was in fine form. From all appearances, the clergyman indeed had taken Mrs Andrews' words to heart. Surely, she would appreciate this sermon. A shame she wasn't present.

"God is compassionate over all He has made, and He has made man in his image. *Let them rule over the fish of the sea and over the birds of the sky and over the cattle and over all the earth, and over every creeping thing that creeps on the earth.* God wants us to be compassionate in our rule over everything He has made. Good and compassionate to the animals and over all the earth. Should Man beat the horse? We would only teach the horse to kick the dog, and the dog, in turn, learns only to chase the cat." Laughter followed this imagery, and Brooks smiled, apparently pleased to have amused his listeners.

"We should be good and compassionate and treat our animals well. God is good and compassionate in all He has made, and God made man and woman. Therefore, we should be good and compassionate towards each other. To that end, I implore you to spend no more time listening to me on this day of the Lord. Let us say a final prayer, sing a final hymn, and then go from here and do something good, something compassionate. Perhaps you need to make amends or ask forgiveness from someone to whom you have not been kind. Rest assured, I have an apology to make. Let me add that the person who inspired this sermon, unfortunately, is not here today. Undoubtedly, she is somewhere doing some good, as she was last Sabbath."

A murmurous buzzing ensued as people glanced around to see who was absent. Nathaniel heard a voice behind him whisper, *He must mean Mrs Andrews. She is always serving somebody*. The thought of her visiting this widower's ramshackle cottage gave Nathaniel an idea of the good he could do.

As the final hymn ended, Brooks stepped down to greet a couple with a brood of children of all ages surrounding them. Moving to head him off, Nathaniel noticed the faded bruises on the woman's face. Mrs Miller, he presumed, clenching his fists while eyeing her husband. He yearned to beat the man senseless but refrained from succumbing to the temptation while in church.

Turning his back to the couple, he told Brooks, "A shame Mrs Andrews wasn't here today. She would have enjoyed your sermon, I am sure."

"Thank you, Colonel. I hope to see you again before you return to your duties," Brooks replied cordially.

"I am sure you shall." Nathaniel left the man to his apology.

~oOo~

Outside the church, many people were discussing what good deed they could do that day, and their conversations faded as Nathaniel approached a small open vehicle parked outside the gate beside the Eastease coach. Two well-muscled horses waited to pull it while a working man in his Sunday best stood at their heads.

To Nathaniel's surprise, a confident Harriet greeted the man. "Mr Robertson, it is so good to see you. How are you and your family?"

"Good mornin', Miss Wyndham. Jacky just left in the cart with the rest of the Redway folk." He pulled off his cap and gestured northward, and Nathaniel peered down the lane at a cart full of people trundling towards the distant buildings.

Harriet introduced the man to her companions. "This is John Robertson, Helena's stable manager. John, this is Mr and Mrs Harker and my cousin, Colonel Ackley."

John pulled at his forelock towards each of them. "A pleasure."

"Ah," Harriet said, "here comes Mrs Harker's aunt and uncle. Mr and Mrs Ridgefield, this is John Robertson."

"Redway Acres' stable manager, I understand," said Mr Ridgefield, nodding to John.

"Yes, sir. I must tell you and your wife that Mrs Andrews sent me ter drive you to Redway."

"Oh, how thoughtful," Mrs Ridgefield remarked. "However, we had planned to stop at the rectory for tea on our way back to Eastease."

"So I wer told, ma'am. Mrs Andrews instructed me ter drive you there from Redway and return you safely ter Eastease after you've visited with Mr Brooks."

At this assurance, Mr Ridgefield handed his wife into the carriage and climbed beside her.

Nathaniel approached the horses to run his hands over their necks and down their legs with a sure touch. Watching him, John asked, "What do yer think of the 'orses then, sir?"

"Excellent specimens. Whatever you feed them at Redway seems to be working. I saw Mrs Andrews' majestic grey in Eastease's stable on Friday. Pegasus, isn't it?"

"Perseus, sir."

"Yes, of course," Nathaniel agreed amiably and then indicated the Ridgefields. "So, you are doing your *something good* for today?" He noted the relief in Robertson's countenance at his change of subject.

"This? Nah, s'pposed I'd stop over at Old Joe's later. See what I can fix up for him, sir."

"He would be the widower in the cottage down the lane? I had the same thought. What time are you planning to go? I'll meet you there."

They arranged to meet after John dropped the Ridgefields at the parsonage for tea.

John climbed up to the driver's seat. Replacing his cap, he tipped it to the Harkers and promised to return their guests to Eastease in time for dinner.

As the Ridgefields departed, Nathaniel's urge was to follow them to Redway, but to what end? While he wished to see Mrs Andrews again, he felt ill-prepared to face her. The sordid business with his father still troubled him. Yet, in some inexplicable way, his brief contact with Mrs Andrews' horses had helped relieve some of his anxiety, perhaps because they were hers and provided a connection of sorts.

Not wishing to be cooped up in the closed carriage, he informed Harker he would walk back to Eastease. Immediately, Harriet insisted on walking with him. She had once told him that Harker and Genevieve could be embarrassingly affectionate in front of her, so he agreed, providing she would ramble with him over the fields. She smiled in assent, declaring how lucky she was to have worn her boots.

Harriet's company turned out to be the tonic Nathaniel needed. They walked through the graveyard, crossed over a stile, and entered a field that would take them back to Eastease. Over the first hill, the house came into view. Harriet expressed how pleasant it was to have him around. Would he stay for the baby's arrival? Surely, he would not want to miss that event. She spoke of books she had read and how her music was progressing. She asked him about Spain's weather and landscape and how much he had learned of the language without mentioning the battles he fought or his injury. He had always shown an aptitude for languages and spoke French and German fluently. He had been learning Spanish and Portuguese and delighted her with some phrases.

At length, their conversation turned to Mr Brooks' sermon.

"Mr Brooks' words reminded me of Helena," Harriet ventured.

"I believe you are correct. I heard several people discussing her as we left the church," Nathaniel confirmed.

"Do you think he likes her?"

"Yes, I think he does. However, any clergyman worth his salt would be shallow and foolish to deliver a sermon based on his infatuation with a woman. I like to think Mr Brooks believes in his interpretation of the text." Nathaniel paused before adding, "Not that he stands a chance with her in any case."

"Because you want her for yourself. I saw how you watched her while she sang. You missed turning several pages."

God be damned; she is teasing me. "I will give you a ten-count head start, Harriet," he warned.

She screamed and, picking up her skirts, ran as fast as she could over the long grass. *It is so good to see her run and laugh.* "That is ten," Nathaniel shouted and then easily overtook her. Taking hold of her waist, he lifted her off the ground and swung her in a tight circle, making her squeal with delight.

After finally putting her down, he hugged her to his chest and kissed her head, as he had often done when she was younger. Nathaniel loved both of his wards and had missed them in the long months he had been away. They were the only remnants left in the world of his cousin and friend, Mark. So he revelled in being with Harriet again.

As they continued walking, she brought up her friendship with Mrs Andrews. How she had met her, and was not Perseus a wonderful horse? How handsome Redway Acres was, and that she hoped he would get to visit the stable.

"I'm not sure Mrs Andrews wants to see me right now," he remarked, surprised to feel a twinge of sorrow.

She cast him a sidelong glance. "I know something happened the other night that no one will tell me of, but I will not worry about it. Helena says wasting time on things you cannot control is pointless. Accept or do not accept a situation, and then move on. I am not accepting that I seem to be the only person excluded from the secret, whatever it is, but since I cannot control it, I am moving on. But tell me this, Cousin. You have been a gentleman towards her, have you not?"

"I have, Harriet, I assure you. We disagreed, and I will apologise if the opportunity presents itself."

He had heard *Helena says* from Harriet many times in his few days at Eastease, so he asked, "What does *Helena say* of riding astride rather than side-saddle?"

She laughed aloud again. "Now, it is my turn to keep a secret. What she told me was meant to stay between us. She did say, however, that she felt it was safer to ride astride. Falling off a side-saddle has killed women because their skirts got caught on the pommel. Is that not awful? Apparently, it is less comfortable riding astride and takes longer to learn. What do you think?"

"I suppose Mrs Andrews is uniquely qualified to know since she has done both. However, I doubt women would have been allowed to ride side-saddle if it was not safe. Does she ride everywhere astride?" A vision of Mrs Andrews hoisting herself up and astride Perseus, as she called her stallion, rose in his mind. He shook it away.

"Of course not. Mrs Andrews only rides that way to train a horse a man will ride or when she is alone, riding around Redway. She says she prefers it. I love the split-skirt riding habit she wears. You can hardly notice that it isn't a regular riding habit when she stands, but sometimes she wears men's trousers underneath her skirts."

"Which do you have hidden in your dressing room, ready for when you get permission to ride astride?"

When she looked at him aghast, Nathaniel laughed. "A nicely executed innocent look, my dear, but you are no cousin of mine if you aren't prepared to take advantage the moment Harker changes his mind."

"I do have some trousers that Helena gave me. They are a bit loose, but as she is as tall as me, they are long enough."

"It would seem that Mrs Andrews wants you to follow her lead." He shook his head. It would not do for that headstrong woman to unduly influence Harriet.

"Not at all, I assure you, Nathaniel. I had to pester her for weeks before she would give me the trousers. When she relented, *finally*, I had to solemnly swear that I would use them only if I had permission from my guardian. You are as much my guardian as Alexander. You could allow me to ride astride, and when I do, you could try riding side-saddle. Then you would have first-hand knowledge in the matter."

Here was Mrs Andrews' influence coming to the surface. The girl made a sound and reasonable argument and cornered him nicely. He felt proud of her despite his concerns. As they approached the house, he contemplated her hopeful face. There was time to spare before his meeting at the old widower's cottage.

Remembering his intention to do her a good turn after she unknowingly helped him speak with Mrs Andrews at the dinner party, he agreed. "Challenge accepted, Harriet. Go and change while I have our horses saddled."

She bestowed a glorious smile. "You should ride Hudson, Nathaniel. He is used to side-saddle commands." Then, she added hopefully, "I could ride Thor."

"That is *never* going to happen."

~oOo~

Grateful to head home, John drove the open Redway coach down the road at a smart clip with the Ridgefields chattering in the back. When Colonel Ackley had said the name *Pegasus*, John quickly corrected him, but he did not know if the colonel believed him. Now John had to meet with the man at Old Joe's place. How could he have refused?

His girl, as he and Ruth considered Helena, had been out of sorts since the dinner party at Eastease, and he suspected that the colonel had much to do with her moodiness. Helena never discussed other people with him except in matters pertaining to horses. And so, earlier that morning, as they worked in adjoining stalls in her stable, she surprised him by asking why men were so smug in their opinions and always felt entitled to tell women what to do. Uncertain if she was venting her spleen or seeking his opinion, he kept quiet.

She continued, "Just because the man is a colonel and used to ordering others around does not mean I have to obey him. He thinks he is so charming and handsome with those blue eyes and that boyish smile. He said he knew Perseus."

Smiling while he worked, John popped his head over the stall wall to scrutinise her. In the midst of rubbing down another horse, she turned to face him.

"I told him he was mistaken," she retorted in response to his shrewd look. "I do not know if he believed me. He is so damn sure of himself. Thinks he is so bloody handsome."

"You said 'andsome twice." John pointed his curry comb at her and then shrugged as they resumed their work.

"Yes, I keep doing that."

When she breathed a wistful sigh, John smiled to himself again. Now that he had met the man she found so intriguing, he understood what she meant by his charm and good looks, to say nothing of his commanding demeanour. The colonel had nearly tricked him into revealing Perseus' history, which indicated a clever mind, but whether the young officer was good enough for Helena remained to be seen.

As John guided the coach onto Redway's drive, he heard Mr and Mrs Ridgefield praising the appearance of the place. Although he worked for Helena and had known her and Redway for years, he took personal pride in the Ridgefields' compliments. As he handed Mrs Ridgefield down from the carriage, he spied his wife, framed in the front doorway, ready to lead the guests to their hostess.

While he waited for Ruth in the entry hall, he could hear her voice emanating from the parlour. "Mr and Mrs Ridgefield, ma'am." After closing the door behind her, she hastened to join him. "What is it, John? I have to see to the luncheon trays."

"What do yer think of them?" He nodded towards the parlour.

"They seem nice enough. Quite gracious, in fact, and Mrs Ridgefield is astonishingly fashionable." She narrowed her gaze and smiled at him. "But that isn't the reason you're standing 'ere. Spit it out, John Robertson."

"Colonel Ackley was there when they came out o' the church. He called Perseus *Pegasus*."

Ruth covered her mouth in shock. "What did yer say?"

"Nothing, o' course, just corrected him. But I don't think he believed me."

"I have ter go." Ruth glanced over her shoulder at the parlour door. "I'll mention it ter her later, but there's not much to do, is there?"

John shook his head. Then, leaving his wife to her duties, he returned to drive the coach around to the back courtyard.

~oOo~

Helena greeted Mr and Mrs Ridgefield with a curtsey. "It's so good to see you again. I am delighted you were able to come."

"Thank you for the invitation, Mrs Andrews." Mr Ridgefield bowed to her. "And for the transportation. It is a perfect day for an open carriage jaunt and such magnificent animals."

"Not mine, I am sorry to say. Those two are a commission, but your transportation was a training exercise for them, so we both benefitted." As Helena had found at the Eastease dinner, she immediately felt at ease with this couple. Genevieve was lucky to call them family.

Ruth and a maid arrived with refreshment trays, oversaw the meats and breads, pies and sweets arrangement, and poured the tea before leaving.

Helena noted that Mr Ridgefield praised the sumptuous fare as enthusiastically as he did everything that pleased him. As they ate, the couple talked of Mr Brooks' sermon.

"I believe you were the source of his inspiration, Mrs Andrews," Mrs Ridgefield said with amusement.

"Indeed." Mr Ridgefield exclaimed. "In the end, he told everyone to do something good for someone else. Bravo!"

"I am all astonishment and am sure I deserve no such praise. I do not look back on my behaviour at dinner that evening with satisfaction. Upon reflection, I may have embarrassed the poor man in front of your niece in my anger over how things had turned out for Mrs Miller. Maybe my good deed for the day should be apologising to him."

"We are stopping for tea with him when we leave here. You would be welcome to join us, I am sure. After all, we will be travelling in your carriage," Mr Ridgefield pointed out. "I would suggest, if you have the opportunity, to make clear your sentiments towards him. I hope you do not mind me saying so, but I suspect he has taken an interest in you, and I believe you do not feel the same?"

Helena gave a quick nod, then paused as an impatient voice arose outside the door. She smiled at the Ridgefields. "I understand from Genevieve that you have several children."

"Yes, we do, and we said today, for the hundredth time at least, how much we miss them. Oh my word, what a pretty girl." Mrs Ridgefield had turned at the sound of the door opening and spotted Issie peering inside.

When Helena gave a quick nod, Issie smiled and entered the room, eyeing the new adults. "Mr and Mrs Ridgefield, may I introduce my daughter, Miss Isabella Andrews? Issie, this is Mr and Mrs Ridgefield, Mrs Harker's aunt and uncle from London."

Mr Ridgefield rose and bowed. In response, Issie performed her best curtsey, provoking happy laughter.

"Adorable," said Mr Ridgefield. "I'm delighted to make your acquaintance, young lady."

"It is lovely to meet you, Miss Andrews," Mrs Ridgefield said and breathed a wistful sigh. "We have five children of our own, but we left them in the care of Mrs Harker's two sisters and mother at Thornbane Lodge in Cambridgeshire."

"Were they naughty?" asked Issie.

"Not in the least, dear," Mrs Ridgefield replied with a laugh. "We miss them all terribly, but it is a long journey, and they have so much fun with their cousins."

"I like you," Issie announced. "Would you like to come and see my horses?"

"Splendid idea, child, splendid." Mr Ridgefield allowed Issie to lead him towards the door.

Helena rose to protest, but Mrs Ridgefield stayed her. "He will be fine. She is delightful, and he will love her showing him around. Besides, he knows I hoped to have a quiet word with you."

Surprised, Helena sat down again. "Of course. Is anything wrong?"

"Colonel Ackley told Mr Harker about his father's indiscretion on

Friday night."

"Oh, I see," was all that Helena could think to say. The heat of embarrassment rose in her cheeks.

"Mr Harker and Gennie wanted to assure you he is doing everything possible to ensure the situation never happens again. So you will be safe at Eastease and here at Redway," Mrs Ridgefield finished sympathetically.

"Here? Of course I will be safe here," Helena retorted, astonished at the thought of being accosted in her own home.

"And what if Lord Aysthill were to visit you? Who here would protect your good name?" Mrs Ridgefield's voice had grown stern. She clearly felt it vital to convey the reality of Helena's situation.

"John and Ruth are here, and my stablemen." Helena realised her tone sounded less than firm.

"Loyal people all, I'm sure, but consider the rank of the man from whom they would need to protect you."

Helena bit her lip, resorting to a longtime nervous habit. "I had not—I did not think." She glanced around worriedly and would not have been surprised if Lord Aysthill were to appear in the doorway suddenly.

"Do not fret, my dear." Mrs Ridgefield patted her hand. "Mr Harker's message was that Lord Aysthill would not dare to come here. Considering Colonel Ackley's mood yesterday, I think he had more to do with it than Mr Harker. Mr Ridgefield was surprised to see the colonel leave Mr Harker's study in his full regimentals, including his sword, after they met with Lord Aysthill. I believe my husband's description of him was formidable."

"Oh," Helena breathed the word as she took in the implication of what Mr Ridgefield witnessed.

Mrs Ridgefield continued, "I have two other questions to ask you, and they are my questions, not those of Mr Harker or Gennie. First, was Colonel Ackley right in saying Lord Aysthill found your door locked, and nothing happened?"

"Yes, he was right. Thank goodness I had thought to lock it. I disagreed with Lord Aysthill before, you see, about horses."

"So I understand." Mrs Ridgefield paused. "Gennie would not be happy with me for asking this, but can you assure me nothing happened between you and the colonel that night?"

Helena rose in shock and stepped back from Mrs Ridgefield, her eyes narrowing. "Why do you ask? Did he say something had?" She fumed at the thought of Colonel Ackley confessing to a liaison that had not occurred. Perhaps he was more like his father than she had credited.

"Not at all," Mrs Ridgefield replied. "I meant no offence, dear. Please mark it down to motherly concern and rest assured that you can confide in me should the need arise."

Returning to her seat, Helena assessed Gennie's aunt. Mrs Ridgefield had shown herself to be a kindly woman. How nice it must be to have a mother or aunt as thoughtful. "Thank you for your concern, but there is no need to worry. After the colonel sent his father away, I gave him a pillow and coverlet to aid him in sleeping on the couch outside my rooms. That was all. He was concerned the earl might return." She hesitated, searching the older woman's face. "You believe Colonel Ackley has an interest in me?"

"Let me put it this way. If a man is not interested in a woman, he does not watch her the way the colonel watched you as you sang that evening. Nor does he threaten his powerful father with a sword to ensure the woman's safety."

"Do you think he is more interested in Redway than me?"

"That question is harder to answer. However, let me ask you this: Have Gennie or Miss Wyndham ever spoken to you of Colonel Ackley's second cousin, Lady Grace Bainbridge?"

Helena thought the question odd. "No, I do not think so, but Lady Aysthill did mention that she has a superior singing voice to mine."

Mrs Ridgefield laughed at this. "I doubt that, my dear. I understand that since the colonel's injury, his parents have been looking to him to quit soldiering and marry her. They want to keep the Bainbridge estate in the family. Yet, here he is at Eastease, protectively sleeping outside your rooms."

"Oh, I did not know that." Helena smiled and then shook herself as if to clear her head. "Well, his interest will avail him nothing. I am not the marrying kind, and I cannot give over Redway to anyone. Let us go and see if Issie has Mr Ridgefield up on a horse."

Eight

Eliot Brooks walked home after a satisfying luncheon at a neighbour's house and thought back to the dinner at Eastease. Youthful but serious, Eliot enjoyed the good fortune of having Mr Harker afford him living arrangements in Eastcambe village. Now that Eliot had firmly settled his path in life, he hoped to take a wife and start a family. When he had found himself seated beside Mrs Andrews, Eliot believed providence was smiling upon him. He thought her attractive, intelligent, and worth pursuing. Eliot soon discovered the folly of indulging his overly eager heart, for their conversation had not gone according to his plan.

After retiring to his guest rooms at Eastease, he had mulled over her points with an open mind, something he failed to do at the dinner table. Eventually, he understood he could not compel her to agree with him, nor should he waste time trying. Though attracted to her, he realised she was far too headstrong to make him a good match. Despite his bruised pride, he still considered himself blessed for having made her acquaintance, for she had opened his eyes. His and those of Colonel Ackley, albeit in different ways. He had seen how the colonel looked at her. Therefore, he, Eliot Brooks, would step aside.

Eliot now recognised that Mrs Andrews had been right to challenge him that night. He had neglected to learn about the Millers' circumstances, so he felt obliged to assume at least some responsibility for the husband's actions. Moreover, he had failed not only the Millers but others in his parish by not trying to get to know his flock. When visiting their homes, Eliot prided himself on not asking questions of a too personal nature. Maybe he should have.

The congregation had received his sermon well this morning, and his conversation with Mrs Andrews had inspired him. He felt confident in his interpretations of the subject matter and hoped his words would positively influence his flock. Today was the first time his congregation had not sat fidgeting but kept their attention on him. He wished his muse had been present to share in his euphoria by receiving his sincere thanks.

Near home, he heard the clatter of horses' hooves and the rattling of wheels behind him. The Ridgefields approached the parsonage riding in an open coach, and trailing the vehicle on horseback was the very focus of his thoughts—Mrs Andrews.

She called out to him from atop her grey stallion. "Mr Brooks, I wonder if I might join you for tea?"

"Why, of course," he replied, even as he worried she had heard about his sermon and now viewed him more favourably. Perhaps the idea that she could influence him flattered her? Watching her rein to a halt, he noted his heart racing again and abruptly constrained his emotions. "I am returning from a very pleasing luncheon with the Cuthbertsons."

Accepting his assistance while dismounting, she said with a sparkle in her eyes, "And are we soon to be calling Miss Cuthbertson Mrs Brooks?"

"Not at all. The food was lavish, but unfortunately, the conversation was less so. I hope you have not exhausted my guests' supply of wit?" he teased in return as the group followed him into his small but pleasantly situated house.

"Mr Brooks, I assure you, my wife and I rarely suffer from a lack of conversation," Mr Ridgefield chortled. "How witty it might be is for you to decide."

As they entered the parlour, Mrs Ridgefield declared, "We informed Mrs Andrews of your sermon encouraging people to do good."

"A good many people are heeding your words," Mrs Andrews added. "John is on his way to see what he can do for Old Joe. I've decided that my good deed should be to apologise to you, sir. I was angry over what happened to Mrs Miller, but I was wrong to embarrass you over dinner. I am truly sorry."

"You mustn't trouble yourself. Please believe I am not upset. You certainly inspired my sermon, but I have never felt so right when preaching as I did today. I spoke with the Millers afterwards and planned to visit them weekly to discuss God's and the church's views of marriage. Mr Miller agreed. I hope you approve."

"I do indeed. Thank you, Mr Brooks."

"You seem to have a nose for finding those in need and helping them in various ways. Perhaps we could work together? At the same time, I hope you permit me to talk of the bible, as you seem determined to spend your churchgoing time elsewhere." Eliot smiled as he spoke. He suspected Mrs Andrews was a non-believer, and he hoped he might persuade her towards his viewpoint. After all, a clergyman's responsibility involved ensuring the souls of his flock arrived in heaven when the time came. He would hate to see Mrs Andrews end up in the hands of the devil.

"I agree," she said, "but with the understanding that I prefer a discussion and reasoned arguments."

"Hear, hear!" exclaimed Mr Ridgefield. "I do believe that Eastcambe will benefit greatly from your partnership."

"Undoubtedly," Mrs Ridgefield agreed. Laughing, she added, "Now, Mr Brooks, would you allow me to talk to you of Mrs Harker's unmarried sisters?"

~oOo~

Nathaniel spotted John Robertson driving the open coach towards him as he turned down the lane to Old Joe's cottage. Evidently, John had left the Ridgefields to enjoy their tea with Mr

Brooks. Now that his walk with Harriet had lifted his spirits from his dealings with his father, Nathaniel had time to recall Joe Baxter and his few previous interactions with him.

As a younger man, Joe had worked at Redway Acres, no doubt for Mrs Andrews' grandfather. When Nathaniel visited Eastease, he and Harker rode to the Davenport manor house opposite Redway to call on Robert. Occasionally, they came across the older man walking in either direction, and if Joe happened to be going their way, Nathaniel would offer to let him ride double on his horse. He always left him at the entrance to the lane, never venturing to the man's house. He wondered if Old Joe would remember him. Robert had moved to London many years ago, but by then, Nathaniel was in the army and rarely saw his friend.

Nathaniel studied Joe's dwelling as it came into view—a single-story cottage with windows so grimy he wondered how the man could see outside. The thatched roof hung low, and the rectangle of thatching that should have protected the front door from the elements looked as though it might collapse at any moment. Joe's home was, indeed, a ramshackle, and Nathaniel hated the thought of Mrs Andrews being anywhere near it.

No one stirred in the house that Nathaniel could tell. As he secured Thor to a rickety fence post, the clip-clop of hooves made him turn. A coach approached from the lane. At that exact moment, a frail form appeared in the cottage doorway. Nathaniel's first instinct was to pull Old Joe out of harm's way for fear the porch roof would crash down on him, but he held back. If Joe wished to take the risk, who was he to interfere?

Joe did not look at him but waited for Robertson to bring the vehicle to a stop, so Nathaniel took a moment to assess the older man. Much older and frailer than Nathaniel remembered, Joe's features had grown wizened over the years, his dark skin folding on his cheeks, his forehead and neck deeply wrinkled. He appeared unkempt and whiskery, and his clothes hung on his gaunt frame like weathered rags on a scarecrow.

He spoke in the thick country accent of a bit further south. "Ol'right, John. Who's this fellah yer got wi' yer?"

"Joe, this is Colonel Ackley. He's acquainted with the Harkers. Colonel, this is Old Joe."

Joe finally looked at him. "'Quainted, ah yer? Ol'roight. Wat yer want wi' me? Colonel, is it?"

"I am pleased to meet with you again, Mr Baxter," Nathaniel spoke with an amused smile. Rarely did anyone address him with less than complete respect. He found it refreshing and thought it might amuse him for a while.

"Ha. Thems all call me Old Joe. Yer say *Mr Baxter* to 'em nah one'll no who yer ah on about." Joe's laughter turned into a cough. After recovering, he said, "I remember yer with Mr Harker an' that Davenport fellah. An' yer ah colonel now, eh? In the army?"

"Yes, the army. Friends call me Ackers—if you would prefer." Nathaniel noticed John raise his eyebrows.

"Colonel'll do. Guessin' y'earned it." Old Joe contemplated him, and Nathaniel smiled.

"I like to think so. Thank you, Joe."

John spoke up, "What we want, Joe, is to help yer. The preacher said we should do summat good in the way Helena does."

"John and I thought we could see if your place required some attention," Nathaniel supplied, noting John's informal use of his mistress' name. Then, all three of them turned to assess the house.

"It 'as sin better days," Joe sighed.

"The roof is saggin', and the doorframe looks rotten, as does this porch roof," John noted. "We'll need the thatcher. We'll 'ave to get the roof fixed before doing owt else."

Joe scratched his head. "Reg Smith'll be at the tavern of a Sundee. Never misses the firs' lesson, does Reg." He entered the house, motioning for them to follow.

"This place will need some money thrown at it," John said, glancing around at the decrepit interior. "We'll need some new wood fer these areas 'ere." He indicated dry-rotted doorframes and floorboards.

"It's a wonder Mrs Andrews doesn't break her neck visiting you," Nathaniel ground out in his concern for the woman.

"She knows where ter walk. She's a good gal, that un." Joe gave

Nathaniel a defiant glance.

"I have some money I won playing cards with my father the other night," Nathaniel told him. "I can use some of that to purchase the wood and thatch. I plan to send the rest to the man who saved my life." He had intended to return his winnings to his father, feeling the money was somehow tainted. Instead, he would put part of it to help Joe and give the rest to Tommy.

Joe grinned. "Well, tha's a deed worth payin' fer."

"All the men we need will be at the tavern," John concluded. "They can work fer free as their summat good."

"An' wat's ta be me summat good if yer'll workin' on me 'ouse?" Joe asked.

"You have done your part in the past. It is your turn to receive," Nathaniel answered quickly.

Joe's glassy eyes looked up at Nathaniel, "Helena would say summat like that. I knew her grandda."

"I wish I had known him. Unfortunately, I never took the time to visit."

"Too busy gettin' inter trouble wi' the Davenport boi, eh?"

"Possibly," Nathaniel replied with a broad smile. "Should we go to the tavern and see what trouble we can get into? What do you say, Old Joe?"

"I don' need askin' twice."

"I have to take the Ridgefields back to Eastease," said John. "Then I can join you. Do you think Thor can manage you and Old Joe, Colonel?"

Nathaniel rubbed his jaw with more than a little trepidation. Nobody had joined him on Thor's back since the battlefield. He looked at Old Joe. "Do you think you are able? It must be over ten years since the last time."

"O'course, but wat about you? Yer look a might pale, Colonel."

Nathaniel harrumphed and headed back outside. Utilising a low wall, he mounted Thor and held him steady. "Give Joe a leg up then, John." He gripped the older man's arm to help hoist him onto Thor. Memories came flooding back—the blood seeping out of him, the dizziness and cold, the terrible prospect of dying before his time—

John's laughter pierced through his stupor.

"I wish Helena could see this," the man guffawed.

Shaking off the past, Nathaniel laughed in return before urging Thor towards the Eastcambe tavern. He could do with a pint or two.

They had left the lane and turned towards the village before Joe spoke up from behind him. "Yer ol'roight, boi? I thought yer wer havin' a funny turn back there."

"Yes, I suppose you could call it that. A fellow soldier, Tommy, was the last man to ride behind me on Thor. After he sustained a leg injury in a battle, I leaned down to help him mount Thor behind me as you just did. A charging Frenchman sliced me across the chest with his sabre. I was—reliving it."

"Sounds ter me like yer saved this fellah Tommy."

Nathaniel considered Joe's words. He had not shared that day's details with anyone, not even Harker. "Yes, but he lost much more and went through hell to bring me home. I am eternally grateful to him for doing that."

"Wa'd 'e lose then?"

"His left leg below the knee. He broke the bone, but rather than letting a doctor treat him, he ensured I received the best possible care. I do not remember much of what happened. For a time, I thought I had died. Tommy got me onto a ship and then to a convent hospital once we landed in England. By the time we arrived there, his foot was gangrenous. They had to remove it. He must have been in such awful pain, yet he thought only of my welfare."

"Wat's 'e doin', wi' on'y one leg?"

Nathaniel hesitated. Tommy's predicament was a source of discomfort for him. While he had recovered from his injury in the lap of luxury, the man he considered a friend still struggled to cope with the hardships of life in a maimed body. "He cannot find work—lives with his parents in Sheffield. His father was a mine worker, but the coal dust got inside him. So Tommy helps his father collect castoff items that others no longer want. They repair the pieces or turn them into firewood. Some they sell, but their profit is meagre."

Joe was incredulous. "Wat yer doin' spendin' money on me? I don' need it. Send it ter 'im."

"I will not have Mrs Andrews break her neck visiting you," Nathaniel spoke in a clipped tone that brooked no argument.

"Yer ain't gonna win 'er over telling 'er wat ter do, boi."

Nathaniel laughed. "And what makes you think I want to win her over?"

"Yer a man, ain't yer? Wat man wouldn't? She's special, that 'un. Like my Bertha. Yer tha on'y man she's ever spoken about ter me."

Nathaniel smiled in surprise. "Am I now? What did she say about me?"

Joe tightened his arms and gave him a little shake. "Don' go soundin' so smug o'er it. She wer angry. Said yer think yer ah so 'andsome an' charmin' an' can tell us all wat ter do."

"She thinks I am handsome?"

"If tha's the on'y thing yer lernt from wat I just said, yer don' stand a chance, boi."

"And charming?" Nathaniel's smile broadened into a grin. Mrs Andrews had not been far from his thoughts these past two days, and he felt pleased that she had been thinking of him, too, no matter what her sentiments towards him might be.

~oOo~

Thinking ahead to a lonely evening spent in his study, on impulse, Eliot climbed up to the driver's seat with John when the stable manager came to collect the Ridgefields and return them to Eastease. "If I am to get to know my parishioners, a tavern would be as good a place as any to start," he declared to his guests seated inside the open carriage.

Eliot had never set foot inside a tavern, and his earlier bravado eluded him momentarily in the unfamiliar surroundings. The common room proved noisy, even raucous in one corner, where several grime-covered men were telling the tale of finally pulling out Mr Taylor's stubborn tree stump. Courtesy of the grateful man, their beers had put them in a fine humour. Eliot spied Old Joe and Colonel Ackley seated at a side table, polishing off their first pints of ale. On seeing Eliot with

John, the surprised colonel caught the barman's attention and held up four fingers.

As Eliot sat down, a thick hand, somehow clasping four tankard handles, placed the drinks in the middle of the table, sloshing ale over the rims. Eliot felt sure the colonel read his discomfit, for he smiled and waved a hand around at the room. "A different side of life, is it not, Mr Brooks? Old Joe, here, has not seen the thatcher yet."

Eliot could only smile wanly at the confident man. How was it possible that the son of an earl was not only at ease in these surroundings but also accepted here?

"Tha's 'im." Old Joe pointed at a tall, slender man just entering the tavern. Eliot viewed the roofer, unsurprised to note a wiry strength in his tall frame, given his occupation.

"Over here, Reg," John shouted, drawing another chair to their table.

Colonel Ackley called across the tavern as the newcomer joined them, "Another jar over here, Big Jim." He shook hands with the thatcher.

"How fares the missus, Reg?" John asked. "Ruth will have at me if I tell her I saw you without asking after your better half."

Apparently, Reg Smith's wife, presently under the weather, had received a great many foodstuffs that afternoon, for which Reg dutifully thanked Eliot.

Nathaniel's voice rose above the din. "To the preacher," he intoned, raising his tankard in Eliot's direction while all around the table and several other men in the room did likewise. A flush warmed Eliot's cheeks, though whether from the alcohol or the embarrassing attention, he could not be sure. Addressing the congregation in his church was one thing, for the armour of his robes and the bible shielded him, but accepting the praise of a tavern crowd was something altogether new and startling.

John and the colonel bartered and drank with the other men until finally agreeing on a plan of action, after which they drank some more. The colonel would meet the tradespeople, most of whom arrived in the tavern at one point or another, at Old Joe's cottage during the week to determine the materials needed to make repairs. He would foot the bill for the materials and the ale they drank this evening. They would all donate their labour as their goodly deed, as encouraged by Eliot.

"Will yer be workin' on Old Joe's house, Mr Brooks?" Mr Taylor asked him. "Yer'll need to do your summat good too."

"Indeed," Eliot agreed amiably, surprised by the pats on the back and cheers around the room.

"Once the horses are taken care of, Mrs Andrews has promised the men at the stable can assist us," John confirmed.

"And Harker will send any willing Eastease men," said the colonel.

When John drove him home, Eliot felt a little worse for wear. They left the colonel and Old Joe at the tavern, still downing drinks and reminiscing about times gone by. Eliot wondered how either of them could bear to swallow another drop.

Joe had not had such a match for a long time and was enjoying himself. But, eventually, the colonel declared that if he drank any more, he would not be able to ride home. And so, they mounted Thor, though with difficulty, and sang songs of obliging women all the way back to the cottage

Nine

At breakfast on Monday morning, Nathaniel seised an opportunity to talk to Mr Ridgefield before the couple continued their journey north. Seating himself next to the man, Nathaniel worked towards his purpose.

"Good morning, sir. I hope all the preparations for your travels are complete."

"Colonel. Good morning to you," Mr Ridgefield's greeting was, as usual, jovial. "We are almost ready. How about you? Did you conclude your business at the tavern? Unfortunately, we retired too early for your return."

Nathaniel sheepishly rubbed his head before answering, causing a loud guffaw to erupt from Mr Ridgefield. "After we settled our plans, I stayed with Old Joe Baxter at the tavern. The man is an accomplished drinker. Were I in full health, I might have fared better."

Mr Ridgefield glanced at his wife. Seeing her in deep conversation with Genevieve, he spoke quietly, "I find the general assumption that hair of the dog should be the traditional remedy is false. My recommendation is a hearty breakfast and a stout cup of tea."

Nathaniel took a mouthful, nodding his agreement before swallowing. "How did you find Redway Acres? I have never seen inside the property."

"Most pleasing, sir. Most pleasing. Our hostess was as genial as ever and the horses magnificent," Mr Ridgefield supplied.

Nathaniel got to his main point. "I understand you know her family, the Billingses? They live in Norfolk, I believe you mentioned."

"Yes, Gregory Billings has mines in the north close to my family's home. I have had some minor dealings with him over the years."

"Do you know the location of the Billingses Norfolk property?" Nathaniel tried to keep his voice merely conversational.

"I have never needed to visit, but I understand it is close to the village of Fairfield Market. You have family near there, am I right?"

Mr Ridgefield smiled, but the man's eyes told Nathaniel he knew precisely the purpose of the questions.

"Yes, my second cousin, Lady Grace Bainbridge."

"Then, my dear Colonel, do you not think she might be in a better position to answer your questions?" the man spoke gently, clearly not bothered by Nathaniel's inquisitiveness.

"I do not believe that to be a wise course of action, sir. My cousin enjoys involving herself in my affairs, but I would rather she didn't. If I may ask one other question?" Receiving a quick nod, Nathaniel continued, "Do you have any idea why Mrs Andrews is not in contact with her family?"

"I'm afraid I do not. Miriam did have the opportunity to speak with the lady in question yesterday, but I am not privy to the content of that conversation. I would suggest you ask her, but I believe her advice would be the same as mine. *Ask Mrs Andrews directly.* She will not appreciate you discussing her with others any more than you want your business discussed with Lady Grace."

Nathaniel nodded and finished his breakfast quickly. Rising from his seat, he addressed the butler overseeing the meal. "Watkins, could you see that Adam has Thor ready for me in an hour? I wish to go to Old Joe Baxter's as soon as Mr and Mrs Ridgefield depart."

Watkins nodded, asking dryly, "Would that be your usual saddle, sir, or should I ask Adam to fit him with the side-saddle?"

Everyone around the table laughed.

"Very amusing, Watkins. My usual saddle will be fine, thank you," Nathaniel said with a laugh of his own before exiting.

Depositing himself at the desk in the library, Nathaniel penned requests to his connections in the army asking of Captain Andrews. He hoped to have at least two replies before the end of the week, at which point he anticipated an opportunity to speak to the man's widow.

Before sealing them, he paused and considered Mr Ridgefield's words. Mrs Andrews would not appreciate his letters, but as she did not know what harm could it do? He was aware she hid something behind her anger towards him, and he aimed to get to the bottom of it. Nathaniel never went into battle without intelligence of his opponent. Captain Andrews, the rift with her family, and, in particular, that grey stallion were all part of the mystery surrounding Mrs Andrews. He aimed to have information of all three before confronting her.

After sealing the letters with renewed determination, Nathaniel completed the rest of his correspondence and sent half his father's money to Tommy in Sheffield. He tucked the other half into his coat to pay for materials for Old Joe's place.

Nathaniel watched as the Ridgefield coach headed down the long Eastease driveway. Then, having given his letters to Watkins to post, he made his way to the stable and Thor. Together, they negotiated a wooded cut-through to the north road before turning down the lane to Old Joe's.

~oOo~

Helena began the week with John tending to Redway's needs. There were various fences to mend and some feed and hay coming in from the farm. Winter plans would begin with restocking the shelters on the outskirts of the property. All of this was in addition to the daily routine of cleaning out stalls, exercising and training horses, and, at some point, foaling two mares.

They agreed Helena would supervise much of the routine work and John the winter preparations. Even though it was September, the weather was fine. She hoped it would stay so for their own purposes but also the repairs on Old Joe's cottage this coming Saturday. Ruth often spoke of how proud she was of Helena inspiring Mr Brooks' sermon, which in turn seemed to have inspired the village. Everyone was being kind and helping others, and a feeling of goodness was in the air.

Harriet visited, glowing with pride over how she had managed to get permission to ride astride around Eastease and Redway. She arrived riding Hudson astride but was most annoyed with Helena for being too busy to notice. Helena had been thrilled for her and laughed heartily at the thought of Colonel Ackley riding side-saddle. He certainly was an unusual man.

~oOo~

Thursday morning, Nathaniel regaled Genevieve and Harriet with stories of his week dealing with tradespeople at Old Joe's as they took a slow turn around one of the smaller Eastease gardens. They were pleasantly laughing when James approached them.

"Your post, Colonel." He handed the letters to Nathaniel and turned smartly to head back into the house.

"Thank you, James," Nathaniel called to his retreating back before looking down at the direction on the letters and pocketing them. He had forgotten all about his inquiries of Captain Andrews.

"Is it your orders?" Harriet asked with concern.

"No. Some information I requested, that is all," Nathaniel confirmed, then replaced a frown with his usual genial smile. "May I impose upon you and stay at Eastease for a few more days, Genevieve?"

A relieved smile crossed his hostess' face. "Of course, Nathaniel. We are happy to have you, and Harriet loves you being here, do you not, my dear?"

Harriet caught hold of Nathaniel's arm as they walked together once more. "I do. I am so pleased we will have time to ride together again. Not today, however, I do not wish to be caught out in the storm Adam says will come later."

Genevieve spoke again, "We must have our luncheon, but I suggest, if you wish to ride Thor today, you do it shortly after. Adam's predictions are rarely wrong."

~oOo~

Alone in the library after their meal, Nathaniel read his letters. Given the sensitive information contained therein, he threw them in the fireplace. Watching as they burned, he murmured, "Nothing known of a Captain Andrews. Who are you? Who was your husband, and why do you have that horse? I think you have some questions to answer, Mrs Andrews."

When Nathaniel entered the stable, Adam was ready with Thor groomed and tacked.

"Yer know there's a storm comin', sir. If yer get stranded there are shelters around. One on the east side if yer head that way, one nearer the farmland an' another over the ridge onto Redway land."

"Thank you, Adam, I know. If I am not back, do not send anyone out for me. I will take shelter."

"Yes, sir."

Nathaniel decided to ride along more of the boundary line. *Who am I trying to fool?* he chided as he directed Thor towards Redway's buildings. *I want to see her today.* Armed with the information from the army and the questions rolling in his mind, he needed to confront her, though all sense told him it was not the best course of action. Thinking to wait until his head was clearer in the brisk wind, Nathaniel changed his mind again and redirected Thor towards the furthest corner where he knew Redway fields ended.

Unsettled by the questions that burned in his throat about Captain Andrews and his own behaviour over the past week, Nathaniel welcomed the threat of the oncoming storm. It suited his mood.

When Nathaniel was not at Old Joe's, he spent his time in the library pretending to read, but in reality, thinking of the redhead in a white nightgown at a darkened window. He had returned to the game room several times and looked up to the window where she had sat. Once he had gone into that bedchamber and looked out from her perspective, then turned and strode away, shaking his head in disgust at how he was acting as a lovesick boy.

Her last words before she rode off on the grey stallion still rang in his ears. *I suggest that you and your father stop trying to tell me what to do and stay away from me.* He had her words for nigh on a week, and he would be damned if he would do so any longer. He wanted to see her again, needed to find out just how interesting she was, and before he could determine that, he required answers. Having reached the outer boundary, he turned Thor towards Redway once more.

~oOo~

Missy has gone, Helena glumly watched the team of stablemen mending the fence to the paddock with John at her shoulder.

"Truly closing the door after the horse has bolted," she stated frankly, not in criticism, despite her concern for her mare.

John's voice was contrite. "I'm sorry. T'was on Dom's list, an' I thought it done before I let Missy out. T'is my fault, and I'll make it up to you any way I can if we 'ave lost her."

"Let's see what state she's in when I find her. I need you here to see to Lady." Helena referred to the other mare that showed the first signs of foaling, as Missy had that morning. "I will take Perseus and some supplies with me. Just hope I find her close to shelter." The air rippled with the feel of a late summer storm rolling in.

"I don' like the idea of yer ridin' that horse in the kind of storm that's brewin'," John spoke with concern.

"John, I will be fine," she reassured him. "Remember, he is a battle-tried horse. He will be steady under me."

"Seems he don' like anyone, 'cept for you," he said wryly. Then added, "Be sure ter take the gun."

Helena went to her rooms and considered what to wear. *Layers*, she concluded. The storm would cool the day, and of course, there would be rain. It didn't matter what she wore once she got the horse to safety. She would require supplies for herself and the horses as well as anything she may need for the foaling. At least they had freshly stocked and repaired the outer shelters on the property earlier in the week.

Helena was concerned that Missy's foaling might not be an easy one. It was just an instinct, but she trusted her instincts. Recalling a difficult foaling from when her grandfather had been alive, she prepared what she would need. He had shown Helena what to do, but unfortunately, it had been too late for the stillborn foal and the mare that lost too much blood. Helena shook herself and turned to concentrate on what she could control.

Dressed, she went to her daughter and explained where she was going. Issie understood as she knew how important horses were to Helena and thankfully felt the same way.

"Good luck, Mama. I will take care of everything here."

"Thank you, my sweet girl. What would I do without you?" Helena gave Issie an affectionate cuddle.

Picking up her supplies from the kitchen, Helena moved outside to the waiting Perseus. Knowing her land well, she mapped the path the mare was most likely to have taken—Missy would not have jumped anything, staying to low ground as much as possible. Her most likely direction was towards Eastease. *Thank goodness Missy is a pale grey and will stand out in this poor light.*

Helena rode out with determination. Within minutes, her hair was flying free, and her bonnet was holding on by its ribbons, pulling at her neck as it bobbed.

~oOo~

Nathaniel's breath caught at the almost ghostly vision that appeared out of the darkening gloom of the day. Mrs Andrews' long hair blew freely in the wind as if red fire chased her, the stormy sky silhouetting horse and rider. Studying her, he realised she was not riding side-saddle. She was up in a half-seat and giving that horse of hers free rein to gallop across the terrain.

As she rode, she scanned the horizon. Recognising a sense of urgency, Nathaniel wondered what caused it. *Could the child be lost?* That was his first thought as she slowed slightly and looked in his direction. His redcoat must have been easy to spot across the terrain. Without acknowledgement, she rode on. Curious and keen to help, he urged Thor towards the racing duo.

Helena saw Colonel Ackley as she scanned the land towards Eastease. The redcoat gave her a jolt as memories tried to flood in, but Helena pushed them back. She had to find Missy. Helena's mare and the foal she was due were the priority. Over the next rise, Helena spotted her. Missy was pacing slowly, obviously in distress. Helena brought Perseus to a trot and then a walk, getting within ten yards of Missy as the redcoat streaked past her.

Raising an arm, Helena shouted, "Slow down, you fool! She will run."

To his credit, the colonel did rein in his horse, but it was a big beast, and there was no hope of stopping suddenly. Instead, he turned the stallion back to the east, and her startled mare did not move far. Helena could see afterbirth hanging from Missy, but clearly, the foal was still within. She walked Perseus a little closer and then slid smoothly to the ground. Leaving her mount, Helena circled wide to approach the mare from the front with a treat in her hand.

"I've got you, Missy. I will get you through this, my sweet," she muttered softly as she deftly swept the halter over the horse's head and affixed a rope. Movement in her peripheral vision caught her attention. Colonel Ackley had turned back towards them. He dismounted and walked his stallion in Perseus' direction.

"Do not approach him," Helena warned, keeping her tone neutral as she shouted over the gusting wind. "He does not like men, especially redcoats."

Perseus, however, was looking pleased to see the colonel.

"We became reacquainted last Friday. Did we not, boy?" The colonel put on his greatcoat and grasped the reins she had left dangling, palming Perseus' nose to soothe.

Reacquainted? Fear crept into her throat, but she looked evenly at Colonel Ackley standing straight and confident between the heads of the two beasts he controlled. A lightning flash split the sky, and the rain poured as the thunder rolled loudly.

"Easy, boys. Easy."

Helena heard him soothing the stallions as she roughly fixed her bonnet and tucked her long hair into her coat.

"I understand from Adam that there is shelter not far from here?" he called over to her.

"You will see it over the next slope and to the left." She pointed out the direction. "Go ahead, as you will be much faster than me. Get the boys settled with a stall between them and light some lamps. There are packs on Perseus' back that I will need, too. Thank you."

To avoid being thrown, Colonel Ackley marched with the two horses over the next slope. He was at the door when she approached the shelter, holding it open for them. The colonel had not put his hat back on to let her in, and his hair quickly became plastered to his head. He closed and secured the door, then removed his drenched coat and hung it on a nail in the wall nearby to dry. The fatigued mare collapsed on the hay-strewn floor he had thoughtfully prepared.

Shrugging out of her large overcoat, she handed it to the colonel. He turned his back on her to hang it alongside his, then looked back just as she was unfastening her gown. With a gasp of bewilderment, he turned away again.

"What on earth are you doing?"

"No need to worry, Colonel. I have the same amount of clothing under this gown that you are wearing. These skirts are wet but served their purpose." She removed the gown to reveal a man's shirt and trousers and handed him the wet garment to hang with their coats. "I can move more freely to attend the mare."

Briefly, she watched him shrug out of his redcoat, noting she preferred the sight of him without it. "Where are my packs?" she asked. "I need a knife from one of them."

Quickly, the colonel retrieved the knife from the packs on the bunk at the back of the shelter and handed it over. Then he returned to pick up the gun John had slipped in there and started to prime it.

"No need to do that," Helena said to him and set about helping her mare. Allowing herself no qualms, Helena set up what she needed, then looked him over.

"Could you give me your cravat? Missy is exhausted. I must pull out the foal, and the rope is too thick." She watched him remove it with a little surprise. She had thought she might have to attempt the knots herself, given how many gentlemen relied on their valets to perform those duties. As he handed it to her, he raised his eyebrows at her amusement.

"Thank you," she said, averting her eyes from his attention. "Could you calm Missy and keep her still?"

She watched for a moment as he stroked and soothed the dam with his strong, competent hands and deep voice. He was good with horses, and Missy seemed to know they were there to help her.

Helena took up the knife and carefully cut into the afterbirth. Blood covered her hands and forearms, but she did not flinch from the job at hand. With her way free, she could see two hooves side by side. The foal would be too wide for Missy straight on. Pushing her hand inside the mare as high up on one foal leg as she could reach, she pressed back to get them staggered and misaligned the shoulders.

Wrapping the cravat around the foal's legs, Helena looked at Colonel Ackley again. Her glance took in his open collar, where she glimpsed a red scar crossing diagonally over his chest. She could not see its beginning or end. His sandy hair curled around his face where it was drying, giving him that charming boyish appearance.

"Ready?" she asked, and he nodded as she put each foot on the mare's hindquarters and pulled at the hooves, the cravat preventing her hands from slipping. Missy writhed in pain, but with it positioned correctly and the afterbirth out of its way, the foal slid out reasonably easily—a colt. Getting out of the way, she untied the cravat and cast it aside. The foal was already moving, and the colonel helped her guide it towards its mother.

Nathaniel had watched Mrs Andrews' actions as she cared for the dam and foal. He was astonished at her confidence and capabilities. As he placed his hands near hers on the colt to help it reach its mother, their eyes met, and she smiled. It was a huge smile of relief, the like of which he had never seen on her face before. My God, the effect was so astonishing he had to take a deep breath before he smiled back.

There was still a lot of work to do. As a practical man, Nathaniel had put all the pails he could find outside before Mrs Andrews arrived. Braving the storm again, he brought in one for them to wash the blood off their hands. That done, they each entered the stall their ride was stationed in and took off saddles and bridles, brushing the horses down with the old brushes left at the shelter. Nathaniel would have offered to assist Mrs Andrews once he had dealt with Thor, but she capably worked as quickly as he.

They gave each horse fresh hay stored in the shelter and a pail of the rainwater. After providing the same to the mare and ensuring the foal fed well, they turned to their own needs.

Other than when helping the mare, they had barely spoken a word to each other, working companionably to provide for the horses. With all possible distractions accomplished, Nathaniel felt the silence become tense, and Mrs Andrews moved to fiddle with her packs upon the bunk. Nathaniel retreated as far away from her as possible and checked the condition of their coats to allow her to regain some comfort.

Enjoying his glimpses of her practical ministrations as she cleaned the knife and returned it, with the gun, to the first pack, his stomach rumbled as she pulled food parcels and a flask from the second. Nathaniel realised how late it had become but had nothing on his person except his whisky flask.

Her voice startled him. "I had planned to eat, drink and sleep if I ended up stranded and have a good-sized meal for one. Still, that could be a reasonably sized meal for two if you would care to join me, Colonel."

Walking slowly over to the bunk, which was the only furniture in the shelter, Nathaniel looked down at her meal and considered while his stomach growled whether he should attempt to ride back to Eastease. The rain still hammered relentlessly on the roof, and the early evening light had dimmed. Journeying back to the main house in the dark and the rain was ridiculous to contemplate, and he didn't like the thought of leaving her here alone.

He stood in front of the bunk, but she gestured to the corner. "Colonel, please take a seat at the dining table."

"I accept, and thank you for your generosity." Nathaniel picked up on her playful tone. Sitting with his back to the far corner, he looked at their meal. Bread, cheese, pie and some cake, with a flask of wine, was spread on a linen cloth. It had been kept dry in her pack. To it, he added his hip flask of whisky.

Mrs Andrews had created a picnic on the bunk, sitting at its foot, her back against the wall. Nathaniel did not miss that she had chosen to sit at the end of the bunk nearest the exit. After the practicalities of dealing with the mare and taking care of their horses, she had become wary of him and the situation in which they found themselves.

"I'm afraid I am inappropriately dressed for dinner, Colonel. I was not expecting company on this mission," Mrs Andrews spoke evenly, merely stating that she would not purposely look this way in front of anyone else.

Nathaniel studied her. Her red hair was coming loose from the tie she used to hold it back when delivering the foal. Her bonnet lay discarded on the floor. She had tucked the man's shirt into her breeches, but without a cravat, it lay open at the neck. Even though it revealed less of her neckline than the gown she had worn at dinner last Friday, it seemed more decadent. He had noticed how her large breasts moved more freely than they would have trussed up in the bodice of a gown but tamped down on the thrill it gave him.

"Your dress may not be suitable for society, but to me, you are more beautiful by showing greater concern for your horses than for your appearance," Nathaniel commented, but she made no response to his compliment. No appreciation, not even a blush rose to her cheeks. She stared at him, still wary.

Frustrated over her lack of trust, the letters he had received earlier sprang back to his mind. "I tried to find a Captain Andrews who died in battle. I received replies to my inquiries today. Nothing known. Who was your husband?"

Mrs Andrews met his question with stony silence and a glare. She looked towards her stallion's stall and then back at him. Fear crossed her eyes before they narrowed in a way he recognised from her takedown of the preacher at dinner.

"As soon as my opinion of you improves, Colonel, you do something that confirms your belief that you are superior to me. You are a man, you have a powerful family, and can do as you please. You are so much like your father."

"I am nothing like my father!" Nathaniel hadn't wanted to shout at her, but there was no worse insult she could have levelled at him. His anger brought hers to the fore, her voice raising in return.

"Then why *make inquiries* about my husband? If you suspected no such man existed, why not ask me of him?"

"Would you have told me the truth?" he asked, exasperated with the woman.

"That we will never know, will we?"

They glared at each other until Nathaniel picked up his whisky flask. He took a long, defiant swig from it before spinning it across the bunk to land beside her.

"You should try some. It will calm you," he suggested, feeling the warmth from the alcohol soothe his temper. "Unless whisky is too strong a taste for you."

Mrs Andrews could not fail to know he was goading her, and Nathaniel knew she would not turn away from the challenge. She picked up the flask and knocked back a considerable mouthful of the liquid it contained. Valiantly, she managed to avoid spluttering all over the bunk and swallowed, but he could see her eyes watering with the effort.

With a small smile at her boldness, he tried a different tack. "Please allow me to apologise and start this conversation again. Mrs Andrews, I know the horse over there is not called Perseus but Pegasus. I knew his previous owner, General Alcott, was killed by him, and they supposedly destroyed that horse. It happened when the general visited friends in Norfolk, and I know you hail from that county. I have no doubt he was beating the animal, as I had seen him do many times before. Mrs Hopkins gave me some wonderful healing ointment that I used on Pegasus, and I would bring him carrots whenever I could. I was sorry to hear he had been killed."

"The general?" she half croaked the word. The whisky must still be burning her throat.

"No, Pega—Perseus. I was surprised and pleased to see him in Harker's stable last Friday."

"Reacquainted," she confirmed, her voice calmer.

"Quite so."

"Carrots are his favourite."

"The general's?" he quipped and raised a small laugh from her. Having broken the tension, he looked at her sincerely. "Would you do me the honour of trusting me? Would you tell me how a supposedly dead horse came into your possession and who General Alcott was to you?"

Colonel Ackley had asked Helena directly, and she could stall no longer. Taking another long swig of the whisky, she swallowed it with more relish now that she was ready for its strength. She considered what she should do. It seemed unfair not to tell him the truth and insulting to try to lie to him further. Could she trust him? She thought so, but how sound was her judgment given her attraction to him?

Mrs Ridgefield had told her he had threatened his father to keep her safe from the earl. This past week, she had heard of nothing but his organising and paying for the repairs planned for Old Joe's house, which had to count for something. Perseus trusted him, which counted for much more in her book—had the colonel not helped with the dam foaling and caring for the horses rather than helping himself to her? They had been together hours, and he had not even tried to touch her, as he had not the night he slept outside her rooms at Eastease. It was a moment to stop being afraid and trust, as he had graciously asked.

"I, too, must apologise, Colonel. In temper, I have compared you to your father twice. I want to assure you that I do not think of you that way. To reveal the truth, I must go back to my childhood and tell you my whole story. It would seem that we have plenty of time for it." Taking one last mouthful from the flask, she handed it back to him.

The colonel nodded his encouragement as he took his flask from her. Then he finished its contents while they ate their meal, and she imparted her tale.

Ten

Helena's mother often expressed that she did not enjoy her childhood at Redway Acres. Miss Joy Stockton hated horses—thought they were smelly, dirty creatures—and married the first wealthy man who crossed her path. Helena learned that Mr Gregory Billings had not inherited his money but made it the new way by investing in mines.

Helena was the older of two children, her mother having a son two years after Helena was born. As children, they would travel north with their father so he could visit his businesses, and when he did so, Helena and her brother stayed at Redway with their grandparents. Away from her mother's demands that she *behave as a lady*, Helena spent most of those days in the stable with her grandfather.

She watched foals being born, helped with the feeding and grooming of the horses, learned to ride, and rode well. She stayed up at night with sick horses and read as much as possible in the Redway library. Helena would have cleaned out stalls if they had let her. She loved horses, Redway and, most especially, her grandparents.

As she approached the age of sixteen, her mother refused to let her *run wild*, and when her brother went north with her father, Helena had to stay at home and be a lady. Her only respite during these years was visiting their meagre stable in Norfolk and spending time with the few horses not driving the carriage north. She enjoyed talking to John Robertson, who was one of their stablemen. Sometimes, she even completed chores for John when he was needed for another task.

These escapades were timed to when her mother was out visiting with local families. On occasions when her mother caught Helena helping John, her punishment was severe. She was locked in her rooms for a day, with no interesting books to pass the time and no meals. However, Ruth was the cook and would bring food to Helena if she could.

Helena's father was able to put aside a hefty sum for her dowry, and a number of suitors visited their house in Norfolk. Helena had no interest in marriage, and her mother could not cajole her into entertaining them beyond the minimum necessary. Most soon lost interest. On the two occasions she received a proposal, she declined, and her father did not force her, much to her mother's disappointment.

After her eighteenth Birthday, General Alcott arrived. He was an older man, close to forty, and an investor of her father's. This man usually met with her father in London, and this was his first visit to their home in Norfolk. He was quite taken with Helena and made his intentions known. Helena refused. Her mother persuaded her father not to spurn General Alcott, but the unhappy Mr Billlings reached a compromise with the man. The general should wait until Helena was twenty years old. The man's visits were few and far between due to his military commitments, but her twentieth birthday hung over Helena—gallows built for the sole purpose of taking away her life.

The general's only redeeming feature, in her opinion, was his horse. A magnificent grey with powerful shoulders and haunches that she often visited while the general met with her father. She groomed him when John was busy and took him his favourite treat. His name was Pegasus, and as she groomed him, she noted welts on his hide that had healed into ridges.

Her twentieth birthday came and went with no sign of the

general. She wondered if he had fallen in battle but scoured each newspaper her father discarded for some news, to no avail. Eventually, six months before her twenty-first birthday, he arrived. She felt trapped—no choice, no way out. It became difficult to breathe, and she had to get out of the house to the place where she felt the safest and at peace.

As she approached the stable, she heard a man shouting abuse of the kind that had never assaulted her ears before and a horse in obvious distress. Helena could not see John or the other stablemen anywhere. Scared at what she might find but entering bravely, out of concern for the animal, Helena peered into the stall from which the commotion was emanating. The general was beating his horse and swearing a torrent.

"Worthless excuse of a beast! You bastard! Startled by a mere fox and trying to shake me off," he railed, his face turning puce with anger and the effort of wielding his crop. "You think I am such a useless rider that you could get away from me, you bugger?"

The horse's eyes were rolling as it pulled at the tether that held it against the stable wall. Helena's empathy for the poor horse, trapped in the terrible situation of being owned by this disgusting man, dissipated her fear, and she ran towards it. She stepped between Pegasus and the crop, shouting as she did so—reaching up to the horse to mollify it.

"Stop it! Stop it! The poor thing is terrified," she pleaded.

"Get out of my way, woman, or I will beat you too," he yelled. "It would not be the first time I have taken a crop to a female."

She refused to move, and the crop came down hard across her back, causing a scream to wrench from her as pain sliced through her body. It ripped her gown and drew blood. Glancing over her shoulder, ready to flinch should another blow follow, she saw the look in the general's eyes change from one of anger to one she did not recognise. He roughly put his fingers into the torn bodice and pulled her to him.

"Take your hands off me, sir!" She tried to sound authoritative and pull away, but now he had an arm around her waist and pulled her back against him—his hot breath in her ear.

"We will be married. I do not see any reason to wait, and you need to learn a lesson." He threw her onto the floor of dirt and straw. Her head banged against the stall wall and dazed her. Kneeling before her, he said, "You need to learn to O-BEY."

As he said each syllable, he pulled her legs either side of him, causing her skirts to rise. He busied his hands with his trousers. Helena recovered somewhat and sat up, crying, "No! Please, no!" Pushing at his barrel-like chest and twisting in an effort to get away. It was to no avail.

Grabbing her wrists, he overpowered her, pushing her back to the floor and forcing himself upon her. Despite her strength, having worked with horses, she could not hope to escape him. Holding both her wrists in one hand, he used the other to rip her undergarments and thrust himself into her. She screamed and writhed to free herself, but he just laughed.

"Oh, you were worth this long wait. You thought you would get away from me, but you are mine now, spoiled for any other, and you *will* marry me. Tell me you will obey me."

Thrust followed thrust, and she thought it might never end. She must be ripping in two, it hurt so much. Tears streamed down her face, and all she felt was despair at this being her life from now on. Neither noticed Pegasus pulling with all his strength against his ties. Finally, the ordeal was over, and the general rolled away from her.

"You will ob—" but his sentence never finished. A hoof came down across his head. The sound was awful—blood spattered over the stall wall behind him, and he sat there for a moment before his lifeless body fell backwards. Blood spilt from his head, which had cracked open from the impact.

Numb, Helena managed to get to her feet and ran to Pegasus, throwing her arms around his neck.

"Thank you," she whispered.

~oOo~

Helena was crying. She had not even been aware of it, but tears streaked down her face, dripping onto the man's shirt she was wearing. She rubbed the heel of a hand across each cheek. By the lamp's light hanging on a hook close to his head, Helena could see Colonel Ackley's face lined with concern for her and the young girl she had been.

"I am sorry," he stated simply. "It is an awful thing to have happened to you."

"You are the first person I have told that story to since my grandfather took me in. At the time, it seemed my life was at an end, but look at where I am and what I have. I am happier than I ever was before. I only wish that my grandfather was still alive."

"Harker told me what happened to your grandfather. Did Perseus kill him?" he asked kindly, causing fresh tears to spill down her face. Helena could only nod, so he spoke further, "You did not think to destroy him after that, given how dear your grandfather was to you?"

"Grandfather's last words were that neither Perseus nor Issie were to blame for what happened. It was an accident. Perseus is that foal's sire from the day Grandfather died." She gestured to the horses in the shelter. "What the general did spared me from a horrible life with him, and Perseus saved me. I cannot perceive of shooting him. I don't regret what happened. It gave me my daughter and brought me here, and I have seen and heard of much worse befalling a woman."

"What happened between that incident and now?" he probed further. "How did you become Mrs Andrews after being Miss Billings?"

"As Perseus had saved my life, I felt duty-bound to return the favour…"

~oOo~

John appeared in the stall doorway, a shocked look on his face. He took in Helena's shredded clothing, blood on her back from the wound and blood spatter across her face.

"Oh no, Miss. What happened?"

"He saved my life." She held on to the massive grey. He was the only thing keeping her upright.

"He hurt yer?" John asked, pointing at the dead man.

Helena nodded, then her words tumbled out of her in bursts as she could not form coherent sentences. "He beat Pegasus—beat me.

Threw me down and—and—here on the floor. I tried—I tried. I couldn't stop him. Pegasus got free. He kicked—he saved me." She could not fathom how she was telling her story without collapsing onto the floor, but she would be stronger than that. She was beginning to realise she would have to be.

"They'll want ter destroy 'im." John tried to pull her away from the horse. "They'll say he's mad and 'as killed 'is master. That 'e won't be controllable."

"NO!" she screamed, tightening her grip around the subdued horse's neck. "I can control Perseus; you know I can, John. I cannot let them slaughter him. I just can't." She released her hold on the horse and turned to John, pleading, "I owe him."

"Let me take 'im. I'll hide 'im until it's all settled. Then, no rash decision will be made. Go ter yer father an' tell 'im what's happened. He'll 'ave to explain it ter the general's family." John led the subdued horse out of the stable through the door that faced away from the house. Helena turned in the opposite direction to go to her father. Neither of them looked at the body of the general.

Helena stood in her father's study, bedraggled, her head bowed. She had gathered herself somewhat and recited what had happened in the stable in a calmer state. He listened in disbelief.

"I want to keep the horse, Father," she asserted.

"Out of the question, his family will insist on its disposal."

"You could tell them that it was, produce a receipt for it even. I am sure you could get one easily." She was determined. "Considering my ordeal, you could grant this request."

"I will not have it in my stable," he stated. "You will not have permission to ride it." She nodded in acquiescence before he strode to the door. "I will go and see to the general. The magistrates will have to be informed."

Her father took care of everything.

Her mother refused to speak to her after stating her opinion. "Why do you have to be so headstrong? Why did you anger the general to such a degree and then allow his horse to kill him? How can you expect a husband now?" she railed. "You had better not think we will allow you to continue living here—disgracing the family name and ruining your brother's prospects. We must make arrangements because I cannot bear to see you again."

"I never wanted a husband, Mother. That was your wish. You have brought this upon the family—upon me."

Helena stayed out of her mother's way as much as possible. She visited Pegasus often in his hideaway with John and his family. A few months passed before Ruth took Helena aside while visiting the horse and explained she was with child.

Helena could not bear to break the news to her family, but she needed money. What could she do but tell her father, at least? He had promised her a considerable dowry, and as Helena turned one and twenty within a month, she hoped he could be persuaded to part with it if she took herself away. She sat at her writing desk and penned a letter to her beloved grandfather, George Stockton.

Within a week, she had her reply, and hope soared in her heart. Revealing she was with child convinced him to release the dowry to her grandfather. He agreed that John, his family and Pegasus would travel with her, and he would explain everything to her mother.

Mother will, undoubtedly, be pleased, Helena thought.

Once Helena arrived in Lincolnshire, she was considered a married woman whose husband was in the military and died in France. Her daughter was born four months later. Her parents told everyone that she had been so upset at the loss of her betrothed she had gone to live with her grandfather. They had never visited her except for George Stockton's funeral. Nor did they acknowledge that they had a granddaughter, not even when she stood right in front of them at his graveside. Her grandfather left her the stable in his will. Although her father had given him her dowry, he had never touched a penny.

She became Mrs Andrews, Pegasus became Perseus, and they were free.

~oOo~

"Your story is safe with me," Nathaniel spoke, aware of the emotion in his voice.

"I do not wish to deceive anyone," Mrs Andrews concluded. "I keep up the pretence for my daughter and to ensure that Redway Acres, on which many depend for their livelihood, continues to do well. You are the only one who has ever questioned how I came here."

"Harker would have, I am sure, but he is far too in love to see his nose in front of his face. I envy them that."

"You mean Genevieve and Mr Harker?" she queried, and he nodded. "They give me hope," she added.

"Hope that you might find love?" Nathaniel asked. *Why am I holding my breath, waiting for her to answer?*

"Hope for my daughter that there might be love in her life. Hope for humanity in general. I do not think I could truly give myself that way to someone. Not anymore."

"Would it be giving up anything, though? You would still have the stable and horses. The money in the bank." He could not understand her reticence if she believed in love, which she seemed to, by the way she talked of the Harkers.

"It would not be mine, though, would it? If I married, I would lose possession of everything, including myself. I would have to *O-BEY*. My husband would make all the decisions and need not even consult me. I could not ride when or how I pleased or assist in the barn with any work. If it had been up to you and John today, the foal standing over there could be dead, and so would its mother. He packed that gun for me to take care of it. Men think they know best, but that foal proves they do not."

She paused after her outburst, and Nathaniel felt she looked as uncomfortable as he at her venting her spleen. At first, he had thought her unreasonable. Still, when she had pointed out how wrong he had been about the mare and remembered how competently she had dealt with the situation, he knew he could not put it down to a woman being emotional or irrational. To be fair, that was usually his father's point of view. Now, she surprised him by setting the subject aside and asking her own question.

"What of you and love, Colonel Ackley?"

"What do you mean?" he hedged.

"Women, Colonel. You do like women, do you not?"

"Of course," he blustered. What possessed the woman to come out with such things? She was laughing at his discomfiture. She had revealed her most guarded secret. Surely, he was brave enough to return the courtesy?

"You are stalling."

"Women—yes. Well, of course—there have been—" he faltered, "women."

"And yet no love. No marriage."

"No."

"But carnal knowledge, yes?"

"What?" He shifted, embarrassed at her teasing. "I mean, yes and all with consent, I might add. But no—no love." His voice held more regret than he intended, and he felt her mood change as he looked at her intently.

"You sound sad," she prompted.

"As a second son, I would once have been happy to meet a woman of means, whom I could live with compatibly. Now I have seen the happiness of real love between Harker and Genevieve. How could I settle for less?"

"Is that why you decided not to marry your cousin—Lady Grace Bainbridge?"

Hang the woman. How does she find out so much of me without me telling her? "That was never going to happen."

"And now?" she prompted him.

"Now, I think to find a woman I love, who loves me in return, no matter the circumstance, would be miracle enough." Why was he telling her all of this? *What is it about Mrs Andrews that induces me to speak of my feelings this way?*

He studied her again. The darkness of the night had crept up, and the rain still poured steadily outside. Her face was half-bathed in light from the lantern, her effect upon him undiminished. She looked at him in return. Her wariness of him had gone, and he hoped never to see it again. He would strive never to give her reason to fear him.

"We should snuff out the lamps before we sleep." He broke the spell. "We do not want a fire to start and become trapped."

She concurred, and he moved to extinguish them.

"Where are you proposing we sleep?" she asked. "There is only one bed and blanket."

"I will sleep on the floor with my greatcoat for warmth. I have slept in worse conditions."

"I doubt your coat is dry at all," she exclaimed. "There is nothing for it but for me to trust you to share the bunk and blanket. It will get cold in the night; we will keep each other warm."

He stared at her incredulously. "I could not possibly risk your honour so."

"What honour?" she asked him. "Truly, you are already entrusted with it. Are you not?"

He looked at her openly, seriously. "You will come to no harm from me this night. You have my word as a colonel in His Majesty's Army."

"Your word as a man is good enough for me, sir."

She lay on the bunk facing the wooden wall, leaving room for him to lie behind her. He lay on his back, with one arm behind his head, and did his best to forget the woman at his side—a woman he found beautiful who was challenging, amusing, quick-witted and strong. Her sleepy voice pierced the darkness.

"One more question, Colonel, if I may?"

"Certainly."

"If, upon entering the marriage state, a woman must be pure and a man experienced, how is that to be achieved?"

Nathaniel softly laughed as he lay awake a little longer. She was right about the hypocrisy of society's views. It made him consider the women he had bedded. All of them were willing and compensated in one way or another. Had there been consequences of which he was unaware? It had never crossed his mind before—maybe it should have.

Nathaniel considered her story. Did it change how he thought of her? No, of course it didn't. Why should it? It was not her fault, and as a widow with a child, he had not expected her to be a virgin.

Her breathing became even and deeper. Nathaniel was comforted that she trusted him while she slept. He had known of what the general was capable—had known his horse better. The sounds of the four horses and the continuing patter of the rain soothed him. He turned towards her sleepily and breathed deeply the fragrance of her hair before drifting off.

~oOo~

Helena woke in the early hours. Sun streamed through a crack in the wood and onto her face. How could she have slept so soundly on this uncomfortable bed, in this man's arms? She would never have thought it possible. She had woken in the night and felt his muscled body pressed against her back, his arm across her, holding her close. Needing to move, Helena had turned towards him, and he laid on his back so she could rest her head on his shoulder. Half asleep, he had pulled her to his side. She had tensed, wondering what he might do next, but when nothing happened, she relaxed her head and slept on.

In the early morning sunlight, she studied his sleeping face. In repose, he appeared much more boyish. He was certainly a handsome man. Tall, lean and muscular, with sandy, light brown hair framing noble features, but his eyes drew her. They were a piercing blue that could show concern, rage or humour. Helena had seen all of those as they talked the night before. But she had seen sorrow and, perhaps, loneliness when he had let down his guard and spoke of love.

Helena did not wish to wake him, so she carefully laid her head on his shoulder again. His shirt was open at the neck, and she could see a section of that scar slicing across his chest from her vantage. *How brave a man must be to go to war.*

The sun had shifted to cast its light directly over the face she had been studying. Its owner awoke with a start and swiped at her hand, hovering over his scar while she wondered if she dared to touch it. Those eyes, she had thought of admiringly only a moment before, bore into hers.

"I—I am sorry," she stammered.

"Think nothing of it, madam. Prepare yourself to depart, if you please." He stood up directly and exited out of the nearest barn door.

Nathaniel had been dreaming of that cascade of red hair and soft lips. He had felt her full figure pressed against his body as they embraced and brought his lips down, in demand, on hers. All the while, he ran his hands through her hair and down her back to those curves. When he woke in a state men often do, Nathaniel needed to escape to avoid frightening her. He may have been brusque in his haste, but that could not be helped.

As he stood looking out towards Eastease, he recalled that her hand had been hovering over his chest. *What had she been doing?* He looked down at his open shirt. *Curious, is she? Better than abhorred.*

He took care of his ablutions in a small copse, using the last pail of rainwater, while he considered broaching the subject of what to tell their respective households. Nathaniel imagined Mrs Andrews would favour saying nothing of it to either. Hers could assume she had managed the foaling on her own. His that he had found shelter for the night, alone.

Knocking first, he entered the barn. "Are you ready?" he inquired. The horses sounded restless and eager to be off.

Dressed with the gown back over her shirt and breeches, Mrs Andrews ducked behind him and outside with her own ablutions bucket before he could offer to take it from her. All they had to do was saddle up their rides.

Nathaniel made a start with Thor, and upon her return, Mrs Andrews tacked up Perseus. They worked in a friendly, quiet atmosphere.

Finishing first, he offered, "Would you like me to check your saddle? The girth, perhaps?"

She smiled at him. "No. Shall I check yours?"

"No." Nathaniel grinned back at her.

They moved out of the shelter, and he cleared his throat. "I will ride with you to Redway Acres."

"I am quite capable of getting there alone, and we do not want anyone to see us together," she spoke with precise determination.

"If they do, we need only say I met you on my ride this morning." He boosted her up onto Perseus' back.

"At this hour?" she questioned.

With the sun just up in the sky, she had a point. "A compromise then," he conceded. She certainly was not a woman to be told what to do. "I will ride with you to the point just prior to becoming visible to your house and stable. Would that suit you, madam?"

She nodded and took the rope attached to the halter around the dam's head as he handed it to her. The foal should follow, but they would have to ride slowly.

Nathaniel looked up at Mrs Andrews on the back of that fine stallion and apprehensively broached the subject of their situation. "I know you do not wish to marry, but should there be any discovery of last night, please know that I would do the honourable thing."

Helena nodded, unsure if that was something he wanted but appreciating him saying it nonetheless. She watched him mount Thor, and then they headed towards Redway.

At the point where they had agreed to part ways, Helena brought them all to a stop.

"Thank you, Colonel. I can go alone from here," she said, hoping he would not insist on coming any further. Instead, he asked her one more question, remaining stationary as she urged Perseus on slowly again.

"Harriet tells me that you had something to say about why men did not want women to ride astride, but she would not tell me what it was. Will you share it with me?"

Helena smiled at him over her shoulder, glad that their parting words should be humorous.

"I said that the only beast a man wants a woman to have between her legs is himself." With that, she turned to Redway and rode slowly over the last rise before the stable came into view, pleased to hear his guffaw before he talked to his horse.

"Well, Thor, I would like some breakfast. How about you?"

Eleven

When a hungry and dishevelled Nathaniel arrived back at Eastease, he dropped Thor at the stable in the hands of the very capable, if cheeky, Adam.

"Spoil him, Adam. He kept me safe in the storm. We found shelter, but I could not care for him as I would have preferred."

"Yes, sir," was the happy reply. Adam knew Nathaniel would reward him.

After James took care of his rumpled appearance, Nathaniel poked his head into the breakfast room. It was still early, so he was surprised by the presence of both Harker and Genevieve.

"You see, my dear," teased Harker, "our Colonel is a resourceful man and survived the night unscathed in the wilderness of Lincolnshire."

Nathaniel rubbed the heel of his hand over his chest and wondered if he truly had.

"I know, I know," acknowledged Genevieve, giving her husband a pained look. "But to survive in battle, only to succumb so close to home, would be a dreadful fate. I am entitled to worry about a dear friend. How did you manage, Nathaniel?" she asked, turning to him.

Flustered because he had been thinking of a red-haired angel flying across the fields on a huge stallion, Nathaniel ran the half-heard conversation through his head before answering. "I saw—I mean, Thor and I found shelter. We spent a companionable evening with my flask for sustenance." He tapped his coat pocket.

As Genevieve studied his face, he knew he had not fooled her entirely. "We are glad you are safe, are we not, Alexander?" She looked at Harker, but he was lost in his paper and gave them a nonchalant wave. With a grin towards Genevieve, Nathaniel tucked into a hearty breakfast, relieved.

~oOo~

Wandering the halls of Eastease that afternoon, Nathaniel found himself consumed with the previous night and wondering how Mrs Andrews fared at Redway Acres. He considered borrowing a horse to ride out there and took two strides towards the stable before realising his foolishness.

Two girlish laughs suddenly caught his attention before some music reached his ears. Knowing that tentative fingering could in no way be Harriet's, Nathaniel pivoted to march purposefully towards the music room.

The scene that greeted Nathaniel brought a smile to his face. Harriet sat on her pianoforte stool with a small girl. The youngster was kicking her stockinged legs in time to the music she was attempting, her shock of red hair groomed into swinging ringlets, too. As she turned towards Nathaniel, something grasped tightly around his heart, and he fell instantly in love. Even without red hair, he would have known at once who her mother was. Thank the heavens, she had not inherited any physical traits from her father. The cherubic face smiled at him.

"Good afternoon," she giggled, "Harry is teaching me to play." It was obviously something that delighted her.

"Harry is, is she?" he replied with a sunny smile of his own. *Harry* was a nickname his friend, Mark Wyndham, had given Harriet, but she had insisted she never wished to hear it again when he died. It felt good to use it.

Harry stood and instructed the young girl to do the same. Then she spoke sternly to her charge, "Isabella, what is it that I have told you about speaking before you are spoken to and of speaking first to people you do not know?"

"Do not do it?" came the reply, with a perfect pout.

"And, what of using the names, Harry and Issie?"

"They are our secret names to use when we are alone." More pouting.

"Isabella," Harriet continued, this time with a kind lilt, causing a smile to replace the pout. "This is my cousin, Colonel Ackley. Colonel, may I introduce our neighbour, Miss Isabella Andrews, to your acquaintance?"

"Indeed, you may." Nathaniel gave a dramatic bow. "I am honoured to meet you, Miss Andrews."

The little girl did a sweet curtsey and giggled again. "A real-life colonel soldier?" she asked with big eyes, taking his measure admiringly.

"I am," he confirmed.

Doubt crossed the girl's face. "But where, then, is your red coat and your sword? Have you lost them? Will you get into trouble? I lost Mama's necklace once and got into dreadful trouble." She clearly held some concern that he not be *in trouble*, of which he directly aimed to relieve her.

"I am not required to wear them when not on duty. They are safe in my rooms. Do not worry yourself, madam. May I ask permission to sit and listen while you are at your lesson?"

Miss Andrews looked towards Harriet and got a quick nod. "Yes, sir." With one more giggle, she sat down at the instrument with renewed efforts.

The girl's fingers were long, and she certainly had the piece's rhythm even though she did not get all the notes right. Nathaniel listened intently and clapped enthusiastically at the end of every piece she tried—the hour quickly passed as Mrs Andrew's daughter enthralled him. Harriet surprised Nathaniel with her patience and humour. The girl's charm did not work solely upon him. He considered taking Miss Andrews home and having another impromptu meeting with her mother. However, before he could make that suggestion, Miss Andrews jumped down from the stool and ran to him.

"Colonel, could you take me home, please?"

"Isabella!" came the shocked response from Harriet. "A lady would never ask a gentleman such a thing. You know full well that Johnson will drive you home."

She turned pleadingly to Harriet, "Johnson cannot fight off any dragons that may cross our path, hoping to make a meal out of me. Colonel Ackley could see them off with a flash of his sword." With that, she sliced through the air with an imaginary weapon while Nathaniel grinned and Harriet primly tutted at the girl's outrageous behaviour.

"I am known hereabouts for defeating dragons. Is that not true, Harriet? I am sure I slew one or two for you when you were younger," Nathaniel's voice was soft and low as he tenderly recalled the much younger twin sisters, Harriet and Maria.

"Still, there is a proper way to do this, Cousin," she said expectantly.

Knowing his duty, Nathaniel stood and turned to the young girl again. "Miss Andrews, would you do me the honour of allowing me to escort you home?"

"I thank you, sir, you may." Giggling, she offered him her hand, and he immediately bowed over it and kissed loudly, smacking his lips and causing her to laugh even more.

~oOo~

Harriet watched as Nathaniel drove the curricle, harnessed with Alexander's Yorkshire Coach horses, to the front of the house where she waited with Issie.

"Thank you, Harriet. Please inform Harker that, unlike last night, I will be back for dinner," he spoke as the noise of the gravel under the vehicle's wheels abated.

"Did you miss your dinner last night, Colonel?" asked the girl.

"Mama missed dinner last night, too. She was caught in the storm and had to spend the night in a shelter. I was in charge. She said I was before she left."

Astonished by the coincidence, Harriet could only stare at Nathaniel. He seemed unperturbed, but she knew from Alexander that he was good at showing impassivity when he complained of how often Nathaniel won at cards. He had not mentioned being caught in the storm *with* Helena. Their two estates were large enough that they may not have seen each other.

Nathaniel leaned into the curricle and pulled out a small step, which he placed on the ground at Issie's feet. Usually, she was unceremoniously lifted into it by Johnson. The stool allowed him to hand the small girl, step by step, into the vehicle with plenty of flourish and aplomb.

How considerate he is, Harriet thought, with a rush of affection.

With a bow, Nathaniel left Harriet with her tender thoughts and suspicions. He rounded the vehicle again to leap into it in one bound and pick up the reins. Harriet was pleased to see him so well recovered.

"Farewell, Harry!" called Issie with a wave.

"Farewell, Harry!" he echoed. "Watch out, dragons. Fearless Colonel Ackley is protecting Miss Andrews on her journey home today. You would do better to stay in your caves."

As the curricle pulled away, his laughter and Issie's delighted squeals faded in Harriet's ears.

The sun was still bright and warm as they left the grounds of Eastease, heading on the North Road towards Redway Acres. Miss Andrews captivated Nathaniel with stories of princesses and the princes, knights or loyal soldiers who saved them from various beasties. Stories she and her mother told to each other at bedtime.

He pointed to a distant peak and a thin greyish cloud, which appeared to be smoke streaming from an unseen source. "I see the Dragon of Lincolnshire is waking up. Can you see his smoke? That is the peak he lives on," he teased.

She looked about his person and the curricle. "Oh no, Colonel!

Where is your sword? How will you slay the dragon if he chases us?"

"Firstly, may I say that the name *Colonel Ackley* strikes fear into the hearts of all in the dragon world for being the best dragon slayer ever known, so I do not think he should dare to chase us. Secondly, if he were to chance his arm—or wing—he would find the going rough because this pair of horses is the fastest in the land." Nathaniel smiled widely at her and elicited another sweet giggle. With continued chatter and laughter, the pleasant journey passed and before long, they were pulling up to the main house of Redway Acres.

~oOo~

Ruth heard Miss Issie run into the house, calling for her mother and talking in a lively fashion of Colonel Ackley driving their curricle and dragons chasing them. She popped her head back into the kitchen and asked Lilly to have John deal with the colonel's vehicle before heading off the man who had already stepped through the open front door.

"Mrs Andrews is through here, sir," Ruth said, gesturing for him to follow her.

Upon the threshold of the parlour, Colonel Ackley paused with her as they watched the mistress of the house with her daughter on her lap. The young girl was relating the story of the Dragon of Lincolnshire and how she had seen the smoke he breathed with her very own eyes. *What a picture they make,* Ruth considered. *How is a man supposed to keep his heart within his chest at the sight of them?* It seemed to her that this man certainly had not. Her girl had an admirer if she was to be any judge.

"Colonel Ackley, ma'am." Ruth gave a bob and smiled at Helena's jolt.

"Colonel, you are very welcome in our home. Especially after saving my daughter from the Dragon of Lincolnshire. Please excuse me from rising, as I seem to have my lap full."

Ruth was surprised at Helena's cordiality. John had told her how annoyed she had been with the man after the dinner at Eastease, and she had not had the opportunity to see him since. *Had she?* Ruth stood silently at the door, listening to the surprising conversation while she waited for her orders.

The colonel bowed and moved forward to sit as Helena gestured. "Mrs Andrews, please do not trouble yourself. Having escorted this princess home, I understand the seriousness of your office."

"Mama, Colonel Ackley missed his dinner last night, too," Miss Issie declared.

"Did he?" Helena looked at the colonel with a slight blush rushing to her cheeks. He looked intently at her, and a smile played upon her lips as she spoke, "Well, that is a coincidence, is it not?"

"As we are having a picnic on Sunday to make up for it, could we invite the colonel? He did miss his dinner too," Miss Issie begged Helena.

It would seem that the colonel has made an impression on both Redway women, Ruth thought.

"What say you, Colonel? Are you one who enjoys a picnic?" Helena spoke in the most flirtatious voice Ruth had ever known her to use.

"I most certainly am. And if you should allow it, I would be happy to supply the provisions."

"It will be such a wonderful day!" exclaimed Issie. Ruth rolled her eyes. The girl would be impossible until Sunday came.

"Do not get too excited, sweet girl," her mother warned. "We have yet to see if the day will be fine. Being caught in one storm a week is quite enough for me. Ah, Ruth, there you are," Helena looked flustered towards her, and Ruth could tell Helena had not realised she still stood there, so focused was she upon her visitor.

"Yes, ma'am," Ruth said with some concern over the unfolding events. "Would you like some tea? And perhaps Miss Issie should go and see Rachel?"

"Yes, thank you," Helena spoke with a look to Ruth as if she had caught her with a hand in the biscuit tin. "Would you like tea, Colonel? Or perhaps you would be more interested in a tour of the stable?"

"Horses are always my preference. I thank you. Please, lead the way."

At that, Ruth disappeared with her charge in tow, who expressed a wish to stay with the colonel. Not even the promise of a treat and seeing her beloved maid, Rachel, would quiet her insistent voice. When Ruth returned to the kitchen, she asked Lilly to run out to John and tell him she needed to speak to him, but he should not disturb their mistress. Then she finished the tray for the youngster Lilly had been working on, giving the cook, Mrs Foxton, a slight nod.

Nathaniel was a very happy man, indeed. His luck was holding, and after a curricle ride with an adorable young lady, he was about to enjoy a tour of her mother's stable. If the weather held, a picnic with this red-headed duo was on the cards for Sunday.

Redway Acres was a country manor—more extensive than a farmhouse and not prestigious, like Eastease, but large and well situated. It was not too grand a home for what it was primarily—a stable. Overall, Nathaniel felt it was functional and comfortable. He loved it, and that was before he saw the grounds where the stable buildings stood.

Leading him out of the parlour and towards the back of the house, Mrs Andrews exited through a wide, dark-wood double door and out to a paved courtyard. When they had stopped to fill two large, secret pockets in her gown with several horse treats from a barrel by the door, she had turned and smiled playfully at him. Taking an additional handful, she dropped some into his topcoat pocket.

Outside, the functionality again meshed with pleasing aesthetics. Two rows of stable buildings extended away from the house, flanking the courtyard. The paving sloped gently down from each, forming a narrow drainage gulley in the centre. Large access lanes between the house and buildings allowed various vehicles access from the front or a route to the fields beyond. Indeed, Harker's curricle stood waiting for Nathaniel's return. The two buildings were joined at the end by the large barn, with a loft and open hatch above where the piled-up hay spilt.

The horses poked their heads over the half doors as they wandered down one side. At each stall, Mrs Andrews gave Nathaniel a bit of history about the horse—their heritage, where she purchased them, and why. She told him which horses were for sale and which certainly were not.

At each stop, she gave the horse a treat from her pocket, or, if she knew his pocket held the favoured treat, she would advise him, and he would dig it out and offer it in his palm to the waiting animal. At first, he felt self-conscious touching her horses, her domain, but she was relaxed, stroking and soothing them all. It made it easy for him to follow suit. Unsurprisingly, he found himself relaxing. It was always the same way for him with horses. That was why he made his way to the army stable often.

John came into the kitchen and smiled at Ruth. "I see Colonel Ackley is visiting. Did you need me for something?"

Ruth instructed Lilly to take the tray to Miss Issie before grabbing John by the hand and pulling him across the hall to the smaller Redway dining room. He grinned at Mrs Foxton, who shook her head in disapproval, and when Ruth closed the door, he took hold of her around the waist and kissed her.

Ruth batted at his chest. "What on earth are you doing, John?" she asked with annoyance.

"Why else did yer bring me in 'ere?" He felt slightly disappointed until she gave him a shy smile and reached up to kiss him.

"That will have to wait. I have to talk to you about Colonel Ackley." Ruth moved over to the small window to peer at the couple strolling down the line of stalls. John joined her, then started at her words. "Issie said he was caught out in that storm too—all night."

"Yer don' think—? It would be unlikely, wouldn't it? Eastease is a big estate; why would he have been over this way?"

"I don't know, but they were very friendly just now in the parlour, and you said she was angry with him. Helena isn't one for playing nice for a man, but she was a few minutes ago. How could she go from being angry to all politeness and charm without seeing him in between?"

"Maybe she saw 'im when she was out? He's been at Old Joe's all week. Perhaps she saw 'im there?" John suggested.

Ruth shook her head as they watched the pair outside enter the stable barn. "She sent Lilly with the food basket in the week because you were all so busy. She hasn't been there since Sunday morning when everyone was at church."

"My God, if 'e has taken advantage, I'll skin 'im. I don't care who his relations are," John said grimly. The thought of Helena being trapped in the shelter during that storm with a privileged man like Colonel Ackley made him feel sick, though she seemed happy enough when she returned that morning.

The image of finding Helena in the stable at her father's home with her clothes ripped and the general dead on the floor flooded his mind. John's mouth closed into a thin, determined line as he stepped towards the door, but Ruth's concerned voice reached him before he grasped the handle.

"Don't go off half-cocked, John. We don't know if they were out there together yet."

"I'll get it out of one or t'other of 'em. If not today, then tomorrow at Old Joe's," he said without a backward glance. Then he headed out the door towards the barn, his long stride quickly eating up the distance.

~oOo~

Mrs Andrews pointed out a few horses to Nathaniel stationed across the courtyard and then entered the barn doors. Inside, they had divided a larger room into several small storerooms for equipment, food and an office. Everything was well organised and labelled. Doors on either side led to corridors and down the inside of the buildings they had just passed. Taking the one to the right, she stopped them at an inner stall, housing the dam and foal from the previous day.

Seeing them again brought the whole afternoon and night into Nathaniel's mind. Heat rose in his body at the memory, and his chest felt tight. Mrs Andrews' face held an attractive blush. Nathaniel grinned and received a sheepish smile in return.

"They look healthy," he said.

"Very."

"And happy."

"Of course," she said with another smile.

"You did a good thing," he offered, thinking of how competently she had dealt with the situation.

"Thank you."

"Who is the foal for?" He had been surprised that Mrs Andrews hadn't provided him with more information about her plans for the colt.

"Me—he is mine," she said with a severe expression. "His sire is Perseus. It is an experiment. Is Perseus the way he is because of how the general treated him, or is it just part of his nature? Will his offspring inherit his unpredictability? So far, he has sired only fillies, all amiably natured. This is his first colt."

The mention of the general made Nathaniel think of her child. He looked around to be sure no one else was there. "You are thinking of Miss Isabella." The concerned look across Mrs Andrews' face was enough to confirm he was right. "She is nothing like him," he said softly, reaching out to squeeze her forearm.

"Regardless, we will see how this horse turns out."

"*We* will?" he asked with raised eyebrows.

"If you wish to come back and see for yourself," she challenged, and Nathaniel realised Mrs Andrews was asking about more than the colt.

"I should like that very much, but first, what did you name him?"

"I have not decided yet, but maybe another Greek god. Perhaps Zeus? What do you think?"

"Maybe you could go with something more along a gambling line. Like Chance or Lucky?"

"Colonel." John approached and pulled his forelock. "She is so full of herself, delivering that foal in the middle of yesterday's storm. I take it she did not mention me having to manage t'other one, all by meself?"

Nathaniel could hear the pride in the man's voice for his Mistress.

"Straight forward, the Dam did all the work. You just watched, so like a man. Then you got to sleep in your own bed," she teased back easily as they moved on a few more stalls. "Lady and her filly. So adorable. Just wait until Harriet sees this one."

"Ruth says you were caught in the storm too, Colonel." John's sharp eyes darted between them. Nathaniel kept his expression impassive, but the man had known Mrs Andrews much longer. Nathaniel had no doubt he could read her response quickly enough.

Although she managed to keep a blush from her face, she said nothing and looked disinterested.

Nathaniel spoke to take the man's scrutiny away from her, "I am afraid my story is not half as interesting as Mrs Andrews' adventure. I was out riding Thor when the storm started. I found shelter, and we had to stay the night. Luckily, I had my flask but was hungry when I returned to Eastease."

"Where did you shelter?" asked John.

"I have no idea." Nathaniel indulged John's questioning. The man was protective of Mrs Andrews, and he approved. "I was over the east side. I have been doing a tour around the boundaries of Eastease, but let us talk of more interesting happenings. What time do you plan to be at Old Joe's tomorrow?"

John accepted the change of subject, though Nathaniel felt it a temporary situation, and they discussed their plans for finishing the repairs for the older man's place.

~oOo~

Though dinner at Eastease was a small gathering, it was lively with conversation. Everyone asked for more details about Nathaniel's eventful evening sheltering from the storm, and he gave them the same story he had given John.

If it came out that he had spent the night with Mrs Andrews, he would have to do the gentlemanly thing and marry her. Personally, Nathaniel did not see that as a problem. He was getting to know her, and he liked her. That he found her attractive was evident by his body's reaction. Her actions and words were challenging, but what she said was right. He loved that she was passionate but sensible in making her arguments. He was beginning to understand why Harker was keen to talk business with her.

Helena Andrews was the best woman Nathaniel had ever met, and he still did not know her fully. He was going to enjoy getting to know her more. No, marrying her would not displease him. However, he knew enough of her story to understand that she was not ready to marry him, or any man. He did not think that she had ever had those kinds of thoughts. Who could blame her, given what Alcott had done to her? He hoped he might be the one about whom she would have those feelings. He was confident she was attracted to him, but did she like him? Could she love him? Suddenly, he realised it was important to him that she did both.

Preoccupied, Nathaniel had only half-listened to Harriet talking of her music lesson with the captivating Miss Andrews. He caught her small smile before she said, "Mrs Andrews was caught out in the storm all night last night, too, according to Issie."

Harker turned his head swiftly to Nathaniel, who felt he was getting a lot of practice at keeping his face impassive. These half-heard conversations would get him into trouble if he didn't pay more attention. His best course of action was to have his say before the questions came, leaving him with only the option of being on the defensive.

"I heard all about that when I drove Miss Andrews home. One of the foaling mares had bolted. Mrs Andrews had to find it and deal with a difficult foaling. She managed to find shelter and saved both the dam and the colt. She is a very capable woman."

"Did you not see her then, Nathaniel?" pressed Harriet.

"From what I understand, my dear, I was on the other side of Eastease. The other mare foaled, too—a filly. I think John is frustrated that Mrs Andrews stole his thunder with a more dramatic event," Nathaniel explained. Harker was appeased and turned back to Genevieve, who was rubbing the large mound of her belly, presumably feeling some discomfort.

The discussion moved to plans for the following day when many hands from Redway and Eastease would work with Nathaniel at Old Joe's cottage. Harker offered to help if Genevieve agreed, saying he felt like doing something physical as he spent the past week behind his desk.

"You will not be far away if needed," she agreed. "I think it would be nice if we could get some refreshments for everyone tomorrow. Perhaps you could arrange that, Harriet?"

"I believe Mrs Andrews was planning to provide some refreshments, too," Nathaniel said.

Harriet jumped at the opportunity. "I will ride to Redway in the morning and discuss it with her. Then I can see the foals."

"I received an invitation to attend a picnic on Sunday afternoon," Nathaniel added as nonchalantly as possible. "Perhaps I could trouble you to ask Mrs Hopkins for some provisions for that, Harriet?"

"Helena asked you on a picnic?" Harriet asked.

"Actually, it was Miss Andrews. She thinks I am a brave dragon slayer." He brandished his steak knife towards Harriet, who looked a little put out not to be invited.

"As it is for Issie, I will arrange provisions for you," she conceded.

"Thank you, *Harry*."

~oOo~

The evening at Redway was quiet. Helena and Issie dined together, and then a bone-weary mother took her daughter to bed, planning to go directly to her own rooms afterwards. Issie was full of talk of Colonel Ackley. She told a story of him saving her from the Dragon of Lincolnshire as they drove from Eastease to Redway and talked of seeing him at Old Joe's the following day.

"Can I make a cake for him?" Issie asked.

"You will have to ask Ruth, for goodness knows my cooking ability is limited at best." Helena extinguished the candle and kissed her daughter goodnight.

As Helena got into bed, she felt sad that Issie longed for a father. She was obviously pinning her hopes on the colonel. Helena hated that she had lied to Issie all her short life, but what was she to do? Tell Issie she was the spawn of a man her mother had hated? That she was created in violence, fear and death? The girl was such a gift that Helena would not tarnish.

She picked up her diary and wrote about her feelings concerning the colonel to see if they would help her understand them.

I think he is attracted to me, which has happened in the past. Men see the outside of a woman and consider the inside empty, waiting for them to fill and mould as they please. I have never met a man who does not think he is better than a woman or knows better than a woman, no matter how highbrow the woman or lowbrow the man. The best man I have ever known was my grandfather, but even he gave me the stable in the hope that I should find a husband to run it for me.

Does Colonel Ackley see the 'me' on the inside? I think he does. At least, he is the only one who has given pause to look and listen. I find myself more willing to explain to him how I feel, although I am sure I stumble over the words under that intense gaze. He knows more of me than anyone, even John. He understood my desire to see how Perseus' foal should turn out. Issie may be spared the meanness of her sire (I hate to say father), but what of her children?

Why do I lie here wishing the colonel's arm around me so I could rest my head on his shoulder as I did in sleep last night? I feel an emptiness that I do not discern when he is present. I did not know it had always been within me until I had experienced a time without it. I enjoy just talking to him. Yes, I have to admit that I do like him very much

Twelve

John and the men working with him at Old Joe's cottage enjoyed the fresh breeze as the day promised warmth with the sun rising higher. Mr Harker and the colonel came to help, and soon, they were taking off their coats and rolling up their sleeves along with everyone else. The skilled tradespeople took over directing the rest of the men, and John found himself working next to the colonel as per his design. He had more to say to the soldier about the storm.

"Did you remember where you sheltered the other night?" John began.

"No," the colonel grunted as he pulled up an old floorboard.

John harrumphed, tackling his board. The man wouldn't make it easy for him, so he decided to be direct. "She is not as tough as she appears." John was going to protect Helena, come what may. Better Colonel Ackley understands that now.

"She is tough. Independent." At least the colonel said it with some admiration rather than the derision of many of his ilk when confronted with an opinionated woman. He crouched down to work another floorboard loose.

"Lonely," John said as he bent to work the other end of the board. "Will not let anyone help her. Afraid of losing what was hard-won."

"Maybe she has to be hard-won?" The colonel glanced towards John, who nodded.

"If someone wer willing to try, and wer worthy enough," John agreed, still unsure that this was the right man for Helena.

"Trying should prove the worthiness, should it not?" They grunted as the nails they tried to loosen proved as stubborn as the woman they discussed.

John snorted. If he knew anything of his girl, this gentleman was going to have to try for a long time, so maybe that *would* prove him worthy. "And patience."

"Not using an unavoidable situation as a reason for rushing?" The colonel gave him a sidelong glance.

John had to admit that the colonel had a point there. His girl would not thank anyone who pushed her into marriage. "No, but—"

"So why are we discussing this again?" the colonel asked brusquely, grasping his end of the board, his muscles working as he yanked it up, almost hitting John in the face.

"Whoa." John fell onto his backside, a glowering face staring down at him. The soldier was losing his patience, but John could never forgive himself for not being there to save the young Helena all those years ago. He scrambled to his feet, pushing away the colonel's proffered hand. He would be damned if he'd stand by and allow this man to effectively do the same thing as General Alcott and take everything away from Helena. *The colonel might be able to beat me in a sword fight,* thought John, *but I don't see any swords hereabouts.*

Nose to nose, they glared at each other. "If you've hurt her—" John began.

Colonel Ackley stepped back and put his hands up in a defensive gesture. "Mrs Andrews would not appreciate us fighting. If I had been there the other night, nothing would have happened. I am a gentleman before all else."

As soon as John released the tension in his shoulders, the man added, "I understand your need to protect her. She thought you had packed the gun for Missy."

John clenched his fist, ready to smash it into that privileged smirking face, just as the door opened.

Nathaniel let his eyes flick to Harker, then back to that enormous, solid hand of Redway's stable manager. John's fingers were unclenching.

"How are you faring in here?" Harker asked with a surprised glance at the floor. "I had thought you would have made short work of this."

His timing was perfect because there was little doubt John was about to swing for Nathaniel, who confessed to himself that he felt like a bit of a brawl. That was why he had tried to goad John with the last comment. It would do him good to release some of his built-up tension over Mrs Andrews.

Instead, he turned his attention back to the floorboards. John had his answers. Nathaniel confirmed his suspicions that they had spent the night together at the shelter and told John that nothing untoward happened. He had indicated where his intentions lay, which, until that moment, Nathaniel had not even admitted to himself.

True to his word, Mr Brooks arrived to help. The garden was a mess, and he began directing the younger boys to clear it. Nathaniel noticed that Brooks hauled and muscled as much rubbish and old machinery as the boys who laboured on the farms. Nathaniel was glad a certain redhead was not there to see the younger man, whose muscles were firm and supple, whereas his own were more steel and granite. He was confident he could flatten the preacher if only the need arose, but even he could appreciate that his hardened and battle-scarred body was not as easy on the eyes.

~oOo~

When Helena drove the Redway cart down the lane with Issie, Ruth and plenty of food and drink for the men, she spotted the colonel standing astride the pinnacle of the roof admiring the finished product of Reg Smith's handiwork. Old Joe's place was single-storey, and the thatch finished low past the eaves. The colonel stood in his shirtsleeves, his sun-streaked hair waving in the breeze and a smile on his handsome face. Helena's dream of being kissed came into her mind, and she sighed.

At that moment, the colonel looked up at the cart approaching and noticed her watching him. Suddenly, he lost his balance and started to fall. Helena screamed as he rolled over and over down the roof's slope.

"COLONEL!"

None of the men were spurred into action by her scream. Leaping from the cart and running when her feet hit the ground, she shouted at them, "Move, you blaggards, move and aid the colonel. What is the matter with you all?"

She rounded the corner and immediately realised why they had not reacted. At the side of the house was a large cart half-full of loose thatch. Safe in the middle of the thatch that had cushioned his fall as he had planned was a grinning Colonel Ackley.

"Thank you for your concern, madam," he said as he sat up.

Realising he had hoodwinked her, Helena picked up a large armful of thatch and shoved it at him none too gently, pushing him back again and covering his face. "You bloody bastard. You have easily taken five years off my life."

Delight that she had used such words showed on his face as he sat up bantering with her, "Only five? You have hurt my feelings."

"It might have been more if your face were prettier," Helena countered, acting up to the crowd of men who laughed heartily. She had learned much of a man's sense of humour, working around them in her stable, but she also covered up her heart's reaction to thinking he was hurt. She turned away to prevent him from reading the fear in her face.

"If prettiness determines years lost, then I would have lost fifty had you fallen half as far," he called out to her retreating back. That got an *Ooooh* from the men, prompting him to add, "But let us deduct ten from that for the unladylike language."

More laughing was followed by a stern Ruth sitting with Issie in the cart. "There is food to be had, you men. Why are yer all horsin' around?"

While they ate, many talked of Helena's expression when the colonel fell off the roof and laughingly repeated their banter. She took it all in good humour, but concern hid beneath her smile. In her mind, she had envisaged that as she turned the corner of the house, she would see him sprawled on the ground with a head wound like the general's, seeping his life's blood into the earth. Back then, she had experienced relief; this would have caused her grief beyond measure.

Surreptitiously, she watched him as he moved easily around the men, laughing with them. He was dirty and sweaty, and his exposed forearms were strong and muscular, scarred too in places. It was hard to imagine that this easy-going man was the same that had spoken to her so formally in the Harker's drawing room. Helena recalled Old Joe's words about her grandfather when he told her to find a similar man to run Redway with her. *For all his rolled-up sleeves an' muckin' in with the men, George were a gen'leman. He were a rare breed tha' cud mix in both circles.*

It occurred to Helena, though she had never considered there would be a man that could capture her interest, Colonel Nathaniel Ackley had seised it in a way she knew no other man ever could. She smiled as he approached her and the other women, thanking them all for the sustenance. They were packing up, and he moved to help Helena carry some boxes. As he took them from her, their hands touched, and their eyes locked.

"Mr Colonel, sir." Miss Andrews broke the moment, and Nathaniel turned and crouched down to her.

"Ah, the pretty Princess Isabella. I have warned all the dragons hereabouts that they must not attack you, or I will hunt them down and cut out their hearts."

"Thank you, Colonel." She smiled, clearly happy to be distinguished. "Did you eat some cake? I helped Mrs Ruth make it, especially for you. Can you fall off the roof again? That was a good joke."

"No," Mrs Andrews spoke immediately. "That was far too dangerous, and the colonel should not have done it at all."

Nathaniel stood again and looked into her eyes, seeing she had been afraid for him. His joke seemed less funny if it had caused her even a moment of anguish. Yet it gladdened his heart that she had been worried for him.

A commotion broke the moment's tension as Harriet rode towards Old Joe's, calling out for Harker. "Alexander, come quickly, come quickly. The baby is coming."

Harker needed to hear no more but sprang from his position of working on a new wooden door frame to leap on his horse and hurry down the lane.

"All is well. Pray, do not break your neck," Harriet called after him before turning to Mrs Andrews. "Gennie is asking for you. Mrs Hopkins says the midwife is in Nottingham, visiting her sister. She thought, given your experience, you could aid them?"

"Of course," Mrs Andrews replied, but Harriet was already retreating up the lane.

Nathaniel watched Mrs Andrews looking around for transportation. Why did Harriet not think to bring a spare horse, he wondered? Ruth Robertson was preparing to take Miss Andrews back with Rachel on the Redway cart, and Jacky Robertson came over to drive it for them, saying he would return on another horse. That could take a while, so Nathaniel moved to pick up his and Harker's coats before mounting Thor and walking him over to where Mrs Andrews stood.

"May I be allowed to provide you transportation to Eastease, Mrs Andrews? It may not be ideal, but you know me to be an honourable man."

"It would seem I have no other option unless I walk. I thank you, Colonel. I will have to sit sideways to accommodate my skirts."

With a stern nod towards Nathaniel, John stepped up and gave her a boost. Mrs Andrews had turned to face John and put her hands on his strong shoulders. Holding the reins in his left hand, Nathaniel wrapped his right arm around her waist and pulled her backwards, helping her land as gently as possible upon Thor and across his lap.

With her in position, he switched arms. His left arm ran across the small of her back, around her side to hold her, leaving his right free to control the reins. He was acutely aware of the feel of her at every point their bodies touched. "It might be more comfortable and safer for you to put your arm around me and hold on. Particularly once we go faster," he suggested as Thor started to walk down the lane.

"I am aware of that, Colonel, but not in front of these men and especially not John. Thank you for holding on to me."

He squeezed her closer to him, causing her to look up, and he looked into her eyes as he spoke, "John knows we spent the storm together."

She looked down, murmuring, "He suspects but has not asked me outright."

"He knows."

"You told him!" she admonished him. "Why would you do such a thing?"

"He would not leave it be. I did tell him that nothing happened and that I was a gentleman. I think he was ready to take a swing at me."

They both laughed at that thought, then turned the corner and out of sight of the men. Mrs Andrews leaned into him and tucked her right arm under his, her fingers running over the muscle ridges of his back and shoulders. "I think it is just as well for John that he did not," she said, resting her head against him.

"If I may say so, I missed sleeping close to you last night," he spoke into her hair. Her breath drew in an indignant gasp. She tried to pull back from him, but he held her tightly. "I mean nothing by it. I wanted you to know that I felt very comfortable and slept much better that night with you than I had for a long time. I suspect that you did, too."

She turned her face into his chest before she nodded. Then he urged Thor into a trot, the rocking movement soon arousing them both. He was sure had she looked up at him at that moment, he could have done nothing but place his lips upon hers.

Nathaniel thought it ideal that Eastease came into view when it did. While slowing his horse to a walk, Mrs Andrews could sit up safely and appropriately. Harriet met them at the door and called a footman to help, giving Nathaniel an accusatory look while he dismounted after releasing her friend.

"How else were you expecting her to arrive after you rode away?" Nathaniel asked as Adam came running around the corner to take Thor from him. The women hurried into the house to Genevieve while Nathaniel took a deep breath to regain his equilibrium after being so close to Mrs Andrews again. Then he pulled on his topcoat and, with Harker's in hand, strode into Eastease to find his friend.

~oOo~

Harriet led Helena past Alexander, pacing the corridor outside Genevieve's rooms. Upon entering, Helena saw her friend lying on the bed, looking worried, but when Harriet came in, Gennie pasted a smile on her face.

"How are you, Gennie? Sorry, silly question, I know that, but you forget most of this discomfort and pain once it is all done and your child is in your arms."

"Really? I have been in pain for hours. I did not see the point in sending for Alexander to have him pacing outside as he is now," as she spoke, Gennie tried to leverage herself further up the bed in a more sitting position. "He came running in here, all of a panic, but Mrs Hopkins and Jenny have banished him." She waved a hand at the housekeeper and her maid.

Helena turned to the two women. "Perhaps you could bring a few supplies to the room, Mrs Hopkins? Two pitchers of hot water for washing and cleaning the baby when it is born, plenty of linens, and a few basins. Some thread and a knife to tie and cut the cord?"

Armed with their duties, they headed for the door, with Mrs Hopkins trying to chivvy Harriet in front of them. "Come now, Miss. This is no place for a young lady such as yourself."

Helena turned to Genevieve, speaking quietly, "It is your decision, Gennie, but do you not think Harriet could be in this position one day, and it would be better for her to know what to expect?" Gennie nodded her agreement, and Harriet bounced back into the room to perch on the bed while Helena grasped the covers. "Would you mind, Gennie, if I take a look at you?"

Not waiting for an answer, Helena pulled back the bedclothes to feel Gennie's contracted belly and then, looking below, noted that not a lot was happening. "It may be some time yet. Your body is still preparing itself for pushing the child out. You do not need to lie in bed if you would rather not. How do you feel about walking around the room? It can help the process if you keep moving."

"I wanted to do that, but Mrs Hopkins insisted I lie down. That the proper place to have a baby is in bed."

Helena waved her hand at that. "We women should trust our instincts more. We have been having babies for centuries without being in a bed. I leaned back in a chair, giving birth to Issie after walking most of the time. Her great-grandfather caught her. How wonderful is that?" While she spoke, Helena helped Gennie out of bed.

"A man in the birthing room? Is that acceptable?" Gennie looked longingly at the door behind which her husband paced in the corridor.

"Who else would I want in there except the man that had delivered well over one hundred foals in his lifetime? Added to that, a man who loved and cared for me and took me in when I was alone," Helena said as she busied herself straightening out the bed Gennie had vacated.

"Why were you alone, Helena?" Harriet asked in a shocked whisper.

Helena looked up from her task and took in the surprised faces of Harriet and Gennie as they stared at her. She quashed the panicked feeling rising in her chest, realising that she had let down her guard in this intimate setting with her two closest friends, as she was happy to call them. Revealing the truth to Colonel Ackley the other night when she had barely thought, let alone talked of it in so long, must have caused a crack in the wall that Helena had built up around the secrets of her life. She would have to be more careful.

"This is not the time for such talk." She tried to wave it off, but Harriet was having none of it. Helena knew that too many people kept too many secrets from the curious young woman.

"This is the perfect time to talk of families and babies. You said it could take some time yet," Harriet countered.

At this, Genevieve shrieked with pain and grasped the railing at the end of her bed. As she leaned forwards, Helena rubbed her lower back, remembering how hers would ache.

"Breathe, Gennie. Remember to breathe. In through your nose and then blow it out, like you are blowing out the pain. How was that?"

"It helped a bit," she said, straightening again and looking gratefully at her friend. "I would like to hear your story. It would take my mind off things."

Mindful that she could not tell these women everything, Helena decided to share what she could. Rather than lie about a non-existent husband, she told them her story from arriving at her grandfather's. "After I was widowed, I became quite sure that I was with child. My parents were not very happy. I wrote to my grandfather and asked him to take me in. He was a wonderful man, tall, strong, handsome, yet so gentle with the foals and Issie."

Genevieve was wracked with pain again but did not shriek this time. She leaned forwards, gripping the bedrails. Clearly, this position gave her the most comfort. This time, Harriet rubbed her back.

"So, your grandfather wrote back to say you could stay with him," prompted Harriet.

"Yes, and it was so wonderful to be back at the stable. John, Ruth and their family came with us, as did Perseus. I grew larger and larger with Issie until I thought I would burst."

"I know that feeling," Gennie grunted, the grip of pain beginning again. This time, much worse, as she screamed. The time between the pains was getting less. Helena was sure there would be a new life in the world within the hour.

The door banged open, and Mr Harker burst into the room, with Colonel Ackley not far behind, smiling at his friend's obvious distress.

"I cannot bear it, Genevieve. I beg you to forgive me. What can I give you to make up for all this pain you are going through?" He knelt before his wife and grabbed her hand while she held fast to the bedrail with the other.

"There is nothing to forgive, my dearest. This is all quite the natural part of the process," Genevieve said, looking lovingly at her husband before another pain ripped through her body, and she leaned once more against the bed rail.

Helena took Harker's hand that Gennie had released and pressed it to his wife's lower back, moving it in a firm circular motion, showing him how he could aid his wife by himself. Helena gave a small smile before speaking again, "Gennie, forgiving him is one thing, but there must be something you can ask of him. You are providing him with the heir of this fine estate. Now is the time to press your advantage, as would any woman worth her salt. How about a diamond necklace?" Helena looked up and winked at the colonel, who had sat discreetly in the room's far corner.

"A new wardrobe," suggested Harriet with a laugh.

"A pair of Yorkshire Coach horses for a dear friend," said the colonel.

"I do not think that any of *my* friends want coach horses," teased Genevieve, amused, seemingly enjoying the process since Helena arrived. It provided Helena with happiness to assist her friend in such a way. Genevieve did not even seem to mind that Colonel Ackley was there, though he sat out of the way, in the corner. Mostly, Gennie looked happy that her husband was there beside her. He was looking at her expectantly, awaiting her command of him. "I had hoped I might be allowed a small garden to tend. To have it walled for our children to play in, and I could teach them all about the different plants and flowers we would grow there." Everyone stilled, the pleasant image that gift conjured in all their minds, so typically Genevieve.

"Then it is yours, my love, and probably some diamonds, too." At which everyone laughed. Mr Harker looked happy to be relieved of some of the worries he had no doubt felt upon hearing Genevieve's cries of pain. Another pain engulfed her, and he quickly moved to rub her back.

"Helena was telling us of the birth of Isabella. Please continue. It is taking my mind off this interminable process," Gennie managed to say when the pain had subsided.

"Not so interminable, my friend," informed Helena. "The pains are getting more frequent and more intense. It is a sure sign your body is almost ready. It will not be much longer. Still, I do not wish to bore Mr Harker and Colonel Ackley with my tale."

"Please," said the colonel from the corner of the room, "whatever is aiding Genevieve is fine with me. We all find Miss Andrews adorable and would love to know of the day she came into the world."

"My pains with Issie started in the night. It was so bad, but she is worth every one of them. She took her time, too, as she did not arrive until the next evening. Her birthday is next month, so nearly five years ago. I tried to keep quiet and not wake my grandfather, but he was used to dealing with foaling in the middle of the night. He heard me moving around and moaning. Ruth arrived in the morning and encouraged me to eat some breakfast. I did not want to, but she was right, and I was glad I had forced myself when I was flagging later in the day," as Helena spoke, she went to the nightstand and poured Genevieve some water from the pitcher. She handed it to Harker to help his wife drink.

"Ruth tried to send Grandfather away, but he would not leave my side. I loved him so much for that. He knew there was no other family to love the baby to whom I was giving life. He made that day special just by being there. It was around seven in the evening, close to this time, that Issie finally decided the time was right. I had been walking around most of the day, and it made sense to crouch by the fire, with a chair for support, as I brought her into the world. Grandfather caught her and wrapped her in a blanket he had ready. I asked him what it was, and he looked so surprised and said, *It is a baby.* I said, *Of course, it is a baby. What did you expect? A foal?*" Her enraptured audience laughed. "*A filly,* he said. My sweet girl. I was a mother, and it was the best day of my life."

Helena looked up into those blue eyes, staring at her intently from the corner of the room. She hoped the colonel understood—the worst day of her life was bearable because it had provided the best.

"Tell us," Nathaniel asked, knowing how much the little girl meant to her, "what gift did you persuade from your grandfather?"

"Missy," she looked at him as she spoke, and he nodded his acknowledgement of her determination to save the mare at the shelter.

"I think I should like to have a chair in front of the fire," Gennie's words startled them both as she looked to Harker, who moved two from around the edge of the room. Harriet perched on the bed, and

Nathaniel remained in his armchair in the far corner. Mrs Andrews' story had held him captive and affected him more than he cared to admit. He fervently wished he had been there for her and was so grateful her grandfather had been present.

"Could I catch the baby, do you think, my dear? Would it be appropriate?" Harker asked.

Thinking if it was his child, propriety could be damned, Nathaniel replied for everyone, "Damn it, Harker, you are the master of this house. If you cannot do as you wish, who can?"

"This is all highly inappropriate," Mrs Hopkins had arrived with the linens and water. "You men should not be in here."

"I am not leaving, Mrs Hopkins," said Harker.

She looked to Nathaniel expectantly. "I refuse to be the only person shut out. I am fine over here in the corner, am I not, Genevieve?"

In the throes of yet another pain, Gennie did not answer, but Mrs Andrews, kneeling at the foot of Genevieve's chair examining her again, came to his aid.

"It is of no matter. The baby is almost here. Mr Harker, you and I should wash our hands in this bowl. Leave the other to cool to clean the baby."

Nathaniel watched from his vantage point as Mrs Andrews instructed Genevieve and Harker to deliver their baby. He was grateful he could only see everyone's upper body as the noises were terrible enough. Of course, he was not squeamish, but he had seen enough blood and guts to last several lifetimes.

Harker held up the baby to show Genevieve, and sensing the sudden cold air, the baby started to cry. "We have a son, Genevieve. Thank you for my son," he declared.

Mrs Hopkins went over with a blanket to wrap the child but did not take him away. Handing him back to his adoring father, she showed him how to clean the baby with the cooled water. Helena finished taking care of Genevieve and helped her over to the bed.

Everyone turned at the surprised voice of Mrs Hopkins, "Oh sir, wonderful luck. He is a caul baby." She got a piece of paper from a nearby desk, removed the caul from the baby's head, and draped it onto the paper for drying and keeping. "He will not drown," she claimed.

~oOo~

"Alexander Jacob Nathaniel Harker!" Colonel Ackley exclaimed again as he rode with Helena across the fields back to Redway. "I expected them to name the child after its father, even its mother's father, but then to add my name? I am honoured."

Helena laughed, her mood buoyant when she considered how they rode this way separately a week ago, both in foul moods. How could she have only known him a week when the surge of feeling in her chest indicated a lifetime together?

"You were wonderful," he continued as the buildings of Redway appeared in the distance. "When we arrived, Genevieve was lying in bed as if ill. Harriet was as pale as ever I have seen her, and poor Harker was at his wit's end. In you came like light shining in a dark place. Despite the pain, you helped Genevieve enjoy it; Harker was involved instead of shut out, and Harriet was no longer petrified. Should her time come in the future, she will know how special it can be."

"And you sat and watched in the corner," she teased.

"It was good to hear you talk of your grandfather," he looked over to her as he spoke.

"It was good to talk of him. All those foals he delivered, and Issie was his only baby." Helena smiled at the recollection.

"How many babies have you delivered?"

"Including Genevieve's? One." She laughed at his astonished expression, then legged Freda into a gallop as they crossed the border of Redway land. The colonel and Thor easily caught up with them.

"One? That baby was the first baby you have ever delivered?" his tone of voice seemed concerned, which Helena found even more amusing.

"Yes," she laughed. "It was miraculous, was it not?"

"I had no idea. Did Genevieve or Harriet know?"

He sounded annoyed now, which caused her to speak rather

indignantly, "I do not know what they knew. You make it sound like I misrepresented myself. I have never said that I have delivered babies before. I have had my own, and my grandfather and Ruth helped me through that. The foal the other day was my first difficult foal, but I had seen many others."

They slowed as they arrived at the buildings.

"But what if something had gone wrong?" he asked.

"We would have dealt with it as best we could, but what other choice was there?"

"You seemed so confident."

"Gennie needed me to be. They all did. Calming everyone was the most important part. The calmer everyone was, the calmer I felt. I trusted my instincts. Babies have been born for hundreds of years."

She dismounted and handed him Freda's reins with a slap to his gloved hand, bringing his attention down to her face. The realisation that he had annoyed her suddenly showed in his eyes before he smiled.

"You are an astonishing woman, Mrs Andrews."

"Is that something you are only just noticing, Colonel Ackley?" She smiled up at him.

"Not at all." He bowed as best he could from his seated position. "I will see you on the morrow."

"Until tomorrow then, Colonel. Please, do not be late, or Issie will be intolerable."

"That will depend on how many dragons I slay on my way here." He laughed and waved, then turned the horses back to Eastease.

Helena watched him from the outskirts of the Redway buildings, assessing his skill. The colonel had a fine riding form, soft hands, strong legs and a straight back. He kept his seat light. *Yes*, she pondered as he disappeared from her view in the fading light. *I do admire his fine seat.*

Thirteen

The following morning, Helena awoke to the delightful sound of her daughter's giggles and running feet before Issie burst into her rooms, where she jumped up to stand on the bed with the carved horse headboard. Wiggling her body from side to side, the little girl sang a made-up song.

"We're going on a picnic
To see what we will see
There's going to be some scrumptious food
For you, the colonel and me!
The sun is shining brightly
We'll smile and be happy
As we eat beside the stream
Just you, the colonel and me!"

Helena grabbed Issie and pulled her down into a warm hug. "Good morning, light of my life. It was too much to hope you might sleep late this morning."

Issie squealed as Helena snuggled her neck, then laughed as her mother tickled all over. "Stop, stop," she said breathlessly.

"Let's get moving then, my sweet girl. We have chores to do first."

~oOo~

After waking in high spirits, Nathaniel hummed to himself as he entered the breakfast room. Mrs Hopkins was the only one present.

"I have never known a grown man to be so enthusiastic about a picnic with a four-year-old girl," she teased.

Nathaniel paused in buttering his bread and pointed at her with the knife. "You will have no effect on my mood today, Mrs Hopkins. The child is disarming. I should suggest to Wellington that we use her to disarm the enemy before going into battle."

"Maybe he should take her mother too, given that they seem to possess the same attributes," she sparred.

"Mrs Hopkins, you always seem to be in the right." He allowed her the point. The day was too good to worry about losing a battle of words. "How is our newest family member?"

Having no chores to complete, Nathaniel tried to pass the time moving from person to person within the Eastease household.

Genevieve threw him out of her rooms when he looked in on his godson. "Nathaniel, you are disturbing him. Go away and allow us both to rest."

In the music room, Harriet admonished him for his pacing.

"Sit down if you wish to listen, Nathaniel," Harriet begged as she practised. "Your constant movement is distracting me. If you cannot be still, then leave. Alexander is in his study. Go and see him."

"Harker, there you are," Nathaniel said as he entered the warm room and sat in the chair opposite his friend. Was it only a week ago he confronted his father in this very spot? Even thoughts of the earl could not dampen his spirits. So much had changed since then.

Harker's quill didn't stop scratching upon the paper as he grunted an acknowledgement.

Nathaniel looked at the pile of sealed letters on one side of the desk. "Who are you writing to now?"

"This is for the Ridgefields," Harker said as he signed the single page with a flourish. "Do you think I should send an announcement to Lady Grace?"

Nathaniel grimaced. "Perhaps to her mother—Lady Agnes?"

Sealing the Ridgefield's letter with wax and the Eastease stamp, Harker picked up the next piece of parchment and began to write *Lady Agnes*.

"I'll be heading off to my picnic at Redway shortly, Harker," Nathaniel said but received no response from his friend. He stood and walked to the French doors. Looking out, Nathaniel saw cloudless blue skies and smiled again. Turning back to Harker, he watched him start another letter before leaving him to it.

Finally, Mrs Hopkins dragged Nathaniel away from the kitchen where he had been pestering the staff preparing his picnic.

"Colonel, I will bring the saddlebags out to you when ready. Here, take this." She gave him an apple for his horse and sent him to the stable.

Adam had groomed Thor so well that he gleamed. Nathaniel rewarded him with a coin and Thor with the apple. He talked with Adam briefly and then walked Thor around the courtyard to warm up. The kitchen hands arrived with two saddlebags packed with provisions for the picnic and a large blanket. Nodding his thanks, Nathaniel headed out towards the road. He was paying his friend's neighbour a visit and should do it via the proper route rather than over the fields as he had travelled last night.

Upon Nathaniel's arrival at Redway, a red-haired animal descended upon him. Holding Thor on a short rein, he leaned down and scooped Miss Andrews up with one strong arm.

"I was so happy when I woke this morning to a sunny, sunny day. Were you, Colonel?" The young face looked up at him from atop the blanket with a smile to rival the sun.

"Indeed, I was," he agreed.

"I am glad to see you again. Did you see any dragons on your way here?"

"I did not. I believe dragons prefer to sleep at noon." He walked Thor around the back of the house to the rear courtyard, and like her mother had the day before, the girl put her arms around him and held on tight. Although a completely different sensation, he was immensely pleased that she, too, felt comfortable enough to hold on to him.

Mrs Andrews was loading a saddlebag onto a pretty, copper-red, chestnut mare with a white blaze on her face. The colour of the horse almost matched the hair colour of its owner. A stableman stood holding a small grey pony, to which Miss Andrews pointed.

"That is my very own pony, Colonel. We call her Elpis for spirit and hope. Do you like her?" She looked up at him expectantly, but he had been distracted by Mrs Andrews' efficient hands, ensuring the soundness of each horse's girth and length of stirrups.

He looked down at Miss Isabella. "I do. How long have you been riding?"

"Mama says in her arms since I was born, but I first remember riding with my G-G-Papa long ago. I was two and a half, but I could not hold on by myself until I was three." She giggled, which was music to his ears.

"Good day, Colonel. Let's get you in the saddle then, my sweet girl." Mrs Andrews moved to help her daughter down from Thor. Nathaniel held her firmly as he lowered her to her mother with his own greeting. He watched them walk hand in hand until they reached the pony, and then Mrs Andrews bent low to give the girl a boost. Miss Isabella stepped into her hands and put her other leg over the animal's back. Noticing the riding breeches underneath her gown, Nathaniel smiled. Her mother moved quickly to arrange the skirts more modestly. She turned and saw him smiling.

"It makes sense for her to learn to ride astride first. It is more difficult and takes longer to master. It is also safer."

He nodded and watched Miss Isabella take up the reins from the stableman, thanking him politely before turning the pony towards the opposite gap between the stable and the house.

"Wait for me," her mother warned. Her tone, though calm, was firm enough to stop Nathaniel from urging Thor on. He turned at a snort of laughter from Mrs Andrews that she tried to stifle and saw her step into the waiting hands of the stableman to swing her other leg over the mare. She, too, was wearing breeches.

They steered their mounts into the waiting green fields, keeping their riding to a walk so they could enjoy the scenery and talk. Mrs Andrews pointed out Redway houses in the distance and told him who rented each—a larger two-storey home that was John and Ruth's, the next a small single-storey that Mrs Dawley, James' mother, was moving into today.

"James, who works at Eastease?" he asked, remembering that his valet had the rest of the day off.

"Yes, his mother lived in a property in the village that the landlord did not tend to. She had been unwell as there was dampness and mould. I happened to be visiting her last Sunday, luckily for me, as it turns out that she is a wonderful seamstress. We always need help with mending horse blankets and suchlike. I am terrible at that type of thing myself. Now we have someone on staff to do those jobs for the house and the help that need it. She gets a small stipend and will live in the cottage. It had just become available. Mrs Hopkins has kindly agreed that James will bring Issie to and from her music lessons with Harriet so he can visit with his mother more often."

Nathaniel looked at her incredulously. *How does she do it?* he wondered. He had told Mrs Andrews how James had come to him when his father was heading to her rooms at Eastease, and she had returned that good deed tenfold at least.

As he gazed at her in wonder, she talked of other staff members at Redway and some of their family members who worked at Eastease and lived in the other cottages. Redway's land to the northeast was farmland on a long-term lease. The workers had stripped the distant fields of grain, and haystacks rested on the stubble left behind by the threshers.

"No Perseus today?" Nathaniel asked as the horses walked.

"He would not enjoy this pace nor be very tolerant walking close to Thor. Last week, I was surprised and impressed when you could walk them both to the shelter. I suppose their horse sense was telling them to get to safety."

"Your mare is beautiful, like her owner; your hair colours almost match."

The mare nodded her head up and down. "We both say thank you,

Colonel. Persephone is good at keeping pace with Issie's pony. I apologise if it is difficult for your horse. Please, feel free to ride circles around us if it pleases him. Issie and I are always happy to do what pleases horses."

"Could I trouble you to call me Nathaniel, do you think? I know it is improper, but we are alone here."

"Nathaniel," she almost whispered it. "I am afraid I'm unable to do so, even though I may wish it, as we are not *completely* alone." With that, she looked pointedly at Miss Isabella, who happily sang to her pony. "What do you think she would tell Rachel and Ruth when she arrives back at the house?"

"Then, I will respect your decision and, with your permission, only think *Helena* when I say Mrs Andrews," Nathaniel whispered her name, as she had done with his and enjoyed the blush that rushed to her cheeks.

Then he rode ahead before swinging back around to bring Thor to the other side of his two companions, so he and the stallion towered over the young girl and pony.

"This is so much fun, Colonel." The small girl smiled up at him.

"It most certainly is, Miss Isabella, and may I be bold and say that you are a very accomplished rider? Where are we heading?"

She pointed ahead, where he could see a small copse of trees, surrounded by luscious grass and cut through by a small stream. "It is our favourite place."

It certainly looked idyllic.

Upon arriving at the copse, Nathaniel helped both ladies off their horses and spread the blanket. He laid down the packs and excused himself and his horse for a quick run before eating. Nathaniel became aware of his audience as he guided Thor up a slight incline along the stream. Careening back down again, he couldn't resist having his horse jump a couple of old, felled trees to halt at the blanket where Helena had arranged their provisions. Enjoying the applause, Nathaniel jumped down and bowed. At his silent command, Thor bowed, too, before Nathaniel led him to the stream for a drink.

"That was wonderful, Colonel!" exclaimed Miss Issie. "Can we teach Elpis to bow?"

"I am sure we could if Elpis is willing, but not today. I am much too hungry, and luckily, we have a feast waiting for us." He tied Thor's reins to a tree as Helena had done with Persephone and the pony so they were loose enough to allow the horse to eat some grass if he wished. Removing his coat, Nathaniel sat down on the blanket.

An hour flew by as they ate, talked and laughed. Issie entertained them with tales of when she was young and her *G-G-Papa*, as she called her great-grandfather, because he worked with horses. It was evident to Nathaniel that she had adored and missed the older man. She could not have possibly remembered some of the stories, so he concluded they were stories her mother had told her often. No tales of her father, he noted. The mother did not talk of him, so neither did the daughter. Of course, Captain Andrews was not real as he now knew, but the child was unaware. Nathaniel wondered if Helena realised what a void that was for her daughter, but even if she did, it would not be a good idea to make up stories about a man who did not exist.

Once they had eaten, Helena encouraged Issie to close her eyes briefly, explaining that she had not slept much the night before with her excitement of the coming day. Helena rolled up the girl's breeches and put them before herself so Issie could lie beside her and use them as a pillow. Deciding to do the same with her own, they both lay looking at Nathaniel. He lay on the blanket opposite them, resting his head on his arm.

"Do you want to start a story, Issie?" Helena asked.

"Long ago, there was a young princess called Issie. Her mother was the Queen of the land because her father, the King, had died in battle, bravely protecting the kingdom and his family."

"Was the queen beautiful?" Helena asked in a way that made Nathaniel believe they often did this. He smiled broadly and nodded. Issie gave a tired giggle and continued.

"The queen was beautiful but sad because the King had died."

"The greatest happiness in her life was her precious daughter, the princess." Helena squeezed the little girl and kissed the top of her head. Issie took up the story again.

"Then one day, the terrible Dragon of Lincolnshire woke very hungry from his one-hundred-year sleep. A passing soldier saw the smoke from the dragon's nose rising from the hilltop. He feared for the life of his Queen and her daughter and rode his horse—" she paused, trying to think of a suitable name.

"Thor," her mother provided. Nathaniel smiled broadly again. He was enjoying this glimpse into the relationship between mother and daughter.

"Oh yes, what a wonderful name, Mama." She turned and planted a sweet kiss on Helena's cheek. "He rode his horse, Thor, in a gallop across the countryside. Faster and faster they went until they were a blur of redcoat and horse." She yawned, and her mother took this as her cue.

"The mighty dragon spread its wings and took to the air. Its favourite things to eat were princesses and queens. The soldier stopped his horse at the palace gates, and the two stood firm as the dragon landed in front of them." Helena looked over to Nathaniel and playfully lifted her eyebrows for him to provide the soldier's words.

Nathaniel played his part. "*You will not pass here today*, the soldier said bravely, although he feared the dragon. *I will protect my Queen and Princess to the death—your death*. With that, he plunged his sword into the dragon's heart. As the dragon died, it reached out a claw and sliced the brave soldier across the chest. He fell off his horse."

"Oh no, the poor soldier! He doesn't die, does he, Mama?" Issie sat up in sudden horror at the turn her story was taking.

Nathaniel was panicked and thought, at that moment, he might prefer to face down a dragon—a *small one.*

Helena gave him a reassuring smile. "Of course not," she said, encouraging her daughter to lie down again. "The queen and princess had seen his bravery and used their secret, magical powers to heal him with a kiss. The princess kissed him on the cheek, but his injury was so bad that it was not enough. The queen kissed his lips until he was completely healed."

Issie's sleepy voice startled Nathaniel as he gazed at Helena.

"Now that they had kissed, they had to get married. The soldier became King and kissed the queen every day, and she was happy again. The princess called him Papa, and they all lived happily, forever." Yawning, her eyes fluttered, and suddenly she was asleep. A talent that Nathaniel envied.

He looked up from the child to the mother, who looked at him embarrassed, presumably by her description of the kisses and the story ending Issie had provided. Thankful she had saved Issie a nightmare over his part of the story, he aimed to lighten the moment.

"I wish kisses would have worked on me. It took much longer for me to heal, and kisses would be much more pleasant."

Helena smiled, but her eyelids looked heavy. With her daughter awake late into the night and the excitement of the birth yesterday, she must be exhausted.

Nathaniel smiled in return. "Sleep, Helena," he whispered.

"Thank you, Nathaniel."

After clearing the food and repacking the saddlebags, Nathaniel took off his waistcoat and walked along the stream's bank, keeping the sleeping duo in his view. He smiled at the thought of himself as the soldier protecting his queen and princess. Briefly, he gave rein to ideas of marriage and fatherhood as he turned his gaze to the babbling stream where the shadows of the trees in the copse waved in the slight breeze. Nathaniel shook himself out of that reverie; he was a soldier, a bachelor, and she had made it clear she did not want to marry.

Movement flickered in his peripheral vision as the child sat up, rubbing the sleep out of her eyes. Walking back over to the blanket, he put his finger to his lips before pointing to her mother, who was still asleep. Sitting back down, he leaned over and picked a nearby late buttercup.

"Let's see if you like butter, Miss Issie."

The little girl laughed as she clambered over his legs and lifted her chin while he held the flower up to it. "Do I like butter?"

"It shines so bright, you must love it," he teased.

"Your turn." She grabbed the stalk from him, clasping his chin in one hand, and her head bobbed out of sight momentarily while she inspected his neck. "You don't like butter," she declared in disappointment.

Nathaniel laughed. "You must have drained all the buttercup

power because I love butter too." With that, he tickled her, and she squirmed in his arms. Issie squealed as Nathaniel rolled on his back, raising her in the air while they laughed.

"Kisses, kisses," Issie said, and he brought her down to his face, where he burrowed into her neck, making loud smacking noises with his lips. Nathaniel turned his head to see if Issie's squeals had disturbed Helena, and his eyes met with sleepy green ones.

"Issie, you woke your Mama," his voice was throaty, as the sight of her beside him again was overwhelming.

"Kiss Mama! Kiss Mama!" squealed Issie.

He wondered if he could. Helena lay there with sleepy eyes and looked at him. He leaned over, with the four-year-old still in his arms, and holding Helena's gaze, he brushed his lips, ever so lightly, over hers.

"And they all lived happily, forever and ever!" Issie shouted, pulling away from his arms and getting to her feet, dancing and spinning joyfully.

Nathaniel looked at Helena, keeping eye contact. He remained still, waiting for her reaction. She lifted a hand to touch his cheek, and then nature intervened as the sun slipped behind a cloud. It was getting late in the afternoon, and the temperature dropped more in the evenings now that they were in September. The spell was broken, and then he heard a splash and a shriek.

"Issie!" Nathaniel called, jumping to his feet and racing to the stream. He knew from his earlier view of the stream that it was not too deep for her at this time of year, but he worried the girl might be hurt. He grinned at the sight that greeted him—the little girl sat in water only deep enough to reach her waist, drenched from head to toe. The shock on her face told him she could either burst into tears or laughter. "Are you hurt?" he asked kindly, wading into the water, his riding boots keeping him dry. With a shaky giggle, she held up her arms, and Nathaniel gathered her shivering body to him, trying to warm her against his chest.

"I fell," she said against his shoulder. "I'm not hurt. Thank you for saving me, Colonel."

"It is my duty, Miss Issie. Evermore." Nathaniel felt her hands squeezing him and looked to the bank to see Helena with the blanket.

"Is she well?"

Nathaniel nodded.

"You can put her down now."

Gently, he put the girl on her feet and watched as Helena quickly unfastened Issie's gown, removing it before wrapping her in the blanket. When she looked up at him, no doubt reading the confusion on his face, Helena explained, "If I left her in the wet gown, she would be very cold by the time we got home. This way, I can carry her on Persephone, lead Elpis behind us and keep her warm in the blanket."

"I will carry her if you can manage the saddlebags and the pony," he suggested, knowing how difficult it would be for her to do all that herself. Nathaniel held back his exasperation at her reluctance to rely on him as he watched her looking about her at the horses, their supplies and then her daughter.

"I can—" she started, but he cut across her gently, wishing he could command her to do the sensible thing.

"Let—me—help—you," he said kindly but deliberately. "I know you are completely capable of doing everything you said, but I am here. You do not need to. This makes the most sense. Your arms will be aching on the ride home if you carry her."

"Please let Colonel Ackley carry me, Mama," Issie said with such an appealing look on her face Nathaniel felt he could never refuse the child. He imitated her pleading expression, smiling when Helena conceded with a harrumph.

"You are wet, too, Colonel," Helena gestured to him, and he followed her gaze down to his shirt, which was sticking to his skin.

"I will survive." He smiled at her staring and strode off to mount Thor.

Helena bundled her daughter up and handed her up to Nathaniel. He made sure he had Issie as securely as possible on his horse, and after confirming that Helena could mount the mare by herself, he headed back to Redway, leaving her to catch up.

Issie snuggled into his chest. His wet shirt was still plastered to him, and he felt her small fingers exploring his scar through the damp material. She gasped, then looked around at Thor.

"I forgot to ask you, Colonel. What is your horse's name?"

"Thor."

She gasped again. Nathaniel wondered why and looked down at her face. She was looking up at him in awe. Then he remembered the story that was peppered with facts about him. From the child's perspective, it must seem like the soldier had come to life.

"You kissed her, and now you must marry," she almost whispered.

"No, sweet girl," he said as gently as possible. "You have to think of your mother's feelings on this. You had a father once who was a soldier."

"He died before I was born," she was matter-of-fact.

"Yes, he did." Nathaniel was not going to lie to her. "When that happened, your mother was very upset. It is hard to be alone. She runs the stable on her own, and she looks after you."

"No, John helps in the stable, Ruth is in the house, and Rachel takes care of me."

"But you are all her responsibility, and you have been since your G-G-Papa died. When you are the one who makes all the decisions all of the time, it is hard to let someone take that from you. She would feel that would happen if she married me." Was he beginning to understand her a little better?

"When G-G-Papa died, I remember her crying a lot, but she is happier when you are here. I am happier." Her pout appeared, and she buried her head into his chest, just like her mother had done the day before.

"I am happier with you, too, sweet girl." He used Helena's term of affection for her child and held her closer to him. He did not want her to be upset and, as a father, would have done anything to relieve her of it. "Sometimes, you have to be patient for good things to happen. Do you think you can be patient with me and for your mother?"

"Yes, sir. I will try."

"Thank you. Here is your mother with the other horses. Hush now."

They completed the journey with very little said. When they got to the stable, Nathaniel carried the *drowned rat,* as he termed her, up to her rooms. As he left her with Rachel, Helena came out of another bedchamber he presumed was hers. He glimpsed her large bed with a wooden headboard ornately carved with horses. He swallowed hard and followed her down the stairs.

At the bottom of the stairs, Helena faced Nathaniel still in his shirtsleeves and tried not to think of kissing him. She had picked up his coat once he was out of sight of her at the stream and hugged it, burying her face into it, inhaling his distinctly male smell. She handed it to him now.

"Please thank Mrs Hopkins for her picnic preparations and assure her we will return a clean, dry blanket to her at the earliest opportunity." She looked up at him as she spoke quietly, "Thank you, Nathaniel, for retrieving Issie from the stream and bringing her home on Thor."

"You are both very welcome. Thank you for the wonderful day. Please let me know if I am featured in any new stories, rescuing drowning princesses." He bowed and made to leave.

"I certainly will."

~oOo~

Issie had another lesson with Harriet, but Nathaniel did not show his face in the music room to hear the girl play, although Harriet told him she had asked after him. He made himself scarce, knowing he had fallen in love with the little girl and possibly with her mother. Some distance was called for, and he anticipated his orders would arrive soon.

True to his word, Harker produced a diamond tiara for Genevieve to commemorate the birth of the heir of Eastease. Harriet had declared Gennie must wear it at a Christmas ball. It had been so long since there had been a ball at Eastease. Nathaniel decided to return then and see if his feelings were still the same for the red-headed Helena.

When Nathaniel received his orders, he informed Harker and Genevieve that he would be leaving for London, and then he rode over to Redway to say goodbye to Helena. He crossed the fields to arrive at the stable in the same familiar way he had done with Helena a few evenings ago. He saw her astride either Perceval or Grenville—he could not yet tell them apart. She put the horse through its paces in the paddock behind the stable. John was watching and nodding, calling out instructions. Nathaniel tied Thor to a post, away from the paddock to avoid distracting her horse, and approached John. Looking at the notes, he ascertained that they were finishing with this horse.

"Colonel," John pulled his forelock.

"John," Nathaniel nodded. Were they ever to be on better terms, he wondered? Maybe not until they had tried to knock each other's teeth out. "He is a wonderful specimen."

"Indeed, got to put t'other one through the same in a minute. Buyer is taking possession at the end of the week." John looked over at Nathaniel, who was staring glumly out at Helena. "You are leaving."

"Yes, tomorrow." He turned to the man who was throwing up his hands in disgust. "I have orders. I am a soldier, remember? I will be back."

Helena had halted the horse and dismounted. Bringing Grenville over to John, she asked, "Perceval next then?"

John took the reins to lead the horse away and retreated, muttering.

She smiled at Nathaniel. "Will the two of you ever stop antagonising one another?"

"I was wondering the same thing myself." He smiled back at her. "Could I talk to you, please?"

"Yes, of course."

John came back around the barn with Perceval, and Helena called out to him, "Could you ride him today, please, John? I need to talk to the colonel."

"Yes, ma'am." The man entered the paddock with the horse and mounted him easily.

Helena turned to Nathaniel and spoke quietly, "Issie has talked of nothing but the picnic, the story and how Colonel Ackley saved her from drowning in the stream."

He laughed at that. "Did she mention—anything else?"

Helena blushed, turning her face away from his scrutiny.

"Surprisingly, no."

Nathaniel said nothing, glad that Miss Issie was heeding his advice. He wondered if Helena had been worried he might ask her to marry him as she looked a little panicked. "I received my orders," he said, noticing her face relax.

Quickly, her concern returned. "You are not going back to Spain, are you?" She looked horrified, giving him hope to know she cared about him.

"Not yet. I am to report to London. I expect to be involved in strategy training of officers and horses, at least until Christmas, when I hope to return to Eastease. I am to tell you that there will be a ball to which you will be invited. Should I make it back for it, I would be honoured if you would save the first two dances for me."

"Yes, of course. And are you a good dancer?"

"I am the son of an earl; of course, I am a good dancer. What about you?"

"I am suddenly glad that my mother insisted on lessons. Those lessons were the only thing my mother made me do that I enjoyed."

Nathaniel looked into her eyes seriously, holding them for a long time as if drinking her into his memory. "Mrs Andrews, Helena, do I ask too much? I mean, could you possibly see your way to write to me?" She made to speak, but he held up a hand. "No, no need to answer right now. This is the direction should you choose to write. It will find me wherever I am stationed. I would love to hear how things are going here with the foals and Miss Issie. As well as any other musings you might like to share." He handed her a note.

"I do not need to think about it. I would love to write to you as a dear friend. Is that acceptable?"

"Friends, then."

"Take care of yourself, Nathaniel." She curtseyed and offered her hand.

"Until Christmas, Helena." He bowed over her hand, turned it over so the palm faced upward and brushed it with his lips. Then he turned to leave.

Helena curled her fingers around where he had kissed as if to hold it in, bringing her hand to her heart.

Fourteen

Nathaniel didn't discover the shop-wrapped gift secreted within his belongings until a servant unpacked them at the Ackley London premises. It lay upon his bedside table with a sealed letter and folded piece of paper. He shook his head at James' secrecy in hiding them within his luggage. Clearly, Helena's help with his mother's accommodation overcame James' duty to tell Nathaniel.

Curious, he sat on the side of the bed and opened the gift. A silk cravat in dark blue was nestled within and fixed to it sat an oval gold pin with the shape of a running horse embossed upon it. The pin looked old and a little worn but shone nonetheless. Unfolding the paper, he was surprised by the quality of the drawing of a scaly dragon. One of its sharp talons dripped with blood, and a sword was embedded deep within the dragon's chest. The unfortunate dragon of Lincolnshire, he presumed with a smile. Leaving those items on the bed, he picked up the letter and fingered the wax seal of Redway Acres. Knowing it must be from Helena, he savoured the moment before breaking it open.

Dearest Colonel Ackley,

Nathaniel, if I still have your permission?

I hope you will accept this cravat as a suitable replacement for yours, which was stained too much to clean. The darker blue will show your eyes even brighter. The pin was my grandfather's, a gift from my grandmother, and I rarely saw him without it. I searched for it recently, intending to give it to you on our picnic, but it was so tarnished you had to wait for me to clean it. It shines well enough now, although a little dented, which adds some character in the same way of scars.

My grandfather would have liked you. He had your sense of humour and would enjoy playing tricks on his wife, much like you did to me, falling off Old Joe's roof last week. So, I think he would be happy for you to have his pin as a thank you for your assistance with Missy in the storm. The foal is doing nicely, and I did decide to call him Chance.

Issie has asked if she may write to you with her stories. Many of them include the brave soldier, Colonel Ackley. Do you like the picture she put in with the cravat? That part of the storyline was yours still I hope it is not too close to bad memories for you.

Issie and I wish you safe travels to London and hope you think of Redway fondly, as Redway will be thinking of you. Your friend,

Helena Andrews

Nathaniel ran a finger over her name and reread the letter. He was touched that she should give him something of her grandfather's, and it pleased him that she related scars as character. He hoped that when she said, *Redway will be thinking of you*, she actually meant she would, as thoughts of her were never far from his mind.

Striding out of his rooms, he went to the study to pen a reply already forming in his head.

Dearest Helena,

I hope I am not being too presumptuous using your given name. Of course, you still have permission to use mine.

You are far too generous to buy me an elegant cravat and very secretive in hiding it within my belongings. There was no need for a replacement; my other one was certainly lost to a good cause. It is gratefully received, however, and when I am unable to wear it due to uniform regulations, be assured that I will have it safe in a pocket about my person, with the pin and an artistic rendering of the Dragon of Lincolnshire.

I am honoured to wear something that was your grandfather's, and I would love to hear more of him in our letters. I believe that I would have liked him, too. I should apologise for the trick of falling off the roof. I saw the pain in your eyes when you talked to Issie of how dangerous it was. I had not considered that you had witnessed violent death before, albeit in different circumstances. Not realising in those few moments that I was safe, you would have had a fair picture of what you might turn the corner to find. Please accept my sincere apology, dear lady.

Chance is an excellent name. Of course, I would say so, as I was the one to suggest it, but given the circumstances of his birth, chance played a large part.

I would love to read Issie's stories. She has a wonderful imagination, something that, too soon, the realities of life can tear from us. Her gift is to share what she loves, and I would be honoured if she were to share them with me.

I do not have much to tell you except that I have arrived safely in London. I report for my duties tomorrow and promised my mother that, when I have time, I will visit Bainbridge in Norfolk. My Father's cousin, Lady Agnes, is a widow, and the whole family concerns themselves with her business interests. However, it seems I am the only one pressed upon to see to them.

Please continue to write with more news of Redway and Eastease. Though I am only gone a few days, I feel it could easily be two months. Your's

Nathaniel Ackley (Col.)

~oOo~

Helena continued to write to and receive letters from Nathaniel informing him of the foals that continued to grow and flourish and how accomplished Issie was becoming on the pianoforte.

At least once a week Helena met Harriet and Genevieve for luncheon. They would coo over the baby and talk of plans for the

Christmas ball. All was going well until Harriet asked what Helena planned to wear. Helena laughed at Harriet's reaction when she informed the young woman she would wear the same gown she had worn to the dinner at the end of August.

Harriet looked horrified. "You—you cannot possibly. No, Helena. This ball is going to be perfect, and you are going to dance with Nathaniel. He will fall in love with you."

"Harriet," Helena let out a short laugh, "Colonel Ackley won't fall in love with me over a ballgown, I assure you. We are dancing the first pair of dances together, that is all."

"I will not have it. Gennie, you agree with me. Helena must wear another gown."

"You really should, Helena," Gennie said apologetically. "I would give you one of mine if you do not have anything suitable, for surely I have many to spare, but I am so much shorter than you."

"One of mine then," Harriet said. "Come with me now. Let us see what would be best."

"Harriet, there is no need," Helena protested but followed the young woman upstairs.

"Annie," Harriet called out to her maid as they entered, and the petite woman appeared. "There you are. My ballgowns, what do we have long enough for Mrs Andrews?"

"Miss, the peach you are wearing at Christmas, but there is the rose from your birthday ball and the blue you had made before that."

"Those will be too short; I've grown at least an inch since then. What about the cream? I got it in London last year, so the style is still fashionable. Could you help Mrs Andrews try it on?"

Helena followed the shorter woman into Harriet's dressing room, stripping down to her drawers and stockings. Annie held the gown out for Helena to step into before putting her arms in the short sleeves. The high waist, just under her breasts, pushed them up into such a magnificent cleavage. Helena would have laughed if the maid fastening the many buttons left her with any breath.

"Let us see it," Harriet called.

"I am not coming out there," Helena argued. "Annie has done her best, but it won't fasten all the way."

Harriet and Gennie bustled unceremoniously into the room before Helena could face the door. They were so silent she wondered if they were as captivated as she over the sumptuousness of the gown. Harriet must have paid handsomely for it. Then, through the mirror, she took in Gennie's shocked expression and Harriet's horrified tears before realising the source—the welt down her back from the crop when General Alcott had struck her. The cream gown had a low back, and the top of her scar would be visible even with all the fastenings connected.

"Helena—" Harriet began.

"Do not worry, Harriet. I can have Mrs Dawley spruce up my old gown. I'm sure she can give it a new lease on life." She tried not to show her disappointment.

"There must be some way to conceal it, ma'am," Annie offered, giving Helena some hope. Having put on the gown, she longed for Nathaniel to see her in it.

Gennie still looked concerned. "But how, Helena? How did it happen?"

Oh, how much harder it is to keep secrets when one has friends, Helena thought, yet she would not trade her friends for anything. How much she had gained in her life from knowing these remarkable women. She decided to tell them as much of the truth as she could.

"An investor of my father's was beating his horse with a crop, and I got in the way trying to protect the beast. He hit my back instead."

"On purpose?" Gennie all but whispered in horror.

"Dreadful man," Harriet said indignantly. "What happened to the horse?"

"The horse was shot after he kicked the man in the head and killed him."

"What an awful affair, but I cannot feel sorry for a man willing to beat a woman," Gennie declared.

"Or a horse," Harriet agreed. "If it were up to me, I would say leave it showing as a talisman to your bravery."

"Kind of you to say so, my dear," Helena smiled at her friend. "However, I do not want to cause a fuss. So, Miss Brown, what ideas do you have for concealing it?"

They all turned to Annie.

Finally, they agreed that Helena could have one swath of hair fall from the top of her head and wave down her back. It should swish sufficiently that no one should be sure of what they had seen, were it to be noticed.

~oOo~

A fortnight later, Helena was disturbed from her work by the arrival of an unexpected delivery. Two men came into the house carrying a small pianoforte. Ruth asked her where to put it, so they found room in the formal sitting room, moving some furniture around to fit it. The older man in the crew handed her two letters and departed with a handsome fee for helping them with the furniture rearrangements. One letter was addressed to Helena and the other to her daughter.

Issie came running down from her rooms with Rachel to see what had arrived. She was thrilled with the instrument and wondered who it was for and where it had come from.

"I should imagine it is for you, sweet girl. I do not know of anyone else here who plays the pianoforte. What does your letter say?" She handed it to her, surreptitiously placing her own letter in her hidden skirt pocket. Her daughter would want her to read it aloud with Ruth and Rachel present, and she did not want to deal with their suspicion of there being more to her friendship with the colonel. The girl sat on the instrument's stool, kicking her legs in happiness, and read out the letter with Rachel's aid.

Dear Five-year-old Miss Andrews,
I understand that you recently had a Birthday and have no instrument of your own to practise your lessons.
I hope you will accept this gift as my effort to rectify this situation and that you have many happy hours playing your sweet music. My only payment, would be to hear your improved playing upon my return to Eastease and Redway.
I am evermore, your dutiful dragon slayer.
Colonel Ackley

The rest of the day, Helena did not get a moment alone to read her letter and had to wait until she was in her bed. Retrieving it from her pocket and climbing into bed, she read it by the light of her candle. In her last letter, and they had exchanged several since he had left, she had not had much to say but had talked of her latest meeting with Mr Brooks. As he had requested after the dinner at Eastease, they discussed the bible, and she asked him pointed questions about it. She was curious about how the bible could be interpreted and put some of her own interpretations to him. It was interesting to have these conversations, but she, in no way, was interested in Mr Brooks as a man, and it seemed his fleeting interest in her as a woman had passed. She was unsurprised, therefore, when her visits to the clergyman were one of the things Nathaniel addressed. From his words, particularly at the end, there could be no doubt that he was unhappy about them.

Dearest Helena,

I hope you are not angry with me for presuming to purchase such a large piece of furniture for your home. From personal experience, I know that practising every day is the best way to learn an instrument. I only wish I could have been there to see Issie's reaction to its arrival. If you can indulge me with a description, that will suffice.

How are things at Redway? It is frigid, although it is only October. I hope you have things in order for the winter. I would happily advise you on any of this, though I am sure John has it all in hand.

Have you been back to visit Mr Brooks? I wonder how often you see each other? Please be careful of people talking. Village news can soon turn into expectations of more from a friendship. Unless, of course, that is how you are thinking, which I admit would surprise me. If so, you had better stop writing to me. Though I confess, I would miss our interactions.

By the time you read this, I will be at Bainbridge Hall, visiting Lady Agnes Bainbridge, and you may send your reply directly there. You know of my family's desire for me to marry her daughter, Lady Grace. I am loath to visit and encourage their views. However, I promised Mother that I would report back to the family on how the businesses of Bainbridge are faring.

I am back writing this letter after my evening meal. I admit that I did drink more glasses of wine than I usually might, as the thought of you thinking of that idiot Brooks in any way other than your local clergyman is disturbing my peace of mind. Please assure me that you will not consider a proposal from him until I return to Lincolnshire at Christmas. Do not forget that you promised me the first two dances at the Eastease ball. I will hold you to your word, even if you are married.

Always, Your's

Nathaniel

Lying back against the pillows, she hugged the letter to her nightgown-clad chest and smiled. The man could charm, annoy and please her all in one letter. Charmed by the gift he had given Issie when she knew he did not have much money to spare, then he asked her to describe her daughter's reaction to its arrival. Annoyed at his assumption, so typical of a man, that she would not have the stable in hand for the winter when they had started their preparations even before he left for London. Pleasure in the last part of his letter, when, obviously inebriated, he had allowed his feelings to flow through to the quill and did not discard this version in the light of day before posting it.

Helena set the letter aside, deciding she could pen a reply first thing in the morning. As she willed sleep to come to her, her mind spun out the words and phrases she should write. She would have to direct the letter to Nathaniel at Bainbridge Hall. At that, her eyes sprang open, and all hope of sleep eluded her. If he thought she was interested in Mr Brooks, might he change his mind about marrying his cousin? What difference would that make to her when she insisted she would not marry? Not sure of that answer, but sighing in frustration, as she knew she would not sleep until she had the words down on paper, Helena relit her candle and padded down to her study to sit at the desk.

The fire had been banked down but soon lit up again as she burned draft after draft, dissatisfied with her efforts. Finally, she felt she had it right. The easy part had been describing her daughter's happiness over his generous gift; easier still, given her annoyance, she took him to task over doubting her abilities to prepare Redway for winter. The harder part was her response to him exposing his feelings. She felt his bravery in doing so deserved that she should respond honestly of her feelings, but she could not raise his expectations of a future with her either. At some point, he would want to marry and, as it would not be to her, it would break her heart. But she could do nothing about that; she was already in love with him. Finally, she allowed the words to flow as he had. Then, without rereading it and before her courage deserted her, she folded and sealed it, giving it the direction to Bainbridge as he had advised.

Leaving the letter on the desk and burning the remaining discarded drafts on the fire, Helena lay on the couch, and finally, exhausted of the words and phrases that had consumed her, she fell asleep.

In the morning, Ruth found her there and seeing the letter to the colonel on the desk, she scooped it up to get it to the post coach with the child's letter of thanks, leaving her mistress to sleep a little longer.

~oOo~

The last time Nathaniel visited Bainbridge, he brought Harriet with him. Though he shared Harriet's guardianship with Harker, the responsibility often fell more to the other man because of Nathaniel's military commitments.

Lady Agnes Bainbridge was a rather timid woman who had become more so after her husband's death. Her only child, Grace, who had enjoyed all the love and no censure of her father and mother, found fault in everyone except herself. So, although he knew Harriet was not keen on visiting her Great Aunt, he wished she was there, as Bainbridge without her was a dismal affair.

Nathaniel arrived the day the pianoforte was delivered to Redway and began with his ritual of touring the grounds. Helena's response to that gift and his revealing letter came two days later. As was her want, Grace perused the post that was brought to her on a tray, before waving the butler over to Nathaniel. He picked up the three letters for him, and though his heart was beating fast, it was belied in his expression.

"I see Harriet is writing to you. What does she have to say?"

He had not even broken the seal. "When I have read it, Cousin, I will read out anything pertinent to you."

Ignoring his surliness, she got to her real point. "Are the others very interesting? I do not recognise the seal."

"Not at all, I assure you."

She noticed him pocket them and narrowed her eyes. Nathaniel, who usually could lie confidently when required, knew he hadn't fooled her. Cracking the seal on Harriet's letter, he hoped to distract Grace with some snippet of news from Eastease.

Harriet teased him about asking Helena for the first two dances. It pleased him to know that Helena had spoken of him to Harriet, and no doubt Genevieve had been with them, too. His smile was not lost on Grace.

"What does Harriet say that is so amusing then, Nathaniel?" she demanded.

He had read on and thankfully came to a part of the letter he could share. "She is to visit here. Actually, she arrives today. Have you or your mother received a letter to that effect?" He was surprised she had not shared it if she had.

"No, indeed we have not." Grace was cross now, although the arrival of her cousin could hardly cause her distress. Bainbridge servants would have to make some swift changes to air out rooms, but certainly, Grace should have little to do. "This is the ill-breeding of that Hopwood girl rubbing off on her. Mr Harker would never have let her travel without informing Mother first."

Grace was unhappy that Harker had married a woman with little to her name and one who did not defer to Grace regarding her cousin's upbringing. She felt that Mark should have appointed her mother and then herself, when she was of age, as guardian to the two young girls rather than two men. Nathaniel thought she had aimed to marry Harker, joining Bainbridge and Eastease and sharing his guardianship of her cousins.

"You mean Mrs Harker, I believe," he said mischievously, knowing she would start a rant about Genevieve that he need not listen to and could, therefore, focus on the rest of Harriet's letter. She planned to stay with him at Bainbridge and leave when he did. From there, she would travel to Thornbane Lodge in Cambridgeshire to collect Genevieve's sister, Martha, who would stay at Eastease until it was warm enough to travel back in the New Year.

While at Bainbridge, Harriet wanted to practise some music for the ball, and she wanted him to help. He was unsure what his ward was up to, but he felt she was meddling.

Nathaniel wanted to read Helena's letter in private as soon as possible. So, making noises to the effect that he would go and talk to the groundskeeper, he left his cousin still muttering about Genevieve Harker.

~oOo~

Nathaniel walked briskly to where he remembered a thick felled tree trunk. He could sit upon it and read his letters. He hurried to keep himself warm and get there as soon as possible. He hardly remembered what he had written in his own letter about her relationship with Mr Brooks, but he knew that he had overstepped the bounds of friendship and hoped she did not push him away because of it. *Finally, here is the log.*

Dearest Nathaniel,

How do you manage to please, vex and perplex me in a single missive?

Firstly, let me thank you for your kindness to my sweet girl. Issie has already written you her note of thanks. I think the gift might make an appearance in a new story, as we talked of how the girl who played it might make magical music, and the effect of the music will depend on the mood she is in when she plays. But I fear I have already given away too much of the storyline.

When it arrived, Issie was astounded and wondered who it was for and from. Your letter swiftly answered both questions, and she was thrilled beyond measure. Immediately, she had to play a tune for us. I was astonished that she could play a piece by heart that she learned from Harriet. My daughter is far more talented than I.

Suffice it to say that you have made a young five-year-old feel very grown up and special to receive such a present. Anything that can make her smile gladdens my heart, so your gift has made two people very happy.

Having garnered my favour thus, you then vexed me into throwing up my hands and declaring, 'How can men be so insufferable?' I think it must be something you are taught in your education, while women are taught posture, sewing and an instrument.

Here at Redway, I started our plans for the winter BEFORE you left for London. John and a team of half our staff have been setting the property straight and ensuring our supplies. He certainly does have it all in hand, as you say, but it was under MY direction whilst I worked with the remaining staff on the daily duties of the stable. I thank you for your concern, but I certainly do NOT thank you for your assumptions.

You perplex me with your comment of Mr Brooks. I agree that he possibly had some interest in me at first, but thankfully, it was short-lived. I certainly have no interest in him as a man, but we have lively discussions about God, the bible and the church. I think he hopes to save my soul, whereas I find these visits more enjoyable than attending church—a negligence for which he no longer reproaches me. If there is a God and He is good, and if I am as good a person as I can be because I firmly believe that we all have a responsibility to help the people we meet, then I see no reason He should spurn me. However, if He were to, then I do not want to know HIM.

I assure you that I will not consider a proposal from Mr Brooks. As I have told you several times, I have no intention of marrying anyone, so the first two dances of the ball remain safely yours.

Confusion is disturbing MY peace of mind regarding your situation with your cousin, Lady Grace. Surely it would be of greatest benefit for you to marry her and live comfortably at Bainbridge Hall? My parents live on the outskirts of a village southeast of there, so I know it well, although we were never in the sphere of receiving an invitation.

You say you hate the thought of me thinking in terms of marriage to Mr Brooks, and I find it equally detestable that you might think of marrying your cousin, and yet how can I ask you not to when I have set our boundaries to friendship and will not marry. I wish I had the power to change the law so that a married woman would not lose her very existence to her husband. It was not something I gave much thought to regarding myself, but then, I had never met a man I could feel that way about because I had not met you.

    I am saying too much and do not have the excuse of too much wine. It is the middle of the night, and I am sitting at my desk in my nightgown, by the light of one candle and the fire burning brightly with all my discarded drafts. I will do you the same honour of sealing this letter before I change my mind on what I have said and feed it to the hungry flames.

    Although I belong to no one, I am only... Your's

Helena

Fifteen

Harriet and Mrs Cornock, her travelling companion, arrived at Bainbridge later that day. Nathaniel came out of the Bainbridge study, where he had been perusing the mountains of papers Lady Grace, who inherited Bainbridge from her father, neglected, to greet his cousin, only to see her retreating form heading into the afternoon sitting room. He scampered after her, eager to protect her from the scathing comments Grace had no doubt been working on since her discovery of the impending visit, only to be brought up short by Harriet's usually gentle voice reaching his ears from across the room.

"I apologise, madam, that you did not receive a personal letter from me informing you of my arrival. I am sure you must have assumed that I did write one, as would be proper, and that it must have been mislaid in the post coach. I am grateful that I thought to mention it in my letter to Nathaniel and that he could inform you so that my arrival was not a complete surprise. I hope that gave Smythe and the chambermaids sufficient time to make their usual, excellent arrangements for myself and Mrs Cornock." She turned to the

Bainbridge butler at this and received a nod in affirmation. Satisfied, she added, "If you would excuse me, Cousin. It has been a long journey. Mrs Cornock and I would like to refresh ourselves in our rooms. I hope if we return in an hour, that would be acceptable to you?" Without waiting for an answer, she turned and exited the room, passing Nathaniel at the door.

"Colonel," she said, with a slight smile that only he could see. He gave her a quick wink and followed her before a stunned Grace could call either of them back.

Nathaniel returned to the study and stood looking at the papers he had been trying to concentrate on. He ran a hand over his face, breaking into a huge smile, as he realised the work of Genevieve and Helena in Harriet's dealing with her cousin. He was thrilled for the young woman he knew had a spine of steel. Now Harriet was learning how to wield it. As Harriet's guardian, he was proud of her and profoundly grateful to the two perfect women he and Harker had found.

He was getting ahead of himself again. Helena was not his, not yet, but perhaps at Christmas. He wished her letter was clear. Her ideas were probably unclear because she still talked of not marrying yet, implying that if she were to marry, she would be willing to marry him. Not only that, but only him, as she had never considered a man before, had never thought she would. He wished he could show Harriet the letter to discover what another woman thought.

In truth, he should burn it, given its content and the location in which he found himself. He resolved to keep it on his person at all times, even in sleep.

~oOo~

After dinner that evening, he elected to forgo his usual cigar and withdraw with the women. Harriet, who had continued to speak in what he termed her *Bainbridge voice* throughout dinner, disappeared to her rooms momentarily and returned with her music papers.

Rifling through them, she found the piece she wanted and asked his assistance in turning the pages. "I want to practise this piece for the Christmas ball," she explained.

Nathaniel glanced at the pages. "This is from the same opera as Mrs Andrews' aria," he whispered so Grace would not hear, giving Harriet a pointed look.

"Yes, it is Florestan's aria. Leonore's husband."

Harriet began to play, and he followed along, turning the pages as needed but quickly realising that she could play the whole piece by heart. The imprisoned man was desolate, pleading to God and accepting his fate as his duty. In the end, he sees an angel who looks like his wife. As Nathaniel knew from Helena's aria that the wife was dressing as a guard to rescue him, he supposed that it was his wife that he mistook for an angel.

"You play magnificently, Harriet," he said with a smile of pride on his face.

Grace called over to them, "You need to practise more, Harriet."

"Quite so, ma'am," she replied genially. "That is why I brought the piece with me. It is a tenor piece, and I was telling Nathaniel that I was sure he could sing it. What do you think?"

Harriet smiled sweetly at him, and Nathaniel rolled his eyes.

"I think you should, Nathaniel. You could cover up Harriet's mistakes with a voice like yours."

He cleared his throat and replied, "I think that might be the other way around, but I see I am outnumbered, so I will try my best."

They practised the piece twice and even managed a smattering of applause from the ladies. During the second performance, Nathaniel noticed Smythe come into the room and speak quietly to Lady Grace. As he did so, she looked at Nathaniel and narrowed her eyes. She whispered something quietly back to Smythe, and he exited.

"I should invite the local Doctor, who is the son of Mr Grosvenor, over for dinner, and you can garner his opinion," Grace offered when the piece ended again. "He needs a wife, Harriet. You would be lucky to make a connection there, and you would live closer to me so I could take care of your interests."

It was Harriet's turn to roll her eyes, and Nathaniel read her mind easily. *Why would I want to live closer to Cousin Grace?*

Nathaniel contemplated Helena's letter in bed that night. He had reread it many times before putting it with the others under his pillow. He was sure his belongings had been searched, but as all his correspondence from Redway had been safely upon his person, they had not been found. He had worn the blue silk cravat but hid the pin behind the knots to avoid answering questions from Grace.

He was getting used to sleepless nights. Nathaniel supposed it came with being in love because, as surely as it was dark outside, he was in love with Helena Andrews. As much as he thought of her declaration of marrying him, had she the inclination to marry, he thought of her sitting at her writing desk clad in nothing but her nightgown. The image was perfectly clear from his memory of her at the window of an Eastease bedchamber. His body reacted to the picture, but as he moved his hand around his hardness, the door of his bedchamber opened with a slight creak.

Had he not been awake already, he should not have heard it. He closed his eyes as a young boy with a single candle crept into the room and set the candle on the dresser. He began to search through Nathaniel's clothes from that evening. Finding nothing, the boy turned and looked towards the bed. Nathaniel had closed his eyes enough to look asleep. He kept his breathing even. Leaving the candle where it was, the boy stepped lightly towards the bed and looked at him.

Nathaniel moved quickly to grasp the boy's wrist. He did not utter a sound but tried to pull free. The boy's expression was not of terror but respect, no doubt at Nathaniel managing to catch him. Nathaniel had seen him often. He was such a small boy that they used him to clean the many chimneys of Bainbridge and probably underfed him, so he had to be quick to steal food. He had already developed a cough that Nathaniel had heard over the past few days, and he doubted the boy's chances of making the age of ten. He had talked to Grace before of new devices that could replace the need for a child. She had refused.

"Stop struggling, Davy. Is Smythe outside my door?" he whispered. Davy nodded, surprise showing at Nathaniel knowing his name. "He wanted you to find a letter?"—another nod.

Nathaniel looked the boy over. He needed an ally, but an ally needed an incentive for allegiance. He took in the sharp, blue eyes, sandy blonde hair curling slightly, and full of coal dust. An uncomfortable thought came to him. "Who is your mother?" He was half afraid of the answer.

"Mary Beckett, she wer a servant 'ere but died havin' me. They said she wer on'y young. No other family."

Nathaniel released a breath he had been holding. He did not know a Mary Beckett, so this child was not his, though their likeness was uncanny. Since his night in the storm with Helena, he had found a few of his assignations to ensure there were no consequences. It had never crossed his mind to do so until he learned of her experience. Such was the effect she had on him.

He put his finger to his lips, slipped the bundle of letters out from under his pillow and tucked them into his nightshirt pocket. He let go of Davy's arm as he got out of bed, confident that the boy would not leave without the letters, and moved to the desk in his rooms. Picking up a few pieces of paper, he put a corner of a page to the dying embers in the fireplace. It caught alight immediately. Competently, he blew out the flame to leave the corners he held intact. He moved back to the boy, who had been watching him intently.

"Take these to Smythe. Tell him you searched my things, under my pillow, but could not find the letters. However, you found this in the hearth and wondered if I had burned them." He smiled at the boy, who returned the smile, surely thinking it fun to trick Smythe, whom Nathaniel knew to be a bully. "Do this and keep quiet, and I will take you with me when I leave."

The boy assessed him warily.

"Do you like horses?" This question garnered Nathaniel another nod and a grin. "I am going to Lincolnshire at Christmas to a place where they raise horses. I can get you some work there and somewhere to live. What do you think?"

"Don' they 'ave chimney boys, sir? Is tha' why they need me?"

Nathaniel suddenly felt protective of the boy and angry at his cousin for her treatment of him. "No more chimneys, Davy. Horses. You would learn to take care of horses. Be outside—a lot." A huge smile cracked the boy's face, and he unexpectedly hugged Nathaniel. "I will take that as a yes. Be ready. I will give you the nod when I leave."

~oOo~

On the second day of Harriet's visit, she walked out with Nathaniel. It was cold but sunny, and they walked the path from the house that skirted the boundary of Bainbridge along the Fairfield Market Road before it turned south. Nathaniel assumed that was the one that led to Helena's parents' house. There were trees on either side of the pathway, and leaves crunched under their feet, making a pleasing sound. Nathaniel commended Harriet on her newfound bravery when speaking with her cousin, and she told him of the help she received from Helena and Gennie.

He told Harriet of his encounter with Davy the night before and his suspicions that Grace was trying to find his letters from Helena and Issie. "She may try to get intelligence from you of Helena."

They discussed how much she should reveal about her. Harriet agreed only to talk of her as her friend and nothing of his interest in her, providing he told her something of their interactions. As she already suspected them of being caught in the storm together, he told her of that day. He talked of the birth of Missy's foal but left out Helena's story from before she came to Redway.

"Nathaniel, you should have offered to marry her!" she exclaimed, horrified.

"Dearest Harriet, you are young yet and see things so simply. If you know your friend at all, then you know her to be an independent woman. I did, of course, offer to do what was honourable if it were to become known. I was a gentleman that night, Harriet. You must know that of me. Why would I want to force her into a marriage she does not want?"

"Why would she not want to marry you?"

Her loyalty made him smile. "It is not that she does not want to marry me, but that she does not want to be married. In law, when a woman marries, she is considered under the protection of her husband. Everything she is, everything she has, becomes his. You should understand this, for when the time comes that you wish to marry. I have to give her time to get to know me and know I would be good to her. She needs to know that she can trust in me."

"You love her. I knew it." Harriet said. "She is definitely in love with you. She gave you the horse pin I saw in the folds of the cravat you wore last night."

"Yes, Helena gave me the pin. As for her love, I hope to have earned it by Christmas."

~oOo~

As Doctor Grosvenor attended dinner at Bainbridge that evening, it was not until tea the following afternoon that Grace got her opportunity to broach the subject of Mrs Andrews. When Nathaniel and Harriet exchanged a shocked glance, she was satisfied to have finally cracked Nathaniel's implacable façade.

"I understand there is to be a ball at Eastease this Christmas."

"Cousin Grace, have you read my letter?" Nathaniel growled.

Grace shuddered at his voice and avoided looking at him. "If you will leave it lying around." She pulled Harriet's letter out of a concealed pocket and waved it in the air, knowing full well he had left it in his rooms and Smythe had found it on his first search.

Nathaniel stood and retrieved it from her. "That does not give you permission to read it."

"I did not know it was not mine until I had read the first few lines."

"Madam, the first line reads *Dear Nathaniel.*"

She waved dismissively at him. He was furious that was plain to see, but she was annoyed not to be able to read the other letters she suspected were from Mrs Andrews. He must conceal those about his person.

"What does it matter when we are all family, Nathaniel?" Grace turned to Harriet. "Now, tell me of Mrs Andrews."

"There is not much to tell, Cousin." Harriet held her mettle, Grace had to give her credit for that despite Nathaniel storming over to look out the window. "She is a widow and runs the stable situated next to Eastease. Her grandfather died a year ago and left it to her. You know how much I love to ride, and she has the most delightful foals right now."

Do not talk to me of foals, Grace's mind shouted, but she remained composed on the outside. "What is her age?"

"I am not exactly sure. At least five and twenty, I should think. Her daughter is five years old."

"And Mrs Andrews is invited to this Christmas ball?"

"Yes, many of the neighbours are invited."

Here Harriet listed several and talked of them. Grace allowed her to run on, hoping Nathaniel, still at the window, was getting his temper under control.

Grace continued to probe. "And Nathaniel here sees fit to ask her for the first two dances?"

"Mrs Andrews does not go to dances and was rather nervous about attending a ball, what with Eastease being so grand. Nathaniel was being gallant and putting her at ease. I am sure that is all."

It was a reasonable reason, so Grace let the matter drop. She could see Harriet had found her spine, and she did not want to push Nathaniel to declare something for this woman. Hopefully, he was only sowing some wild oats. Once he was done playing soldier, he would see sense and settle down with her at Bainbridge. She should keep her eye on him, though. She was not pleased, not pleased at all.

~oOo~

At Redway, Helena had been waiting for a reply from Nathaniel. When she had awoken the morning after writing to him, she had lain on the couch wondering why she was there before recalling the letter. She would have to rewrite it. She could not possibly send it, given its content. He would be horrified. What if the letter was to get into the wrong hands? She had walked over to the desk, but the letter was nowhere to be found. Looking out of the window, she realised how late it was. Ruth must have come in and picked it up.

Now, sitting in the parlour, she groaned for the umpteenth time and rested her head in her hands. Ruth entered with a tea tray, and Helena immediately accused her, though it had been a familiar refrain between them these past few days. "Why did you pick up that letter when I was asleep? In the light of day, I realised I would have to rewrite it, but it was gone."

"It is too late to worry about that. What's done is done," Ruth replied annoyingly calm.

Helena harrumphed. "It would be quicker to drive to Norfolk and collect his letter myself. Harriet will be with him at Bainbridge Hall by now."

"Why is it so important to you if you insist you will not marry?" Ruth smirked.

"What am I thinking? You are right, Ruth. I should be concentrating on Redway." Helena shook herself. Ever since she met this man, her life had seemed in turmoil. She was preoccupied thinking of him when she had more important Redway Acres business requiring her attention. She still felt she was leading him towards a proposal that she could not accept, which was unfair. Her feelings were such, however, that never seeing him again seemed unacceptable.

Standing, she decided to get to work when there was a knock at the door. Ruth returned smiling and holding up a letter. Helena pounced upon it and headed up the stairs.

Ruth did not regret sending that letter. In her opinion, her girl needed a push towards this handsome soldier. He was good for her, would be good for Redway and certainly good for Miss Issie, who already adored him as much as he did her.

Running up to her bedchamber for privacy, Helena sat in the chair in the corner, bringing her knees up to her chin in a childlike pose. She rested the unopened letter on her knees and placed her cheek on it, grasping her hands together as she wrapped her arms around her legs. The moment was exquisite, between happiness and pain, with the outcome decided as soon as she opened the letter. If she did not open it, then the pain would not come if he had not been happy with her reply. If opened, she might not experience the pain, as he may be happy, and her own happiness could burst forth. Huffing out a breath, she broke the seal and unfolded the letter.

Helena,

    Firstly, let me say that your last letter was most gratefully received. I am sure you have waited with trepidation for this reply, as I did your last one. I am endeavouring to keep our correspondence in friendship, but you know what I feel for you is more than that. I am afraid to push you if you are not ready because I do not want you to send me away. I am satisfied that if there were to be anyone significant in your life, you would want it to be me.

    You must know I feel the same way. While in London, I looked for the women that I had before. Not for the same purpose but to ensure I had not left them with consequences. I am unsure what I would have done had I discovered any, but I hope I would have done something to aid them. One or two of the women were happy to see me and to offer more of the same, but I declined. If I were to lie with another woman, I would only wish I was with you, and how would that be fair? See how you have affected my behaviour. I would have considered myself an honourable man before.

    I assure you that I will never propose to my cousin. Let that thought trouble you no more. She has been trying to get hold of your letters to me. She hates to think that something is happening in my life of which she knows nothing. I believed I had been outwitting her, however, I forgot to keep Harriet's letter about my person. She found it in my rooms and read it. It contains how Harriet discussed our dancing at the upcoming ball, and now my cousin is pursuing information about you. She is displeased, and that is when she is most formidable. She barely hid the fact that she had my things searched for your letters. The woman has no shame.

    I know you will hardly be able to believe this, but Grace sent a small boy to my rooms one night to retrieve your letters under my pillow while I slept. I stopped him, of course. My sleeping of late has not been that deep, something which has a considerable amount to do with you. I burned some paper in the fire and gave the boy burned pieces to show the butler—hopefully, it saved him a beating. I should have burned your letters so she has no hope of reading them. Although I have committed them to memory, I cannot do it.

    Davy is about six years old, and I am ashamed to tell you that they use him as the chimney sweep for the many flues at Bainbridge. He already has a cough, and they keep him underfed so he fits in the chimneys. I plan to abduct him. He is in favour. I promised him stable work and horses by Christmas and hope that is acceptable. I think he needs you.

Please understand that I am not his sire. He looks so like me that I had to ask who his mother was, but I did not know her. She died in childbirth. He says she was very young. What do you say to a new apprentice?

Would you please accept my thanks and pass them on to Genevieve for helping Harriet face her cousin? She has been respectfully outspoken, held her ground when questioned about you, and played the pianoforte marvellously. Lady Grace still finds fault, as she always will, but Harriet bears it well and does not let it affect her, which takes the wind out of Grace's sails.

I have not partaken of too much wine this time. I want you to know that my feelings for you are not conditional on whether you return them, nor are they dependent upon marriage. They just are, and forever more will be. I do not believe our story has played out to the fullest yet, so let us move forward step by step until we see it through. Whatever the outcome.

I am, as always, Yours,

Nathaniel.

Helena's fears of his displeasure washed away with his beautiful words, and tears of relief coursed down her cheeks. He had mentioned *My feelings for you*. Although he had not precisely stated what they were. That they were not conditional in any way alleviated some of her concern over his expectations. But if not marriage, how would their story end, if not in heartbreak? A man like Nathaniel would not want only friendship forever, and her body's reaction to the dreams of kissing him almost every night seemed to demand something that she suspected was only permissible between husband and wife.

Christmas seemed too far away.

Sixteen

As Nathaniel rode southeast towards Fairfield Market, unease settled in his belly. Helena would not appreciate this imposition. However, he could not ignore the opportunity to discover more of the family that had produced the woman who had captured his heart. His most burning question—*why desert her in a time of greatest need?*

The collar of his great coat turned up against the prevailing wind, his hat fixed securely, and his warmest gloves protected him from the cold, but the sight of the local tavern and the thought of a rousing beer were still welcome.

For a moment, a scrawny barkeep's eye followed the shining flash of coin that Nathaniel flicked between his fingers, and then he pointed to a young man of about twenty at Nathaniel's inquiry about the Billingses accommodation. "Tha' be Master Billins roight thare. He's 'ad a fair few ales t'day."

Nathaniel spun the coin in the air to land in the gnarled hand of the barkeep, then turned his attention to the young man alone at a far table.

Master Billings was not a tall man, but he was undoubtedly significant in other areas of his person, as his stomach stuck out far enough to touch the table rim, and his fingers did not all fit in his tankard handle. Nathaniel could see no resemblance between the siblings and estimated he could take Billings down in five seconds. He would have to ensure he avoided the man toppling on him.

As Master Billings rode his horse slowly home, Nathaniel followed—his task much easier due to the man's inebriation. He located the Billings household a mile from the village down a lane he had passed that morning. It was small compared to Bainbridge or Eastease but a good-sized country home. Riding around a few hedgerow-bordered lanes, he ascertained it had a reasonable amount of land with it but no smallholdings. All the family money, therefore, must come from the mines Helena had said her father owned. It was less substantial than Redway, but the estate earned more money if you added the businesses.

Nathaniel dismounted at the front of the house and rapped loudly on the door. It was a good twenty minutes since the younger man of the house had returned. Giving his card to the maid, Nathaniel asked to speak to Mr Billings and waited in the hallway, which, although large, was crammed with small tables and cabinets covered with knick-knacks. He felt if he knocked anything over, that small action would send one thing after another crashing to the ground until nothing was left but shards of glass and china. He could not imagine Helena here at all.

Mr Billings, a tall, lean man, stood and bowed stiffly when Nathaniel entered the study that also served as a library. It was similarly crammed full, but unlike the hallway, it contained books and papers on every surface, stuffed animal heads on the walls and dark, bulky furniture, including the enormous desk behind which his host now sat, having gestured Nathaniel to the chair opposite.

"Colonel Ackley, I am honoured to make your acquaintance."

"Mr Billings." Nathaniel tried to shake off guilt over kissing this man's daughter. However, in Nathaniel's opinion, the man had lost all right to be indignant over that when he sent her away as if the attack on her had been her fault. Even now, the man left her to fend for herself. However, Nathaniel was not here to judge Mr Billings; he wanted to pose as a potential investor, so he put on his amiable persona.

"Would you like some refreshments—tea perhaps? Or is it too early for something stronger?"

"It is a bracing day, something stronger will be warming for me, providing, of course, you are joining me." The older man smiled, the lines on his face crinkling at his eyes, and reached for the decanter and two glasses behind him. He poured, then handed one glass to Nathaniel. They both drank, Mr Billings rather more heavily than prudent. It would seem that the saying, *like father, like son,* was as accurate in this household as it was opposite regarding himself and his father.

"How may I be of service?"

"I was acquainted with General Alcott. I understand he was here when he died." Nathaniel noticed Billings blanch at the general's name. "He mentioned he had good investments with you, and I wondered if you were still taking on investors. My father is generous, and I want to make my money work long-term."

"I am sorry to have wasted your time, Colonel. Presently, I have all the investments I need. I can certainly contact you if the situation changes."

Nathaniel had no interest in investing. He had wanted an excuse to see the house that Helena grew up in and meet her family. In reality, she was as far removed from them as anything Nathaniel had expected. Still, he should not mind more information, as he was there already.

"Not at all. I was nearby anyway, visiting my family."

"Ah, yes, my wife often speaks of Bainbridge. Perhaps if you have a little more time, you would allow an introduction? She would be honoured to meet you."

"Of course, but first, can you tell me what happened to the general's investments? Did you pay them back, or did the family keep them? I might see if they are interested in selling."

"No, the family has kept them, but I hear nothing from them." He rose to show Nathaniel out of the room. Nathaniel followed the older man through the hallway and into a parlour where Mrs Billings sat. She stood when she saw them. Mr Billings made loud introductions to wake his son, who was asleep on the couch, but his attempt was futile. Nathaniel ignored the son and turned to the mother with a bow.

"Mrs Billings, a pleasure." Though it was nothing of the sort. He saw a mean-looking woman who was rake-thin. Her brown hair was pulled back tightly on her head. He could tell her gown was refined, but there was no lustre to it because there was no lustre to her. Helena, dressed in a rag, would have more shine.

His hostess ordered tea, and they talked of simple pleasantries. The parlour was as fussy and crammed with furniture and ornaments as the hallway. Although he was at least warm, Nathaniel felt itchy to be out of the house. Understanding Helena's need to escape to the stable came to him easily.

"I thought I understood from my cousin that you have a daughter and a son?" He did not miss the exchange of looks between husband and wife.

Mrs Billings spoke bitterly, "Our daughter lives in Lincolnshire with her grandfather. Her husband, Colonel, was also in the army but died in battle."

"I am sorry to hear that. You must get to visit often, with your business being in the north, Mr Billings?"

Billings was shifting in his chair, obviously uncomfortable. It seemed they liked to forget they had a daughter, a fact that sickened Nathaniel, given what a wonderful woman she had become. They should be proud of her, not ashamed. Look at the oaf that they did acknowledge and would leave everything to. He could not even be awake to acknowledge a distinguished guest. It did irk Nathaniel when people with such high hopes of their own importance, as Mrs Billings obviously had, could not address him adequately.

Again, the wife replied, "I do not travel well, I am afraid, Colonel, so when my husband goes north, I stay here. To get back to me promptly, he does not indulge in a diversion to see our daughter."

Indulge! What was the woman saying? For goodness sake, she was their daughter, and they had barely seen her or their adorable granddaughter in over five years. They did not even acknowledge Isabella existed.

He had met Issie two months ago, spent a fortnight in the vicinity of her and her mother, and already missed them terribly. He put his hand to his coat pocket, wherein he kept Helena's letters. Six so far, one a week, and he had replied to each and every one. He did not think he could contain his temper if he had to sit there a minute more. There was a knock. The maid entered and addressed Nathaniel.

"I am sorry, sir, your horse is frantic in the stable, and no one dare go in. We think he might sense—"

"Mary, that is enough." Billings shot to his feet and headed out to the back of the house. Happy to escape and eager to ensure Thor was unharmed, Nathaniel followed him, grabbing his greatcoat, sword and hat from the maid as he passed. He assumed that Mary was referring to the ghost of General Alcott.

They approached a small stable that had been the haven of a young, red-headed girl who did not fit into this family. Nathaniel heard Thor upon exiting the house. He was whinnying so loudly it was almost a scream, and his hooves were battering on the stall they had contained him in. Nathaniel lengthened his stride and overtook Billings to reach his mount quickly.

"Please leave," he shouted over the men in the stable, who were all advising the stable manager. They quieted but did not move. "LEAVE!" he bellowed as he hooked the side of his greatcoat over the hilt of his sword. The men scattered at the sight of the weapon, but he sensed eyes peering around every corner they could to see what he would do.

Hearing his master's voice, Thor stopped thrashing his hooves, but he still whinnied and paced in the stall.

"Colonel, can I just say—" Billings began.

"No, you cannot," Nathaniel shot it at the man. "I take it this is where the general—died."

Billings nodded.

Ignoring the eyes on him and Billings to his right, Nathaniel approached the stall door that had been completely closed.

Cautiously, he opened its top half, talking to Thor in a soothing voice.

"Hey there, boy, it is me. Whoa there, whoa there. Come on now, we are leaving, but you have to calm down. Come here, boy. There now." Still in full tack, Thor continued to pace, but the whinnies had stopped, and his pacing calmed with each word from Nathaniel. Although Thor was a battle horse, he would not be cooped up like this in battle. Blood spatter still stained the wooden slats from the general. Blood was like that—it hung around for years. Thor could probably smell it.

As he continued to soothe his horse, Nathaniel looked around the stall where General Alcott had forcibly taken Helena's virginity. The metal rings attached to the walls that Pegasus had been tethered to while he was beaten. The floor the man had thrown Helena to after he had whipped her for trying to protect the stallion. The wall she had banged her head against, the general over her, raping her. Nathaniel could see it all in his mind's eye but was powerless to stop something that had happened over five years ago. Pegasus had strained and pulled against his ties. Finally, he got free, and a loud crack seemed to go off in Nathaniel's ears—a hoof connecting with the general's head. He opened the lower door without realising it and stepped in to reach Thor, grabbing his bridle and palming his nose to soothe.

"I know, boy, I know, she was here. It happened here. You know. Our big man saved her, though. Perseus saved her and she is safe now, safe. There you are, there you are." Nathaniel hardly knew what he was saying, but tears stained his face at the thought of all Helena had gone through. Nathaniel held on to Thor, who rubbed his face against him as they comforted each other.

Silent, he marched Thor out of the stall and out of that dreadful stable. If he had been Helena's father, he would have burned the whole building down, preferably with the general's body inside. Billings followed him, but he did not care.

"Wait! You know my daughter?" the man called to him.

"I have nothing to say to you, sir." Nathaniel swung his leg up and over his horse. "You have no right to call her your daughter, as it is plain to me that you do not know her or care about her at all."

~oOo~

A few days after Nathaniel's visit to the Billingses, a letter arrived with a wax seal of a large, decorative *A* that he did not recognise. Upon reading it, he was surprised that Dowager Alcott, General Alcott's mother, requested he attend her at her London home. The letter gave Nathaniel the perfect opportunity to make excuses to leave Bainbridge. Grace's questioning of Harriet about Helena was becoming more and more obvious. He tried pointing out a few eligible and well-connected bachelors that might be more suited to his cousin. It was to no avail. He had to make his escape, and this was his chance.

Nathaniel turned to Harriet. "I have to go to London urgently. Can you leave today?"

"After luncheon, if that is acceptable. Is anything wrong?"

"Not at all, but I must deal with this before I report back for duty."

Nathaniel left to see the Harker carriage prepared while Harriet returned to her rooms to ensure the maid would complete her packing in time and inform Mrs Cornock they would be heading to the Hopwoods in Cambridgeshire.

Nathaniel hunted up Davy in the kitchen, where the scullery maid pointed to a cupboard under the servant's stairs. Nathaniel opened it to see Davy nestled in swathes of old, dirty blankets, making short work of a biscuit. He made a mental note to pocket a few things from the luncheon table for the boy on their journey.

"Davy, I am leaving after luncheon," he whispered. "Can you be ready?"

As his mouth was full of food, Davy only nodded.

"Do you have any belongings?" Nathaniel saw nothing but the boy within the blankets, and Davy's face showed only confusion. "Um—do you have anything other than what you are wearing?"

Davy shook his head.

"Keep a look out for me and be ready then."

Receiving a smile and a nod, Nathaniel headed off to his rooms to see his bag was packed.

After a satisfactory meal, where Grace complained at them all leaving so suddenly and did her best to persuade Harriet to stay a few more days, Nathaniel waved Harriet off before gathering his pack and helping himself to a blanket—the boy would be cold riding on Thor.

Bidding his cousins farewell, he strode out the door to the welcome sight of Thor waiting for him. A slight figure came running around from the side of the house with Smythe in hot pursuit. Smiling, Nathaniel affixed his bag to the back of the saddle, mounted Thor and reached down to swing the running Davy up in front of him. Though over a year older, he weighed no more than Issie had last summer. He wrapped the blanket around the boy and addressed the butler.

"Goodbye, Smythe. I fear this little fish is jumping out of the net and coming with me. Tell Lady Bainbridge not to use any more children in her chimneys."

Thrilled to be so high up on the enormous horse and feeling very safe with the colonel, Davy gave Smythe a cheeky wave from within the blanket.

Nathaniel was grateful Harker allowed him free reign at his London house, as he had no wish to take Davy to his family's town residence. He asked Harker's butler to see to Davy's needs. The boy needed feeding up, more clothes, and to start working in Harker's London stable, as he would be moving to Lincolnshire and working with horses there come Christmas.

"May I also recommend a bath, sir?" Jenkins suggested.

~oOo~

Nathaniel promptly arrived at Dowager Alcott's large London property and was shown into her parlour. He was astonished at the woman who greeted him. The general had been a bull-like, barrel-chested man, but the sight that greeted him was completely opposite. She was a delicate-looking but not frail woman of about sixty years old. Her blonde hair showed only slight vestiges of silver-like grey, and her smile was warm and genuine.

The house had large windows, letting in plenty of light, and brightly coloured cushions on sturdy but decorative furniture that was not overly ornate. Nathaniel bowed towards the lady who had stood graciously to meet him and curtsey herself.

"Colonel Ackley, I am so happy you could find time in your busy schedule to visit Alcott House." When she spoke, he picked up an accent, slight though it was, as she had obviously lived in London for many years.

"I thank you for the invitation, madame, though I was surprised to receive it." Nathaniel waited until she was seated again and sat on the opposite couch as indicated. "I hear an accent. Am I right in thinking you are French? Parlez-vous français ?"

"J'ai commandé quelques rafraîchissements si cela convient, Colonel ?"

He nodded and waited for her to continue.

"I have received a letter from Mr Billings in Fairfield Market, with whom my late son, General Alcott, had investments. Before he died, he had informed me that he was engaged to Mr Billings' daughter. Not the best match for a man of his stature, but he was taken with her. I understand she was very young. Did you know my son, Colonel?"

"I did not have reason to talk with him at length, but I knew him by reputation. I knew his horse better, as I was often in the stable." Nathaniel observed her reaction to him mentioning Pegasus, but she merely nodded.

The ordered refreshments arrived, brought into the room by the housekeeper, Hester, who was as tall as Nathaniel. The dowager continued with the conversation.

"He was a fine animal, but like many things my son laid a hand on, he was ruined."

Nathaniel was surprised. She was Alcott's mother, and mothers usually forgive all, especially to an only son. He had only to look to the Billingses for that example. He did not venture any further opinion.

"As I was saying, I received a letter from Mr Billings, who mentioned you visited him and asked him about my son's investments. He was concerned that you might attempt to swindle me by offering very low. After which, he offered me an extremely insulting, low amount."

She paused, presumably to gauge Nathaniel's reaction to her disclosure. He attempted to remain impassive and calm; at least, he hoped on the outside, waiting for her to continue.

Dowager Alcott decided to be more direct with him. "Colonel, please would you enlighten me as to your purpose at the Billingses?"

"Curiosity." Nathaniel had been pondering, while she spoke, how much he should tell her. He obviously could not tell her of Isabella. To the world, the girl was the daughter of Captain Andrews, but he saw no reason not to mention that he knew Billings' daughter. "I met their daughter while staying with friends at Eastease in Lincolnshire. Her grandfather left her his stable when he died. She had been staying with him after the death of her husband on the battlefield. She does not have any contact with her parents. She had mentioned that the general had visited due to investments he had with her father, and I knew he had died visiting friends in Norfolk. As I was close by, at Bainbridge, I thought I should visit them."

"I see," she said, and he felt she saw a lot more than he cared. "So she married another military man instead of my son, and he died, too? That is very unlucky. What is the name of the stable?"

"Redway Acres." Nathaniel saw little point in keeping this information to himself. Dowager Alcott could find out quickly enough should she wish.

"Interesting. Now that my husband has died, everything falls to me. I am still working out what investments he had that I am truly interested in, and I do not believe that I am interested in mines. I am tempted to sell. Am I to understand that you are not actually interested in buying, Colonel?"

"No, I am a second son and do not have that kind of income at my disposal. If it interests you, I recommend you sell back to Billings and squeeze him for every penny."

She laughed aloud. "Oh, I do like the way you think, Colonel. Perhaps you would indulge me in some more advice?"

They spent the rest of his visit talking of some of her husband's other investments, and he gave her his opinion of them, glad that he had listened to Harker. He agreed that she could use his name to glean more money from Mr Billings and promised to visit again when he was in town. She wished him good luck, if he found his way back onto the battlefield.

~oOo~

A month after Colonel Ackley visited Alcott House, Janine Alcott received her solicitor, Mr Davis. Following her recent instructions, the subject of his report was Mrs. Andrews and her stable. Janine listened intently from behind her desk.

"My investigator travelled to Redway Acres and posed as a horse buyer."

"Excellent. What did he discover?"

"The stable is well if not optimally run. My man said he would have bought a horse if he could have afforded it, as he's seen none better. Mrs Andrews inherited from her grandfather, George Stockton, a little over a year ago, so she has not had much time to get her feet under her. Everyone agrees that her best course of action would be to marry. The consensus in the village is that she could, very fortuitously, marry Colonel Ackley."

"And does she have any children?"

"A daughter who recently turned five years old. Born after Captain Andrews died. A charming girl, by all reports. I have the exact date here." Mr Davis passed her the document.

Janine nodded as she calculated in her head once again the months of a pregnancy. Her excitement could barely be contained.

"And, could your man ascertain who Captain Andrews was precisely? The location of his family?"

"No. His contacts afforded him nothing on that front. It would appear possible that no such man existed."

"In which case, given the date Miss Andrews must have been conceived, I could have a grandchild."

"Indeed. How do you wish to proceed, ma'am? Unless the mother can produce proof of Captain Andrews and a marriage certificate, you would be within your rights to claim guardianship for the child."

Janine sat back with a hand over her mouth and tears in her eyes, temporarily overcome. Then, she eagerly leaned forward again. "Send your man back to the area. I will pay for the horse he wanted, and he can inquire about a property in the area I can purchase. I am sick of London, where Hester and I have too many bad memories. We will find a new purpose near the only family I have left. Once everything is in place, I will contact Mrs Andrews myself."

Seventeen

Nathaniel turned Thor into the Eastease estate with more anticipation than ever before. It was over three months since he last laid eyes upon Helena, yet he believed he knew her better through their letters than he did back then. Davy sat in front of him and had not complained the whole journey. At least this time, he wore suitably warm travel clothes, although they still had the blanket.

Davy leaned back in the saddle to look up at him. "Tis bigger 'an Bainbridge. I'm ter stay in the stable?"

"Yes, Adam will take care of you. Mind you heed what he says."

"Yes, sir," Davy said smartly. "I will meet the new lady two days after Christmas?"

Nathaniel sighed. They had repeatedly gone over this, but he supposed Davy needed reassurance. "Yes. She will be at the ball the day after Christmas and will take you to Redway the following day."

"You're sure she's nice?" Davy asked.

Nathaniel's stomach squirmed again, wondering how he would feel when she was before him. "Very sure."

He tamped down on those thoughts. Christmas would be family time, and he would see his godson, who was now three months old. The day after Christmas, Helena would be busy with her horses in the morning and then should come to Eastease. Harriet had planned to whisk her away to prepare for the evening, so the first time he would see her, after more than three months, would be when she appeared before the ball started. As much as Nathaniel felt this dramatic entrance was ridiculous, he couldn't deny that it would make the moment of laying his eyes upon Helena special. He felt tightness in his chest just thinking of her.

What were two more days, Nathaniel wondered—but those two days seemed to take as long as the three months preceding them. Everyone was busy preparing, and Thor did not need a ride after the long journey from London. Nathaniel's only respite from his impatience was a trip to Old Joe's on the afternoon of Christmas Day.

~oOo~

"Where's tha yung 'un? Thought yer might bring 'im ter see me," Joe said as he scooped tobacco into the bowl of the pipe Nathaniel had bought for him, pressing it down with a gnarled finger.

"Helena told you of Davy?" Nathaniel was pleased she shared information of him with Old Joe, provided she didn't tell him *everything*. Old Joe's laugh told him he saw right through him.

"Don' worry none. She din' tell all—blushed plenny though. A' yer gonna pour that liquid before Oi die o' thirst 'ere?" Joe lit his pipe and, after a few puffs, tamped down on the tobacco before lighting it again.

"Davy is earning his keep with Adam in the Eastease stables," Nathaniel explained, relief soothing his sensibilities as he poured generous servings of Harker's whisky he had procured into two glasses on the table between them. "I was concerned when I saw him that he was mine. He looks so like me. I feel protective of him. I have to admit it."

"Nuffin' wrong wi' tha'. Sounds like 'e's had a rough go o' life. Helena'll do roight by 'im."

Nathaniel nodded his agreement, sipping his whisky as Joe

knocked back a healthy dose before puffing on his pipe again. Fragrant smoke began to fill the parlour.

"I have to ask her to marry me, Joe. I'm for Spain again in the New Year. It would be better to face the battle knowing I have her to come home to. Helena and Issie, even Davy."

"I don' know how yer do it, boi. Injured as yer've been an' yer goin' back fer more."

"I have to make my living in some way. I'm a soldier. I'm good at it."

"Can't say as killin' men is a way ter earn a livin'. An' yer more than tha'. Yer mus' know it."

"Better than letting Napoleon set foot on British soil. Besides, it's more about the men for me. Training them to survive the battles and leading by example."

"There's summat ter tha' I s'ppose. Yer can' imagine Helena's goin' ter like it, though."

"But, if we can marry before I leave, the Ackley name will protect her if the worst happens."

Joe shook his head, drinking heavily again.

"What?" Nathaniel was exasperated with the man. His good name was his biggest asset.

"She don' care about yer name, or yer sol-jerin'. She don' wan' ter marry. Yer knows tha'."

Nathaniel's gulp of whisky matched Joe's. "All I can do is ask, Joe. Then we will see."

"Well, don' say I din' warn yer, an' if she refuses yer, don' give up. Yer'll find yer way if you love her enuff."

~oOo~

Genevieve watched as servants rushed around the Eastease ballroom. Several rooms adjoined it that would be used for serving food and playing cards, the gentlemen enjoying a cigar or the ladies refreshing themselves. Mrs Hopkins stood at the centre of it all in the same way as a conductor with an orchestra. Gennie nodded in satisfaction at the arrangements.

"Mrs Harker, I assure you everything will be perfect," the housekeeper said proudly.

"You are a miracle worker, Mrs Hopkins."

"Mrs Harker," a deep voice came from behind her, and she turned to see the butler looking perturbed.

"What is it, Watkins?" she asked in trepidation.

"Lady Bainbridge and Lady Grace Bainbridge have arrived. They are in the main parlour."

"We did not invite them." Gennie supposed she shouldn't be surprised, given Harriet's information about Grace's inquiries of Helena. "This is not unexpected, is it?"

The usually stoic Watkins shook his head.

"Please inform Mr Harker and have him advise the colonel. Goodness, Nathaniel will not be pleased. Mrs Hopkins, could you order tea for the parlour? And rooms will have to be prepared for our new guests. Do you know where I can find Harriet?" Music drifted to Gennie's ears, and she turned back to Mrs Hopkins. "Never mind. She and I will greet Lady Bainbridge. Please ask Martha to stay out of sight. I have a plan."

Upon entering the parlour and after the usual greetings, Gennie explained the reason for all the disorder in the house. "I am afraid you find us in a state of upheaval this afternoon as we prepare for our Christmas Ball tonight."

"Oh, a Christmas Ball, how wonderful and festive," declared Grace. "You must be excited, Harriet."

Gennie could not but admire the audacity of Grace's words when it was apparent she knew of the ball back in October when Harriet visited Bainbridge. Nothing was to be done but invite both ladies to the ball and stay overnight. Once again, Gennie grimaced at how displeased Nathaniel was going to be.

"My Ladies, we would be honoured if you would join us. We could send to Aysthill for your clothes," offered Genevieve.

Unsurprisingly, suitable attire was produced from their carriage and taken to their rooms. Harriet's maid was pressed into service of these two women, while Harriet agreed that she and Mrs Andrews would share the service of the less experienced Rebecca.

"Ah, then I will finally have the pleasure of meeting this, Mrs Andrews," Grace said, though to Gennie, she sounded like it would not be a pleasure at all.

~oOo~

Nathaniel had been in the stable with Adam and Davy when the Bainbridge carriage had come round to the back of the house after dropping its passengers at the front.

"I'm not going back," Davy had shouted, sprinting up the ladder to the hayloft.

"Damn and blast the woman," Nathaniel muttered, rubbing at his face, while Adam nodded beside him. "Assure Davy I will not allow him to return to Bainbridge. I am going to have words with my cousin."

"Yes, sir," Adam said, making quick work of climbing the ladder.

Furious, Nathaniel strode towards the parlour door where Watkins had informed him his cousins were partaking of tea with Genevieve and Harriet.

"Ackers," Harker called out to him just as he reached for the door handle. "In here, man." He gestured towards his study.

Nathaniel turned and took a step towards his friend but stopped. His anger still bubbled, and he did not want to let go of it before confronting Grace. "You know what she is about coming here. I will not have it."

"Get control of yourself," Harker ordered, pointing again into his study and disappearing.

Defeated by his friend's common sense, Nathaniel followed him. It was Harker's house, after all. He could hardly presume to throw someone as connected as Lady Bainbridge and her daughter out of it, even if they were related.

Harker shoved a brandy into Nathaniel's hand as soon as he entered. "If you are as serious about Mrs Andrews as Gennie believes you to be, Lady Grace will be very disappointed tonight."

"That does not give her the right—"

Harker held up a hand, cutting Nathaniel off. "Despite her

attempts to manipulate you by turning up uninvited, you should let her down gently."

"I am still dancing the first two dances with Helena," Nathaniel said belligerently, ignoring Harker's raised eyebrows at his use of Helena's given name. "Grace will have to wait. Then I will need to dance with Genevieve and Harriet."

"No need to worry about that. As host, I will insist I dance the first two with Lady Grace. I owe you that much from the twins' sixteenth birthday ball. You can dance the second two with her." Again, Harker held up a hand as Nathaniel made to object. "Gennie and Harriet have already decided upon it. If you wish to argue the point with them, Ackers, you are a braver man than me."

Nathaniel shook his head and obediently sipped his drink.

~oOo~

Finally, it was time for Grace to descend the curved staircase at Eastease dressed in her new ballgown with the Bainbridge diamonds sparkling in the candlelight. Since Nathaniel's visit back in October, she had made plans to wrest him away from Mrs Andrews' clutches. Grace could easily tell that Nathaniel was not pleased with her arrival in time for the ball, but she had been to the best shops in London and purchased a ballgown in the latest fashion. The Bainbridge diamonds had been cleaned and shone more brightly than she had ever known. She would dazzle compared to this stable owner, and with them side by side, he could not doubt which of them was the proper lady for a man of his stature.

After Genevieve and Harriet descended the stairs with a third woman that she presumed to be Mrs Andrews, Grace's mother had gone ahead of her. Grace watched unseen as Nathaniel approached the last step and offered his arm to her mother. He was a thoughtful and caring man. All eyes looked up at Grace as she lived up to her name, moving fluidly down towards them—towards him.

Nathaniel did look handsome in his regimentals. He hardly ever managed to make his appearance perfect, which she could help with when they were married, but that added to his charm. His smile was rueful, as if he could not deny her loveliness. Grace knew her gown made the most of her figure as it floated around her. His blue eyes sparkled with the reflected light of the diamonds at her throat, hair, and wrists.

Grace was annoyed when Nathaniel did not approach the stairs to greet her as he had so effortlessly with her mother.

"Nathaniel," she demanded in a half whisper, and he seemed to startle before walking over to offer her his arm. Her annoyance changed as she decided her beauty made him forget his manners.

"You look very handsome this evening, Cousin."

"Thank you, Nathaniel," she replied, wishing he would use her name rather than their relationship.

Grace enjoyed the compliments of the Harkers and Harriet before Nathaniel stopped her in front of the woman she didn't know.

"You remember Miss Martha Hopwood, I am sure," Nathaniel said, gesturing to the lady she had assumed to be Mrs Andrews.

Grace recovered herself quickly. She had met all the Hopwoods at Harriet's sixteenth birthday ball and immediately forgot they existed until she learned that Alexander Harker was to marry their oldest daughter. "Of course, it is a pleasure to see you again."

Realising Mrs Andrews still had to descend the stairs, Grace moved away and tried pulling Nathaniel towards the ballroom. "Surely we do not need to be in the greeting line, Nathaniel?"

When he didn't reply, and she could not move him an inch, Grace turned to see his eyes glued to the figure on the stairs. She had never witnessed such an expression of desire and admiration in her whole life. Nathaniel pulled his arm away from her grasp and started walking towards the bottom of the stairs—a man entranced.

Everyone below looked at Helena as she stood on the top step. Helena did not see why Harriet insisted she make an entrance like this. She was embarrassed, especially when she found out that Lady Grace would be there and would, indubitably, be making a grand entrance to impress Colonel Ackley. She could not compete with the resplendent noblewoman who could outdo her borrowed ballgown and jewel with a simple day gown.

Harriet had told her that Grace would want to be the last to make an entrance and that Helena should wait until Lady Grace descended before doing so herself. As planned, Lady Grace must have assumed she was Martha, forgetting she had met her before.

It seemed like a lot of fuss to Helena, but then she saw the look on Nathaniel's face, and her cheeks heated. She smiled and decided Harriet was right; that look was almost worth the three-month wait. Despite his cousin standing next to him, a glimmering vision in white, his eyes stayed on her with a look that she could only interpret as hunger.

Helena's doubt at her only adornment, the jade pendant her grandfather had bought her, vanished. She felt her confidence and courage rise at the thought of George Stockton. She had been looking forward to this evening, admittedly a new sensation for her, and this woman would not spoil that.

Helena felt caught in his beautiful blue eyes. As he drank in her appearance, the stare of them caused her to vibrate from head to toe. She felt like she was a tuning fork and would not have been surprised, had she put her ear to it, to hear her skin hum. He reached the bottom of the stairs at the same time she did and bowed.

Nathaniel's feet moved of their own accord when he noticed Helena standing at the top of the stairs. Her red hair was piled high, and one long, thick tail curled from the top to cascade down her back like a horse's tail. The cream gown was off her shoulders, and the neckline scooped low, skimming the top of her ample breasts. Nestled between them was her only jewellery, a large teardrop of jade on a long, simple chain. Cream flowers were in her hair, and her skirts were full and moving with her body as she walked down the stairs. Nathaniel found himself at the bottom stair as she reached it.

"Mrs Andrews, it is an absolute pleasure to see you again. May I say you look beautiful tonight?"

"You may, and I thank you. It is wonderful to see you, too. It has been too long."

"Far too long," he agreed, looking into those enchanting, green eyes and offering her his arm so he could walk her over to greet everyone.

"Cousin, would you allow me to present Mr Harker's neighbour and owner of Redway Acres stable, Mrs Helena Andrews? Mrs Andrews, my cousin, Lady Grace Bainbridge."

"Mrs Andrews, a pleasure to meet you."

"My Lady." Helena curtseyed and received very little in return. "Your gown is beautiful."

"Naturally. I recently purchased it from the best tailor in London, so it is the latest fashion, in case you did not recognise it. Where did you get your gown?"

Nathaniel had been dreading the moment of these women meeting, considering what they knew of each other. Though he could see the difference between the two women's attire, he thought neither lacked suitability for this event. With a smile, Helena straightened her back, rising to her full height of an inch or two taller than Grace.

"Actually, you will have to ask Harriet that question. I borrowed it from her. Of course, we had to let it out somewhat, but I have a wonderful seamstress in my employ who managed it rather well."

Nathaniel smiled at Helena's mettle in dealing with Grace's set down. All they had to do now was negotiate her expectations of the first dances.

The guests began to arrive, and Nathaniel walked in with Helena and Grace as the ballroom filled. He found seats and left the ladies together while he obtained some refreshments. He hoped to get back to them quickly, but at every turn, there seemed to be someone else greeting him and saying how good it was to see him in Lincolnshire again. Nathaniel directed a servant with a tray of punch glasses towards them.

When he could, Nathaniel looked back to see how things were faring between Helena and Grace. Sat side by side, he tried to determine what he thought of each and why Helena was the one that had captured his heart when Grace had failed to do so. One glimmered and shone from the diamonds about her person, while the other glimmered and shone seemingly from within. Her only jewel was the large jade teardrop pendant. Nathaniel could not determine if the jewel enhanced the green of her eyes or if it was the other way around.

The long tail of her red hair down her back reminded him of the copper-red, chestnut horse she had ridden on their picnic.

People were approaching the two ladies often, and each time, Helena would rise, curtesy and make the introduction between her neighbours and Lady Grace. That Lady seemed little pleased and did not even rise out of her chair, even though all present were very respectable families. Between greetings, the two women seemed to have little to say to each other.

Where is Nathaniel? Helena scanned the ballroom for him, frustrated that he had left her with his cousin yet unable to abandon the woman who must know so few people present. The least she could do for the Harkers was to entertain their most prominent guest and introduce her to those who greeted them.

"Mrs Andrews, I hope you understand that my cousin will, ultimately, do what his family desires and ensure Bainbridge is kept within the family. I only warn you, as I would hate to see you disappointed."

"If that is what you think, you know nothing of your cousin at all," exclaimed Helena, knowing full well that Nathaniel had no intention of marrying Lady Grace.

"It is you who do not know him. Your arts and allurements are distracting him, that is all."

"Arts and allurements?" Helena laughed. "If you are talking of allurements, you could do no better than to look in the nearest mirror." More people approached them, Helena made the introductions, and the guests moved on.

"I know you better than you would like, madam." There was anger in Lady Grace's grey eyes. No doubt she thought Helena should be cowering before her and realising how far short of the level of a wife for Colonel Ackley she was. "I visited your family in Fairfield Market. Your mother was most anxious to assure me that she had cut off all ties with you to ensure the respectability of the family name. She hoped that one *bad apple* would not ruin the reputation of the name Billings. I was sympathetic, and she told me everything that happened. Perhaps I should tell my cousin? I wonder what he would make of the lie of your marriage, *Mrs Andrews*."

"My mother only knows the lies she chooses to tell herself because she cannot face what she allowed to happen to me. Your cousin knows the truth and has known for many months. He does not seem to be perturbed by it."

Yet another family approached, and as Helena dutifully made the introductions, realisation dawned about this woman's plans should she not get her way where Nathaniel was concerned. She did not disappoint.

"What would all of these respectable families, that seem to hold you in such regard, make of this news, however? I insist you step aside, leaving my cousin to do his duty to his family and me. Otherwise, I can start tonight while they are all assembled. This ball has made my task very easy."

"What do you think you will achieve by doing so?" Helena said with some satisfaction as the vicious woman looked shocked at how calm she was. "You will alienate your cousin, who will never forgive you, and you will force his hand in offering for me."

"He would never offer for one so disgraced."

"He would, when it was a member of his family who had exposed her to that disgrace and—if he was in love," Helena spoke the last more softly as she watched Nathaniel's progress around the room. He turned, and their eyes met. "As I said, you do not know your cousin, My Lady. He is exceptionally dutiful and loyal, but to those he considers *more* than family."

Once all had arrived, Mr and Mrs Harker entered the ballroom to great applause. Helena watched as Mr Harker walked over to Lady Grace, bowed and asked for the first two dances.

"Surely, Alexander, you should dance with your wife. Nathaniel will dance with me."

"My Lady, I insist. As your host, I do not think you can refuse me." He smiled warmly and gave her no choice but to accept his hand so he could lead her to the top of the dancing lines. He gave the musicians who had been playing quietly instructions to start the dancing music.

Formally, Nathaniel stood in front of Helena and bowed. "Mrs

Andrews, I believe you promised me the first pair some time ago."

She smiled, acknowledging what the Harkers had just done to allow them these first two dances together, stood gracefully and accepted his hand. They looked across at each other as they lined up for the first dance. She was determined to be happy even if these were the only moments they had together tonight.

Helena was unsure how she managed not to miss a step or fall over. All she saw were his eyes, and all she felt were the sensations that ran through her at being in his presence again. Sparks ran up her arms and through her body every time their hands touched. From the looks he gave her, she thought it was the same way for him. No conversation passed between them, but his words from his letters ran through her head as if he was saying them at that moment, and maybe his ideas ran along the same lines—

Do not forget that you promised me the first two dances at the Eastease ball. I will hold you to your word, even if you are married.

As I have told you several times, I have no intention of marrying anyone, so the first two dances of the ball remain safely yours.

I want you to know that my feelings for you are not conditional on whether you return them, nor are they dependent upon marriage. They just are, and forever more will be.

I wish I had the power to change the law so that a married woman would not lose her very existence to her husband. It was not something I gave much thought to regarding myself, but then, I had never met a man I could feel that way about because I had not met you.

I am, as always, Yours.

Although I belong to no one, I am only... Yours.

The dancing continued, and, as he must, Nathaniel danced the two next with Lady Grace. She was an exceptional dancer, and they were well-matched, but their dancing was formal and technical. Flawless but devoid of emotion. It held no joy for him, as had the previous two dances with Helena. When he danced with her, he was aware of every part of him that touched her, and their dancing had flowed.

"Is my dancing so bad, Cousin, that you have to scowl through the whole process?" Harriet teased when she partnered with him.

"My apologies, Harriet, my thoughts were elsewhere." Nathaniel glared at Helena dancing and laughing with *that damned fool* Brooks.

"Mrs Andrews holds no interest in Mr Brooks. Though I fear you would scowl even if she danced with Old Joe."

He laughed and paid his ward more attention. He managed two more dances with Helena before the music stopped, and everyone took a welcome break for refreshments. Tables of food lined an adjoining room, and while they moved to take their fill, the servants speedily set the tables around the ballroom for people to sit and eat, then they milled around with wine to fill glasses and help with requests. Nathaniel spent most of his time sitting with Helena, enjoying an opportunity to talk at length with her and forgetting Grace completely.

As the conversation took a lull when bellies were full, Harker called for some entertainment. Harriet rose to take her position at the pianoforte, and Nathaniel joined her as promised. He cleared his throat of his nerves and spoke in his commanding voice to reach across the large room.

"Some time ago, at a dinner here at Eastease, Mrs Andrews treated those in attendance to a beautiful rendition of the aria of Leonore from Beethoven's opera. Miss Wyndham recently informed me of the aria of Florestan, Leonore's husband. He has been unjustly imprisoned, and Leonore is trying to save him. I apologise for inflicting my singing upon you, but the blame must fall on Miss Wyndham, who persuaded me to sing it tonight. Thankfully, her playing is marvellous and should more than makeup for it."

Everyone laughed, and as silence fell, Harriet started her playing. Nathaniel searched out the green eyes he loved so much and began singing.

Helena was shocked at his announcement. Harriet had told her about having the music for the Florestan aria but did not mention getting Nathaniel to sing it. She must have practised it with him when she was in Norfolk. She had explained how Florestan sang of his despair over his imprisonment and his resignation to his fate as he prepared to die. Then, he saw what he thought was an angel who looked like his wife, but in truth, Leonore was dressed as a guard to rescue him.

Nathaniel's voice was rich and powerful. Helena had no idea he could sing so wonderfully. She knew he could speak German, so he was able to emote the words because he understood them. He sang to her, his eyes locked on hers. Her tears sprang forth at the thought of the man in the song suffering so much. There was silence for a moment when he had stopped singing, then the room erupted in applause.

Helena felt a pinch on her arm and looked to her right, where Gennie sat and clapped. That pinch brought her back to the room, and she clapped with everyone else.

"I had to pinch Nathaniel the night you sang, too." Gennie grinned.

Nathaniel graciously accepted praise from people as he gradually approached Helena. "Nathaniel, I had no idea you could sing so beautifully," she said as he stopped before her.

"Neither did I. I think my view of an angel of my own inspired me."

Helena smiled warmly at the compliment, but his eyes glanced at something or someone beyond her. "What is it?" Helena asked him as she turned towards the door.

Adam from the stable was trying to catch the colonel's attention from around Johnson's large body as the bigger man tried to prevent him from entering. Helena never did feel warmly towards that footman.

"I think it might be about Davy." Nathaniel strode towards the door, and Helena did not hesitate to follow him.

"Colonel, 'tis Davy, 'e fell asleep in tha stable and now 'e is screamin' and won' stop." Adam was breathless.

"Is he hurt?" Helena spoke from behind Nathaniel, and he moved aside to allow her into the conversation.

"No, ma'am, he don' seem ter be. 'is eyes are wide open, so not sleepin', but 'e's screaming. Mrs Hopkins is tryin' ta comfort 'im, but 'e int having none of it."

As they started towards the stable, Helena kept pace with the men in her finery. She knew it was inappropriate, but if Nathaniel cared, he did not show it. Not that it would have garnered him any luck if he did. She was close to tears over this put-upon child, and the way she felt, no one would be able to stop her from taking care of him at this moment.

Eighteen

It was cold but not far to the stable, and as they rushed in, Helena could hear the screaming. *Poor child.* Men and women from the stable and kitchen crowded around the stall where Davy was rigid in the arms of the Eastease housekeeper sitting on a stool. The colonel stared upon the scene along with all the other bystanders.

Helena placed a hand on his arm to get his attention. "Make everyone leave, Nathaniel. Please."

"Everyone about your business. We have this in hand," he commanded, cutting over Davy's screams. Everyone scattered, leaving them alone. Mrs Hopkins held tight to Davy, and Adam worried at the cap in his hands. Helena touched his shoulder gently, nodding when he looked her way to assure him he had done all he could.

"Nathaniel, you said he was a chimney boy?" confirmed Helena.

"Yes, that is correct."

"Mrs Hopkins, I do not know for sure, but if he is captured in a nightmare, despite his open eyes, it could be of being in a confined space like a chimney. Although you are trying to help, it might add to the nightmare. What do you think? Should you perhaps let him go?"

"Oh, I hate to, ma'am. I want to make him feel better, poor, poor boy."

"Indeed, Mrs Hopkins. But please, could we try it? This does not seem to be working."

"Yes, ma'am." The housekeeper released Davy and placed him on the floor, which was well-banked with straw. Helena stepped forwards and sat down near him. Mrs Hopkins moved to protest, but Nathaniel stayed her. Davy continued to scream, even though the screams were hoarse and his breathing laboured. His body was still rigid.

"Davy," Helena said firmly but kindly. "Davy, I am Helena. You are safe. You are safe, Davy. You are not in a chimney. You are in a stable with wonderful horses. Can you hear me, Davy?" Still, the screams came.

"Davy, listen to my voice. You are safe. The colonel is here. Hear my voice and wake up. Wake up, Davy, you are safe." The screams were not so loud now. Encouraged, Helena continued talking to the boy but did not touch him.

Gradually, the screams lessened until only the panting of his breathing remained. And then—

"Ma."

A sob hitched in Helena's throat. She had been near to tears for this boy, who she knew to be almost two years older than her child but was so small and malnourished. "Yes, it is me. Come here, Davy. Come to me. You are safe."

The boy sat up and threw himself into her outstretched arms. Then the sobs came. She leaned back against the wall as the boy's tears soaked her breasts and her gown.

Nathaniel looked at Helena in her fine gown and large jewel, sitting in the straw and dirt, leaning against the rough wooden wall, with this ragamuffin boy crying in her arms. Would any woman back in the ballroom do what she was doing here? Would any of them have known what to do, as she seemed to, so instinctually? Grace certainly would not. Look at what her family had done to the boy already.

"The blanket, Nathaniel." Helena pulled him out of his reverie, and he strode over to pick up the Bainbridge blanket from the floor and drape it over her and the boy.

"You cannot possibly be comfortable," he murmured, trying not to be jealous of Davy, who was crying more quietly but still had his face resting on Helena's breasts. The picture they made was disturbing, given how much Davy looked like him. It could almost be his wife and child sitting there.

"It is of no matter." She smiled, but he moved her away from the wall so he could sit behind her and she could rest against his chest. "Thank you, Nathaniel."

"Colonel, this is highly inappropriate." Mrs Hopkins exclaimed as she and Adam continued to look on.

"Propriety be damned, Mrs Hopkins. Davy is calm, and that is all I care about. Please inform Mr and Mrs Harker of the reason for our absence. I will explain all to him tomorrow. Adam, get yourself to bed. Davy can sleep on the couch in my dressing room tonight in case of any more nightmares. Thank you both for your assistance."

"Yes, sir." They left.

~oOo~

Grace scowled as Nathaniel exited with the Andrews woman. *Harriet is a minx.* They had practised that song in her very own drawing room. She had known it was for this ball but not that Mrs Andrews had sung the wife's aria before. Lady Aysthill had written some time ago of Mrs Andrews singing at a dinner party and that her voice in no way compared to Grace's. Grace had planned to sing and play tonight. *With Nathaniel out of the room, what is the point?*

Grace followed the pair exiting the house to see the Bainbridge chimney boy. He was upset from what she could hear of their exchange. She rolled her eyes, such drama over the annoying boy. She found a room with a window that looked out at the back of the house and could see the comings and goings of the stable from her vantage point. When Mrs Hopkins returned to the house, Grace headed her off.

"My Lady, the boy was having some difficulty, but Mrs Andrews seems to have it in hand. She remains out there to settle him again."

"With Colonel Ackley?"

"Yes, ma'am."

Grace allowed her to pass and decided to see what was happening for herself.

~oOo~

Nathaniel's glance over Helena's shoulder gave him a view of Davy falling back to sleep and a tantalising glimpse of the soft breasts the boy rested on.

"This is not how I had hoped to talk to you alone, Helena, but I am not particular. You were wonderful with him. He has not had a spell like this before. I wonder why it happened now?"

"Maybe because this is a grand house like Bainbridge, and it brought up old nightmares?"

"How did you know what to do?"

"I did not. I thought of an idea and tried it. If it had not worked, I would have thought of something else."

"Thank you, and thank you for sheltering him at Redway. I have grown quite fond of him, I have to admit. He is smart and funny."

"He looks so much like you, Nathaniel. I know you said he is not your son, but have you considered he might be your father's? The earl has visited Bainbridge. Davy could be your brother. Well, half-brother, I suppose."

The tightness in Nathaniel's chest caused him to clench his jaw. Then, recalling their location and Helena's previous experience, he forced himself to relax and speak in an even tone, "My father will never acknowledge him."

"He called me *Mama*. Perhaps I should take him in as my own. He would still learn of horses and be a big brother. Rachel could teach him, too. What do you think?"

"This is new," he laughed, all thoughts of his father gone. "Mrs Andrews of Redway is asking for my opinion."

"I believe I asked your opinion of the name for Missy's foal," she pointed out.

"That is true, and my answer seems the same. Chance. Take a chance on this boy and take him in. As you said, he already seems to think you are his mother. Life so far, for him, has not been good. He deserves a better stab at it."

~oOo~

Unseen by either party, Grace had entered the stable and listened to this last exchange. Nathaniel was so different with Mrs Andrews than he was with her. His voice, though still deep, was gentle and soothing. There was humour between them as they teased each other. She could see him looking at the woman as if he could hardly believe she was in his embrace.

Grace had suspected the chimney boy was Lord Aysthill's bastard, so she had instructed Smythe to do as he wished with the child, providing he was not seen or heard. The boy was lucky to get that much. They could have turned his mother out, and she and the baby would have died. It could not be borne that the boy should be allowed to grow up close to Aysthill, or worse, if Nathaniel married this woman, he would be Lord Aysthill's grandson.

She turned away to go and find her footman. They would have to take him back to Bainbridge.

~oOo~

Warm in Helena's arms, Davy was not asleep. He had been confused when he woke and had thought he heard his mother calling to him, though he had never known her, so that could not have been right. Instead, Davy saw this caring woman holding out her arms and felt such a pull in his chest he could do nothing to prevent himself from sobbing and falling onto her. She held him while he cried and did not care that his eyes and nose had run all over this soft gown she was wearing.

She continued stroking his head and playing with his hair, even after his crying had eased. It was so comforting and warm, with the blanket the colonel had put around them, that he feigned sleep to stay there as long as possible. The woman had shifted when the colonel sat behind her, and he had dismissed the others, so the three of them were sitting on the straw, one leaning on the other, like a family. It was the happiest moment of his life.

They had talked in a friendly way that soothed him. Then, the woman had suggested he might be the colonel's brother. Could that be possible? It would be wonderful to have a brother like the colonel and think he could grow up to be like him. It did not matter to Davy when the colonel had said his father would not acknowledge him. To know the colonel was his brother was so was enough. She said he had called her Mama. He thought he had dreamt that part but must have spoken aloud. Then she said she could take him in. What did that mean? What she said seemed to suggest that he would be her son. She asked the colonel what he thought, and Davy held his breath. What would the colonel say? Finally, he said she should. That settled it then—this was now the happiest moment of his life.

~oOo~

Helena got undressed in the same room she had been in the night of the dinner when she first met Nathaniel. After help with her hair and dirty gown, for which she had received surprised gasps from Rebecca, she dismissed the girl and changed into her nightgown. As she brushed her hair, she was reminded of that night nearly four months ago, when she had seen Nathaniel from her window while he played cards with his father and brother.

Her hand reached out to the curtains, but she hesitated. Would he be there? Of course not. Everyone had gone to bed. Would he see it as a sign to come to her if he was? No, he would not do that, although the nearness of him in the stall had not gone unnoticed by her. It had been so pleasing to lie against his strong body. If not for the hard floor causing discomfort, she would have stayed there all night with a wonderful man at her back and a small boy in her arms. She wanted to take Davy in, but she had to admit partly that was because he provided a connection to Nathaniel she would never have unless she married him. Nathaniel was infuriating and opinionated and loved to tease her. He was also handsome, thoughtful with Issie and now Davy, and courageous. She loved him and was unsure what to do about it.

Regardless, she wanted the curtains open so the early morning light would wake her. Decidedly she pulled them apart and looked down to the games room. Colonel Ackley sat in his shirtsleeves, his waistcoat undone and cravat hanging loose around his neck. The decanter of brandy and a snifter were in front of him on the table. His face rested in his hands, and he rubbed at it, as she had seen him often do when he was agitated or frustrated. *Usually with me,* she thought with a smile.

Nathaniel had wondered if she would come to her bedchamber window, as she had after the dinner at the end of August. He had left the boy in his dressing room with James after a brief explanation and a promise to return shortly. Nathaniel told himself he needed a drink anyway but was disappointed when she did not appear directly at her window. He sat down with the brandy to calm his nerves. He could still smell her on his clothes where she had leaned back against him. From that position, he could see the top of the scar on her back where Alcott had struck her for protecting his horse. Fury bubbled within him, but it had not been the time to talk of it.

He had been alive for over thirty years and had never met a woman who challenged him the way she did. She was opinionated, loved to shock him and was frustratingly often right. She was also kind and thoughtful to those closest to her and those in need, and he found her beautiful. He loved her. He wanted to share in all aspects of her life. He hoped that she would see that. He had to find out, at least. If only she would come to the window. He dropped his face in his hands.

Once more, Nathaniel lifted his eyes to Helena's room again. She was there. He stood and smiled. He never tired of drinking in the vision of her. Red hair and a white nightgown, kneeling on the window seat for him. The same feelings stirred in him as had stirred that night back in August. He wanted to rush to that room and claim her for his own, but this time, he loved, too, and it was even harder to look at her and not take action. She smiled and put her hand to the window. He did the same, then stepped back and bowed. Standing, she bobbed a curtsey and stepped away. He downed the remaining brandy and headed to the emptiness of his bed.

~oOo~

Why does my heart beat so fast at the sight of Nathaniel and this young boy, who looks so much like him, walking towards me and the curricle?

Nathaniel appeared tired, ruffled, and improperly dressed in his shirtsleeves, yet his smile warmed her. Davy seemed no worse for his screaming and crying the night before. Indeed, he seemed excited to begin this new part of his life.

"Are you to come with me then, Davy?" she asked. "What say you?"

"Yes, ma'am." He looked at the colonel, who gave him an encouraging nod.

"Mrs Andrews, may I call on you tomorrow?" Nathaniel asked her with a pointed look. "I would love to see how Davy is settling in."

"Yes, of course, Colonel. Until tomorrow, then."

~oOo~

As pleasant as the anticipation of his visit was, her greater concern was his true purpose. She suspected that he would propose to her. The thought equally excited and appalled her. *It is your fault for leading him to believe a proposal would be welcomed despite your frequent protestations that you will never marry*, she chastised herself.

Preoccupied with ideas of Nathaniel and what he was planning to say to her the next day, Helena was startled when Davy pulled on her sleeve.

"What does it mean to take me in?"

Her eyebrows raised. "You were not asleep then?" After receiving a cheeky smile, she continued, "It is when a child with no parents finds a new one. The child then becomes a part of that family."

"You want to make me part of your family?"

How sweet and innocent his expression was. He clearly believed no one would want him.

"Yes, I do. I do not have a husband but I have a daughter, Isabella—Issie. Her father died. He was a soldier. She is five years old, so you would be a big brother."

"And your son."

"Yes. If you wish it."

"And the colonel's brother?"

My goodness, the boy was sharp. "You have big ears, young Davy." She swiped gently at an ear. "We were only speculating there."

At his confusion, she rethought her wording. "We thought it might be possible because you look like the colonel. His father is Lord Aysthill, and he would never acknowledge you. Lord Aysthill may have been with your mother and made you but was not married to her."

"At Bainbridge, they called me a lot of names and said things about my mother because she was not married. I hated them for that."

"I think the best thing you can do for your mother is to think fondly of her, even though you did not know her. She gave life to you when she died, and she would have wanted you to do your best with that gift, do you not think?"

Davy nodded. "The colonel is a good man."

"Yes, he most certainly is," she sighed.

"If he is my brother, then can I be like him, even if he is only my half-brother?"

"I think you can choose to be like the colonel, whether he is your brother or not. Do you have any more questions? We are almost there."

"When can I call you Mama?" There was the cheeky smile again.

"Whenever you are ready."

Not long ago, she thought she could never lose her heart to a man—now, she had lost it to two.

~oOo~

Issie insisted she show Davy the rest of the house immediately after Helena had explained the new situation to her daughter. After that, Helena would take them both out to the stable. She told John, Ruth, and Rachel about the latest addition to the Redway family and warned them of his nightmares.

Her next vocation was attending to the letters Ruth had left on her desk. One was addressed in a neat hand she did not recognise, and the seal had a large A pressed into it. She had seen that A before; she would never forget it. It stood for Alcott. The walls of the room seemed to press in on her. Helena grabbed the side of the desk to steady herself and sat with a thump in the chair. Ruth walked into the room with the tea tray and quickly put it down on the nearest surface to rush to her.

"Are you well, Helena?"

She showed the letter to Ruth, who looked at her questioningly. "Alcott."

That one word had the housekeeper collapsing upon a chair, too. "Whatever can the ghosts of the past be wanting, Helena?"

Reaching over to clutch the older woman's hand for a moment, Helena gained the courage to break the seal on the letter.

Dear Mrs Andrews (née Billings)

Please allow me to introduce myself. We have never met, and I know it was never announced, but I understood from my son, before he died, that you were engaged to him. Then he passed, and I heard no more from you or your family. My son's investments in your father's businesses reverted to my husband's portfolio and remained untouched. When my husband died, all of his property and investments fell to me.

Imagine my surprise when I received a letter from your father, who had a visit from Colonel Ackley, with whom I believe you are acquainted. He felt that the colonel might be interested in buying the investments and wanted to offer to buy them first. To say his offer was insulting is not saying anything at all. I think he assumed that I would not know much of money matters as a woman. He soon found out to the contrary, and I have now cut all my ties with Mr Billings.

Prior to selling, I met with Colonel Ackley to ask him if he was interested in buying. I was unsurprised when he confessed that he did not have the income. Despite being in mourning, I do keep up with social circles. It prompted me to ask why he was visiting your father.

'Curiosity', he said, as you have no contact with your family, and he knew that my son had died in Norfolk. He mentioned that you now lived in Lincolnshire, at the stable you inherited from your grandfather.

My curiosity peaked, and I wondered why you had left your family after my son had died. Colonel Ackley is under the impression that you married another military man and had a child by him before he died in France. Men do not understand these things the way women do, or perhaps he does because he did not mention your child. I found out about her when I sent a man to inquire about you.

Let me say that I understood more about my son than he thought I did. His father was cruel to both of us, and his son learned to be the same way, if not more so. I am under no illusions that my son imposed himself upon you but died before he could marry you. As I know he beat that fine horse of his, too, I would not be surprised if it lashed out in self-defence. I was sad when my husband insisted that the handsome beast be destroyed. Its life was too short and harsh.

I have worked it out and am sure I am not without family, as I believed. I have a grandchild, and she is a pretty, talented, and sweet child. I am sure all of that is a credit to you and the fact that she knows nothing of her father.

Please, do not be fearful that I wish to expose your secret. Neither do I wish to take the child from you. I know both things have crossed your mind reading this, as I would think the same in your situation. However, I find I do not like living alone here in London. I have only bad memories of this house, and I prefer to find land and purpose further north, close to the only family I have left in the world, even if the connection is not acknowledged for the child's sake.

I have met with your Colonel Ackley and find I like him very much. I think he likes me, too, as he has promised to visit me again. Perhaps you can speak to him of me and decide whether I could visit Lincolnshire in the spring and wait upon you and your daughter.

I wish you the best felicitations for the season and hope to hear from you in due course. Your's

Janine Alcott

Helena scanned the letter, breathed in relief, and handed it to Ruth to read. The housekeeper read it herself, nodding a few times.

"Well, that is somethin'."

"It certainly is," Helena agreed. "The audacity of the man. To see my father, to meet with this woman." She gestured at the letter. "I thought he was beginning to understand me, and then this."

"You should give him a chance to explain."

"He is visiting tomorrow afternoon. He might ask me to marry him, but I cannot."

"Why child? Is he not the best man you have ever known?"

"Yes, he is, but I cannot give everything to him and leave nothing for myself. He would control me and be in charge of you, Ruth, and John. Look what he does before he even has that right?" She shook the letter.

"But you need someone to love you, my dear."

Nineteen

Nathaniel had received correspondence of his own—his orders. He was to report to London in the New Year and return to battle. He would have to get into the right frame of mind for it. He needed to ask Helena to marry him and, hopefully, get that part of his life settled.

He rode from Eastease to Redway the following day, as agreed. The low sun and chilled wind felt good on his face. Around his neck, he wore the cravat and pin Helena had given him. When she had appeared at the window the night of the ball, his hopes soared that now was the right time to ask her to be his wife.

Despite having little to offer in fortune or property, Nathaniel always considered it simple to ask for a woman's hand, even one of means. He was a distinguished gentleman and soldier from a well-connected and powerful family. However, Helena cared nothing for that, so Nathaniel hoped she cared enough to accept him. He hoped she would share her life and daughter with him, for he could love that little girl no more if she had been of his own loins. They would have a son, too, in Davy. A son that he had brought to her and a daughter to whom she had given life. With these thoughts, he turned into Redway.

~oOo~

"Colonel Ackley, ma'am." Her housekeeper announced.

He bowed formally. "Mrs Andrews." He smiled stiffly at her, aware of his nerves, as he wondered if she would refuse him.

"Colonel Ackley." She curtseyed. "Would you like some refreshments?"

"No, I thank you."

Ruth bobbed and left.

"Mrs Andrews," he began. "You cannot doubt that I am in love with you. You captured my heart from the first, with your singing, riding, caring, headstrong opinions and logical arguments, and most especially your strength in overcoming some harsh realities. If it is within my power, I will never see you feel pain again. I love your daughter and Davy as if they were my own. I would lay down my life for any of you and think it worthwhile. Please, Helena, would you do me the honour of allowing me to be your husband and the children's father?"

"Thank you, Colonel Ackley. If there were any man I could marry, it would be you, but I have always maintained that I cannot. I will not marry. I cannot give everything I have and everything that I am over to the control of a man, even if that man is you. No matter how much I love you. I do love you, Nathaniel."

He stared at her, rubbing his hand over his face in frustration.

"Why do you not trust that I will allow you to continue as you have before? That we would work together, side by side. Raise our children together. Live here in our house *together*. Your life need not change, except I would be a part of it."

"Yet, you said, *I will allow you.* I would have to ask your permission. No decisions would be mine. You could decide that John and Ruth should go. I know you have had your disagreements with him. You could decide whom Issie should marry, as my father did for me. You love how I care about people, yet I would have to ask your permission before every good deed."

"I prefer to think that we would discuss all of these decisions. I do not want to rule over you. I want to share in your life, and I want you to share in mine."

Her eyes narrowed in an expression he recognised from their verbal sparring. *What is she going to say next?*

"Is that so, Colonel Ackley? You would consult me before taking actions that would affect me if we were married? Why should I believe that when you show no sign of consulting me even when we are not?"

She turned to a small desk behind her and picked up a letter. Although fury was on her face, she walked calmly to hand it to him. It was a letter from Dowager Alcott, inquiring after the possibility of Isabella being her grandchild. He was astounded. He had not told the dowager of Issie, but he could see how she had come to that conclusion. He cursed her timing, although he was unsure it would have made a difference to this conversation.

"Three times you have meddled in my life without consulting me. First, you inquire about the existence of Captain Andrews, then you presume to visit my family, and now you put my relationship with Issie at risk by talking to her grandmother. Not one time did we have a *discussion*." She continued, clearly noting his confusion. "What if Dowager Alcott had decided that she should be the one to raise Isabella? She could easily take her away from me. I am an unmarried mother who has lied to all around her about a non-existent husband. She has the money and power to do it, but I can see you did not think of that."

"I did not. Forgive me." Nathaniel handed the letter back to her.

"I do forgive you. It seems my fears were unfounded, as you see from the letter. However, you still did not consider my opinion or even inform me of your actions. If we were married, you would continue to make decisions because you think you are right. It would not cross your mind that I might have a viewpoint you had not considered. Men will always think they know better than women, and you have not shown yourself to be any different. If we were married, the only difference is that I would be wrong in taking you to task over it. I would belong to you. My opinion would have to be yours."

"I have not done these things in the best way, but believe me when I say I have done them with the best intentions. I will learn and want you to keep taking me to task. I value your opinions, and I have always enjoyed our discussions. I do not want to be your captor, although you are mine. You are the captor of my heart. I have no choices because of my feelings for you."

"You are the captor of my heart too. Please do not doubt that. I have never allowed a man as close to me as I have you, and I should not have. Now we are here, and neither of us will be happy with the outcome. But what of my free will? If I am married, I will not have free will and belong to you. My heart belongs to you, but my free will must always be mine, as yours remains with you."

"Why do you suppose they are exclusive of one another? I have no free will because my heart gives me no choice."

"But I would have no free will because the law gives me no choice, regardless of my heart or yours."

"Then, if you will not change your mind, I must bid you goodbye. I leave for France in the New Year."

Perhaps the thought of him in harm's way prompted her next question. "If I accepted your proposal, would it change your plans? Would you stay here and not go to war?"

How tempting it was to say he would stay if she accepted him, but he knew his duty, and with the allied forces so close to defeating Bonaparte, he could not leave it for others to risk their lives and stay safe at Redway. "No."

"Please be safe." Tears filled her eyes and poured down her face as she blinked them away, but she held in the sobs that threatened to wrack her body.

Unable to witness her distress nor offer comfort, Nathaniel turned on his heels and exited the room. Once the door closed behind him, he heard the sobs come, but it was not his place to go to her and wrap his arms around her, which was all he wanted to do. His hand remained on the doorknob, his forehead resting on the door.

Ruth Robertson stood to the side, watching him. "Don' give up on her, please, Colonel."

"My heart will not allow me to do that, but I must leave and return to my duties. My place is in battle."

"Come back safe, Colonel. Victorious and safe. John and I will take care of her for you, the same as we always have. I think you will work out a way to be together."

Nathaniel pried himself away from the door.

~oOo~

When the door closed upon the man who took her heart with him, Helena sank to the floor, her sobs engulfing her mind and body. Only the couch, which supported her head and arms, prevented her from falling entirely to the floor.

He could not have asked her in any better way, but why did he have to ask her at all? Her heart beat out, *say yes, say yes, say yes.* But she knew that she could not. She could not give herself to any man, not even him. She had known all along that this moment would break both their hearts.

Ruth sat down with her and did her best to comfort, but no one could mend her heart but herself, and she refused to save her independent existence.

A small pair of arms appeared around Helena's neck as her daughter draped herself over her back. Davy's hand brushed through her hair as he sat on the couch. "Do not cry, Mama. Please do not cry." It was the only thing that could stop Helena's convulsive sobs.

"What is the matter, Mama? Are you ill? Why are you so sad?"

Helena could not tell her daughter that the colonel had asked to be her father, and she had refused. Not when she knew how desperately her daughter wanted a father and loved the colonel so much. She was, however, not one to shield either child from the realities of the world.

"My darlings, Colonel Ackley was just here, and he told me he has to go back to France to fight Napoleon Bonaparte with the allied forces. I am sad because I will miss him, as I know you both will, and I worry for his safety. He has promised to do all he can to return safely to his family and us, his friends."

The small girl took in this news, and her face screwed up as she began to cry. Helena pulled her to her lap and held her to her bosom.

She made room for Davy, too. He was not crying, but he was very close. With tears still streaming down her face, she held her family to her. The wracking sobs abated for now.

Nathaniel may not be their father or her husband, but their grief was equal to what it would be if he were.

~oOo~

"James! James!" Nathaniel shouted the moment he entered Eastease's foyer. Upon the valet's appearance at the balcony rail, he barked instructions, "Pack my bags. I am leaving at first light. I can't bear another minute in Lincolnshire."

The ladies crowded the doorway to his right, their shock evident, but his mood held no room for abashment. Harker's lean figure beckoned him further down the corridor, and he strode gratefully towards his friend.

"Did you ask her in the right way?" Harker asked as he poured stiff brandies from his study's supply. "Women look for the correct wording and a good dose of feeling. I botched it the first time with Genevieve."

Nathaniel accepted the drink, taking a sizeable mouthful as Harker joined him at the other end of the couch. "I could not have asked her in any way and received a favourable answer. She refuses to marry, not refuses to marry me."

"She is independent, but I had hope. She obviously loves you."

"We view marriage very differently. I imagine sharing our lives, but Helena sees it as giving up her freedom. I tried to explain that I would not rule over her and that we'd make decisions together, but unfortunately, I said, *I will allow you—.*"

"She needs to know you better. We will all talk favourably of you while you are away. Absence is sure to soften the heart."

Nathaniel downed the remaining brandy, trying to swallow the hope that rose at his friend's words. The alcohol's heat barely warmed his innards and did not soothe his bruised heart. "Please explain to the ladies. I do not think I can summon the words in front of their pitying glances."

"Of course."

A knock at the door disturbed their silent contemplation.

"Come," Harker ordered, then stood with Nathaniel as Lady Grace entered.

"Might I be allowed a moment alone with Nathaniel?" she asked.

Harker looked at him, so Nathaniel gave a resigned nod with an accompanying eye-roll unseen by Grace. Harker left the door ajar.

Nathaniel remained standing and did not offer her a seat.

"I wondered where you were hiding. I wanted to talk to you of Mrs Andrews before I leave. She refused you I take it, given your mood. She is a fool."

"She has good reasons." Defending Helena stuck in Nathaniel's craw, but he did not need sympathy from Grace, of all people.

"I know she thinks she does. I went to see her family in November. I had you followed the day you went there."

"Really?" Nathaniel ground out. He recalled feeling uneasy when riding out to the Billingses but had put it down to knowing Helena would not thank him for it. Certainly, did not thank him for it today. "Whoever it was, they were good. I did not spot them."

"Her mother told me all that had happened with General Alcott—how her daughter put herself between him and his horse and made the general angry. She wanted the horse to kill him. She made her father lie about destroying the horse and give it to her."

"The general forced himself on her, Grace. Threw her to the stall floor and—. No gentleness, no caring and no marriage."

"They were engaged. It would have happened eventually."

"She was a virgin." Nathaniel was unsure how he was keeping his temper.

"So she says. Regardless, it was his right."

My God! If she were a man, I would hit her.

"For God's sake, Grace, do you not have any compassion? He had no right, not until he had stood up in church with her. I knew him, and he was a violent man, Grace—violent with his horse and with Helena. She had not consented to the engagement."

"It was not up to her to consent."

He rubbed at his face. He could not understand Grace's lack of compassion for her fellow woman. Helena had shown sympathy for and assisted many women who had landed in misfortune. At the ball, Grace had fallen short in every comparison to Helena he had made. Now, she was doing so again.

"We are not going to see eye to eye on this Grace. We would do better not to discuss it."

Smiling, she stepped towards him, her tone entirely changed to light and coquettish. "I agree. Instead, let us talk of when we should be married."

Has she gone completely mad, or have I? His heart was in tatters, and she thought he would marry her instead. Why would she even want him? Does she have no self-worth? Now was the time to be blunt.

"Grace, I offered for another woman just this morning, and she turned me down—"

"That does not matter. It is all forgiven and forgotten." She waved away his explanation. "She was a distraction, that is all. Now you are free to do your duty to your family and me. We can marry when you return from France."

"I must be clear, Grace. Helena *was not* a distraction. I love her. There can be no one else. There will never be anyone else. If I cannot marry Helena, I will never marry. I will remain a bachelor and a soldier. My only duty to my brothers in arms and His Majesty's Army." He moved to leave, but she blocked his path and put a hand to his chest.

"You need more time, I understand. Go to France, fight, and work her out of your system. I will take the chimney boy back with me to Bainbridge, and when you come to us, we can be the family you want. He is, after all, my relation as your father's son. He should remain at Bainbridge, where he was born."

"Good God, woman, how low will you stoop?" As he stepped around her, his mouth moved close to her ear. The temptation to throttle her had abated, but his temper still roiled. "Hear me well, Grace. You will leave Davy at Redway with Helena—you have no rights after mistreating him. If I return from France and find that you have taken him away, you will experience firsthand how violent a man can be."

She stepped aside, and he slammed the door behind him as he exited.

Am I to protect the inhabitants of Redway Acres from all my family? Nathaniel slumped against the doorframe as the shame of being related to them overtook him. He wished, ever more fervently, that he could call Helena, Davy and Issie his family instead.

Shaking himself, he pushed away from the support, his decision made. He would follow Grace's coach to ensure she did not head to Redway Acres.

"Watkins!"

"Yes, Colonel." The man appeared instantly.

"Have Adam resaddle Thor. I am leaving immediately."

He strode to the stairs, unceremoniously passing Grace's mother as he bounded up two at a time.

"James! Double your efforts, man. I am leaving now with a mind never to return."

Soon, he was heading down the stone steps of Eastease to a waiting Thor. When he got to the bottom, a cry made him turn back.

"Nathaniel!" Harriet ran towards him, throwing her arms around his neck. "I am so sorry she refused you. I wanted you to be married and live only five miles away."

"Me too, Harriet. Me too." He held her to him and patted her head with his gloved hand.

"Please be careful, Nathaniel. I could not bear to lose you."

"You will not lose me, Harriet. We will defeat Bonaparte and return victorious. I have not given up on Mrs Andrews either. I am only retreating to lick my wounds." He released her then and managed a smile. "Now let me be off. I have dragons to slay."

1814

Twenty

Nathaniel paced in Dowager Alcott's parlour, relating the details of his proposal to Helena while she patiently sipped her tea.

"I apologise, Colonel, that my letter might have spoiled your proposal."

He sat for only a moment to press home his assurance. "You only provided her with an excuse. Please, do not fret."

"But it did not help."

He rose and began his pacing once again. "Entirely my fault. However, Helena is grateful that you will have contact with Issie. Have you heard anything?"

"Yes, I received a letter yesterday and have been invited to stay at Redway Acres. However, I have been in touch with Mr Harker, who has offered rooms at Eastease for Hester and me while we peruse the manor house I hope he will sell. I expect to divide my time between both locations to ensure I do not outstay my welcome."

"You could never do so, I am certain."

"Very kind. What do you intend to do now?"

"What can I do? I love her, she loves me, it should be simple. We marry and be happy for the rest of our lives. She insists on making it complicated."

He sat opposite the dowager again, at least long enough to sip his tea.

"Perhaps because it is only simple for you?"

"She knows I do not want to rule over her. I apologised for being heavy-handed with some of my actions and will learn from those. I would never berate her for pulling me up over some perceived disregard."

"You do not hear yourself, Colonel. *I would never berate her for some perceived disregard*. These actions would be perfectly within your remit if she married you. That you would choose not to do them is entirely up to you, never your wife."

In his agitation, he rose to his feet again, not missing her small smile. "I do hear it after I've said it. I am so used to that language that it will be hard to change what I say. It does not mean that I would act in those ways."

"My dear Colonel. I do not think you could ever understand what it means to lose your freedom of will. And she would lose it by marrying you, regardless of your intentions after the fact."

Resigned again, he sat back in the chair and ignored his cup. "So, for now, I go to France and fight. Perhaps some distance will help us both."

"I hope so, for both of you. If I am to move opposite Redway Acres, I cannot deny it would be a blessing to me to have you as my neighbour."

"The old Davenport place?"

"I will call it Bernier House after my father."

~oOo~

"Well then, Colonel, a happy New Year to you." Nathaniel raised his glass to his reflection in the study window of Harker's London Town House. His mirror image obligingly returned the toast with the same grim look, swaying slightly.

After picking at a lonely evening meal, he had cheerlessly made a dent in the contents of Harker's port decanter, but its benefits did not improve his mood. This year was not beginning at all how he had anticipated. During Christmas at Eastease, hope flew on love, but now only bitter disappointment filled his chest. Pain of the heart was a new sensation for him.

As he sipped the next glass of port and with a few days of insight behind him, he conceded Helena's point. He had done everything of which she had accused him. He had gone to see her father and Dowager Alcott without telling her or asking permission.

Nathaniel closed his eyes to the image of them laughing gaily, lying on a blanket on a sunny day. If he had been a painter, he could have reproduced every detail—*Not enough port.* He moved to the side table and refilled his glass.

Helena let me kiss her that day. His lips had brushed in a gentle caress over hers. Emptying the glass in one long gulp, he refilled it—*No, not nearly enough port.*

Sipping at his port again, Nathaniel considered Ruth Robertson's words that he and Helena would find a way to be together. However, being together how he wanted would mean being married, and Helena would not marry him. He had no solution.

Downing the last of the port in his glass, he put his hand on the decanter to pour another. Then he realised there was not enough port in the world to make him forget her, so he went to bed.

~oOo~

Nathaniel shrugged into his uniform coat and stood before the mirror while his valet fussed over straightening and brushing it. The pride and excitement of dressing in his regimentals had all but gone. Annoyed, he dismissed the servant, then picked up a bundle of letters and stared at them briefly before adding the blue cravat with the horse pin attached. Nathaniel stuffed the whole bundle into an inside pocket. He patted his chest against them, resting his hand there for a moment.

He stepped outside the house to a gleaming Thor and mounted, heading down the street with his back straight, head high and mind focused.

Nathaniel's breath huffed out of him in a fog as it met with the cool morning air. He had slept off the port most of the previous day and woke to a clear head at dawn. He trotted Thor purposefully down the street with his orders tucked alongside a picture of a dragon and Helena's letters. The discipline of a soldier's life was called for, removing all other matters from his thoughts by putting his mind and body to work.

A month passed quickly, and, all too soon, Nathaniel was onboard a ship headed to the French and Spanish border. Invited to eat with the captain and other officers, Nathaniel found it hard to be as jovial as he might once have been before. As soon as considered acceptable, he headed into the depths of the vessel to check on Thor. He glanced in the cramped and smelly accommodations of the regular soldiers being shipped across to fight with him. They appeared as happy as his stallion, who stomped in the close quarters he shared with a dozen other animals. Thor nudged him in the gut, causing Nathaniel to regret the indulgent meal he had just eaten.

"Not long now, Thor. Once we dock, you will soon be sick of marching to the battles."

After making swift work of the carrot and apple core, Nathaniel had spirited away from the galley, Thor nipped at his waistcoat. Nathaniel ran his hand along the scar beneath that fabric.

"Mebbe Old Joe 'as a point, eh? Killin' men ain't a way ter earn a livin'." Nathaniel chortled at his attempt at the older man's accent. "You would like to live at Redway, would you not, boy? No war, grassy fields and plenty of young fillies for you. Perhaps I'll offer my services as a manager. I know I could help improve the place for Helena. Still, I cannot imagine living and working there but never holding her in my arms." For a moment, he rested his head against his friend's solid neck, then he patted him. "Get some rest, Thor."

~oOo~

This was the most challenging time for a soldier—the long days of travel, after which he would spend a long time rubbing down Thor. The best way to have the horse ready for battle was to treat him well. His man could be imposed upon to deal with Thor, but most men could not work with the troublesome horse. He missed Tommy.

Rain had stopped the allies' offensive earlier in the year, but with a break in the weather, word was coming back to the troops that the battles had continued with many victories. Halfway through their journey, the weather changed again, and rain poured down, which made marching and camping a miserable affair. The ladies in England saw the red coats as dashing men honoured in battle, but they never knew of the dreadful conditions they often suffered. It was not a lie when Nathaniel told Helena he had slept in worse conditions than the dirty floor of Redway's shelter.

After a few days of rain, they reached the Allies' encampment in southwest France. As an officer, Nathaniel was required to report to headquarters. After leaving Thor at the makeshift stable, he went to the central French house where they had positioned their headquarters. While men put up tents in the surrounding fields, the officers drew plans of attack and later, plans dependent on possible outcomes were discussed.

"Ackley," the general called out to him.

"Yes, sir," Nathaniel responded quickly.

"I hear you can speak Portuguese."

"Yes, sir. Passably."

"Passably is good enough. You will command the Portuguese regiment under their Captain Matias."

"Ca-pit-o Match-e-a—never mind. Yes, sir."

On the day of the battle, word spread down the lines of a French regiment trying to flank the primary battle. Nathaniel's new order was to thwart it. He issued clipped commands to Matias and his regiment of Portuguese soldiers as they moved to intercept the enemy to the east. Their skirmish was successful, but it cut them off from the Allied forces. Surrounded, Nathaniel, Duarte Matias and their surviving fifty men were marched away. Ordered to dismount, he had to relinquish Thor, who had been taken away as a spoil of war.

~oOo~

Helena's cold and broken heart matched the winter, but life continued at Redway. The horses thrived under her expert hands with the assistance of John and their stablemen. Issie was doing well with her pianoforte lessons and tried her hardest to pass on her skill to her new brother, but Davy did not have the same musical bent. Instead, he quickly learned to read and write. The boy's thirst for knowledge soon outstripped Rachel's learning level, and he began writing out Issie's stories. She would draw pictures, and then they would send them to Nathaniel. Helena tried to write to him, but what was there to say other than she missed him?

When Helena accompanied Issie to one of her pianoforte lessons, Mr Harker asked to speak to her in his study. As they made to exit the music room, Helena stopped at the door upon hearing Issie talking of Nathaniel.

"Harry, do you remember when I played for Colonel Ackley?"

"You are much improved since then," Harriet replied, and Helena smiled at her attempt to divert Issie from talking of him.

"He took me home and fought off the dragon of Lincolnshire."

Helena turned to Mr Harker, who stood at her shoulder and gave him a weak smile.

"She talks of Ackers whenever she is here," he said.

"She misses him," Helena said with a sigh.

"We all do," Mr Harker confirmed, gesturing down the corridor.

Once his back was turned, Helena wiped away a tear, then squared her shoulders. She would not cry in front of this gentleman, though she wondered at having any more tears left within her.

Helena sat opposite Mr Harker and expected him to ask her questions about her business and a discussion to ensue as usual. However, he startled her this time with news that she thought she would never hear.

"Lord Aysthill has requested you meet with him at Aysthill House. How would you feel about that?"

"Why?" Helena could not hide her astonishment at such a turn of events. But then, an unbidden thought entered her mind. "He cannot want to talk of Davy, can he?"

"He does, but he will never acknowledge the boy, so you have nothing to worry about. I will be with you the whole time."

She nodded her agreement, curious as to what the earl could want.

~oOo~

Helena had hoped to feel brave in meeting the stout man again but stood slightly behind Mr Harker in her wariness. Also present was a smaller, balding man who held a large ledger. He bowed smartly but said nothing.

Lord Aysthill cleared his throat. "Mrs Andrews, as I am sure you are aware, I am under a request from my son, Nathaniel, and Harker here to make amends for my misdeeds with women in the past and provide restitution. My son's part of this demand was that I not see you again, and let me say, he was so persuasive that it is unlikely we would meet like this if he were not in France. This, therefore, being my first opportunity to speak to you in person, I would like to formally apologise for my behaviour at the end of August last year. I assure you, nothing of the sort will ever take place again."

"Apology accepted, My Lord."

Helena barely managed to get the words out. Her mind was whirling over what had been said. They must have assumed that Nathaniel had told her what he had made his father do. All these months had passed since the rattle of her door handle that night, and he had never uttered a word. Because of that minor incident, which, admittedly, could have been a lot worse than it turned out to be, he and Mr Harker had insisted that his father make restitution to all the women he had harmed in the past. She recalled correcting Nathaniel, saying that the first time Lord Aysthill had forced himself on a woman was going too far. He had listened to her, and knowing Nathaniel, as she knew him now, he had most likely felt some responsibility for it.

Additionally, Nathaniel requested Lord Aysthill never see her again and was so persuasive that he only dared to see her because Nathaniel was so far away. Helena recalled Mrs Ridgefield saying her husband had seen Nathaniel leave Mr Harker's study looking formidable. What had he said to his father, she wondered? Whatever it was had ensured her protection.

Now, the detestable man talked about his relationship with a young girl at Bainbridge when he visited his cousin seven years ago. He admitted she was only fourteen years old. Helena felt physically sick at the thought, and then the name he mentioned caught her attention—Mary Beckett.

"I understand from Davidson here that she died giving birth to a son. Davidson did some asking around at Bainbridge and interestingly found out that the boy worked in the chimneys there, but Nathaniel had taken him away with him. Davidson tracked him down to you at Redway Acres, and I understand you have taken him in. Were you aware he is my bastard? Is this an attempt at embarrassing me?"

"I suspected. He looks like Colonel Ackley, but the colonel did not know Mary Beckett. So, the logical assumption, given your proclivities, was that he was yours." Helena, by this point, was barely containing her temper. There was no enduring this man, but she was unable to leave. He talked of the people he had affected so severely as if they were nothing. As honourable as Nathaniel had been in getting his father to make this restitution, his father held no such honour, as he felt no remorse for his actions whatsoever.

"And so," he continued with a smile on his face, as though he was bearing some gift, "I would like to give you an annual stipend for the care of this bastard and provide a small fund for him for when he is old enough to marry and enter into whatever trade he decides upon."

"No."

"No? What on earth is the matter with you, woman?" Lord Aysthill did not bother to cover up his anger. Mr Harker turned to Helena and looked at her questioningly but said nothing. He knew her well enough by now.

"There is nothing the matter with me, Lord Aysthill, but I am seriously considering that there is something the matter with you. These are people you are talking of, children, in fact, including the fourteen-year-old you forced yourself upon. She probably had no other experience of a man than you, and then because of what you did to her, she bore your child and died giving birth to him. You murdered her with your so-called *misdeeds,* and you think that offering her son money makes up for that? That is your restitution? Where is your shame? Where is your remorse?"

"Now, wait just a minute."

"No, you wait a minute while I finish what I have to say. Mary Beckett bore your child, and you allowed her son—*your son*—to be put to work in your cousin's household as a chimney boy. He climbed up into hot, narrow flues and swept them by hand when Lady Grace could have paid for a device to do it. They starved him to keep him small enough to do that job. He was only four years old the first time they sent him up there. He would not have seen adulthood had his brother, Nathaniel, not saved him. I have no need to attempt to embarrass you, sir. You do an excellent job of that all by yourself."

"How dare you use my son's given name and relate him to that mongrel?" Lord Aysthill shouted.

Mr Harker stepped between them, no doubt to protect Helena from herself as much as Lord Aystill, but she had more to say to this despicable man and promptly moved around him.

"I do dare, and I dare to call your mongrel by his name—Davy. He was named with his mother's dying breath, as I am sure you are aware from Mr Davidson. Now, he is my son. You lost all rights to him when you mated with his mother and left her to die. I have taken him in; he calls me Mother, and my daughter calls him Brother. He is very clever and will not *go into a trade* as you suggest but will go to school and be as qualified as your other sons to do whatever he wishes in the world. So, I do not need your money to raise my son. And when Nathaniel returns from France, we will marry as he has promised. Our son will be known as an Ackley and will be your grandson. You know Nathaniel well enough to be sure he will give the boy his name. If you want to set aside some money for Davy, you should do it, and he can decide what to do with it for himself when he comes of age."

"Marry Nathaniel? He has said nothing of this to us. It will not be borne."

"I have nothing further to say to you. Please do not contact me again unless you can offer more than money to the people your misdeeds have hurt. Good afternoon."

With that, she turned and fled.

What on earth have I done? What on earth have I said? Helena had been so angry she wanted to make that dreadful man see what he had done to a poor young girl. That the price she paid for his moment of pleasure had been the highest of all. He had compounded things by allowing six years of mistreatment of the baby she had brought into the world. In her anger, Helena had said she would marry Nathaniel because she wanted to shock Lord Aysthill into realising his connection to Davy could not be discarded so easily. *Now, what am I going to do?*

Mr Harker joined her outside, and they mounted their horses to make their return journey. They said nothing while they made their way out of Aysthill House grounds. Once they had turned onto the main road, Mr Harker looked at her and finally broke the silence.

"Are you going to marry Ackers? Have you changed your mind?"

"No."

"Then what are you planning to do? You know they will write to him and demand he does not marry you, so he will know you said you would. He does not deserve to be hurt a second time."

"I do not know. I let my temper get the better of me." She glanced his way and snorted at his rueful smile. "Why did you not stop me?"

"I did try. I do not think anyone has ever spoken to Lord Aysthill like that except when Ackers threatened him the day after you came to dinner. Ho! You called Lady Grace a skinflint. Wait until I tell Gennie that." He gave a chortle.

"You are not angry with me?" She realised suddenly, and with some surprise, that Alexander Harker's approval was important to her.

"Not at all. You have said many things, many times, that none of us have even considered. Your reproof to Ackers in August spurred me into appointing Davidson to oversee the restitution we have made Lord Aysthill pursue. Now I see money is not enough. I did not know what had happened with Davy's mother. It truly was murder. However, because she had no family and he is who he is, the earl will not be called to answer for it until he meets his maker."

"Mr Harker, could I trouble you to relay the events of the day after that dinner back in August? I had no idea that so much had been done. I thought the matter was dismissed and never spoken of again."

"Ackers never told you himself?"

"No, never, but so like him, is it not?"

"Yes, very like him." He told her how Mrs Hopkins talking of Rachel and others Helena had helped gave Nathaniel the idea of making his father provide restitution, the conversation he had with Lord Aysthill, and a description of Nathaniel threatening him. He included how, after Helena refused Nathaniel's proposal, he still had only those at Redway in his thoughts when Lady Grace threatened to take Davy back to Bainbridge.

Helena listened in rapt attention. She had no idea these two fine men had taken her words and deeds in such a way. Her heart was breaking again over having to refuse Nathaniel's proposal. She had been angered by his actions concerning her family, but now she was considering his actions on her behalf, against his own.

He certainly was the best man she had ever known. She would willingly share everything in her life with him if only the law would allow it. She would share Redway, her children, her bed, and even her body.

Helena had no solution and was moved to tears yet again.

Twenty-One

Nathaniel sat in his *cell*, a room on the upper floor of a French mansion in Toulouse that had been turned into a prison in one wing and a barracks in the other. The battle south of Toulouse had not gone to plan for him and the men he commanded. Although the Allied forces had prevailed and the French had fled, he and his men had been captured and marched north.

His men were Portuguese soldiers. Fifty had survived and were imprisoned here with him, mostly in basement rooms. They had marched for three days and then stopped here. It had been several days, and apart from the men bringing sustenance, such as it was, he had seen no one but Capitão Duarte Matias, the captain of the Portuguese regiment. When captured, they were relieved of all their weapons and their horses ridden by the French. On arrival at the mansion, their captors held them at knifepoint and stripped them of their possessions and coats, leaving them in trousers and shirts. Nathaniel and Duarte talked quietly in English and Portuguese. Learning more of each other's language passed the time for them both.

Finally, Nathaniel was brought before the prison leader. A primped but mean-looking man, Capitaine Henri Arbour, sat at a table upon which were the personal items taken from the men. Particular to Nathaniel were the blue cravat and horse pin Helena had given him, her letters and a drawing of the dragon of Lincolnshire.

"I have read your letters, Colonel. It seems you have a fine young woman waiting for you at home," he spoke in French but seemed to know Nathaniel understood him. "You look like a stoic kind of man. It seems commanding this prison full of Portuguese scum will provide some entertainment after all. Bring in the other man," Arbour commanded.

The door opened to reveal a soldier from the regiment under Nathaniel's command—young Mateo, whom Duarte had often expressed concern about in the past day. He was injured and held his arm against his body. There was a lot of blood on his clothes, and his face was pale and sweaty. "You will tell me what I need to know of my enemy, Colonel Ackley. I need numbers, positions, strategies, and next moves. If you do not provide me with information, I will kill a man for each day you refuse." With that, the Capitaine drew and raised his sword. He pointed it at the young man's chest.

"Por favor, eu imploro coronel!" Mateo's frantic eyes flicked between Nathaniel and the point of the sword.

Before Nathaniel could respond, the Frenchman laughed and plunged the sword into the man's heart. As he withdrew it, the soldier's lifeblood poured from the wound, a spreading stain that saturated his shirt. He fell to the floor, dead.

"You did not even give me a chance to respond."

The capitaine dismissed his objection with a wave. "You would only have said *Non*, and I would have had to kill him anyway. Now you know I am a man of my word, and you have a day to think about the man I will kill tomorrow. Hold out his arm."

Two guards grabbed Nathaniel, who struggled to free himself as he wondered what the man planned to do. Reaching for Nathaniel's left arm, Arbour almost tenderly rolled up the sleeve to expose his forearm. He pulled a sharp dagger from a sheath at his waist and sliced a thin line into his flesh. "One slice for one man, I will see you tomorrow, English bastard."

Nathaniel was feeling nauseous when he returned to his cell. Blood was on his sleeve, and Duarte came directly to him with a worried look.

"Colonel, are you injured? You are bleeding. What did the bastards do to you?"

"It is nothing, nothing at all." He pulled his arm away from the young capitão, annoyed with his fussing. "They killed a young man from the regiment right in front of me. One man for every day I refuse to tell them of the allied forces' plans and strategies. I am sorry, it was Mateo."

"No! He was so young."

"He was severely injured. Not that it is any consolation."

Duarte shook his head. "Why did he slice your arm, my friend?"

"For the man. Tomorrow, I will receive another. Whatever I know of plans will have already been changed for security's sake. Yet, I fear that if I tell him anything at all, he will have us killed. We have to hope the allied forces break through soon. I think Capitaine Arbour is a man who enjoys himself by making others suffer. What are your thoughts? They are your men."

"We are all your men, Colonel. You can tell them nothing, and we cannot attempt an escape with so many soldiers stationed here."

"And what if they bring you into the room, Duarte?"

"I am your man too, Nathaniel. Tell them nothing."

~oOo~

Day followed day, and each day at no particular time, soldiers removed him from the room he shared with Duarte. Arbour beat him and asked for information of the allied forces—he refused.

"Kill me if you must kill anyone, Arbour. Kill me and spare my men," Nathaniel offered.

"These bastards are not your men, Colonel," Arbour had said. "Why would you sacrifice yourself? To me, you are all scum, and it would make no difference whether I killed you, but where is the fun in that?"

"If I tell you anything, what then? Do you kill us all?"

"I haven't decided yet." Arbour pouted. "Perhaps I will spare half."

"Anything I tell you could be a lie, a trap, or plans could have been changed after my capture. Nothing I tell you could possibly be of any use."

"Let me be the judge of that. All you have to do is talk. Reveal all you know."

"No."

He had to refuse, though he wanted to shout it from the rooftops, to stop having to hear one more plea, before a man died and he received another slice to his forearm for remembrance. He would wake in the night sweating and screaming, *No!* Then, he would lie there and think of Helena.

Helena, who had been so strong in her own life, made him strong. He imagined her talking to him in the same soft, soothing tones she had used with Davy when he had been screaming. He thought of what she would say to him as she played with his hair while his head rested in her lap. *Nathaniel, you are safe in my heart. I love you. You must return to us. Come back to Redway, where we need you. I know this is hard, but you can do it. If there is anyone who can withstand this, it is you. You are strong, Nathaniel.*

"I understand now, Helena," he whispered to the vision he had conjured. "I understand how you would not want to lose your independence. I would never have hurt or abused you if you had married me. I would have worked every day to make you happy. To give all of yourself to anyone, no matter that person, and to never have that back in the eyes of the law is too much."

"Who are you talking to, my friend?" Duarte's voice reached him through the darkness.

"A lady. I am in love with her, but she will not marry me and become my possession. I understand her now."

"I have a wife and son. They live in Torres Vedras." Duarte shared with him. "I hope one day to see them again. Hold my beautiful wife in my arms."

"I hope you have that, too."

Nathaniel could do nothing to control what was happening. He just prayed each day that the allied forces would break through to Toulouse and save him from witnessing one more death, in the same way Pegasus saved Helena from a life of abuse and sadness at the hands of the general.

~oOo~

The door opened, and the soldiers beckoned Nathaniel out—head high, with thoughts of Helena giving him the strength he needed. Capitaine Arbour was in fine form, sitting with his feet up on the table and loading a pistol. He was wearing the blue cravat Helena had given to Nathaniel, and the horse pin shone within its folds.

"Ah, here he is. Colonel Ackley, how are you today? Talkative? Non?" He walked around the table and backhanded him across the face. Nathaniel tasted blood. This was not an unusual tactic. He had bruises up and down his body of varying colours from the past week of abuse. The door opened again.

"Here is our other guest."

"Duarte," Nathaniel said with a weak voice, "no, not you."

Pleased with the response, Arbour pranced around the room like an excited child. "Not you, Duarte," he repeated, leering into Nathaniel's face.

In his excitement, he got a little too close, which allowed Nathaniel to rear his head back and butt him. Blood poured from the capitaine's nose, and he reached for the pistol he laid on the desk, pointing it at Nathaniel.

"Do it, you bastard, do it." Nathaniel pushed his chest up against the barrel of the gun. The Frenchman wiped at his nose with his sleeve. Nathaniel waited, his body shaking but his mind determined.

"Non, Colonel, you do it. Pull the trigger on your friend, or tell me what I need to know. Do neither of these things, and I will cut him into tiny pieces in front of you."

Arbour pressed the pistol into Nathaniel's hand, turned him to face Duarte and hovered at his shoulder. Nathaniel's body sagged. He could not bear to watch Arbour slice another man in such a cruel and gruesome way, especially not Duarte, but he did not wish to shoot his friend. Duarte had tried to follow the conversation in French as much as he could.

"Eu perdoô você, Nathaniel."

I forgive you, as simply as that, but Nathaniel shook his head.

"Forgive me, Helena," he said instead. Bringing the pistol to his head, he pulled the trigger.

Nothing happened. Nathaniel stared at the pistol in confusion—he had seen Arbour loading it. He crumpled to his knees, denied the escape and a way to save his friend's life, at least for a time. Behind him, the manic laugh of the crazed man raged.

"That one was not loaded, Colonel." Arbour bent over laughing. "A sleight of hand. But this one is." With that, he was suddenly sane, standing straight, raising the loaded pistol from his coat and pulling the trigger.

The bullet struck Duarte's chest, right through his heart. He gasped, eyes wide, and then he fell forward, his head hitting the floor by Nathaniel's knees. Blood pooled out from beneath Duarte's body as Nathaniel laid a hand gently on Duarte's head.

"Goodbye, my friend."

Nathaniel was pulled away from the body by the guards. He did not feel it when Arbour cut his arm to mark Duarte's death.

He spoke calmly and coldly, "When I am free, I will kill you. There is nowhere in France you will be able to hide."

"Then I must kill you before then, Colonel, but not yet. Non, I am not done with you yet."

The men manhandled Nathaniel back to his cell before they threw him in. He fell, sprawled on the bare floor. The loneliness of the sparse, desolate room without Duarte overcame him as he cried. He tried to summon Helena to his mind to soothe him, but why bring her to such a place, even if only in his mind? The music came to him as he lay there, his cheek resting on the hard floor—the aria he sang at Christmas. The aria's words flowed in his mind, and he spoke them softly in English, replacing Leonore's name with Helena's.

God! What darkness here!
O awful silence!
My surrounding deserted; nothing,

No living thing apart from me.
O difficult trial,
Yet righteous is God's will!
I do not complain,
The measure of misery stands beside you.

Nathaniel pushed up to his elbows and then knees.

In the springtime of life,
Happiness has escaped me.
The truth, I dared to speak,
And these chains are my reward.

He held up his arms in frustration as if chained, then slumped back to the floor.

Readily I endure all the pain,
A humiliating end is my fate.
Sweet comfort in my heart,
My duty I have done!
Sweet, sweet comfort in my heart,
My duty, my duty I have done!

Nathaniel rolled over to stare at the ceiling, moving closer to the wall where he had slept.

And do not I sense a gentle,
Soft-whispering air,
And is not my grave lit up?
I see, how an angel with a rosy scent,
Stands comforting by my side.
An angel Helena! Helena so like my wife.
Who will lead me to freedom,
To the Heavenly kingdom!

A faint Helena appeared to him, sitting on the floor and leaning against the wall. Nathaniel rested his head on her thighs.

And do not I sense a gentle,
Soft-whispering air,
I see, how an angel with a rosy scent,

Stands comforting by my side.
An angel Helena! Helena so like my wife.
Who will lead me to freedom, to freedom,
To the Heavenly kingdom!
To freedom, to freedom,
To the Heavenly kingdom!
Who will lead me to freedom, to freedom,
To the Heavenly kingdom!
To freedom, to freedom,
To the Heavenly kingdom!
To the Heavenly kingdom!
To the Heavenly kingdom!

Helena's hand moved across his face and into his hair. He turned to her for comfort and fell asleep with her fingers combing his hair.

~oOo~

Spring came to Redway, and Helena welcomed it. While it was still cold and often wet, it was a little warmer. On a Sunday towards the end of the month, she paid her usual visit to Old Joe, leaving the children with Rachel.

Helena paced in front of the grimy windows, barely registering the pouring rain hammering against the windows. When she turned, she saw Joe surreptitiously pour some whisky into his tea. Hers was cooling by the chair that used to belong to Bertha.

"I can barely believe it, Joe. Mrs Hopkins told Nathaniel about me helping Rachel, Lilly and others, then Mr Harker and Nathaniel confronted the earl and made him make restitution to all the women he had hurt over the years."

"Oi 'eard tha'."

"From Nathaniel?"

"Mostly."

"After I refused Nathaniel's proposal, he still protected Davy from Grace taking him back to Bainbridge. I was angered by his actions concerning myself without considering his actions on my behalf against his own family. He protected me from his father, went against his mother's wishes for him to marry Grace and refused his cousin's demands. He chose Redway over a Bainbridge—a life of hard work with horses over leisure and a grand estate. He saved Davy from a hard and very short existence, and when we learned who his father was, Nathaniel asked for the honour of being his father."

"He's a good 'un."

"The best 'un, Joe. But what did I do in return? I let him face the battlefield without the promise of returning to a life with me. What on earth have I done, Joe?"

"Yer've fair broke this lad's 'eart, Helena."

"I broke both our hearts. If I marry Nathaniel, he will own everything. What if he turns out like his father after we marry? It's been a week since I met with Lord Aysthill, and he will have written to Nathaniel by now, telling him he disapproves of our marrying. I have to write something to him."

"Yer can't hurt 'im a second time," Joe reasoned.

"Mr Harker says the same. I don't want to. Why did I let my temper get the better of me with that despicable man?"

"No 'un prob'ly ever spoke to 'im like that a'fore," Joe chortled, coughed, and then supped a bit more of his tea.

"What am I to do, Joe? What would you do?"

He looked at her kindly. "I never cud get Bertha ter marry me."

She was astounded. "But you were husband and wife and had children together." she knew that the two children Bertha bore died of illness in childhood.

"Well, as far as we were concerned, we were. I loved that woman as I had never loved another a'fore and never since. I made a vow ter 'er in my 'eart, and she did the same ter me. We never needed no church or law to say what we wer ter each other. That made no never mind. Gawd could see in our 'earts that we were man and wife. What more mattered? We bought this place, moved in and tha' were tha'—husband and wife. No one knew different. No one minded."

"Thank you, Joe. Thank you for trusting me with that. I never met Bertha, but I would have liked her from all you told me."

"I like your young man and so wud ha' George. When 'e comes

back from France, you make sure 'e comes and sees me. I need ter talk ter tha' boi, and then I need ter drink 'im under tha table. I need a soldier for that. The bag o' lightweights 'round 'ere are no good for a piss up."

~oOo~

The month passed in a blur of beatings and the killing of men. Nathaniel, however, had a new purpose—revenge. He was going to kill Arbour.

He had found a spoon within the blankets Duarte had used. His friend had ground the handle to a point. Nathaniel used his time well, and despite the meagre food given to him, he paced the room and worked his muscles. He lifted the only chair in the room above him to strengthen his arms. From the barred window, he could see the mansion's courtyard. Arbour practised his sword fighting with his men, and Nathaniel watched his techniques to learn a defence against him. He practised the sword moves he would need. Never before had Nathaniel planned to kill a man, but every death of those under his command strengthened his resolve. Saying no to Arbour became easier, for how could he stop the death of another soldier if he would not stop Duarte's? The pleas of the men were more difficult to take, and should he live, Nathaniel doubted he would ever forget them.

A few days into April, Nathaniel watched Arbour in the courtyard, his fingers running absently over the row of scars on his forearm– *thirty-five.* When a distant boom rented the air, everyone below stilled, waiting. Another boom—cannon fire. Nathaniel's heart leapt with hope. The fight was upon him again, and here he knew what he was doing—waiting, killing, misery all finally over.

"For you, Duarte," he said as Arbour looked up at his barred window before indicating the two men with him to Nathaniel's room. Nathaniel pointed at him, and Arbour all but sprinted away. "Cannot face me yourself? Quelle surprise. You can try running, but I am coming for you."

He had to succeed. He had to take his revenge and return to England. As long as he remained alive, Helena and the children were safe from his family. He repeated his oft-thought mantra, "Kill Arbour and return to Helena."

As the two guards arrived, Nathaniel stood a few paces back from the door with his hands behind his head. Clasped in one hand was the sharpened spoon.

"He's just surrendering," the man who looked through the peephole said to his fellow. "I guess Arbour has him whipped."

Think again. Nathaniel sneered as the man opened the door, walking in and pocketing the key, still grinning back at his friend.

Nathaniel lunged, wrapping his arm tight around the man's throat and kicking the door closed into the face of the second guard. As the man in his arms scrabbled for purchase on his sword hilt, Nathaniel thrust the sharpened spoon handle into his abdomen. The door opened slightly again, and a sword and forearm appeared first. Nathaniel kicked again, and the door slammed onto the arm. Its owner roared in pain and dropped his sword inside the room before Nathaniel manoeuvred his back to the door, bringing the struggling guard with him. Leaning against it, he pushed the door closed.

Grasping the hilt of the sword of the man he still held, Nathaniel let it unsheathe as the man fell to the ground. Picking up the second sword, he opened the door cautiously. Pointing both blades at the unarmed man. "Lock him in, then take me to the prisoners, and I will spare your life."

They saw no French soldiers, probably because they had fled or had been sent to fight. Nathaniel held a sword in each hand as they proceeded downstairs. The men in the cells were in poor condition but eager to fight. The guard unlocked the cells and then was locked in himself. Other guards arrived, but they soon overpowered them. Those not killed were locked up. Nathaniel left the keys with one of his men.

"Search the house," commanded Nathaniel. "Bring any Frenchmen down here. If you find Arbour, he is mine. I will avenge your brothers and Capitão Matias."

Nathaniel headed off on his own search and found Arbour as he was trying to exit the house to the courtyard, carrying bags of money and other collectables. He still wore the cravat and pin that belonged to Nathaniel.

"Hell waits for you, Arbour," he boomed, causing the Frenchman to pause in the doorway long enough for Nathaniel to kick him through it. Everything he carried spilt onto the courtyard stones.

Nathaniel followed him out, and the man unsheathed his sword to fight. As Nathaniel had seen from his window, Arbour attacked in vigorous, predictable movements. Nathaniel parried each attack with minimal effort. He knew he had little strength and had to conserve it. He nicked the man on the left forearm with an inch-long slice. "Un." A second on the right. "Deux." And a third across his back as Arbour performed one of his favoured, fancy turns. "Trois."

Nathaniel's sword fighting was among the best in the British army and had served him well through many battles. When he had time to study an opponent, he was unsurpassed and had spent weeks studying this man. Nathaniel made slice after slice across Arbour's skin until his shirt hung from him in tatters. "Trente-quatre." Thirty-four, and not a mark from this fight on Nathaniel. Arbour's breathing was laboured, and in a final effort to take the weaker man down, he lunged for Nathaniel, who sliced a deep gash over the Frenchman's heart and disarmed him. Blood seeped from the wound, and Arbour knelt in front of him, spent. "Trente-cinq, that one was for Duarte, you bastard. I feel him around here. I think he waits to escort you to the gates of hell."

Holding a sword to the Frenchman's heart, he slipped the other between the blue cravat and Arbour's neck. He sliced the material and put the blade through a loop, pulling it and dropping it on the ground by his feet. Nathaniel joined the swords together at the man's heart. "What say you, Arbour? Feeling talkative? Want to plead for your life, as you made thirty-five good men plead?"

"Colonel, I beg…" He got no further as Nathaniel coldly plunged both swords into the man's chest. Removing them again, he allowed the body to fall to the ground as he turned on his heel, picked up the cravat, unhooked the pin and pocketed it. Discarding the fabric, Nathaniel noticed the bundle of letters from Helena on the ground with the rest of Arbour's collection. He picked them up and walked to his remaining men gathered at the door to the courtyard. They had been watching his display, and as he reached them, they crowded around him to pat him on the back and offer their thanks.

Nathaniel led his remaining men back to the allied forces, once more riding astride Thor. He reported to his commanders behind the battle that still raged outside Toulouse. Only days later, Napoleon abdicated and was exiled to Elba. British troops began to make their way home. Before boarding a ship to cross the English Channel, he received three letters that had waited a long time for him.

As the ship sailed towards England, Nathaniel stood at the railings, staring at the horizon for his first glimpse of home. He pulled out the letters. The first was from his father, informing him of a meeting with Helena where she had declared that he, Nathaniel, had promised to marry her on his return to England. His father expressed unhappiness about Davy Beckett being considered his grandson and urged Nathaniel to reconsider.

The page fluttered in his hand as Nathaniel wondered why Helena had declared herself this way to his father. He allowed the wind to take the page away and into the sea.

His mother's letter held no surprises for him, as she had heard of his apparent engagement and was most displeased. She insisted he do his duty to the family and propose to Grace the moment he set foot on English soil. The paper flew from his hand and away, catching on the white crest of a small wave.

Finally, he turned Helena's letter over in his hands. What had happened that she had declared herself such, and would the letter make him the happiest man in the world or make him want to jump over the side of the ship?

I have tried many times to write since Christmas, but the words did not flow because I did not know how your heart would accept them. However, I finally have something to say that might rectify the situation. Mr Harker asked me to accompany him to Aysthill House to meet with your father and Mr Davidson.

Nathaniel's expression hardened. "You and I will be having words over that, Harker."

Lord Aysthill told me of your persuading him to make restitution to the women he has wronged. I had no idea you had done this. The fact that you did it because of me is astounding, and I am exceedingly grateful. I was, however, less than grateful towards your father, who offered to make monetary restitution for Davy and his mother but showed no remorse for his actions. He sickened me, and I am afraid I told him so.

"Oh, I bet you did. I wish I had been there to see it." Nathaniel let out a snorting laugh.

In my temper, I told him we were to be married, and you would give Davy your name, making him an Ackley after all. He was displeased to hear it, which was my aim, and I am sure he has written to you, asking you not to marry me.

"He most certainly did."

Your feelings may have changed after my refusal; if so, no further action is needed.

"Oh, Helena, I would be a sorry specimen of a man if I gave up on my heart so easily. You should know me better by now." He scanned the horizon once again and shook his head at the fanciful idea that she might be standing on a cliff watching for his ship. The dark line remained determinedly blue.

However, if your feelings remain the same, and please know that my heart has not changed regarding you, I would like to meet with you when you return to England. I wish to make a proposal that should, I think and hope, make us all happy. Well, all except for your parents and your cousin.

"But what? What can it be?"

If you are thinking of me, then know I am thinking of you. If you are in battle, I wish you strength and skill to defeat our enemies and Thor, fleet of foot.

"You have no idea how often I thought of you and how your

strength helped me through, my love."

I love you, Nathaniel. Come back to your home. To Redway, to me and our children. Forever and only ever, Your's Helena.

Nathaniel folded the letter carefully, slipped it inside his coat, and then covered the place it rested with his hand. The blue line of the horizon had changed to white with a fine green line above it—England's Dover coastline. A chink of light shone brightly onto the hope he held in his heart that they would one day be together, and it warmed him in a way that he had not felt since he had sat in a stable stall with her and Davy in his arms.

Though he still had several hundred miles to travel once they docked, Nathaniel smiled. "Home—you, our children and Redway Acres."

Twenty-Two

As Nathaniel and Thor crested the hill at a fast pace, he saw Helena leaning in the doorway. She looked the same as ever. His breath caught in his chest. There had been several times, in that French prison, when he thought he might never see her again. He loved her, and she loved him, and apparently, she had a plan about how they would be together.

When Nathaniel arrived at Eastease the previous day, her note awaited him. *Meet me at the shelter tomorrow afternoon.* He had taken some of Harker's whisky over to Old Joe's to pass the time, and they drank heartily. Under the influence of alcohol, Nathaniel divulged his experiences in France.

Nodding, a sombre expression on his face, Joe asked, "Now yer 'ave experienced loss of yer free will, would yer give it up agin? Fer anyone?"

Nathaniel stared into those brown eyes, surrounded by the deep crevices of age. He knew what Joe was getting at—would he give up his loss of will to marry Helena, which is what she would have to do to marry him? To never have it back in the eyes of the law? "No."

"Not even ter be married ter a woman like Helena?"

"No. Not forever, which is how long I want to be with her."

Joe smiled, nodding. "Ah, now, Helena. Known her since she wer' seven. As headstrong and stubborn then as she is now. Put me in mind o' me Bertha tha' one. With a woman like tha', a man takes what she's willin' ter give yer and no complaining mind, cos she's werth it."

"That's just the problem, Joe. I don't know what she is willing to give me or whether it will be enough."

"Enough, eh? Ask yerself this. If yer wer' ta list everything you want from 'er, and then list everythin' yer are willin' ter give up for 'er, wud tha scales balance?"

"I don't have property to match Redway," Nathaniel explained, his hands outstretched.

Joe slammed his empty glass down on the table, waving a hand of dismissal at Nathaniel. "Ah, boi, as usual, yer ain't listenin' roight. I'm not talkin' bout Redway. I'm sayin' wha' ar' yer willin' ter give up fer 'er? If yer not willin' ter give up yer free will, yer can't expect 'er ter, can yer?"

Nathaniel shook his head, ashamed that tears were so close. He needed Helena so much that his chest hurt, and he could barely catch a breath.

"Ah now, yer ain't gonna blubber all o'er me a'yer."

Nathaniel smiled and shook his head, refilling their glasses.

Thrilling at the vision of the storm clouds gathering in the wake of his charging steed, Helena stepped aside to allow Nathaniel to lead Thor into the barn as he stopped shy of the door and dismounted with a flourish.

Neither spoke as he moved Thor into a stall and untacked him. She watched his movements. Nathaniel looked a little thin, but the aura of strength still exuded from his presence. She had heard of his capture after she had sent her last letter. His task complete, they locked eyes.

Although Helena stood stock still, Nathaniel knew her well

enough to see the signs of her nervousness, so she unclasped her hands that were tight at her waist and stopped chewing her bottom lip. His eyes dropped to her mouth, causing heat to rise.

He stepped out of the stall towards her, but Helena held her ground. He was so close that his head almost touched hers with his slight bow. Nathaniel broke the silence, seeming annoyed, which always brought out her own temper.

"This is highly inappropriate."

"You came, though," she pointed out.

"As you wished."

So, Nathaniel was not going to make this easy on her. Helena could not blame him. Many could say she had led him to believe she would welcome his proposal, as it would have been if she were the marrying kind. Helena wondered if he thought she did not want to share her property. It was time to make her proposal and see what fate awaited her.

Walking around the area where she had delivered Missy's foal last summer, Helena cleared her throat. "I am taking on partners." Nathaniel stared at her intently but said nothing. "You and John."

A furrow appeared on his brow. *Is he angry?*

"I do not have enough funds to buy into your business," he stated bitterly.

"No, that is not what I meant. I mean to give you forty-five per cent of Redway. John would have ten per cent, so when you and I disagree, which I am sure we will, he will be the deciding vote."

"You want to give it to me?" he asked incredulously. "You would not marry me because you did not want to part with Redway."

"You know that is not true."

"So, this is your plan? We would work together side by side, but not be together as husband and wife? As much as I love Redway, I do not think I could bear it. I love you far too much. I hoped you should feel the same way."

"I do, and that is the second part of my proposal." Suddenly aware she was speaking to the ground, Helena lifted her head. Dazzling blue eyes momentarily took her words away. She took a deep breath. "I propose that we live as husband and wife. Appear to the world as such but without the actual ceremony and legality."

Nathaniel felt the pain of her suggestion. He had offered her his hand, love, protection, and the prestigious Ackley name and connections. Helena presented him with a business proposition, so much for Joe's idea of balancing the scales. He was hurt.

Then, her second proposal hit him like a physical blow. *Has she gone completely mad?*

"This is what you think of me?" he finally exclaimed. "That I would compromise you. You think this is what I want?"

"I am already compromised, as you know. That does not bother me. I think this gives us both what we want."

"I need to sit down." Nathaniel looked around and became aware that a door was now closed between the stable stalls and the back room, where they had slept the night the storm trapped them. "Why is there a door here? What have you set up?"

He slammed the door open against the stall wall with Perseus in it, causing the horse to whinny in protest. He came to such an abrupt halt after walking through the doorway that Helena bumped into his back.

"What the—?" Nathaniel's breeding was the only thing that stopped the expletive erupting from him as he took in the changes in the room. The narrow bed was wider, with new bedding. The chimney had been cleaned, and a fire set ready to light. A pretty table contained food and drink supplies, and a small closet was enclosed for privacy.

"It seems you were confident that I would agree to this. I am sorry to disappoint you. This is not what I want. It goes against everything I was taught about being a gentleman, and I take my leave of you, madam." As he spoke, the rain started to lash against the barn. There was a flash of lightning and a roll of thunder. Their horses snorted and stamped around their stalls.

"You cannot leave in this," Helena exclaimed.

"Eastease is not that far. I will dry off easily enough when I get back," he countered bitterly.

"Then go, but realise you leave me stranded here alone. Redway is too far in this weather. What does your good breeding think of that?"

There was no escape then. Had Helena planned it? She must have known he would baulk at her suggestion. With rain due, Nathaniel had thought her asking to meet him at this location was perhaps a coincidence or a female sense of romance. Had he known it was a trap? Who was he fooling? He had hoped they should be stranded again.

Nathaniel took a deep breath. A night of torment, as he resisted his basest instincts or, the bed flashed in his vision, capitulate. He could, of course, let it be known they were stranded here a second time and force her hand, but she would resent him forever, and he could not bear that.

"Let us start this conversation again," he suggested, recollecting their argument the first night they spent here. "If we are to discuss such a course of action, I suggest we sit and drink a glass of wine."

Moving behind a chair, Nathaniel held it out for her to sit in, ready to push her to the table.

"Thank you, Nathaniel."

With a nod, he sat opposite her. In silence, he poured some wine for each of them and sipped. After Helena sipped some herself, she seemed to gain some confidence.

"If we had met when I was still under the control of my father, I would have felt very differently about marriage. Oh, my mother would have loved you, Son of an Earl. She would have insisted on marriage, and I would not have refused." She blushed, becomingly. "But I have spent so long and been through so much, making my own decisions. I cannot give that away. Still, the two parts of my proposal are separate. I have decided I need partners and have already signed over John's ten per cent. I gave Ruth their house in her name, even though that makes no difference, as they are married. Those are your papers." She gestured at the thick document on the table.

Nathaniel glanced at them, then back into her eyes. "It was never about Redway Acres for me." He took a more sizeable drink of the wine and felt better for it. "I would have wanted you if you were penniless. I would have wanted Issie and Davy, too. To be a family."

Her tears welled at his words, and she covered her mouth to stifle a sob. Old Joe was right she was worth it—whatever she asked of him.

He would take whatever she could give him. At this thought, Nathaniel stood, rounded the table, and pulled her to her feet so fast she gasped. Helena had wept once before, and he had left because she had refused him. Now, she was the one proposing. He would not refuse and leave her crying again.

"I love you, Helena." He crushed his mouth against hers. His hungry lips moved as Nathaniel gave reign to his desire. It only took a moment for him to realise that she was not responding as he expected—she was still and tense. Stopping, he pulled back from her. Though he didn't let her go, he did gentle his grasp on her arms. Horrified to see the fear he had put in her eyes, he swore lightly. "Damn it all." She misinterpreted his anger as directed at her.

"I am sorry. I—I will do better. Give me some time. I fully understand a man's expectations and will not deny you."

"Helena, no. I was angry with myself for treating you so roughly. I should have known better, but I have waited so long to kiss you and hold you—I let my emotions get the better of me. *I will do better.*"

He cupped her face. Bringing his lips close to hers, he gently brushed them over her swollen ones. He knew he had done the right thing when she lifted her hands to his arms and moved her lips against his.

"Helena, I assure you that you do not understand a man's expectations. Your experience was brutal and cruel, and I will never treat you that way. You have my word on that, as the man that loves you more than life."

"Does this mean that you are accepting my proposals, Nathaniel? Both of them?"

"It would seem that I am, though I reserve the right to continue to persuade you to marry me, and I want our children to have my name. All of our children, including Davy and Issie, too. Additionally, you must remove this immediately."

Nathaniel took her left hand in his and took off the plain gold band she had put on in pretence of being Mrs Andrews. Then he foraged around in a pocket before pulling out a posey ring and showing her the words engraved upon the inside. *With free will...*

Yours.

As Nathaniel moved to put the ring on her finger, Helena stopped him. Confusion stopped him, but a smile appeared on her face.

"I, Helena Billings, do take thee, Nathaniel Ackley, to be my husband. I will always love you and no other. I share everything in my life with you and promise to raise our children and horses together—to work side by side with you. I cannot vow to obey you, but I will consider all reasonably stated requests."

Nathaniel gave her a wry smile, then spoke his vows, "I, Nathaniel Ackley, do take thee, Helena Billings, to be my wife. I will love you for all my life, and there will be no other. I do not have much to share with you, but I vow to protect you and our children forevermore. I promise to discuss all decisions with you, though I may need some practice."

As he slid the ring onto her finger, he said, "I love you, Mrs Ackley."

Helena nodded in agreement. "Now you may kiss me again, Husband." She tilted her face to him, and he kissed her gently, applying more pressure and encouraging her to part her lips.

"I love you, Nathaniel," she murmured when the kiss finished, and this time, she pulled his head down to hers to initiate another.

Realising his earlier mistake, Nathaniel was gentle, although her words thrilled him. Truthfully, she was much like a virgin; she had only one violent experience, which took away the physical, but in all other aspects, she was inexperienced, and he would consider that when taking her. He would have to stem his desires and be patient. However, he had wanted to hold her for such a long time, so he indulged in feasting on her lips, gradually increasing his passion.

Helena was surprised by her reaction to Nathaniel and realised she wanted him to put his hands on her body and run them over her curves. Deciding to feel her way without overthinking, she tentatively leaned towards him and pressed herself against him. She was pleased when his hands slid down her arms and around her. One strong arm held her back from waist to shoulder while his other hand slid over her bottom. He pressed her closer as if trying to meld their bodies together. With a groan of pleasure, he released her lips to kiss her face and ran the tip of his tongue down her neck to her collarbone. Desire shot through her body through the points he held her pressed against him. She gasped, and he reclaimed her lips, his tongue sliding inside her open mouth.

Shocked, Helena pulled away to see the desire in his eyes and the humour that was never far away. The intimacy of it was powerful, and she responded in kind. Seemingly pleased with her daring, he swept her into his arms to walk to the bed, their lips still locked together.

Helena had expected him to throw her onto the bed, but instead, he sat her gently on its edge and took off her boots, then his, too. He removed his top coat and waistcoat, then, moving over to the grate, lit the fire.

She watched him lovingly; they were finally together, and all the obstacles disappeared. She was nervous about what would happen next, but although this felt very intimate, she was fully clothed, apart from her boots. He was in his shirtsleeves, as always in her dreams, but this was much better. Kissing him was wonderful. She would not mind the other thing so much if kissing happened first.

Nathaniel moved back to her, smiling when he noticed her watching him. Then he pushed her gown off her shoulders and bent his head to kiss the exposed skin before standing her up to reach around her back and unbutton her gown. While he was at his task, she decided to kiss his neck as he had done to her, but his cravat impeded her, so she started untying the complicated knot. She smiled at him. "James ties a very intricate cravat."

Nathaniel looked into her eyes. "Are you sure, Helena? Be very sure."

She tugged harder at the fabric at his neck, growling in her frustration. "I am sure this knot is preventing me from kissing your neck as I wish to."

His intense look had her hands falling away, and she returned his look with as much sincerity as she could muster. "I am sure, Nathaniel." Then she gasped as her gown fell from her body into a heap on the floor. His eyes flared at the view of her breasts only covered by the thin fabric of her chemise. His desire caused her own to soar at him seeing her this way.

Reaching up again, she finally freed the knot of his cravat and clamped her mouth on his neck. She licked and kissed as he had done to her and elicited another groan of pleasure from him. He reached around her again and untied her petticoat—it joined her gown on the floor. Helena was enjoying this process and continued to follow his lead but was unsure when they should get on the bed. Surely, he did not intend for them to get completely undressed? She only wore her chemise, drawers and stockings, and he was in only his breeches and shirt.

Nathaniel, however, fully intended to get Helena naked. She had told him of her treatment before, and if he could make this time any different, he would. He knew she fully expected an end result of him forcing himself into her and that it would be painful. He was about to show her how different it could be. At first, he had been surprised by her intuition in copying his actions, but he thought back to her coping with Davy's screaming and helping a foal into the world in this shelter. He realised he could show her what to do to him by doing the same to her first. As always, Helena had learned quickly, and now she was pulling his shirt out of his trousers. He loved the feel of her strong hands running over the skin of his back but stiffened as he wondered what she would make of the scar on his chest.

"I love your body, Nathaniel. You are so strong," she murmured, moving her hands to his chest.

"You make me strong," he said, clutching her hands under his shirt. He had spoken with such feeling it surprised even him, and he knew it to be true. Nathaniel had survived the prison and Arbour because of the escape that thoughts of Helena had provided him. As he released her, she ran her fingers along the raised skin of his scar. His voice was deep with emotion as he asked about what worried him, "Can you love even that? It is not a pleasant sight."

"Especially so because this scar shows how brave you are." She pushed his shirt up, and he grabbed it, reaching up with his arms to pull it over his head. "You are beautiful, Nathaniel."

He laughed. Leaning in, Helena pressed kisses along the scar, right down his rib cage.

"My turn," he said hoarsely and, keeping eye contact with her, lifted her chemise so he could run his hands over her back before moving to cup her breasts. His thumbs caressed her nipples, and he captured her lips again. He continued those ministrations before lifting the chemise over her head. In her embarrassment at being so exposed to him, Helena covered her breasts with her arms. Ignoring her reaction, Nathaniel unpinned her long hair, ran his fingers through it, and pulled it forward over her arms. Gently, he took her hands so he could pull her arms away and allow her hair to cover her nakedness.

Slowly, he picked her up again, lifting her out of the swathes of her discarded clothing to gently lay her on the bed. Then he joined her. He did not lie on top of her as she might have expected but passed over her to her right side, leaving her free to get out of bed if she so wished. Leaning over, he kissed her again and, pushing some of her hair aside, continued his attentions to her breasts with his free hand.

Surprisingly, after kissing his way down her neck again, he continued to her chest and over one breast, taking her into his mouth to lick and suckle as Issie once had. The sensations this action delivered to her body were highly different from those she had experienced when feeding her child. He released one nipple to go to the other and licked in circles, almost driving her mad until he finally took it into his mouth.

Helena was so distracted by the new sensations that were running through her body and the familiar throbbing between her legs she had not realised that he had untied her drawers until he moved to kneel on the bed and remove them. Her stockings followed them to the pile of discarded clothes.

"Nathaniel," she breathed his name, unsure yet not wanting to be anywhere else.

"You are so beautiful," he scanned her body with a look of hunger that instilled her with confidence. "I am going to take off my breeches so we are both naked, but nothing will happen until you are ready."

She nodded, noticing his hesitation as she leaned on her elbows to watch him reveal his body as he lay beside her. Perhaps he thought she might look away, but her curiosity was intense as she had never glimpsed anything of a man's body. He smiled and unbuttoned his breeches, releasing himself from their constriction and pushing them off his legs with his feet.

Helena enjoyed the sight of him—every inch muscular and sinewy. *A magnificent beast* were the words that came to her mind. Nathaniel recaptured her lips and ran his hands over her body. It was glorious lying naked next to him. He loved her, he loved her body, and he was just as naked as she. He was suckling her again and ran a hand down to her thigh, where she pressed her legs together. He caressed up and down as if waiting for permission. Her body responded as she opened, but he didn't rush.

"I will not hurt you, Helena," he said, moving his fingers to apply the gentle caressing to that private area. His mouth over hers as his fingers moved expertly, parting her gently and finding a particular point they liked circle. That point seemed to be the centre of the familiar throbbing. She pushed herself against his hand and pulled away from his kiss to take in breath after breath. His actions were making her pant as if she had run from Redway.

"Look at me, Helena," she met his deep blue gaze as his finger slipped inside her. The feeling was not at all like her recollection from her nightmares. He moved the finger, adding a second, his thumb continuing the circling of that throbbing point. All she could think was that had he thought of asking her to marry him, she would have been able to do nothing but agree.

"Nathaniel, what are you doing to me?"

"I am giving you pleasure, Wife. It will peak in a moment. Enjoy it."

Moving his mouth to her breast was enough to send her over the edge, and the throbbing moved to waves of incredible sensation that rippled through her body until she found out what he meant by a peak. This sensation was what her dreams had lacked. She clamped her legs together, trapping his hand as her body pulsed, then relaxed, completely sated. He moved to kiss her, removed his hand and lay back on the bed.

"I have never experienced that before." She turned her head and looked at him.

"You never thought to touch yourself?" he croaked, the thought of it driving him mad with desire. He desperately wanted to take Helena immediately but knew he still had to wait.

"No, I suppose it is thought sinful and not appropriate for a woman to do. Do you?" She looked at him and then down his body.

"Yes," he almost groaned the word. Since he met Helena, his thoughts at those times had been only of her, and often outside in long grasses or a pool of cool running water. He closed his eyes. He had to stop looking at her momentarily to regain control. He felt her hand on his chest, moving down his stomach. His breath caught and held. This woman was so instinctual that he knew they would have a lot of fun as he taught her about pleasure.

His stomach quivered under her touch. Her fingers were light as she reached for him and stroked his length. He moaned, and she lifted her fingers to stroke again. Quickly, he captured her hand and, wrapping his fingers around hers, helped her make a fist encompassing him. Their hands moved together, and she understood. Nathaniel dropped his hand to his side as Helena continued to pleasure him, his eyes still closed. Soon, his breathing became as laboured as hers had been.

Helena's soft voice broke into his concentration on holding his control. "Now I am giving you pleasure, Husband."

His eyes flew open and took in the astonishing view of her flushed face, watching her hand upon him with fascination.

"There is another way," he suggested softly, promising himself not to be disappointed if she refused him. His heart leapt as she nodded and lay back in the bed. "I promise I will not hurt you, Helena."

Slowly, so as not to startle her, he moved over her and inserted a leg between hers. Still, he did not push her but allowed her to open for him. He vowed to rein in his control. "Be sure, Helena. I am unsure I could stop myself, but I will try."

"I am sure, Nathaniel." She ran her fingers through his hair. "I love you."

Taking as much care as he could, he gradually pressed inside her. As he had planned, she was wet from his arousal. With each stroke, he could penetrate a little further. As he did so, he ran a hand from her buttocks down to the back of her knees so he was able to bring her knee higher and allow him deeper.

Nathaniel had never felt anything like it before. He had known women but had long waited for Helena and loved her deeply. He found that being in love with the woman you were taking to bed made all the difference in the experience.

Helena was surprised by the feeling of Nathaniel inside her. It felt incredible that she was giving pleasure to him with her body, that he wanted her and had said that he probably could not control himself and stop. Helena did not want him to stop. Instinctually, she lifted her feet, wrapping her legs around his waist.

Though surprised, he was obviously pleased and continued moving. His strong muscles bulged in his arms with the effort of holding himself above her. He was strong, like an animal taking its mate and as she thought of these things, the pleasure within her increased. She was moaning again as her pleasure built, and when her body peaked, the muscles within her contracted around him. Nathaniel must have felt it as he emptied himself within her with a series of guttural groans and collapsed on top of her.

When she could gather her wits, Helena smiled. "You are an astonishing man, Colonel Ackley."

Nathaniel lifted his head. "Is that something you are only just noticing, Mrs Ackley?".

"Not at all."

Twenty-Three

Nathaniel lay on the bunk, the night surrounding him as Helena breathed softly at his side. He had never been happier and started thinking about their life together. How happy they would be. How many children would they have? How many horses would they raise—would he finally get a pair of handsome Yorkshire coach horses? They had kept warm by enjoying each other's bodies. Between those times, they talked of their plans to elope and return married.

"I do not want to spend another night away from you," Nathaniel had said, his emotion high in his throat, grateful she concurred. She turned in her sleep, and Nathaniel ran his fingers along the six-year-old scar on her back. He kissed along the fading line of it, claiming it for his own. No part of her would ever belong to the general again. She was all his, as he was all hers. Pressing himself close to her back, he slept.

"Não, Duarte!" he screamed in his sleep and woke her.

"Nathaniel, I am here. It is me, Helena."

"An angel, Helena. Helena so like my wife."

"I am your wife," then she realised he was still caught in his nightmare of being imprisoned, "Nathaniel, wake up," she spoke firmly, using the voice she had with Davy in the stable at Christmastime. "Come to me, Nathaniel, you are in a nightmare. I am real. I am here. You are at Redway. You are home."

"Helena." he woke groggy to see her sitting in the bunk. She was naked, with her arms reaching out to him. The sob caught in his throat as it wrenched from his chest. "Tell me that I am not dreaming." He threw his arms around her and pressed his face to her breasts.

As he cried, she was reminded of comforting Davy and held him to her in the same way. He told her in a wavering voice what had happened, told her of Duarte, of the cuts to his arm and of putting the pistol to his head. Then he told her how he had killed the man responsible.

"You are so brave and strong, Nathaniel. To bear this alone is too much, and I am glad you shared it with me." She brought his arm up to her lips. She had wondered what had happened to him, and now she knew. Gently, she kissed each scar. Thirty-five kisses— "These belong to me. He is dead and controls you no longer."

He put his head to her breasts, and thinking he wanted her to hold him some more, she placed her hand on his head. She felt his tongue on her skin and then a nipple and laughed. "You are taking advantage of my compassion, sir," she exclaimed playfully.

Lifting his head, he looked thoughtfully at her. "I kissed the scar on your back when you slept so that no part of you could be his ever again."

"You did?" She was surprised they had thought to take the same action. "Can you do it again, do you think? I want to be aware of it."

He turned her gently onto her stomach and, moving her hair aside, spread tiny kisses up and down the scar on her back. Aroused once more, he moved his body over her and pushed a leg gently between hers. Bending his head to her back, he ran his tongue along the scar. She moaned quietly and opened her legs for him. After all their loving, he slipped into her easily and then, scooping a hand under her, he lifted her to her hands and knees. As he moved within her, his hands roamed over her breasts and then between her legs to that spot that he had such a talent to make throb.

Spent, they collapsed on the bed, entwined their bodies together and slept peacefully until dawn.

~oOo~

"Ackers," Harker spoke with exasperation, "at least wait a couple of weeks and marry her from Eastease. We can give you a wedding breakfast to rival my own."

"Neither of us wants that." Nathaniel hovered over James as he packed a bag for him, handing an occasional garment to the servant in a vain attempt to speed things up. He'd left Helena at Redway Acres two hours ago, and his hands itched to hold her again, but the methodical and efficient James would not be hurried.

"Nathaniel! I promised George Stockton that I would look out for Helena. How would I be honouring her own grandfather's wishes by allowing this? At least marry her in the Eastcambe church where everyone can witness it."

He turned back to Harker, his eyes narrowing. "What are you implying? Do not forget I am still unhappy with you for taking Helena to Aysthill when I was gone. We will marry, Harker. I give you my word that my life will be devoted to Helena and our children. If George Stockton were here, he could not ask for more. One of these days, I will tell you the details of my month of imprisonment, and you will understand why I cannot bear another moment without the woman I love."

Nathaniel's only other stop was Old Joe's cottage. He had badgered Mrs Hopkins for a basket for the man, given that Helena would not be making her usual Sunday trip. He laughed when he went to add a jug of whisky, only to find Mrs Hopkins had already done so. Old Joe would be delighted with two.

"Yer came ter yer senses then, boi?" Joe greeted him.

"Thank you, Joe." Nathaniel held out his hand to the wizened man, who shook it firmly and grasped Nathaniel's shoulder.

"Yer treat 'er roight, Colonel. Oi might seem 'alf tha man I use' ter be, but Oi still 'ave me ways. An' if Oi'm dead 'n gorn, Oi'll haunt yer."

"Yes, sir." Nathaniel didn't doubt it.

Old Joe held up his glass, and Nathaniel did the same.

"T' Colonel an' Mrs Ackley."

~oOo~

The sun had barely risen when Helena arrived at Redway rather dishevelled. Ruth shooed her maid away to finish packing so she could help Helena herself.

"We will be gone maybe a week, Ruth. We will come back married."

"You are getting married, or you will come back married?" Ruth asked her, eyeing the gold band on her left hand.

"Does it matter, my friend? I never knew it could be like this."

"Of course you didn't. What experience did you 'ave? Well, I said to him that you would find a way. I've sent John on an errand in the village, so Jacky will drive your carriage. It should be John, but you know that he's not happy about this. He and the colonel are always butting heads. Jacky will be discreet. Where are you going?"

"We will find a place to stay for a few days, so we will have been away long enough to have married. Nathaniel has a friend in Sheffield he wants to visit before we make our way home. I am so happy, Ruth."

"Then I am happy for you, my girl."

They embraced tightly.

There was a knock at the door, and none other than Nathaniel poked his head inside. Helena could not help the heat that rushed to her cheeks when his eyes slid to the bed.

"Everything is ready, my dear. I just need you," he whispered. They had decided not to wake the children who would want to come with them.

"I'll be there in one moment, my love."

When he disappeared again, she looked at Ruth whose eyes filled with mirth. "It's like 'e owns the place already, coming right up ter yer bedchamber," she commented.

"He does—some of it, at least. He signed the papers before we left the shelter this morning, Ruth."

"Then 'eaven 'elp us."

~oOo~

To Helena's mind, the several days spent at the Lakes in a secluded Inn contrasted the hard days of work to come at Redway. They arrived as Colonel and Mrs Ackley, and most of the time, were in their rooms, but they did take in some pretty walks. Helena desperately wished to assist Jacky in caring for their carriage horses and Thor but did not want to raise suspicions about her relationship with Nathaniel. She satisfied herself with checking upon them when they rode around the lakes.

What surprised Helena most was how Nathaniel opened up to her about his upbringing, his father's anger and his ultimatum that he marry Lady Grace. She learned of his childhood friends, of whom he only saw Mr Harker now. She remembered some of his stories from her grandmother's tales of the boys. And, of course, they talked of Old Joe. He agreed with Helena's insistence that they care for her grandfather's friend as much as he would allow them.

Spurred on by Nathaniel's openness, Helena talked of her own family. She missed her father and brother and yearned for a connection between them. He was able to tell her of his visit there the previous October. Unsurprised about her brother, she was pained to hear of her father's drinking.

They discussed Dowager Alcott's wish to live close to Issie, and Nathaniel promised to influence Mr Harker in any way he could to allow her to buy the property and land opposite Redway. The dowager was looking for a purpose and held an interest in how Helena helped people. In particular, women who found themselves in desperate circumstances.

One stormy night, as they lay in each other's arms, Nathaniel told Helena of Tommy Smithson, how they had saved each other, and that he had very little to keep house with his mother in Sheffield now that

Tommy's father had died. Nathaniel had sent money when he could but wondered, as Tommy was so good with Thor, if they could give him work at Redway.

Building had already begun on adjoining cottages further down the North Road. One was planned for Jacky and Rebecca when they married, but the other could be for the Smithsons. It would be small with just two bedchambers, but it should do until something else worked out. Assuming, of course, that mother and son would wish to move away from Sheffield.

Their visit to the Smithsons on their return journey proved fruitful. They would have a new stable man at Redway and, if Helena managed to work on Tommy to allow it, a blue roan mare from which to breed.

Married life was making her happier than she had ever experienced.

~oOo~

Helena's joy lasted only until their return to Redway.

Expecting to be greeted with congratulations and calls of *Mrs Ackley*, Helena was surprised at her children, *their children*, she corrected herself, crying as they ran to her. She gathered them to her skirts as she noted their tear-stained faces.

"What has happened, Ruth?" she asked her housekeeper with fear.

"Tis Old Joe, Helena. John went ta look in on him this mornin' and found him dead. He went peacefully in his sleep, holding a letter from Bertha to his chest. Even if you had been 'ere, you wouldn't have been with him when he went. Bertha was with him, I'm sure."

"Bertha was always with him, in his heart." Helena's tears threatened at the thought of never seeing Old Joe alive again. How much she and Nathaniel owed him, and she had hoped to care for him for many more years yet. Not that he would have appreciated it had they successfully persuaded him to move to Redway.

"No one much accepted him until you showed them different."

"He was a kind and loving man, once you got behind the gruff exterior—and the smell." She gave a short laugh. "What is being done?"

"Mrs Dawley and I went and laid him out. John asked Dom ter make up a coffin for him. He is the best we have with wood and is using the workshop here. I hope that is all acceptable. Mr Brooks has been to see Old Joe, and we have put plenty of flowers around the room. Mr Brooks says he has a plot in the church graveyard for him, next ter Bertha. We are burying him on Saturday."

"That all sounds acceptable, thank you, Ruth. There is no other family that we know of?"

Ruth shook her head sadly.

"I will go and see him myself tomorrow," Helena confirmed before glancing up at Nathaniel, who also had tears in his eyes. "We shall go and see him tomorrow," she corrected.

"Now, children," Helena continued, looking at Davy and Issie at her sides, "let us sit in the parlour. Colonel Ackley and I wish to talk to you. Though it is very sad about Old Joe, we do have some happier news to tell you."

Ruth left to get some refreshments.

Before Helena even began to talk to the children of her *marriage* to Nathaniel, Davy piped up in his straightforward way.

"Where did you go on a trip with the colonel, Mama?"

"Colonel Ackley asked me to marry him, and I said I would. We did not want to wait because we missed each other while he was away, so we married."

Before she could say anything further, Davy and Issie threw themselves at the man.

"Papa! Papa!" they exclaimed as they clambered over him.

Nathaniel was overwhelmed with emotion. The news that Old Joe had passed had barely sunk in before the two children that he loved most dearly in the world vied for a place on his lap. His tears flowed as happiness enveloped him. He managed to manoeuvre a child to each knee.

"Papa, why are you crying?" Issie was concerned.

"Because I am happy. Sometimes, you cry when you are happy."

"Even men?" asked Davy, a little concerned. The last time Nathaniel had seen the boy was the day after Davy's crying in Eastease's stable.

"Even men. Come to us, Helena," he said gruffly, and she came, removed the two children from his lap and sat on him herself. Then she gathered their children on her own lap so he could wrap his strong arms around them all.

"Kiss Mama!" squealed Issie.

"Kiss Mama!" repeated Davy.

Their lips met gently and then more passionately before Issie joined in with a kiss to her father's cheek and Davy to his mother's.

At that moment, Ruth walked in and stared at the happy group. She thought how wonderful it was that her girl finally had a family.

~oOo~

They buried Old Joe on a bright, late-May afternoon that held the promise of summer. Helena was surprised by how many people had bothered to turn up in the church and at his graveside. Many were the men who had worked on Old Joe's house with Nathaniel the summer before. Colonel and Mrs Ackley had allowed all their workers the afternoon to pay their respects, and there was food and drink aplenty for everyone back at Redway Acres.

Mr Brooks completed the graveside service, and as Old Joe's casket was lowered into the ground, Helena sang an old folk song that she had often heard sung in the stable. It was fitting that it was about an old tramp who had not been accepted at the local tavern.

> I'm sitting quietly in my chair,
> They think I only sit and stare,
> But I don't miss much a sitting here,
> And here comes poor Old Joe.
>
> Puts his money on the bar,
> Likes to buy us all a jar,
> Always asks yer, how y'are,
> But they don't ask poor Old Joe.

Redway Acres - Helena

Seem to think he's a disgrace,
Say he low'rs the tone of the place,
Wasn't born with a silver spoon in his face,
So, they don't want poor Old Joe.

He sits him down to drink his beer
They'd like to have him out of here
Don't like the way he wears his hair
No, they don't like poor Old Joe.

He's on his feet, he's on his way,
And as he leaves us every day,
The only words yer'll hear him say,
Gawd bless yer, Gawd bless yer,
But they don't like poor Old Joe.

I'm sitting quietly in my chair,
They think I only sit and stare,
Well, I don't miss much a sitting here,
But I do miss poor Old Joe.

Gawd bless yer, Gawd bless yer,
Gawd bless yer, poor Old Joe.

Twenty-Four

Nathaniel quickly adjusted to the routines of Redway Acres and was grateful Helena tried to make adjustments by including him in discussions and decisions. Nathaniel had no plans to make sweeping changes that his wife would not appreciate. Instead, he learned her way of doing things and made suggestions when asked. Used to balancing the books and sorting papers at Bainbridge, Nathaniel quickly undertook that work. It was a good way for him to understand the business, and he had valuable connections. His name went a long way in greasing the wheels where needed. Nathaniel prided himself in working well with the men, whose respect he earned by handling Thor and Perseus. Perseus was the more dominant of the two horses, but Nathaniel was the dominant male in the stable.

Unsurprisingly, the one person who did not accept him was John, and Nathaniel knew that things would come to a head sooner or later.

Persephone, Helena's copper-red mare, was two months shy of foaling. Nathaniel had been surprised to hear that Thor was the sire. It must have happened when they were on their picnic last September.

Thor had managed that day, what had taken Nathaniel several months more, and had his way with a redhead. Nathaniel congratulated the stallion as he leaned over Thor's stall, feeding him some carrots when John picked his moment.

"Are you as surprised as I was to discover you will be a father? You got to Persephone when we were distracted at the picnic. I will have to tie you more securely in future. I wonder how long it might be before I get the same outcome with my own mare?"

"Bloody full of yourself yer ar'," growled John as he passed.

Nathaniel put out a hand to stop him. "Are we going to do this now, John? This has been brewing since you met me."

"Since you took advantage of her in the storm last year, yer mean."

"I thought we had settled that. I did not take advantage of her."

"Didn't offer to marry her though, did yer?"

"She did not want to get married."

"Then yer forced your bastard on her."

"Call my son a bastard again, and I will knock you into next week."

"Yer can try. If yer wanted to marry her back then, why not do it instead of going to war? She said she would take yer. She cried for days and yer were off playing soldier."

"I wanted her to want to marry me, not as a duty to save me from battle. She had already refused me but would say yes if I stayed. I was sorely tempted, John, sorely tempted. I had already received my orders. Would you have me desert King and Country and my brothers in arms? How honourable would you think me then?"

"If yer ar' so honourable, why did yer compromise her the other week in the shelter and then have to whisk her off to a rushed marriage? Her stable is good enough for yer to take from her, but she is not good enough for a lavish Aysthill wedding. Yer 'ave never introduced her as yer wife to yer family."

"My father is not welcome here, and I have not taken her stable away. You had better stop talking," Nathaniel warned.

"I am not afraid of yer. Yer might best me in a sword fight, but I will take my chances with fists."

"You would only have one chance, John. I have let you have your say, and now it is my turn. I have wanted Helena since the day my eyes landed on her. She will not marry me. I did not have to marry her to get the stable. She gave me half her share. I do not own her. She gives herself to me every night, willingly. You do not like it because you are no longer the man she turns to."

John's fist landed squarely on Nathaniel's jaw—it staggered him. The man had a hand like a rock. Nathaniel blocked the next one and landed a punch to John's stomach. Doubled over, John charged and took Nathaniel down to the floor, his roar attracting some of the other men who started cheering them on. They rolled over, fists flying but mostly ineffectual as each tried to get the upper hand. Nathaniel managed to get on top of John and straddled him so he could punch him again.

As he pulled back his fist, Helena's arms wrapped around his and hung on, preventing him from using it. She pulled him to his feet. John scrambled up while Helena released Nathaniel and stood between them, arms stretched out and keeping them apart. Each was rubbing some smarting part of his own body.

"Oh, you are such—men!" she exclaimed, trying to find a suitable insult but realising the one that fit. "You are worse than the horses, fighting to see who is the dominant male. Even they did not resort to this. Well, I have news for you: Redway Acres has no dominant male. There is a dominant female, and you are looking at her." She stood with her hands fisted on her hips and glared at each.

Turning to scour the other men, who still watched the show, Helena bellowed at them, "All the rest of you take note of that. I am still in charge here. Now get about your business and leave."

As they scattered, she stayed John and Nathaniel. "Not you two."

Rolling her eyes towards John, she defended her husband. "I never want to hear you say that Nathaniel *played* at being a soldier. His services to King and Country are considerable, as was his suffering when injured and captured. I will NOT have you belittle that. There has not been a lavish Aysthill wedding because we are not married. I will not give over my free will, John, you know why, and Nathaniel has accepted that, although he is not entirely happy with the situation. The pretence is for society and the children. Nathaniel and I have made our vows to each other in our hearts. He is the best man I have ever known and would never hurt me or the children. In fact, he would give over everything for us.

"I will not have you talk of Davy like that, John. I'll have your guts for garters if you repeat it. He looks like Nathaniel because he is his half-brother. Now, he is our son, and you will give him the respect he deserves in the same way we respect Jacky. The earl is not welcome here because he threatened me some time ago, and Nathaniel swore to kill him if he came near me or Redway again. If you cannot accept any of this, John, I am sorry for it. If you feel you have to leave, I will understand, but be very saddened, and we will buy back your share in the stable."

John's shoulders sagged, and he nodded at her points, which gave Helena hope that he would not leave. She still cared for the big lump and was grateful he still felt the need to protect her.

Nathaniel harrumphed and made to turn away from them.

"Oh, I'm not done, Nathaniel." With John at her back, she said her peace to her husband, "How dare you fight with John this way? You need to show him some respect. He is no longer a paid worker here at Redway; he is our business partner, and you have decided to resolve your differences with fisticuffs? Where is your good breeding now— *son of an earl*?

"That aside, this man has taught me all he knows of horses, helped me keep Redway going, and been more like a father to me than my actual father. You know that to be true, as you have met my parents. At a time when they were more interested in what their neighbours thought, John and Ruth were there to comfort me, not blame me. They left all they knew in Norfolk to travel with me here and protect me and my secrets. They are the rocks I leaned upon when my grandfather died. Had your father come to Redway when you were away, John would have stood up to him for me, no matter the cost."

Looking from one man to the other, she finished. "I do not want to see either of you again until you can be civil to each other." Turning on her heels, Helena left them to it with a fervent hope that they would sort it out more civilly.

"She set yer down," John had humour in his voice. "Yer had to take it, and she's not even yer wife."

"She set you down, too, and she is no longer in charge of you," Nathaniel pointed out.

John nodded, conceding the point. "I am sorry for disparaging yer, Colonel, and Davy. I love that boy. I didn't mean any of it and certainly didn't want Helena to hear it."

"I am sorry, too, John. I thought that I did not have to ask permission from anyone to marry her, given her situation here and with her own father, but I was wrong. She has a father, and you have done a fine job raising her." He moved towards the man and bowed. "It is too late to ask permission, but I hope you accept me as her husband. I love her, John, more than life itself."

"Son of an earl, eh?" He grasped Nathaniel's arms. "She has done pretty well for herself."

~oOo~

Without Old Joe to visit on a Sunday, Helena had taken it upon herself to sort the contents of his house. Either Ruth or Nathaniel would accompany her. There were no valuables to speak of, just the house he had told Helena he had bought with Bertha. He had no family, so she supposed the house should revert to the Crown. As she scanned a box of papers, she found a note in Joe's handwriting dated the day she met Nathaniel at the shelter to present her proposals.

This paper is to stand as the last wishes of Joseph Baxter of the cottage down the lane off the North Road, Near Eastcambe, Lincolnshire.

I don't have much in this world except the love in my heart for my dearly departed wife, Bertha and our two children, who were taken from me far too early. Since Bertha died, I have sought to live for the day when I could join her, but I was surprised to find I still had some room in my heart for a dear woman with a child of her own who cares for me—I know not why. Mrs Andrews spurred a village to come together to repair my home and brought a young soldier into my life. I hope I was able to help by listening to him talk of his soldiering experiences. Something he felt he could share with no one. I advised him to put his pride aside and accept this woman for who she was.

The cottage and its land are all I have to leave behind in this world. I had thought to leave it to either of them, but as they already have a home at Redway Acres, they would probably give it to a worthy person.

So, it is my last wish that this home that gave Bertha and me so much happiness and sadness, such as life is, should be given to the young man who saved Colonel Ackley in Spain in June 1813. I believe his name is Tommy. Such bravery and heroism deserve reward, and he is in need.

Thank you, Tommy, and I wish you a good life and perhaps a Bertha of your own.

Old Joe

With tears in her eyes, Helena showed it to Nathaniel, who nodded in approval. Tommy and his mother could move to Redway Acres sooner than hoped.

~oOo~

Nathaniel loved his married life. He worked hard in the stable and made decisions with Helena and John, with whom he was finally friends. Issie and Davy accepted him as their father, and he shared his bed with the best of women every night. There was, however, one problem bothering him, and Nathaniel had an idea how to solve it.

Now and again, in the stable, Helena would flinch in recollection of her brutal experience at the hands of the general. If she were alone in a stall with a man, she would step out and lean over the stall door instead, even if it was him or John. He did not think she was even aware that she did it, but it hurt him that she should, even unconsciously, turn away from him in fear.

He recalled how he had reacted a year ago when Old Joe got on the back of Thor with him to go down to the tavern. That had been the first time someone had ridden on the back of Thor with him since his injury in battle, and the recollection had been painful and raw—until John had started laughing. On the journey to the tavern, he had told

Old Joe all about Tommy. Nathaniel's fond memory of Joe's humour and wise council had given him a different memory, leaving the old one on the battlefield where it belonged. He wanted to do that for Helena, give her a new memory in a horse's stall alone with a man—him.

He smiled when he thought of his plan because it was not entirely selfless. Helena had been almost virginal when he first enjoyed her body, and gradually, he expanded her horizons. She was undoubtedly an eager student. This was another step on that journey they could take together—one he planned to enjoy immensely. He had made sure that John kept the stable clear of people while he took his pleasure in his wife.

It was a warm summer day, and he entered the stable to find Helena alone. She was wandering the corridors, searching for everyone.

"Where have they all gone?"

"I have no idea. Come over here with me," Nathaniel beckoned her to the empty stall. It was banked with straw, not a sight of the dirt floor, as there had been on that day when she was only twenty. She hesitated at the doorway. He was lying in the straw on a thick woollen blanket and patted the empty side for her to lie on it with him.

"It is the middle of the day."

"As it was when you first seduced me, as I recall," he retorted. He wanted to reach up and pull her to him as she stepped cautiously closer, but he waited patiently so as not to startle her. She sat on the blanket and looked at her husband's lean body.

"I love you. Do you trust me?"

Helena nodded. "I love you, too, Nathaniel." she sighed in contentment and slowly lay beside him. He moved above her and kissed her gently. His kisses roamed her face and down her neck to the hollow where it met her shoulders. There he licked with his tongue and sucked gently. She moaned in pleasure. She loved how he would do these things before taking her.

Taking her—she tensed, and her eyes flew open. *Why am I panicking?* She was safe. She was with Nathaniel. He loved her—*why am I tense?* Because it was the middle of the day? Because any stablemen or even John could walk in at any time? Neither of those felt right. Because it was a stall, and that was where *it* had happened—*that was it.*

She had tensed and knew he must sense it, but he continued his gentle exploration of her lips, neck and face. He slowly loosened her bodice and flicked his tongue inside to the soft skin of her breasts.

Now that she thought of it, the only part of him that was touching her was his tongue. He was not holding her down so she could get away. She could escape, but why should she? His exploring tongue had found her nipple and was rubbing across it. Another gasp escaped her, and her tensed body relaxed, enjoying only the sexual tension that he brought out in her.

"I do love you so, Nathaniel." His eyes raised from his vocation, humour and desire warring in them. "I love your tongue." She nodded towards her exposed breast.

"Do you?" he asked, and after she nodded eagerly, he added, "Do you trust me?"

"Yes, my love, of course I do." Oh, when was he going to put that tongue to good use again? He moved his hand to reach below her skirts and between her knees. Slowly, and while keeping his eyes upon her, he pushed gently one knee aside and then the other.

"Trust me, my love. You need never be afraid of me."

She looked down at her breast, where her nipple waited for his mouth. "I think," she said tartly, "you should stop talking and use that tongue better."

He smiled broadly. "For once, we agree." He playfully lifted her skirts and disappeared underneath them.

"Nathaniel, what are you doing?" she could feel his hands exploring the insides of her thighs and his fingers parting her drawers to expose her and then, was that his tongue? "Nathaniel, oh my!"

She could say nothing more as his fingers moved from holding her drawers apart to holding her apart, and she pushed herself against his mouth. He continued to lick and suck her. His tongue flicked quickly, then washed over her. His fingers were moving again, and one long, strong finger slipped easily inside her, caressing in and out while he continued to lick and then a second finger. She was losing control.

He had brought her to a peak, as he had termed it, many times before, but never like this. Her skirts rose up her legs, and his head appeared beneath them. She plunged her fingers into his hair, moaning and writhing. With a final groan, her body bucked, and a last big wave of pleasure engulfed her. She clamped her legs on either side of his head. Her body continued to wrack with pulses as he withdrew his fingers and raised his head with a self-satisfied smile on his face. He had enjoyed it, too, it seemed, and she was glad because that meant he should be more inclined to do it again.

Looking at her husband kneeling between her legs, she smiled and then noticed a sizeable bulge in the front of his trousers. Oh, she would knock that smile off his face, and he should enjoy it. A thought had come to her while he was pleasuring her that she must be able to reciprocate in some way. She had learned how to give him pleasure with her hand and body, but now she had another idea. Sitting up suddenly, she barrelled him over into the straw and straddled him. He laughed with her and pulled her to him.

"Oh no," she said as he made to roll her over onto her back. "It is my turn to use my tongue."

Nathaniel was not sure he took her meaning, but her hands were getting busy on his body as she pulled his shirt from his trousers and pushed it up so she could kiss his chest. She undid his trousers while she slowly lowered her tongue onto his nipple and teased him. Then she ran her tongue, inch-by-inch, down the middle of his body, leading down to where he strained against the last vestiges of his clothing.

He moaned as she released him, and she looked up at him from all fours. My god, Helena looked like a temptress, with her red hair falling around her face, her bodice undone and revealing those full breasts he loved to touch, and her skirts raised high on her thighs. Was she going to do what he thought she might? Was it a sin to pray to God that she would? Or perhaps he should make a deal with the devil?

"Do you trust me?" Helena asked with a smile.

"Stop talking," he growled. Obliging, she licked her lips to moisten them and then stuck out her tongue and licked him from base to tip. All the while, she kept her eyes on his, and he held his breath. Then she took him into her mouth. *Thank you, God.* He let out all the air he had been holding on a single moan.

He could barely control himself, but he tried, how he tried, because he wanted the sensations she gave him to continue forever. She licked him, sucked him and scraped her teeth lightly along his length as her mouth moved over him. Her hand joined her mouth, wrapping around him and moving in time.

He tried to stop her. "You have to stop, or I will empty into you."

She pushed his hands away and continued until he could no longer restrain himself. It was his body's turn to buck and groans to escape his lips. Thoroughly spent, he lay on the straw, unable to move.

She lay on top of him and laughed lightly. "Nathaniel, you are full of surprises. That was so much fun."

"I am full of surprises?" he groaned and wished he had his breath back so he could take her to bed and do it all again.

Twenty-Five

As Helena sat working in the barn's office, she heard a commotion in the corridors and Nathaniel's angry roar, "Argh! What the blazes? Shit? Get back here, you little bugger. I will beat the shit out of you and throw it on your head. Let us see if you find that funny, boy."

Davy ran past her door and scampered up a ladder to the loft above. Stepping out of the office to look in the direction from which he had come, Helena saw Nathaniel striding her way, brushing straw and horse dung out of his hair and off his clothes. She laughed.

"Did you fall for the bucket on the door trick?"

Nathaniel did not return her amused look but walked into one of the storage rooms and picked up a crop. Horrified, Helena backed up to the ladder to prevent him from climbing it. She took one step up backwards so she faced him nose to nose. His anger was still bubbling, and my god, he smelled foul.

"Get out of my way, woman."

"Or what?"

"I beg your pardon?"

"What are your intentions if I do not move out of your way?"

"Just move out of the way. I need to discipline my son."

"Our son."

"Regardless, he still needs discipline."

"Because he played a trick on you?"

"Because he covered me in horseshit."

"That will wash off your skin and clothes, although I imagine you will still be full of it. How quickly will the sting of this crop wash off Davy's skin? Should I warn Issie to expect the same treatment?"

"No, of course not."

"What of me? Will you beat me if I do not let you pass?"

"No, never. I love you. I would never treat you that way. You should know that by now." In his anger, he failed to see the trap his own logic made.

"I thought I did, but here you are threatening Davy, whom you also profess to love. A grown man with a crop against a small boy. Perhaps these are your true colours?"

"You do not understand. It is different with boys. Boys need to experience tough love to help them face the realities of the world. They are beaten at school and in the army."

"Are they the reasons your father gave for beating you?" Helena watched his eyes as realisation dawned, sympathy drenching her heart. "Davy is not at school nor in the army. He is at home, where he should be safe. I think he has faced enough of *the realities of the world* for a seven-year-old, do you not?"

"Yes." Nathaniel hung his head, and she felt for him at the shame she knew to be washing over him.

She wanted to hold him to her. Hold the seven-year-old Nathaniel, whom his father had beaten. However, that would have to wait until later, as she had more to say.

"He's probably thinking you are going to send him back."

"No, never." His eyes showed defiance as he raised them again.

"I know that, but he does not. You would have done better to laugh when it happened. Rolled around in it with him, cleared it up and then had a bath together."

"Maybe I will play this trick on you so we can bathe together." He moved to press his smelly body to hers. His voice lowered with mock menace, "Do not think I missed that *full-of-it* comment."

He was deflecting her from his behaviour, and she knew better than to press him further. She jumped swiftly down from the ladder, pulling the crop out of his hand as she passed. Instead, she gave him a promise. "You do not need to play a trick on me for that, sir. I will ask Ruth to get a bath ready for you both." She laughed, tapping him on the bottom with the crop.

"Helena," She glanced back on her way out. "Thank you."

She nodded, and he climbed up the ladder.

"Davy, are you up here still?" There was no reply, but he heard a rustling that sounded bigger than a rat, so he thought it must be his son, "I am sorry, Davy. I will not beat you. Will you come out?"

"No, I do not believe you and I will not go back to Bainbridge."

Nathaniel sat at the hole's edge with his heels resting on the ladder's top rung. As was his habit, he rubbed his hand across his face. What was the matter with him that he had thought it acceptable to beat his son? He, who had cursed his father and cousin for their treatment of the boy, would do no better by him. Thank the Lord, he had Helena to talk him down from his temper. Why had he not just laughed at it like she said? It was, after all, a splendid trick. Not with horseshit, but possibly water or clean straw would be funny.

He started to laugh, and the more he laughed, the funnier it got. "You got me good, Davy." A snort of laughter came from the same direction as the rustling.

"Your face was funny." They laughed together now.

"Come on out, Davy. We need to talk."

"You will not send me back? You can beat me if you want to, but do not send me back."

Nathaniel closed his eyes on the tears he felt forming there. His heart was breaking for his boy. *What have I done? Have I irrevocably lost his trust?*

"Davy, men do not talk of love much. When I asked your mother to marry me, I did not just ask for the honour of being her husband but of being a father to Issie and to you. I said I would give my life for any of you, and it would be worthwhile. I still believe that." He opened his eyes and saw the boy standing next to him. "I love you, Davy. Nothing you can do will ever change that. Nothing."

"What if I were to—"

"Nothing."

"But what if I—?"

"Nothing"

Davy sat down next to him. His legs dangling into the hole, too.

"I am new to being a father. Neither of us started this when you were born. I am sure I will lose my temper with you again, and you will get angry with me, too. But I promise that I will never beat you, and I will never send you away. One day, though, you will leave me. It is what sons do."

"Will you teach me how to fight?" The question surprised him.

"Yes, I will and will teach you when it is right to fight. That is just as important. Also, I am warning you that I am good at playing tricks on people and will retaliate for today. You will not know when or where, Davy, but I am going to get you good."

The boy giggled, and Nathaniel reached over and ruffled his hair.

"We have some shit to clean up, my boy and then we will have a bath."

Nathaniel leant out over the hole, clasped his fingers on the opposite side and swung himself effortlessly into the barn below. Looking up, he was shocked to see Davy follow suit. He hung there, afraid. "Let go, Davy. I will catch you."

Davy let go immediately, and Nathaniel safely caught him. As his heartbeat steadied itself, with his son safely in his arms, he realised that his son's trust in him was restored.

~oOo~

John was preoccupied with his own ideas for several weeks. When the colonel asked him to clear the stable as he wanted to cure Helena of her unconscious fear of being alone with a man in a stall, he refrained from reminding the colonel that he had cleared a stable in the same way once before—when the general was beating Perseus.

No matter how wrong he considered it, John had wanted none of the men getting in the way of that. Of course, Helena had gotten between the general and his horse instead. John regretted his part in that often, so, this time, he decided to keep an eye on proceedings in case things did not go as the colonel hoped.

John did not consider what he would be seeing because he had not thought the whole thing through. He was no peeping tom, but once things had started and Helena was receptive, he could not move without making noise and alerting them to his presence. So, he closed his eyes tight, covered his ears, and sat there wondering because, in all their married years together, he had never put his mouth on Ruth in the place the colonel had with Helena. *How would Ruth taste?* Now, this idea was in his head, and he couldn't think of much else.

One particular day, he stopped over at the house with one excuse or another to see Ruth and look into her eyes, sweep her up in an embrace, or run his hands down her back.

"What has got into you today?" she said with a laugh after he had visited her for the third time that morning, but her eyes looked soft.

"You." He kissed her neck lightly. "How about an early night tonight?"

"But it is not even Saturday, John!" she exclaimed.

Once they had children, their time alone together had lessened, and though the children were older, they had not diverged from routine.

"How about sneaking home?" he suggested with a teasing squeeze of her bottom.

She batted at his hand with the cloth she was holding. "Have you been drinking, John Robertson? We both have work to do, so you had better go and get on with it." She swiped at him again, and as he left, she flicked the towel at his behind, slapping it. Pleased, he headed back to work.

Later that evening, Ruth lay on her back waiting for him, as she had often done. She said nothing as he got into bed, leaving the candles burning. *What has gotten into him?*

Leaning over her, he kissed her fondly and then with more passion. She returned his kisses, surprised at his attention to her lips, as over the years, the time spent just kissing had waned, as it did with married couples, she assumed.

"Do you trust me?" he asked.

"Of course I do, you silly bugger. I married you."

He didn't laugh as she expected but surprisingly moved his head below the covers.

"Where are you going, John?"

Suddenly, she felt his tongue—down there. What was he thinking of doing such a thing? After a moment, she didn't worry any further.

The next morning, Helena noticed a glow about her housekeeper that she had not seen before. It was the kind of glow that she had seen in herself ever since allowing Nathaniel into her bed. She sidled up to Ruth, who had mentioned how amorous John had been the day before.

"Did you have an early night last night?"

Ruth explained how John had surprised her. "Aren't yer shocked?"

"The first time Nathaniel did that to me, I thought he was mad for about two seconds, and then I no longer cared as it felt so delightful. Did you reciprocate, Ruth?"

Ruth stared at her. "You mean you—? Really?"

Helena explained what she had done, watching Ruth leave the room looking thoughtful. Helena chuckled; John should be getting a pleasant surprise.

~oOo~

Helena marvelled at the months passing so quickly as summer turned to autumn, and she added a governess to Redway's staff for Davy. As promised, Rachel was permitted to learn with Davy while still maintaining Issie's studies.

Isabella Ackley, as she liked to be introduced, continued to improve on the pianoforte and write her stories, which included a father and son dragon slayer. The new Ackley family spent many afternoons riding and picnicking as Davy learned his horsemanship skills. Persephone gave birth to Thor's foal—a colt they named Mjöllnir.

In September, Tommy and Enid Smithson moved into Old Joe's cottage. Their blue roan, Bessie, divided her time between Redway, when her master was at work, and the excellent stable Dom and some Redway men had built for her in Old Joe's garden. Enid started plans for her new, bigger garden for the Spring and worked with Mrs Dawley on the mending and sewing needed for Redway and the families that worked there. They added to their workload, now that there were two of them, by taking in washing as well.

By the end of October, the preparations for Dowager Alcott's property opposite Redway were completed. Everyone was excited for her arrival, but Davy most of all, as he had been working on his French with his father and wanted to impress the older lady with his burgeoning talent.

The timing of Dowager Alcott's move was perfect, as Mr and Mrs Ridgefield were visiting Eastease once again and brought with them Gennie's youngest sister, Milly. Everyone was invited to a lavish Eastease dinner.

~oOo~

As this was the first time Helena stayed the night at Eastease with her husband, she found it oddly pleasing that they were in the same rooms she had inhabited before. As she readied for dinner, she stood at the window and looked into the games room, where she had seen her husband twice before and wished herself in his arms. Almost as though he read her thoughts, Nathaniel embraced her from behind, whispering how much he loved her and what a view she had made at that window.

Dinner was full of good food and lively conversation about what had happened since their last dinner. Mr Brooks laughed amiably at Nathaniel's teasing of Helena's reprimands at that time, and she cast her husband a disdainful look as she bolstered the clergyman's pride over his more recent accomplishments with those in his parish.

In the drawing room, while they waited for the men to join them,

Mrs Ridgefield, sitting with Helena and Dowager Alcott, asked, "How are you enjoying Eastcambe, Janine?"

"I find myself very happily situated, I thank you. The maids and kitchen staff are settling in well, many of whom are escaping unfortunate circumstances. With Mrs Ackley's aid, I hope to help them help themselves. We have several soldiers currently on the opposite side of the house to my quarters, on whom they will practise their serving duties. Some of those men are in a terrible way, even if they are mostly healed from their injuries. The local doctor helps where he can."

Mrs Ridgefield seemed impressed. "It is an excellent service you are offering."

"My initial thought had been only to provide shelter for women, but then Mrs Ackley suggested the soldiers would provide them with someone to serve."

The bustle of the gentlemen joining them prompted Dowager Alcott to ask, "Are we to have some entertainment? I fear I am not much of a musician, but I enjoy listening."

"Have you had the pleasure of hearing Mrs Ackley sing?" Mrs Ridgefield asked. "She sang an aria at our dinner a year ago."

"Marvellous, simply marvellous," Mr Ridgefield added as he joined their conversation.

Dowager Alcott turned to Helena. "Oh, please do sing, Helena."

"Harriet has persuaded Nathaniel and I to sing together this time."

Needing no further encouragement, Harriet excitedly sprang up and walked quickly to the pianoforte. Confidently, she stood to its side and waited for a lull in the conversation.

"Many of you were here when Mrs Ackley, Mrs Andrews as she was then, sang a moving aria from Beethoven's opera, Leonore. It was Leonore's song, hoping for her love and sense of duty to give her strength to pose as a guard and free her husband, Florestan, from unjust imprisonment. At our Christmas ball, Colonel Ackley sang Florestan's aria. An emotional song of his loneliness, suffering and acceptance of death, only to see an angel in front of him who looked like his wife before realising it was her. So I have persuaded both singers, now married, to sing Leonore and Florestan's duet together upon finally being reunited. Colonel and Mrs Ackley."

Light applause followed them to the instrument, and they stood side by side next to Harriet, who had taken her seat and was ready to play. They had practised the piece often, with Harriet and alone with no accompaniment. Line after line, they alternated Helena and then Nathaniel in German,

O Nameless joy!
O Nameless joy!
O Nameless joy!
O Nameless joy!
My husband at my breast!
At Leonore's breast!

Then they sang together, their voices entwining and soaring higher with each repetition.

After unspeakable suffering,
So great desire.
After unspeakable suffering,
So great desire,
So great desire,
So great desire.

Alternating lines again.

You again now in my arms!
O God, how great is your mercy.
You again now in my arms!
O Thank You God, for this pleasure!
My husband, my husband at my breast!
My wife, my wife at my chest!
At my breast, at my chest!
It's you!
It's me!
O heavenly delight!
It's you!
It's me!

O heavenly delight!
Leonore!
Florestan!
O Helena!
Florestan! Florestan.

Stunned that he had used her name and not Leonore's the second time, Helena looked at her husband's face, taking in his tears. She faltered with her own tears at the second Florestan, bringing her head down to rest on his chest. He wrapped his arm around her. She could not tell if he had meant to say her name or said it accidentally, but she did not care.

They had missed the repetition of *so great desire,* but Harriet continued playing. They gathered themselves for the last part, alternating again and then singing the last two lines together in that embrace.

O Nameless joy!
O Nameless joy!
O Nameless joy!
O Nameless joy!
My wife, my wife at my chest!
You again now at my breast!
You again now at my breast!
O Thank You God, for this pleasure!
For this pleasure!

Reaching up, she gently wiped his cheeks. He brushed away her tears with his fingers and then caught her lips in his in a quick but nonetheless passionate kiss.

The applause, which had held off until they kissed, was loud in appreciation, as much to allow them to compose themselves. Helena looked around and noticed several ladies brushing away a tear.

~oOo~

Later, when everyone had gone to bed, Nathaniel entered the

games room in his shirtsleeves, his waistcoat unbuttoned, and his cravat hanging untied around his neck. Helena had gone to their rooms, where Rebecca was helping her undress and prepare for bed. He had looked at her pointedly and said, with a smile, that he would get a drink from the games room as a nightcap and should rejoin her shortly. Helena gave a smile of understanding and hurried Rebecca into helping her with her gown before shooing her away to her own bed so she could be alone.

With one candle lit, she went to the window she had looked out of earlier and pulled open the curtains. As before, Nathaniel was there, sitting with his head in his hand and rubbing at his face. This time, she knew he was waiting for her and would come to her.

He lifted his face out of his hand. *What is keeping the woman?* He looked up for the hundredth time. How often had he fantasised of this moment, when he could see her there and then go to her? There she was on the window seat—a vision that could take his breath away. Kneeling, she dropped the nightgown from her shoulders, letting it fall to her knees. He stood completely still for several seconds, shocked and thrilled, in equal measure, at her brazenness. Raw passion shot straight through him, from his eyes to his loins. He moved to raise a hand as if he could caress her over the distance, but he heard a noise behind him and spun around as if caught in the act of something illicit. Harker was in the doorway.

"What the blazes are you doing down here, Ackers?" he demanded. "Do you not have a wife to see to?"

"What of your wife, my friend?" Nathaniel smiled at Harker, praying Helena had closed the curtains again.

"I am on my way; you can count on that. First, pour me a brandy and pray, tell me more of your imprisonment in France," he glanced down at the scars on Nathaniel's forearm, visible below his rolled-up sleeve. Before Harker could sit down, Nathaniel approached his friend and put an arm around him.

"I will tell you, Harker, as I promised. But this kind of talk is not conducive to returning to our wives ready to please them. So I suggest we save this conversation for another day."

They walked out of the games room and up the stairs together, parting at the top to go separate ways.

Meanwhile, Helena wondered where Nathaniel had got to. She was hoping he would race to her as such would be his passion at seeing her naked at the window. It had felt very daring, and she could feel herself aroused at his stare, even from such a distance. She had seen him spin around and was talking to someone not in her sight, so she quickly closed the curtains and put on her dressing gown.

Peeking back out, she saw him leave with whomever he had talked to, and she moved to her door to look out for him in the corridor. His long legs were striding purposefully towards her, with that half-smile and half-bemused look only she could put on his face.

Nathaniel saw her standing there as he turned the corner. She was dressed in the white, silk dressing gown he had seen the night he had slept outside her rooms. He remembered wishing then that he could pick her up and walk into that bedchamber with her and deposit her on the bed to overpower. Well, now he could.

"My god, woman, you almost killed me with that trick." Taking the last stride to her, he scooped her up in his arms without stopping. "You are so very beautiful, Wife." He brought his lips down hard on hers. Gone were the days when his rough passion scared her. She felt thrilled that the sight of her naked body had driven him to this behaviour and answered his passion with her own.

Walking through the open bedchamber door, he kicked it shut, letting it slam. Striding to the bed, he threw Helena upon it, then joined her boots and all as he continued with his passionate kissing. He fully intended to enjoy every part of his wife's body, and before he took off a single boot, he had her naked on the bed.

1815

Twenty-Six

Helena stretched lazily in her bed with the horses carved into the headboard. The sun was well up in the sky, and it was unusual for her to be in bed at this time of day. She smiled.

In the same way as every day, she had woken just before dawn to get dressed and check on the horses and the men caring for them before she had her breakfast. Nausea had hit her immediately as she sat up, and she only just managed to get her face to the chamber pot when she cast up her accounts. A hand stroked her hair out of her face as she retched.

"Helena," Nathaniel's voice was groggy as he reached across the bed for her, but she could hear his concern. "I thought this illness had run its course."

"So had I. Perhaps it was just something I ate last night. I feel better for ridding myself of it." She pulled away, placing the pot on the nearby shelf and covering it with a cloth. Going to the washstand, she picked up a cloth and dipped it into the frigid water in the basin, applying it to her face to clean and her head to stop the pounding there.

Helena heard the bed move as her husband got up and walked over to her, buttoning his breeches as he approached. She had been sick several times over the winter and knew it worried him. He took the cloth from her and gently applied it to her pale face himself.

"Get back into bed, woman, and rest. I will see to the horses."

"But I must—" she protested, hating that he told her what to do, yet knowing more rest would be for the best.

"No. You must not. Rest, and I will ask Ruth to bring your breakfast to you. I will let you out of bed later if you can keep that down. Or perhaps I will get back into bed with you and assure myself of your wellness in my own way." He kissed her then but pulled a face. Her mouth tasted as bad to him as it did to her.

She shivered, so he picked her up easily and walked over to the bed. She forgave his hands for roaming over her curves before he covered and left her. It was reassuring that he still found her desirable after watching her vomiting into a chamber pot.

As Helena curled into a ball in the bed, she wondered what Nathaniel was doing. The horse stalls would all be cleared, and John would distribute the work list between the men, as discussed last night. Nathaniel had said he would ride Perseus today. She had planned to do that herself, but the stallion needed exercise, and she doubted her husband would allow her to ride today.

She cursed the timing of her being sick. Nathaniel probably would not have witnessed it if it happened later in the day, but then she wrapped her arms around her stomach and wondered contentedly how many children they might produce together over the coming years. Only the keenest eye would notice the swelling, and when she was naked, her husband's keen eye was not looking at that part of her body.

She felt she knew the time it happened. The time his seed had finally connected with her body to start a life—the dinner at Eastease when he had come to her after a nightcap, swung her into his arms and entered the bedchamber.

Nathaniel's kiss had been hard and urgent in its demand before he threw her onto the bed. He partook of her body in every way he could conceive. She had taken it all from him, and when he finally left them both, exhausted and satiated, she felt that, though his clothes, for the most part, remained upon him, he was as stripped bare as she.

A familiar sensation snaked through her at these thoughts, and she hoped he might make good on his promise to check how well she was in his own way, but she chastised herself. There was work to be done, and it was not her way to shirk her responsibilities.

Ruth had brought her breakfast earlier and voiced her suspicions to her mistress.

"When are you going to tell him?"

"When I feel it move within me. How long have you known?" Helena raised her eyebrows.

"Speculated about a month ago. So unlike you to be sick, but the colonel has not known you long enough to know that."

"I could never pull the wool over your eyes," she mused.

"Never. He is worried, though. Might worry less if you tell him." Ruth would not tell her what to do directly, as Helena was her mistress, but in the way of a mother could not resist making suggestions. Helena loved her for it.

"I think he would worry more, and then he will stop me working in the stable. He might even stop me riding." Despite Nathaniel tolerating her independent ways for the most part, sometimes he would put his foot down, and Helena would try to acquiesce as best she could. If possible, she would prefer to avoid having to do that.

"It might be for the best for a while."

"Nonsense. I rode with Isabella until I got too uncomfortable, about two months before she came. Even then, I could do a sidesaddle at a walk when I had no choice."

"Mr George said she would be born with hooves," Ruth said with obvious affection for her prior master.

Helena felt a pang of grief at the mention of her grandfather, and she nodded sombrely.

Ruth spoke again, "Now rest up, my dear. I will check on you later, or himself will have me up on charges of neglect of duties."

"Himself, your John, or himself, my Nathaniel?"

"Both of 'em colluding, I shouldn't wonder. I miss the time when they used to fight."

Dutifully, Helena ate breakfast and slept. Now, she gratefully found her stomach settled. She got out of bed and began to dress. Her maid, Mary, must have heard her and entered with some fresh linens to put away and her new day gown.

~oOo~

In early March, Helena set out for her weekly luncheon with Genevieve and Harriet—a habit they started while planning the Christmas ball well over a year ago. She had missed a few weeks over the winter due to bad weather and several bouts of sickness.

Thankfully, that all seemed in the past, however, Nathaniel insisted on driving her there, and he would visit with Mr Harker while the ladies lunched together. Helena planned to talk to Genevieve of her suspicions that she was with child, a fact that she had not told her husband, as the baby had not quickened, and she did not want to tell him until it had.

The visit did not turn out to be the pleasant diversion either of them had hoped. Within minutes of Nathaniel leaving the ladies to join Harker in his study, Harriet started crying.

"Harriet, whatever is the matter?" Helena asked.

Genevieve spoke above Harriet's sobs, "We have news that Napoleon has escaped his exile and is already gathering his armies in France once again."

"No. Oh no." Helena rushed from the room and towards Harker's study. The door opened before she could, and Nathaniel stood resolute in its frame.

She paused just feet from him, neither of them moving. He knew she would not want him to leave, but he would have to do his duty. She knew he would go out of a sense of loyalty but was scared for his safety.

"Colonel?" she asked, the word catching in her throat. He nodded before pulling her into his embrace and muffling her sobs on his strong shoulder.

~oOo~

Nathaniel's orders came through shortly after their visit to Eastease. In the nights leading up to his leaving, he joined his body to Helena's often. She would wake in the night and move into his arms. Their joining, which had frequently been playful and loving, became wistful and tender. They promised to write letters, and he vowed to return safely, their words whispered into the night air. After her first bout of tears in his arms at Eastease, she had not shed another, at least none he had seen. He knew when he left, she would shed more, but she was being strong for him.

Sleep eluded Nathaniel. Physical exhaustion from the day's labours and the night's loving were all that brought him peace, short-lived as it was. Otherwise, he would lie awake with visions of a Frenchman slicing his chest open or, worse, Duarte and the other men killed at the prison in Toulouse. He was not afraid for himself, but the stakes were higher than ever. If he were to die, he would be leaving Helena and the children, and that hurt him more than any sword could.

On a cold March day, when Nathaniel prepared to mount Thor, wearing his red coat and sheathed sword, Helena stood with her back straight and her head high. Their children ran to him and clung to him, with fresh tears on their cheeks, and all she wanted to do was the same. Cling to him and never let go, but she could not.

"Davy, Issie, that is enough now," she called gently.

Nathaniel straightened to gaze into her eyes as the children returned to her side. It was as painful for him to leave as for her to stay without him.

"I will be back before you know it," he said.

Would, but it was true, she thought. "Slay a dragon for me, brave soldier."

He smiled his wide, bright smile and put his hand over his coat pocket that held a new silk cravat, a dented horse pin and a drawing of the Dragon of Lincolnshire.

He bowed low, and Thor did the same.

"Anything for you, my Queen."

Nathaniel exited Redway Acres and spied the injured soldiers of Bernier lined up. They saluted him and played drums and fife while singing the marching refrain, 'The Girl I Left Behind Me'. Nathaniel had Thor do a passage-controlled trot in time to the drums as the two of them headed south.

The hours sad I left a maid
A lingering farewell taking
Whose sighs and tears my steps delayed
I thought her heart was breaking
In hurried words her name I blest
I breathed the vows that bind me
And to my heart in anguish pressed
The girl I left behind me

Then to the east we bore away
To win a name in story
And there where dawns the sun of day
There dawned our sun of glory
The place in my sight
When in the host assigned me
I shared the glory of that fight
Sweet girl I left behind me

Though many a name our banner bore
Of former deeds of daring
But they were of the day of yore
In which we had no sharing
But now our laurels freshly won
With the old one shall entwine me
Singing worthy of our size each son
Sweet girl I left behind me

The hope of final victory
Within my bosom burning
Is mingling with sweet thoughts of thee
And of my fond returning
But should I n'eer return again

Still with thy love I'll bind me
Dishonours breath shall never stain
The name I leave behind me

~oOo~

In the three months Nathaniel was gone, facing Bonaparte's armies with his brothers in arms and trusty steed, two notable visitors came to Redway. Both were part of his family but not seeking him out. Helena knew that the visits came because her husband was not there.

Firstly, a most astonishing visit came in April in the form of Lord Aysthill, with the other man, Davidson, walking close behind him. With Davidson present, Helena felt safe in accepting his request for a meeting with her. Ruth had left her study door ajar, and Helena, who could see out of the door from her vantage point, was grateful when John appeared outside. She subdued the small smile that crept to her lips.

"Mrs Ackley," Lord Aysthill began. His hesitancy surprised her, but she waited for him to continue, "I realise that the last time we met, I offended you with the offer of a stipend to assist in raising, ah—your son. Please accept my apologies."

Helena nodded, failing to see why she should make this meeting easy upon him.

He ploughed on, "I have done what you suggested and set up a fund for Davy Beckett."

"Davy Beckett Ackley," she corrected.

"Ah, quite. Well, we can add Ackley to it." He looked at Mr Davidson, who had been reaching in his bag for some papers. Nodding, he returned them. "And send them to you for safekeeping."

"You could have done that anyway. Why come here?"

"At our last meeting, you indicated that monetary restitution is not sufficient, and I would like to make an apology to the boy if you will allow it. Providing he will understand that I cannot admit that he is my—," he paused at the warning look she gave him, "that he came from me."

"He understands where he came from and does not seek that

acknowledgement. As far as he is concerned, he is proud of his father, whom he now considers to be Colonel Ackley, your son, which makes Davy your grandson. Perhaps you might consider acknowledging him as such?" Helena rose to leave. "I will go and talk to him and see if he is willing to listen to what you have to say. However, I will explain that he is not obligated to accept your apology or acknowledge you as his grandfather."

Moments later, she returned with Davy.

"Davy, do you know who I am?"

Davy nodded.

"I would like to apologise to you for what I did to your mother, that is, your other mother. I am sorry that she died. I am also sorry for not doing something about your situation at Bainbridge."

"J' accepte vos excuses."

"He said…" started Helena, but Lord Aysthill held up a hand.

"Je vous remercie, mais pourquoi en français ?"

"Je ne suis pas prêt à accepter en anglais."

"J'accepte vos conditions, monsieur," Lord Aysthill bowed. "If there is anything I can do that might help towards further acceptance, please advise me at once."

"I wondered if that old hag at the big house had got another chimney boy. Father told Smythe to be sure she didn't and told me there was a new device they could use instead. I should not want to think that I was lucky to get away from her, but another boy took my place."

Lord Aysthill gave an indulgent smile at Davy calling his cousin an *old hag,* but did not reprimand the boy.

"I will see to it immediately and ensure we are using the new devices at Aysthill House, too. Is that acceptable?"

Davy nodded. He never used more words than necessary.

"Would it be acceptable to you to call me Grandfather? I am, after all, Colonel Ackley's father."

"And Issie, too?" Davy asked, to Helena's surprise.

"Yes, Issie, too."

"I will go and ask her." With that, he ran from the room.

Lord Aysthill turned back to Helena. "Thank you. He is a tough nut to crack, like Nathaniel."

"And did you ever manage to *crack* Nathaniel?" she said with a toughness in her voice. After the incident with Davy, Nathaniel had told her of the beatings his father had perpetrated upon him.

"No." Lord Aysthill gave her a hard stare before sighing. "Young Davy doesn't only look like him. For now, He will only accept my apology in French. I expect the acceptance in English will be worth the earning. I had no idea how smart he is. I suspect the French is Nathaniel's doing?"

"And that of our new neighbour, Dowager Alcott."

Helena did not elaborate as he seemed to want to say more. "I—I would like to assure you that my behaviour with his mother was the only time with one so young. My only defence is that I had drunk far too much that evening."

"Well, let us hope for the sake of all fourteen-year-old girls you refrain from drinking so much in the future."

"Will anything I do ever be enough to please you?" he asked bitterly.

"I do not know, but I do not understand why it is so important to you."

"Neither do I."

The two children raced back into the room. Issie curtseyed. "Grandfather, I am Isabella Ackley. Would you like to hear me play the pianoforte?" With that, they each took the older man's hand and led him to the drawing room, where the instrument stood waiting.

~oOo~

Helena's second visitor arrived in the warmer month of May in a formidable carriage with many footmen in attendance. The Bainbridge crest was emblazoned on the side, and the sight of it sent Davy into a panic, thinking that she had come to take him back. Despite his mother's assurances, he ran to the stable and shadowed John the whole time the woman visited.

Lady Grace Bainbridge stood in Helena's parlour, refusing a seat or refreshments. She spotted Ruth's small garden out of the window and gestured to it.

"That seems to be a small but well-tended garden, with no horses roaming around. I should like to take a walk there, Mrs Andrews."

"Mrs Ackley, Lady Grace," Helena corrected.

"Hmmm. We will see."

Upon reaching the garden, she took a turn around it, criticizing everything. It was not a prim garden; the various flowers and vegetation were allowed to mix and meld together to form a complementing whole. Ruth would have been hurt to hear the critical words, but Helena allowed the woman to have her say and waited for her to get to her real point for the long trip from Norfolk.

"Do you remember who I am?"

"Yes. You are my husband's cousin. We met two Christmases ago at the Eastease ball."

"I am Colonel Ackley's cousin," she said in a tone that made Helena feel she was being corrected. "Being family, I am, therefore, interested in what he is making of himself." She looked back at the house and towards the stable and sneered. "I demand to be satisfied as to whether you are actually married to him."

"I believe I have already confirmed, twice, that I am." Helena was shocked at the question, wondering what the woman knew. She was unsure how long she would tolerate this woman's snide looks and insulting comments about her and her property. If she preferred Bainbridge so much, she should have stayed in Norfolk.

"I understand that you would like the whole world to think that, Mrs Andrews, but I had a man follow your route almost a year ago. You never made it further than the Lakes."

"I am of age. There was no necessity to go all the way to Scotland. It makes no difference where we were married."

"My man informs me that no record of any ceremony exists. You do not acknowledge propriety? You do not give my cousin his due? No respect or trust."

"I have shared everything with my husband. What you see here is *our* home, *our* business and *our* children. I do not understand. Do you want me to be married to him, or do you not?"

"It seems you are doing neither."

"You are severely deluded to think that Nathaniel would marry you *if* we were not. He could have done that at any time had he the inclination. Why do you want to marry him?"

"He is the son of an Earl from a powerful family, a respectable soldier, injured in battle. He would not have had to return to battle if he had married me. He would own a grand estate larger than Eastease, and with his marriage to me, granddaughter of the previous Earl of Aysthill, his position in the world would be far greater than that of his friend. He would be accepted in all the best society."

"You mention all these great places and wonderful society, but you do not know Nathaniel at all. He would not be happy with any of that. You want him only for his name and position, to mould him into something he is not. You sneer at Redway, but he loves it here. It is his home, and it suits him. He works with me and the men to care for and raise horses. He teaches our children to ride and work—to achieve something with one's endeavours. I married him because I love him. You mentioned nothing of love. He loves our children and me. He will never leave me."

"And yet he is not here."

"Duty calls him away. He could have chosen to stay here, but he is an honourable man. I am proud to call him my husband."

"Perhaps he wishes to remove himself from your brood of bastards." Lady Grace's snide glance took in Helena's swollen belly,

Helena felt as if Lady Grace had physically slapped her. Without a response, she turned to walk away from the woman, around to the front of the house where the carriage was waiting. Lady Grace followed, calling out to her retreating back, "You have no secrets from me, *Miss Billings*. All of your children were born outside wedlock, and this one will be no different. How about I spread that all around the county? The respectable Mrs Ackley no more. Unmarried and three children, every one a bastard, each with a different father. Two of the fathers are from the same family. What would Nathaniel do then?"

They had reached the carriage, and Helena laughed, which confused the other woman to no end. How happy his cousin would make Nathaniel by putting about the rumours that would ensure she would have to marry him.

"Madam, you have left no stone unturned in your insults. I ask that you leave our property immediately."

"Do you admit that you are not married to him?" Grace asked after climbing back into the carriage.

"I admit that I have made my vows to my husband, and he has done so in return. Where and in front of whom this took place is of no concern of yours. Good day."

~oOo~

Nathaniel felt the force of the cannon blast behind him and heard the scream of his horse as half of its rear flank was blown away.

Thor landed heavily on Nathaniel's right leg and thrashed around in agony. Nathaniel's sword, drawn in battle, had been thrown from his reach. With each thrash, Thor moved the saddle and stirrups painfully against Nathaniel's trapped leg, but he could not extricate himself. He tried not to scream with the pain, as he was vulnerable and sooner or later the enemy should discover him, but he would rather it was later. Looking back, he saw Thor's left leg and hind quarter were utterly gone. His trusted friend was done for, and he grieved.

Withdrawing his pistol, Nathaniel aimed the barrel at Thor's head. He heard running and hoped it would be allied forces, but he heard French spoken. If he shot the first man, the second would kill him anyway. He only had one shot, and his sword was out of reach. Not wishing his friend any more pain, he pulled the trigger.

"Thank you, Thor. It was an honour."

When a blade was placed in front of his neck, he closed his eyes and pictured Helena lying on a picnic blanket, reaching for him. As he waited for the slice, he prayed the Frenchman's blade was sharp.

Instead, the blast of a pistol assaulted his ears, and the body of the man fell across Thor. Nathaniel grasped the fallen man's sword, but it was not needed. His own men surrounded him. They lifted Thor enough to get him out from underneath the animal, but his leg was bad. Agonising pain shot through him as he attempted to bear weight on it, and he passed out.

Twenty-Seven

Helena was close to a month away from giving birth to their child when word reached Redway of Nathaniel's injury. Travelling as far as Aysthill would be difficult, but why did they send him back to Aysthill instead of Redway? If he considered her his wife, his place was with her, even if he was injured. Mr Harker had been to see him and reported back that his leg was crushed when Thor had died and fallen on him. She knew that he would feel the loss of Thor badly. The doctor recommended the removal of the leg at a point above the knee before gangrene set into the damage, but Nathaniel refused. Helena knew why.

She had talked to Tommy of a young woman from the village who always seemed eager to see him when her work brought her to Redway. He had said he would not be a suitable husband with a missing limb. Nathaniel would be thinking the same. Tommy, however, did not have a wife already as Nathaniel did. Unless, of course, he was considering that he did not, and what did that say of the vows he made with her in the shelter? She couldn't bear to think of it.

"John's back," Ruth said, peering out of the window at the sound of a horse outside. A moment later, John entered the kitchen and placed a sheaf of papers on the table while taking off his coat and hat.

Helena, still seated at the kitchen table, eyed the document sceptically. "What is that?"

"He wants you to sign. He's relinquishing his share of Redway back to you."

"Has he lost his mind? Did he say why he had them take him to Aysthill instead of here?" Helena knew her anger to be covering her heartbreak.

"He says he wants to die in his family home. He said he wouldn't burden you. I'm sorry, Helena."

"He does not need to die. He could still do so much with only one leg. Did he say anything about my letters?"

She had written to him several times, but the letters remained unanswered. She was unsure if he had even received them, knowing his mother wanted him to marry Lady Grace.

"I told him a loss of a leg would make no difference to you, but he wouldn't listen. He's stubborn."

"He has decided that he should choose for the both of us. Did he learn nothing from our courtship?" Helena demanded of John, appealing to the kind, weathered face of the man who had been more like a father than her own.

Here was the one man who had been a constant in her life, who had comforted, protected, and advised her. He had taught her all he knew, as a father would, and now had done the best he could to bring her husband back to her.

"I reckon his brain got a knock when he fell with Thor," John sighed.

Her love, her heart was fewer than ten miles away, and he refused her upon the misapprehension that he would burden her. That decided it then—she should go to him and either talk or knock some sense into him.

"Saddle up Colossus, please, John," she said with a determined look. "I will talk some sense into Nathaniel myself."

"Get some sense into yourself first. You cannot ride in your condition, not even that big ol' softie. That bairn is almost ready to pop out."

Helena stared at the man she had just been considering like a father, and now he was behaving like one. He must have seen the determination in her eyes, for he relented. "How about I drive you in the coach?"

After she had readied herself to be received by Lord and Lady Aysthill, she collected one of the new wooden legs Tommy had made and climbed into the carriage. The new style leg included a joint to enable an amputee above the knee to ride.

~oOo~

As the journey progressed, she felt riding the horse might have been more comfortable. She braced herself as best she could in the rocking carriage. Halfway there, she felt a dull ache in her lower back, another mile, and unmistakable pain ripped through her body. Her child had picked an inopportune time to begin its journey into life. Recollecting the long process of birth and that she was nearly a day bringing her daughter into the world, Helena was determined to see her visit through and get home in time. She worried that the bairn was a little early, but perhaps her calculations had been wrong.

Only one more pain gripped Helena before her journey's end, and by the time John opened the carriage door, she had composed herself again. Gathering her skirts and the wooden limb, she walked to the door, confident that a servant would have spotted her arrival. Sure enough, Edgars opened the door promptly and led her to a small feminine sitting room, requesting she wait for Lady Aysthill. Laying the leg on the pretty coach, she remained standing. Given her condition, she could not fathom attempting to rise from a chair in that woman's presence.

"Mrs Andrews," Lady Aysthill greeted her as she entered.

"Mrs Ackley, Lady Aysthill," she corrected.

"That will be all Edgars. Mrs Andrews will not be staying for refreshments." In the countess' hands were Helena's two unopened letters. She threw them on the sofa next to the leg. "Take these and that monstrosity with you when you leave. As you see, they are unopened. My son does not wish to see you."

"He never even saw these letters. You kept them from him."

"No, he did not want to open them. He does not want you."

"I know your son, Lady Aysthill. He thinks giving me up is best for me. However, he does not know of the child that I am carrying. I told him of it in those letters. If he had read them, he would reconsider."

The pain of the oncoming child ripped through her once more, and she grasped the back of the sofa to steady herself.

"A bastard child because you refuse to marry him." Lady Aysthill used Helena's pause to interject as she interpreted her vice-like grip on the sofa back as anger. Helena realised that Lady Grace had been busy imparting her knowledge to Nathaniel's relations.

"I refuse to marry any man and relinquish my property. To become property myself, no matter the man. I do, however, love and respect your son and would marry him in an instant if the law would change to make man and wife equal, as I believe they should be. I have already shared my property with him as an equal partner. I have given him more than his own family. He gets nothing from you because he is your second son."

"What is the use of ownership of a stable when he cannot run it? When he cannot work with the horses and has to watch others' enjoyment because he can only sit and not ride. I know my son, too, and he would not be happy when horses and riding are such a passion for him."

"Is he happy now? Is he happy without me? Would he be happy never knowing he has another child?"

"No, he is not happy." Like an engine that had run out of steam, Lady Aysthill sank into the armchair close to her side. "My angelic boy, with the happy smile and infectious laugh. He no longer laughs or smiles. He will not try and plans only to die."

"I can make him happy again. I know I can. He is a strong man, and he can ride with this leg. I have brought a horse with me that will suit him." Helena hoped she was getting through to the woman and thought to try and remove a thorn. "I know you cannot be happy that

Nathaniel and I took in Davy, but he is a wonderful boy, and so like Nathaniel. An angelic boy with a happy smile and an infectious laugh. What happened to his mother was never his fault." With a sudden understanding, she added, "Neither was it yours."

The countess paused at that observation. "That is very astute of you. I have blamed you for so much. Father and son have been at odds since that dinner at Eastease. My husband apologising to all the women he has wronged, taking time and money. Your success in hiding behind the notion of a dead husband, but most of all, you taking Nathaniel's heart and refusing to marry him."

"I am sorry you feel that way."

"None of it is *actually* your fault, of course. I know that. I have written to Grace suggesting she visit and tell Nathaniel that he could marry her. All ease would be afforded to him, being her husband and the master of Bainbridge."

"And what was Lady Grace's response?"

"I heard nothing despite all my efforts in promoting that woman in the past. Even at the cost of my relationship with my son."

"She fears the stigma of a husband with only one leg."

"Why do you not?"

"Because I love him. I know what he is capable of, even if he doesn't, and because I would do anything for my children who need us both."

"You do love him. You have come here and withstood all my ill-judged insults. You have done right by the son of the young girl, my husband wronged so badly, and then sympathetically tell me I am not to blame. He has not apologised to me," she said simply.

Helena guessed she meant Lord Aysthill. "Men are stupid."

"Nathaniel will die if he does not have that leg removed. Do you think you can persuade him to do it?"

"I can try."

~oOo~

"Helena, you should not be here."

"It is you who should not be here," she looked at Nathaniel in his bed in a grand bedchamber, "you should be at home, at Redway."

"We are not married, Helena. Everyone here knows it. My home is here."

"I will not sign those papers, Nathaniel." There were tears in her eyes. "Redway is your home, I am your wife, and you have three children. This one is making its way into the world right now."

He suddenly noticed that she was carrying his child. In his pain, he had not seen it, "I am sorry, Helena. Once again, you have borne so much while I have been away. I cannot burden you with more."

"What I cannot bear is a life without you in it." A pain ripped through her again and tore away all her patience with him. Her eyes narrowed as she looked at him. "My vows to you were real, Nathaniel. I meant every word. It does not matter to me that we were not in a church before your God. No matter that there is no legal document to attest to my vows, so I am under no obligation to keep them. Yet I do, every one, because there has never been another man I have cared for in this way, and as long as you are in the world, there never will be.

"We vowed forever to each other's hearts. We vowed in sickness and in health, but you are not sick, Nathaniel. You can recover from this and are strong enough to work beside me. You would not be a burden. What of your vows? Were they only words? Did they not matter to you because they were not legally bound or in a church?"

"Of course, I mean them. Of course, they matter, but if I were to let them do this, I may be in pain every day."

"Why do you not understand? If you die, I will be in pain every day." Another spasm ripped through her. She groaned loudly, suppressing a scream and grabbed his hand, squeezing tightly.

"Now is the time to press your advantage, Wife. Any woman worth her salt should make a request of her husband."

"You have to choose this, Nathaniel. Ask yourself this—if our roles were reversed and I was the one choosing to die rather than live my life without a limb, willing to leave you to raise three children with no mother, willing to leave you with an empty bed. What would you say to me? I have to leave and have our child at Redway. Please choose this, and get strong and well again. Come back to us. Do not let this be the last time we see each other."

She bent to kiss him, a soft, gentle kiss, and then hurriedly left his rooms, only to run straight into Lord Aysthill.

"There you are, my dear. Did you talk him into it?" She shook her head, tears streaming down her cheeks. "Leave it to me; I think I have just the right thing to say."

"Excuse me, Lord Aysthill. I must leave." She walked as quickly as she could to the stairs but paused to look back at him. "My Lord, there is a woman you forgot to apologise to—your wife."

~oOo~

Helena all but collapsed into John's arms when she managed to get out to the carriage.

"What is it? What happened?" His concerned face swam in front of her.

"The baby is coming, John. Take me home."

"But you should stay here. They could get you the care you need."

"I will not have my baby here. Get me back to Redway. There is time. Issie took all day."

John helped her in and closed the door. Helena braced herself in a corner when it rocked as John climbed up to start the horses.

Her relief at being on her way home did not last long. Another pain engulfed her as her stomach tensed into a tight knot, and she felt pressure between her legs. Had it even been ten minutes since her last pain? She knew the closer they came, the sooner the baby would arrive. Was it more painful than with Issie, or was it just her predicament that sent a lance of fear down her spine? How much she missed her grandfather's presence. He had been so reassuring during Issie's birth.

I won't let anything happen to you, Gal. How she wished she believed in an afterlife—some place from where her grandparents could send the strength she needed to see this through. Tears assailed her at the realisation that she had imagined Nathaniel would be with her during this time. He would have held her hand and caught the baby as she pushed it out. Instead, she was alone and faced a future without him simply because he refused to live with only one leg. Why couldn't he understand he was forcing her to live the rest of her life without her heart?

I will survive this. I will survive heartbreak, and I will care for our children by myself.

When the next pain came, anger emanated through her, and she swiped at her tears before her scream rent the air.

~oOo~

Nathaniel cried out as an incredible pain shot through his crushed leg. He tried to blow out the air captured in his chest as his body spasmed. Was Helena's child birthing pain greater than this? He couldn't imagine worse.

Unannounced, Nathaniel's father barrelled into his rooms, seemingly jolly despite Nathaniel's pain. After seeing Helena in the throws of childbirth, all Nathaniel wanted was to wallow in self-pity as he waited for death to claim his miserable, sorry soul.

"I just saw that *wife* of yours', boy. Still a fine-looking filly, even with a belly full of your bastard."

"Keep your eyes to yourself, old man," Nathaniel managed to growl as the wave of pain swept out of him. He was in no mood for the man's antics. Hadn't Helena written that he had apologised to Davy? It wouldn't be beyond his father to have been playacting.

"What are you going to do about it, boy? Once she has had that bairn, I might go and console her on the death of her husband. See if I cannot get her to give me some of what you have been having for the past year."

"She would not have anything to do with you."

"What could she do once I let it be known that I had her? Your share of Redway should be mine as your next of kin. Unless, of course, she can produce evidence of your marriage."

"Harker would stop you."

"Harker? No, he should not bother me overly. You, on the other hand, were ruthless. I imagine you could protect that woman even with one leg, but you will not be there. I could even get Harker to let me stop with this ledger idea of his."

The older man stood up to leave. Then he was stayed by that chilling voice he remembered from when Nathaniel threatened him.

"Get Doctor Grosvenor here and tell him to bring his saw."

~oOo~

Halfway home, Helena had a strong urge to push but did not feel right. She called out and banged on the roof of the carriage. It stopped, and the door burst open. John stood there looking worried.

"You have to help me, John. Something is not right." She had already manoeuvred out of her petticoats and drawers before pulling at her skirts, but he stepped backwards.

"No, I can't do that, Helena. 'Tis a woman's business."

"John, how many foals have you delivered? Get in here and help me, for goodness sake. I need to know what is going on."

John glanced briefly beneath her raised skirts, his expression changing from embarrassment to practical at observing Helena's predicament. "Baby's wrong way round. I can see a foot. Don't look like that—we can do this."

"Thank you, John." Panic rose in her throat, but his calm manner soothed her somewhat.

"I could try pushin' the foot back in and turnin' tha bairn around."

She nodded, but before he could try, she was wracked with another pain. The urge to push was too strong, and John reached out to support the baby.

"I 'ave two legs an' a bottom. There's one hand, but only one. I could reach in for t'other?"

Helena could only nod, groaning with the discomfort of him reaching inside her.

"One arm is still up inside the womb with the head. I'm goin' to hook a finger around to bring that down. Then yer'll have ta push the head out."

With that done, she took two immense pushes with the most incredible pain she had ever felt, but she had no other option. To Helena's relief, the baby started crying immediately, and after John had cut the cord, Helena wrapped him as best she could in her petticoats. Then, she staggered into the nearby wood to deliver the afterbirth.

Unsteadily, she emerged to see Doctor Grosvenor's curricle stopped beside her coach. He was not within it but inside her own, no doubt examining her son. What a relief it was to see the kindly man.

John spotted her leaning against the last tree and came over to scoop her up easily in his arms. "Doctor's orders," he imparted before she could protest, though honestly, she felt very weak.

"Mrs Ackley," the doctor greeted her as John deposited her in the carriage. "Your son seems healthy aside from being rather small. Congratulations."

"Thank you, Doctor. It was an ordeal. We could have done with you a quarter-hour earlier."

"Nonsense. You both managed admirably. I will come by and check upon you on my return. I am heading to Aystill House to see your husband. I assume that is where you have been."

"Yes, though I don't think I reached him. Will you try, Oliver? Please try."

"Of course I will. I have brought my equipment with me in the hopes that I will need it and can save him. May I tell the colonel he has another son?"

"Yes, please do, Doctor."

He handed the baby to her before turning to head into the woods. No doubt he intended to inspect the afterbirth. As John closed the door and moved to the driver's seat, Helena decided to try feeding her son. It would take her mind off how painful it was to sit in a rolling carriage. When they were on their way again, she allowed the tears to fall upon the tiny bundle in her arms.

~oOo~

Nathaniel screamed at the first cut of the knife into his thigh. He tried to take his mind away from Doctor Grosvenor, slicing through his flesh as the pain continued unabated. Earlier, he could not imagine worse but needed no imagination now. Still, this pain, like Helena's in the Redway coach, was purposeful. How scared she must have been to give birth to their son the wrong way around, still she had done it and then gone into the woods alone to take care of the afterbirth. He knew no one as strong and determined as Helena and was proud to call her his wife.

When they had lifted him onto this table, his father insisted on aiding the men pinning Nathaniel to it. Two men from their stable held his hips and legs while Edgars and his father held down his shoulders.

I will survive this. I will hold my son in my arms and protect my family. Helena. Helena. Nathaniel hadn't realised he spoke aloud until his father replied in a most caring voice that was so unlike him. Nathaniel was distracted from the pain momentarily.

"You will, son. You will. I have a confession. I could not bear to see you throw your life away. I could not bear to continue to watch you die when it is only recently that I have come to appreciate the kind of man you have become. I said what I did to make you take this action and save your life. Your sense of duty is so strong you would bear anything yourself to protect your wife and children. I am proud of you, Nathaniel."

Sweat beaded on Nathaniel's forehead and poured down his face to join the tears in his eyes. "Thank you, Father," he whispered before the grotesque noise of saw on bone began bringing more unbearable pain. His screams faded in his ears as blessed oblivion consumed him.

Helena struggled to open her eyes despite the sound of her baby crying. John had carried her to bed upon their arrival, and Ruth had tenderly taken the baby from her arms to clean him. She couldn't remember the baby being brought to her. She must have fallen asleep instantly, but a glance to the side of her bed confirmed he was within the small cradle and had kicked off his swaddling.

She tried to move, but every limb was as heavy as lead, and her head throbbed an objection.

"Ruth," she called, but it came out of her as a weak whisper. "Ruth."

Thankfully, the baby had no such constraints and filled his lungs, protesting his hungry belly and the cold air. The door opened to a stern Ruth, whose face was immediately swathed in concern at seeing

Helena. Helena thought, *I must look very unwell*, but then succumbed and knew nothing further.

Twenty-Eight

Nathaniel lay in a sweaty mess for over a day while a mild fever raged in his body. Though no longer in excruciating pain from his crushed leg, the stump that remained was swollen and painful. He tried to concentrate on the hope of seeing his newborn son soon—of holding Helena in his arms once more and enjoying the laughter and antics of Davy and Issie. He knew he was recovering within a few days because he wished to be out of bed as much as possible.

He was surprised not to have further word from Redway or even a visit from Doctor Grosvenor or Harker. Determined to know of more beyond the four walls of his bedchamber, he moved to the edge of the bed and looked down at his shortened limb still wrapped in bandages. A wave of regret assailed him. He would be dead by now if he had gone through with his plan. Doctor Grosvenor had only given him a couple more days had he not had his leg removed.

He shook himself. If he were dead, he wouldn't have the prospect of seeing his son grow. But how would he live? How would he ride? He would have to get used to riding with a wooden leg as Tommy did. Thor was dead, and most likely, a docile horse, like Brownie, who they used for other soldiers to learn to ride, was in his future.

The door to his rooms opened, and his long-time friend entered just in time to lift Nathaniel's spirits.

"Harker, how are you? Thank you for coming to visit. Have you heard of Helena? Are she and the baby well?"

Harker's sad, brown eyes locked on his. Nathaniel felt like he had been run right through the heart. "What is it, Harker? Helena? The baby? Tell me, for God's sake, man."

"The baby is fine. Helena is in a bad way, Ackers. She has an infection."

"Help me, Harker, I have to go to her." He made to stand, but Harker touched his shoulder and pushed him back.

"No, there is no point in risking an infection yourself. Helena does not know where she is or who is around her. You have to get better for your children."

"Oh, my God!" Nathaniel rubbed his hands over his face as the tears welled inside him. He could not hold them back. "How can I live without her?"

"How did you expect she would live without you?" Harker said it without recrimination, but it hit home much the same.

"This is my fault. If I had been at Redway or had this damned leg removed straightaway, she would not have been visiting here. She would not have had the baby in the coach and got an infection. I have been so wrong. She called me on it. She said her vows to me meant everything to her regardless of where they were said, but that I did not act the same way because they were not said in a church, with a legal document. I saw it as a way out for her, but she did not want one." He looked at his friend. "We are not married, Harker."

"I know that." He looked at Nathaniel with a wry smile. "What woman would take you?"

Nathaniel allowed him the poke. "Is she going to pull through?"

"The doctor does not know. We have to wait."

"This is how she felt. I never considered it. Will you keep coming back and let me know how she is? Please?"

"Of course. Either the doctor or I will visit. Every day if we can."

~oOo~

Nathaniel's father came back to his rooms. "I am sorry to hear of your wife, son. I hope she pulls through."

Nathaniel stared at the man before him. Who was he? His father had never spoken to him the way he had during the surgery. Nathaniel assumed his father did not give him any thought at all. He was the spare, not the heir.

"Thank you, Father," was all he could think of to say again. He had confirmed with Edgars that it had not been a figment of the pain and feverishness that had caused him to hallucinate his father's confession.

"Heal up quickly, Son, and get back to her. She needs you." He put his hand on Nathaniel's shoulder, and Nathaniel leaned his head against the man's arm for a moment. His father quickly left before things got embarrassing for them both.

~oOo~

Helena was conscious before she could raise even a finger. Everything ached. As had been the case the few times she recalled surfacing from the depths of her illness for mere moments, Harriet sat across from her, reading a book. Helena moved her head, gasping at the pain the simple movement caused, and Harriet looked up from her book before springing into action.

"Helena, are you back with us?" Harriet placed a cool hand on Helena's forehead. "Your fever has broken. Thank the Lord." She ran to the door to call for Redway's housekeeper.

"Nathaniel?" Helena managed to croak, ready to hear the words that would add a broken heart to her broken body. There had been moments these past few days that she could have succumbed to the pain and let go of her earthy coil, her spirit floating off who knew where. Only the thought of her children without a mother or a father kept her connected to the world.

"He is well, Helena. Do you not remember me telling you before? His leg is gone, and the word from Aystill is that he is getting stronger."

Helena's body shook in its attempt to cry in relief at the news of Nathaniel, but she did not have enough moisture to form tears. She touched her dry, cracked lips, and Harriet reached for a cup to help her drink.

After a few sips, she felt able to say more. "The baby? Tell me everything. How long as it been?" Helena managed to sit up a little and shakily hold the cup while Harriet fussed with her pillows before sitting down again.

"Little Nate is five days old now. We have a wet nurse for him, and he is growing well. Everyone is healthy. We are so blessed, Helena. So blessed to have you back with us."

"Little Nate?"

"You never gave him a name, so we thought, as he is Nathaniel's son—Little Nate."

Helena gave a small laugh, but pain ripped through her chest at the effort.

The door burst open, revealing a surprised-looking Ruth. "Oh, my child. My poor, dear child. I knew you would be spared. You had to be, but you gave me such a fright."

Ruth rounded the bed and sat on the edge before pulling Helena into her arms. Harriet grasped the cup to avoid a spill, and Helena managed a weak embrace of Ruth.

"Hurts, everything hurts."

Ruth stood and collected herself, brushing the creases out of her apron. Helena clasped her hand and squeezed a little.

"Lilly is bringing a tray up for you. Eat as much as you can. You need to eat to get your strength back."

"Yes, ma'am," Helena responded with a smile. "Stay and join Harriet in telling me what has been happening."

With a tray groaning with food that she could not possibly eat entirely, Helena lay propped up in the bed and listened to two of the women who had cared for her. Everyone in her household and beyond had stepped up to help, for which she was humbly grateful.

"This silly girl would not leave your side," Ruth began with a gesture to Harriet and then the couch, which held a pillow and several blankets. Her voice was tinged with respect, however, and no doubt gratitude that Harriet being there spared her double duty of caring for Helena and running the household.

How tired everyone must be, Helena considered.

"My mother died of an infection after the birth of her stillborn child. Oh, Helena, I could not bear to lose you too."

"On those times when I surfaced briefly, I remember seeing you the most, Harriet. Thank you so much for being here."

"Still, Ruth insisted I take some breaks. She and Enid Smithson took over my duties at that time."

"Oh, Enid!" Ruth exclaimed with a roll of her eyes. "She's a hard worker and such a treasure, but every time she saw the children, she spouted such doom and gloom. *Poor babies. Father and mother are both battling their problems and who knows what the outcome will be? They need them both but might end up with neither.* I told her to keep her voice down. Your babies didn't need to hear that."

"Have you told them I am well?"

"They are having their meal and can see you after they are ready for bed. They have been reading to you, so I'm sure they will want to continue. You need a wash first, though. I would open that window if it weren't so cold tonight."

"I'm going to stay the night and return to Eastease tomorrow. We've sent word, and I have no doubt Gennie will want to see you."

"Has word been sent to Aystill?"

"Alexander has been visiting Nathaniel. He will go tomorrow and inform him."

Helena was exhausted. Her eyes drooped, and when she woke again, it was getting dark outside, and the children were creeping into the room. She was wearing a different nightgown, so someone had washed and changed her, but Helena had no idea. She smiled to reassure Davy and Issie before they leapt upon the bed. Helena had enough energy to embrace them and listen to a story before she slept again.

~oOo~

It was fully dark when she woke to a baby's cry. Ruth had promised she would bring the baby in when he woke again. A wet nurse had been feeding him, but Helena hoped it wasn't too late for her milk to come in. Her happiness soared at the sight of her and Nathaniel's son. Red tufts of hair covered his pate; his eyes were his father's startling blue. Time would tell if they remained so.

She tried him at her breast, knowing the wet nurse was waiting in the wings to take over if she failed. Tears filled her eyes, blurring the image of her baby kneading her breast to encourage the milk forth, but her body was not obliging. He cried in frustration, and she willed herself not to believe it was a rejection of her.

"Keep trying," Ruth sympathised. "You will manage it. Just make sure you try to feed him before the wet nurse each time." She took the screaming baby and handed him to someone just outside the door. In only moments, Little Nate was quiet again.

Ruth returned to straighten out her blankets and fuss over her.

"Sit down, Ruth."

The woman Helena had thought of more like a mother than her employee perched on the bed, and Helena grasped her hands more firmly than she had managed earlier. Their tears breached their eyelashes and ran down their faces.

"Thank you, Ruth," Helena spoke with more emotion than expected. "What would I do without you?"

"What would our world do without you, Helena? You are pivotal in the lives of so many people and animals. I hope that thick-headed man has finally realised how lucky he is to have you in his life."

"He will be happy that we must now marry, given his cousin's revelations around the village and beyond."

"We will see."

~oOo~

As soon as he could get out of bed, Nathaniel insisted on going out to the stable. His mother had told him that Helena left him a suitable horse, and he wondered which it was. Nathaniel managed to manoeuvre to the stable using a crutch, followed by his manservant, as were the man's instructions from Lady Aysthill. It took all his effort, and he was breathing hard when he got there. The stable manager greeted him with a pull to his forelock. "Colonel."

"Frank, my wife left a horse under your care before she left."

"She did indeed, sir. Bit of a handful, not sure you can handle him."

Nathaniel's head snapped around to look at Frank and then

moved more quickly towards the stall the man indicated further down the row. Could she have left her favourite horse for him? It would be just like her to think of such a thing. He looked in at the stall.

"Perseus!" The horse was thrilled to see Nathaniel and came to the half-door, putting his head over it. He nuzzled against Nathaniel, nearly knocking him over. "Whoa there, boy, you have got to be gentler with me now. I only have one leg to stand on."

Frank came over and gave Nathaniel a letter. "John said to give it to you when you came to see him." He gestured towards the horse.

"Thank you, Frank. Can you get me some carrots for him?"

Frank left him to read the note that Helena must have written before she visited him. Nathaniel sank gratefully onto a nearby stool.

My darling Nathaniel,

I am so happy that you have decided that your life is worth living, and to live it with me and our children.

Come to us when you are ready. Tommy can visit and show you how to use the leg with the saddle. He has adjusted your spare saddle to accommodate it. He will help you learn.

Perseus is yours. I give him to you with all my heart. I know you mourn Thor, and no horse can replace him. He was so wonderful. Perseus will, I am sure, understand your injury and work with you.

Ride him home when you are ready. We will all be waiting. I love you, my husband.

Helena Ackley (Mrs)

Nathaniel looked up from Helena's letter and saw Harker striding towards him, holding two carrots by the stalks. He had a big smile across his face. Nathaniel's heart raced in anticipation of his words. Surely, only one thing could make him smile like that, and it was not the carrots.

"Her fever broke," such was Harker's greeting. Nathaniel blew out a long breath that he had not even realised he had been holding. "Look at you, up and out of bed. Today is a good day." Harker grasped Nathaniel's arm that he had held up for help to stand and retrieved the crutch. Perseus had already reached over the stable door and helped himself to one of the two carrots that Harker had forgotten. He gave the other to Nathaniel to feed to the horse himself.

"Is that not Helena's horse?"

"Mine now, she gave him to me," he handed Harker the note.

"Hell of a woman."

"Yes, she is."

"Are you going to marry her properly?"

"In a heartbeat, but I do not need to own her. She is mine. She has been more of a wife than I have been a husband. We made vows to each other, and she took them as seriously as if they had been said in church. I did not see it that way, and I should have. Do you think she will forgive me?"

"As parched as she was when she woke, her first word was *Nathaniel*."

"Then I have a chance."

"With all the speculation your cousin unleashed after Helena threw her off Redway property, you need to marry her."

"I have something else in mind, but I will need the help of my father and Mr Brooks."

"Really? Let me know if you need me at all."

"Maybe a celebration?"

"Genevieve and Harriet will love it."

After Harker had left, Nathaniel made his way back to his rooms. The manservant tried to help him as sweat poured profusely from his forehead and into his eyes, but Nathaniel stubbornly pushed him away. At the bottom of the stairs, he stopped to catch his breath and peered upwards where the treads waved like the ocean and the handrail coiled and stretched like a snake. His head swam with nausea, and strong arms surrounded him before he could fall to the floor.

"It seems I arrived just in time," Tommy's deep voice boomed as he scooped Nathaniel up in his arms and climbed the stairs, his wooden leg thudding with every other step.

Plonked unceremoniously on his bed, Nathaniel finally caught his breath. "Where did you come from?"

"I got to the stable barely a minute after you'd left, so I followed you in. Just as well I did."

Exhausted, Nathaniel rolled over, and purpose filled his mind. *I am going to learn to ride a fiery horse again. I'm returning to Redway the way I left it—healthy, strong and able to work side-by-side with my fiery wife.*

Promptly, he fell asleep, comforted by Tommy's presence.

~oOo~

Tommy was gone when he woke in the night, and a tray of cold meats and bread with wine was left on his table. He was hungrier than he had been since arriving at Aysthill and was no longer tired, so he ate and set his mind to write the apology Helena was owed.

My dearest wife, Helena,

How can you forgive me for the pain I have put you through? Still, I know you have a generous heart, and therefore, I feel brave enough to ask you… Helena, I beg of you to please forgive me.

Your words did reach me—I want you to know that. When I woke after the surgery, Harker arrived to inform me of your illness. Suddenly, I was the one in the position of possibly facing the rest of my life without you. The pain of my leg was nothing, nothing compared with the pain of my heart, and to think that I could have inflicted that upon you, all the while thinking I was doing what was best.

I should know by now that you would be right.

Please forgive me for not honouring our vows as I should have. I put the emphasis on the venue rather than the words. Vows said between husband and wife are what is binding, not the location in which they are said. If God is everywhere, surely He was in the shelter with us when we spoke of what was in our hearts so softly to each other. He should be equally angry with me for breaking the vows of my heart I made to you then, as He would be if I had said them in church.

You have proven yourself my wife in everything, and I only ask you to give me another chance to prove myself equally, as your husband.

I love you more than life. I am ashamed that I was too quick to give up that life when the most important thing is to live my life as long as possible and spend every breath that I have remaining with you, with our children and in your arms.

I will return home to Redway and our family soon—riding to you on the magnificent horse you gave me when I least deserved it.

Thank you for getting yourself well again and sparing me such pain. I wish you a speedy recovery and send my love to our three children.

Ever your faithful husband,

Nathaniel

Twenty-Nine

On an early August day, Helena sat in the drawing room with her three children. Her six-week-old son was in her arms, her six-year-old daughter was at the pianoforte, and her eight-year-old son was reading a book and lying on the floor at her feet. All of them, but the baby, looked up when they heard hooves outside the front of the house, and the two older children ran to the window to see who had arrived.

"Papa! It is Papa on Perseus," they sang in unison and ran to the door. Helena's heart was singing, too. She stood, breathed deeply and then followed them.

Nathaniel sat straight and tall on Perseus. She could see the wooden leg strapped to the saddle supporting the thigh of his right leg. A crutch was strapped to the side of the saddle so he could use it when he dismounted. She smiled up at him. He looked strong and healthy. Just to look at him was delightful.

Nathaniel was not fully prepared for the sight of Helena framed in the doorway with his three children. He stared at her, trying to imprint this vision into his mind. Despite her recent illness, she still took his breath away. He smiled at her and then dismounted as fluidly as he could. He had to lead with his left leg swinging over the horse to the ground, and then his stump came out of the hollow of the wooden leg, leaving that still strapped to his horse. Finally, he grasped the crutch and pulled it out of its strappings to use.

"Papa!" Issie and Davy ran at him. Helena wanted to call out to them to be careful so as to avoid bowling him over, but she stopped herself in time. She had decided that she was not going to fuss over him. She stared as he held tightly to the boy and girl who loved him and had missed him so much, afraid he would disappear if she stopped looking.

She did not move but held his gaze as he came towards her.

"Helena, my love, my heart, my wife. Please forgive me." He picked up her hand that was not holding the baby and brought it to his lips.

"There is nothing to forgive, my husband." She moved her hand to his cheek. He looked at the baby—his son, his second son.

"What did you call him?"

"I have not. I wanted to wait for you. I seem to recall you are good with names."

"How about Nathaniel Joseph Harker Ackley?"

"Perfect. He is already known around here as Little Nate."

"Kiss Mama," demanded Issie. Nathaniel looked at Davy.

"Could you please hold your brother a moment, my son?" Davy smiled.

"Then will you kiss Mama?" he asked.

"If she will allow it."

"Nathaniel, be very sure," she handed the baby to his brother, "the infection left me unable to give you any more children."

"You have given me a daughter and two sons, and we have each other. What more could a man ask for?"

"Marriage," she whispered, unheard by the children who were happily chanting their 'Kiss Mama' request, "your cousin—"

"No," he cut her off, "I do not need to marry you. My vows remain the same as when I made them to you. They would not be better or stronger if they were legally binding. I will be better at adhering to them, though."

"Are you sure, Nathaniel? Please be sure."

He leaned heavily on the crutch and put his hands up to her cheeks. A sob caught in her throat and was smothered by his passionate kiss.

~oOo~

That night, as Nathaniel prepared for bed, he felt as nervous as he had when he was a virgin. How was she going to react to the stump of his leg? She had not worried about the scar across his chest, and she had healed the scars of his heart, but this was greater than any of those. Now he only had one knee for support, Nathaniel was unsure of his ability to do what he had been able to before. Helena had straddled him in the past and may be willing to do so again, but he wanted to take his wife, not just be ridden himself. He was also unsure how she was feeling. Was she even well enough to receive his attentions? He had not asked.

Putting on his nightshirt, he left his dressing room and entered their bedchamber. They had always shared the large bed with the horse-carved headboard. Helena watched him approach with a welcoming smile. "This bed has seemed too big without you to share it." She frowned as he got into bed, still in his nightshirt. They had always been naked in bed before, and she was naked now. She sat up in bed, pulled back the covers, kneeled, and faced him as he lay there.

"Look at me, Nathaniel."

He was looking at her. How could he not? "You are extraordinarily beautiful, Helena," his voice was thick with emotion.

"And yet I see how much my body has changed since you saw it last, and I worry you will no longer find it appealing. While feeding our son, my breasts are heavier and lower, and the tips are sometimes sore and cracked. My belly is soft and lined from carrying him within me, and I was stretched once again from birthing a second child. Within, I was so ravaged by infection that I can no longer bear you children, and I wonder if that makes me seem less womanly in your eyes."

"None of that makes any difference to me. You are as you have always been, Helena. The most magnificent woman I have ever known, and I will always be in love with you."

"Then why do you not think that I should feel the same way about your body, my love?" She looked at him expectantly.

Smiling though still nervous, Nathaniel once again wondered

how the woman managed to be so right all the time. He sat up and pulled his nightshirt over his head. When he summoned the courage to study her reaction, his smile turned wry at her gaze, taking in the part of him showing her he still found her beautiful.

Reaching out with a firm hand, she stroked his hip and ran her hand down his thigh to the stump. He flinched, but she was looking at him with affection and love. Leaning back on one hand, he brought the other up to her face, then down her neck and to her breast and felt the heaviness of it before running his thumb up and over her nipple.

Moving closer, she straddled him and caught his lips with hers. It would seem she, too, thought this might be a good starting point for them as they relearned each other's bodies. He pulled her to him with one strong arm and ran his tongue down to a nipple. However, before she could warn him, he received a mouthful of her milk for his efforts.

She laughed as he spluttered and swallowed, and he looked up at her. "I am sorry, Nathaniel. My body is not entirely mine or yours for the moment, while our son needs me to feed him. I am afraid you will have to be a little less rigorous."

His laugh died in his throat at her moan as he moved himself against her. "Some things are different; some remain the same," he managed as she rose above him and slowly took him into her. "I missed you, Helena."

"Oh, Nathaniel, I missed you, too."

~oOo~

He lay naked next to his wonderful wife. She had turned to sleep on her side, and he had moved his body up against hers, in the same position they had adopted two years ago when they had been caught in that first storm together. He ran a finger down the familiar scar on her back. He kissed that scar to claim it for himself the night they had first come together. She had opened up for him then, and they had enjoyed an animal kind of mating, which he had fantasised of whenever he spent a night away from her.

He had thought her asleep, but she moved her bottom against him and rolled onto her stomach in encouragement. He pushed his stump between her legs, and she allowed him to push one of her legs up with it gradually. She did not flinch or move out of his way. He loved her so much for her acceptance of that part of him, but he was worried about keeping his balance on one knee while he took her.

A pillow hit him in the face.

"Take me, Nathaniel," she moaned. Helena had worked it out, of course. He rested his stump on the pillow, moved entirely between her legs and pulled her up to him. She was strong and gave him some support so he could reach a hand around and find that spot between her legs that she loved him to please.

This was right. This was being a man and taking the woman you loved. He had won her trust, her love and the right to her body that no other man had ever had. She did not consent for him to use her body this way because she was married to him and owned by him. She did it because she wanted to, chose to because she loved him. She made him feel strong and whole. He heard her breath quicken, and her moans become more demanding. Thrusting faster and using his fingers in the way she loved, he felt her body peak. Her muscles pulsed around him as he emptied into her.

~oOo~

Helena could not take her eyes off her husband. She was so happy he was there and would not leave again. She had been the strong one for so long that she had forgotten how to be anything else. However, while she was ill, everything had gone on without her. Now she was back at the helm, but she realised, in a way that she had not when they were together before, that she no longer had to do it alone in any area of her life.

Every time they came close together, they touched somehow, somewhere. Nathaniel would run his hand down her back, she would touch his hand or cheek, he would tuck a tendril of her hair behind her ear, she would put her hand up to his chest, and their eyes followed each other all day. Everyone else kept laughing at the pair, but they were all happy to see them back together.

During their early morning walk around the stalls, when

Nathaniel could catch up with all that was happening, Helena did her daily inspection of Missy, who was close to foaling. On this day, the horse was restless in her stall, swishing her tail and looking at her sides. Helena narrowly avoided a hoof as the mare kicked at her own abdomen.

"Let us keep a close eye on her today. Her udder is distended, too. She could be in the beginnings," she soothed the horse, assuring her they would be there for her. "Have you checked the paddock fences, John?" she teased, recalling the last time Missy had foaled. Almost two years ago, Missy had escaped Redway's paddock and foaled in an outlying barn, where Helena had then spent the night caught in a storm with Nathaniel. They locked eyes, both thinking of that night and how far they had come.

This would be Thor's second foal. Mjöllnir was almost a year old. She knew this would mean a lot to Nathaniel. He had told her during the night of his choice to kill Thor, as he had lain trapped under him. She understood because she would have made the same decision. "He knew you loved him right to the last." Then, they both cried over the loss of a dear animal.

Missy gave birth to a filly later that day. They named her Freya. Thankfully, there were none of the complications Missy experienced during her last foaling, and the skies remained clear, not a drop of rain in sight.

~oOo~

With Nathaniel's return, the rumours about Helena's husband were rife. She told him she had heard from their neighbours of a man visiting the village who talked of no marriage between her and Nathaniel. No one could give her a name for the stranger, and she had asked how much stock should be put into a stranger's words, putting doubt into their minds of his validity. Most of Eastcambe's inhabitants agreed they should rather believe the word of the colonel, who had earned their respect working on Old Joe's house, and Helena, who had served so many people. Still, some would stoke the fires, for their own amusement, without considering the ramifications to their children.

Helena had detailed Lady Grace's visit. While she had no evidence, she suspected the man who had talked of them in the village was the same one who had tracked their progress last spring when they were supposedly on their journey to get married.

With the discovery of his father's improved opinion of Helena, Nathaniel had broached a subject with him that might deal with the rumours and continue to allow him to be with Helena without compromising her wish to be a person of her own free will. To that end, he met with his father at Mr Brooks' house a fortnight after his return to Redway.

"A pleasure to meet you again, Mr Brooks," said Lord Aysthill, having been shown into the clergyman's small parlour.

"My honour, Your Lordship, I assure you. Colonel Ackley." He bowed to each man in turn. Various pleasantries were exchanged while refreshments were served. "How may I be of service?"

"We think you can help with a woman's reputation. As you may know, some people say that my son here and Mrs Helena Ackley are not truly married," began Lord Aysthill. "Complete nonsense, of course. Admittedly, they did not take the more traditional route to matrimony, but I can swear they are married. We felt an acknowledgement of the marriage in church, as part of the Sunday service, might put the matter to rest. What say you?"

"It is a little unorthodox, but I suppose I could come up with some suitable wording to bless the union."

Nathaniel doubted the clergyman could refuse Lord Aysthill anything. However, the man surprised him with his following words.

"I would not have refused Mrs Ackley such a service, even if she had asked me directly. I am happy to help friends and neighbours. Mrs Ackley, if I may be so bold to say so, has made a big difference in my life."

"Mine, too, Mr Brooks," replied Nathaniel.

"And mine," agreed Lord Aysthill. "Quite a woman you have saddled yourself with, my boy." With that, the ennobled man let out a loud guffaw as he smacked his son's shoulder.

"Father, you are exactly right."

Epilogue

And so it was that two years to the very day of their first meeting, Helena attended church with Nathaniel for a blessing of their *marriage*. Family, friends and neighbours crammed the church pews to observe the first of this kind of event in their church and the rare sight of Helena's attendance.

"I am enjoying having you in my church, Mrs Ackley," Mr Brooks informed her as they waited for the crowd to settle.

For her part, Helena had submitted herself to the ministrations of her friends and her maid. She was dressed in a lovely gown and a small veil. Nathaniel stood by her side in front of the pastor, looking resplendent in his regimentals and using the new leg that Tommy had made for him, he stood without a crutch.

Mr Brooks' voice rang out clearly.

"Nathaniel and Helena, you have committed yourselves to each other in marriage, in the will of God, the union of a man and a woman, for better, for worse, for richer, for poorer, in sickness and in health, to love and to cherish, till parted by death. Is this your understanding of the promise you have made?"

"It is," they both said, exchanging smiles.

"Nathaniel, have you promised to be faithful to your wife, forsaking all others, so long as you both shall live?"

"Willingly," he said fondly and then in a clearer voice, "I have."

"Helena, have you promised to be faithful to your husband, forsaking all others, so long as you both shall live?"

"Always," she said softly and then, "I have."

"Heavenly Father, by your blessing, let the ring already given be to Nathaniel and Helena a symbol of unending love and faithfulness and of the promises they have made to each other through Jesus Christ our Lord."

"Amen," bellowed through the church.

Having bowed his head for the prayer, Mr Brooks looked up at the congregation. "Nathaniel and Helena have affirmed their promises in their marriage here today. Will you, families and friends uphold them in their marriage now and in the years to come?"

"We will," echoed behind them, followed by a raucous cheer. Everyone not attending the Eastease celebration knew that Colonel Ackley had provided a generous sum to the tavern for free drinks.

~oOo~

Helena's friends generously hosted a lavish party at Eastease. Many local families and friends attended, including Mr Brooks, of course. When an opportunity arose, he approached Helena.

"My first time doing that kind of ceremony, but a special request from Lord Aysthill is not to be ignored. Does this mean I will finally see you more often at Sunday service, Mrs Ackley?" He smiled at his own humorous comment.

"It was very good of you, Mr Brooks. It would seem I have much for which to be thankful." Helena returned his good humour.

"Undeniably," he agreed, his wry smile acknowledging she had not answered his question. He tried another. "Am I right in thinking that you and the colonel are not *actually* married, Mrs Ackley?"

"My vows to Nathaniel are steadfast, and I hold them in my heart.

Do you think God sees that, Mr Brooks?"
"Indeed, I do."

~The End~

Poor Old Joe (sheet music)

Redway Acres
Maria (sample)

By
Trish Henry Green

1812

Prologue

The first words Maria remembered hearing were, *Why are you not more like your sister?* She and Harriet were so identical not even their mother could tell them apart until she spent a minute with either one. Their mother would often lament that Maria cried more than Harriet as a baby, demanding more attention, whereas Harriet would coo and be content to look at her surroundings or play with her toes. Harriet received more cuddles because she would lie still, and many praised her good behaviour, amiable nature and pleasant temperament. Everyone found it much easier to love Harriet.

"And how can I blame them? When I am the one who loves Harriet the most."

"I beg your pardon, Miss?" Maria's maid looked up from fashioning her hair into a suitable style for dinner while Maria tried not to fidget on the cushioned seat.

"Just thinking of my poor, dear mother giving birth sixteen years ago today."

"Two identical babies. God bless your mama's soul," the maid replied. "How did she manage?"

"I am sure I did not help. I was so inquisitive and, after being set down, would get up, insist on doing things for myself, and be frustrated when I was not allowed."

"If you can sit still for just two minutes more, I will have finished this style. You look beautiful, if I may say so."

"Thank you, Lottie. You are very patient with me."

"How did your mother tell you apart? I am sure I can't."

"Harriet would be the one with her nose in a book reading aloud to me. I would be the one relaying what we learned to all and sundry. I knew every country in the world by heart. Their trade, their capital city and the languages spoken and would make up stories about explorers discovering new countries," Maria said as she wistfully recalled driving her mother, nanny and governess to madness with her constant questions and then questions about the answers she received.

But her thoughts turned sad, recalling Eliza died in childbirth six years later with the baby who had never taken a breath—the son of Maria's stepfather, Lieutenant Mark Wyndham, a naval man.

That man was one of two people in Maria's life who accepted her for the curious, mischievous creature she was. Mark had been a wonderful stepfather with infinite patience when answering her questions, giving her the confidence to know, figure out, and be up and about. She still missed him. Mark Wyndham had died at Trafalgar several years prior when she was nine years old.

The second person was her cousin, Nathaniel Ackley, who joined the army. Maria wished she could join the military. It seemed to her to be an extraordinary life, full of travel and danger, sword fights and excitement—much more interesting than music and sewing. Nathaniel was fun-loving. He enjoyed playing tricks and sneaking food from the kitchen. Their stepfather had named Nathaniel as one of their guardians. The soldier sometimes visited with his younger friend, Robert Davenport, who had engaged Maria's attention with exciting stories of London and Europe.

Maria sighed. For the first time in many years, Mr. Davenport arrived this afternoon and gave gifts to herself and Harriet. He was charming and attentive in the absence of their other guardian, Alexander Harker, the owner of the Eastease estate in Lincolnshire where they lived. Two new feelings had assailed Maria's sensibilities upon Mr Davenport's arrival—a desire to feel this man's attention upon her and resentment that Harriet seemed as determined as herself to dominate his time.

Despite their early losses, Maria could not deny that life had been good for herself and her twin. Though their mother had only a short time with Lieutenant Wyndham, they both understood how much that couple loved. The handsome lieutenant would arrive home and look lovingly into their mother's eyes. Growing up, Maria wondered if a man would ever look at her with such love. After this afternoon, she pinned her hopes firmly upon that man being Mr. Robert Davenport.

~oOo~

Earlier that afternoon, Maria practised a fun piece of music on the pianoforte with Harriet when the Eastease butler, Watkins, opened the drawing room door. Unfortunately, Maria had just bumped Harriet off the instrument's stool more violently than she intended and was bending over to help her sister when a man in his late twenties entered the room. Their laughter came to an abrupt stop.

"Mr. Robert Davenport," Watkins announced. "Should I arrange for refreshments?"

The servant exited when Harriet confirmed he should.

"Mr. Davenport," Maria greeted him with a curtsey, feeling the heat of a blush rising in her cheeks. "Welcome back to Eastease. It has been several years since we have enjoyed your company."

"Miss Maria?" Mr. Davenport asked, bowing and smiling when she nodded confirmation. "Miss Harriet."

"This is a surprise, Mr Davenport," Harriet confirmed. "Please take a seat."

As one, Maria and her twin moved to the couch of a conversational grouping, and Mr. Davenport took the armchair across from them.

"I made my way north as soon as I realised the date's significance. A happy birthday to you both. I can hardly believe you are sixteen already."

"Thank you, sir," they replied, exclaiming over his offer of neatly wrapped gifts.

Maria quickly secured the jewellery around her neck and wrist whilst Harriet demurely set hers aside, placing the delicate lace handkerchief neatly on them.

"You are very generous, Mr Davenport," Maria confirmed, admiring her wrist adornment and fingering the silky handkerchief lace.

"It is the least I could do for two young women after missing several birthdays."

"Then you are entirely forgiven," Harriet said politely. "Alexander returns today from visiting a friend in Cambridgeshire, and the colonel hopes to escape from his duties for the weekend."

"It will be good to see them both and enjoy some Eastease hospitality while I visit," Mr Davenport confirmed.

Maria could not contain herself. "But Mr. Davenport, there is to be a ball on Saturday to celebrate our birthday. You must attend. I insist."

Harriet was less forthright, but Maria could see the excitement in her eyes. "If you can attend, Mr. Davenport, we would be most grateful. I would be."

He turned his hazel-eyed gaze upon Harriet, and Maria keenly felt the sting of losing his attention. "I would be delighted. There is, however, one problem. How do I choose which of you wonderful ladies to dance with for the first pair of dances? Would that it were possible to dance with you both at the same time."

"Mr. Davenport, you are incorrigible. You will have to choose one of us," Maria said coyly, pleased when he turned his whole body towards her, his gaze running up and down her figure before resting upon her eyes. He ran a hand through his thick brown hair, his mouth opening slightly. *This is it*, she thought. *He is going to ask me first.*

"I believe it will be expected of us to dance the first and second pair with Alexander and Cousin Nathaniel as they are our hosts and guardians," explained Harriet, who was always aware of what was appropriate.

"Oh pooh!" exclaimed Maria. "You are right, Harriet. I am afraid, Mr. Davenport, that we will have to disappoint you. Assuming, of course, that the colonel makes it here in time."

"He will be here," defended Harriet. "He made a promise, and I have never known him to break one."

Maria nodded her agreement.

"Then I will have the equally difficult task of choosing who to dance with for the third pair," Mr. Davenport interjected into their discussion.

"The third pair I have already promised to the younger Mr Parker when we visited his grandmother last week," explained Harriet, properly saying no more.

"Then, my dear Miss Harriet Wyndham, if you will consent to dance the fourth with me, I would be honoured," declared Mr Davenport, seemingly not put out by being delayed. Harriet agreed.

Maria, however, was most put out. He graciously asked Harriet for the fourth and assumed she should be available to dance the third with him. She cleared her throat.

"My dear, Miss Maria Wyndham, if no young, local gentleman has been so lucky as to procure *your* hand for the third pair of dances, could I ask you to honour me?"

Maria beamed, pleased he realised she wished for the same deference as her sister.

"Yes, thank you. It would be my pleasure."

Alexander strode into the room with Watkins close upon his heels and a footman carrying the refreshments tray. Alexander greeted them with affectionate embraces and best wishes for the day, calling them *his girls*, as he always did.

Bowing, he addressed his friend. "Davenport, to what do we owe this unannounced pleasure?"

"Sorry for not writing ahead, Harker. It was a spur-of-the-moment decision as soon as I became aware of the day's importance. I came to wish these delightful young ladies a very happy birthday and brought several gifts for the occasion."

Dutifully, Maria showed Alexander the gifts Mr Davenport had brought them, holding out her wrist to allow a closer view of the trinket.

"We have invited Mr. Davenport to stay at Eastease and attend our ball on Saturday night," she declared as a fait accompli.

"If that is acceptable to you, sir," Harriet added, glaring at her.

Maria shrugged. *How can Alexander expect us to do less after the man's generosity?*

"Of course," agreed Mr. Davenport, "Harker must approve first."

"You are welcome, Robert, but do you not wish to stay with your father?"

"I will visit with him while I am here, but seeing you and Ackers and enjoying the Misses Wyndham's entertainment should be much more fun."

Ackers was Nathaniel's childhood nickname.

Maria let out the breath she had been holding, a broad smile spreading across her face as she gazed into the warm eyes of Mr. Davenport.

One

In his opinion, Robert was proven right. Dinner with Harker and the Misses Wyndham was a much jollier affair than it would have been at his father's household. He entertained them with impressive tales of his travels around England, parties and balls in London, pretty ladies and dashing gentlemen. Miss Harriet and Miss Maria regaled him with details of the ball on Saturday night.

"I wonder if I might get Ackers to play the pianoforte, and we men could entertain the ladies with a song or two for a change," Robert speculated, looking forward to seeing Nathaniel. He had hoped, of course, to see his closest friend while he visited, but you never knew with the man's soldiering duties when he might get leave. Still, as a colonel now, he should be able to come and go more freely, surely?

"Providing you sing songs suitable for our girls' ears, Davenport," said Harker with a teasing smile. "I am not just considering Harriet and Maria. I have invited the Hopwoods to stay at Eastease, and they have three young daughters."

"And is Mr Woodhead joining us too?" Miss Maria asked. "You said he was interested in one of the Hopwoods, I recall."

"Yes, and it would be a good match for the Hopwoods should Samuel secure Miss Martha's hand. Mr. Hopwood has little by way of income to maintain his property of Thornbane. Therefore, it is imperative for at least one of the girls to make a good match."

"Would not a connection to Eastease be considered a *good match*, Harker?" Robert asked with a laugh as he turned to the young women who joined in his amusement. "Are we to see the most eligible bachelor in Lincolnshire snapped up, finally?"

Robert was surprised to watch his friend's cheeks suffuse with colour as he almost choked on his wine.

"Oh, which is it, Alexander? Do tell us? Which Miss Hopwood do you like the best?" Miss Maria asked with a laugh, but her guardian refused to answer her probes.

Instead, he continued, "Samuel and the whole Hopwood family plan to stay here for a month at least. They should arrive tomorrow afternoon."

~oOo~

When the ladies withdrew from the dining room, Harker poured two glasses of port from the decanter, handing one to Robert. "I am glad you will visit your father while you are in the vicinity, Robert. When did you see him last?"

"It has been several years. With Ackers in the military, I have not had cause to come this way until now."

"Except to meet with your father," suggested Harker gently. "Don't forget I am your friend too. You are always welcome at Eastease, Robert. Life in this area would be cheaper for you than London."

Robert gazed over at his friend. Harker was aware, of course, of the rift between himself and his father, but had the older man revealed why? "Yes, well—" Robert began, looking a little sheepish.

"Did you know your father has not been well lately?"

"I did not. Thank you for keeping an eye on him." It was just like Harker to care for his neighbours' health.

"I have not visited as much as I would have liked as I have been in Cambridgeshire with the Hopwoods recently. However, I did ask George Stockton at Redway if he could send someone to check on Mr. Davenport."

"I will go while I am visiting here," Robert assured him.

"I urge you to make things right between you before it is too late."

Robert nodded. *How old was Harker when his father died? Eighteen?* "I'm not sure if that is possible, my friend. I will go tomorrow if you allow me to stay the night here."

Alexander agreed, "You are welcome to stay until after the ball, but I need you to be on your best behaviour with five young ladies in the house as of tomorrow afternoon."

"Are the Hopwood daughters beautiful?" Robert asked, his eyes shining brightly.

"Yes. I want your best behaviour, Robert. Your word."

"All three?"

"Yes, all three," Harker did return his smile then.

"Better and better," Robert said, rubbing his hands together before holding them up in supplication to Harker's frown. "I know, I know, my best behaviour. You will have it, Harker, but at least allow me a little fun."

"Respectable fun," Robert's host confirmed, and at that, they both smiled.

~oOo~

"Finally!" Maria exclaimed under her breath when Alexander and Robert joined them in the drawing room. Harriet launched into the song they had agreed to play and sing upon the men's return. When they finished, both men, who had taken up seats at either end of a couch, stood and applauded.

"Our girls' playing and harmonious singing are unsurpassed by all attempts we hear in any house to which we are invited, Robert."

Mr. Davenport moved over to them, "I can believe it, Harker. These young ladies' talents are angelic. Let me see what other pieces you have here if I may be so bold as to make a request?"

Harriet giggled while Maria, who had stood to sing while Harriet played, encouraged him. "Of course, Mr. Davenport. We would be honoured to play something to your liking."

The man manoeuvred between them to look over Harriet's shoulder at the music while she turned pages and said little.

"What is your favourite piece, Miss Harriet?" Robert asked her sister gently, which caused Maria a brief sensation of misery.

Ungraciously, she wondered whether Harriet's reticence was a ploy to garner more of Mr. Davenport's attention. The less Harriet said, the more consideration Mr. Davenport paid to her, which, Maria thought, was often the case with her sister. It usually did not bother her overly, but she really liked him and wanted his attention to be on her. Harriet monopolised Luke Parker's attention when he visited. Wasn't one man enough for her sister?

Now Mr Davenport sat beside Harriet, turning the pages of the music himself. Maria leaned towards him, which afforded him an excellent view of her breasts. He looked up from them and into her face, so she gave him a pert expression that would tell him she knew exactly where his eyes roamed. She leaned further forward, addressing Harriet and pointing at a piece of music that perfectly suited her own voice.

"I love singing this piece. What do you think, Mr. Davenport?" Maria looked again into his eyes. He seemed to be swallowing hard.

"How can I refuse?" his voice came out with a rather strangled croak.

Harriet unceremoniously launched into the piece, causing Maria to straighten quickly and cast a glance at Alexander, who seemed distracted by his thoughts. She started singing and afforded a quick apologetic glance at Harriet, whose playing then took on a lighter touch that suited the piece better. Maria's heart sank a little. It had been mean of her to try and take Mr Davenport's attention away from Harriet by using such tactics. *What on earth possessed me?* she wondered, then she glanced at the man again, his beautiful eyes locking on to hers. In that instant, she knew, as only a young heart could, that if it wasn't love she was feeling, it was very close to it.

"I—I was wondering why Ackers is not here with you today, celebrating your birthday?" Mr. Davenport managed to stammer when the song had finished.

"His duties did not allow him to make it here today, but he will be here soon and in time for our ball," Maria defended her cousin quickly, excitement over seeing Nathaniel taking over her emotions for a moment. Harriet nodded her agreement.

Maria decided Harriet had enjoyed sitting next to their guest long enough. "Budge up, my turn to play," she said, bumping her hip into Mr Davenport, who in turn knocked Harriet off the other end of the stool, only just grabbing her arm in time to stop her falling to the floor. Maria chanced another glance at Alexander, surprised he had not curtailed Mr Davenport's flirting with them, but again Maria noticed Alexander's distraction. Given his embarrassment over her earlier question about which Hopwood daughter he liked best, she surmised Alexander was genuinely interested in one of the three. It should be an amusing pastime to find out which.

~oOo~

When Harriet's maid left her room that night, Maria crossed their adjoining sitting room and opened her sister's door. "Harriet?" she whispered. When there was no reply, she crept to her sister; the route in the dark was well known to her. How many nights had they shared a bed? Especially when they first moved to Eastease after their mother's death. Maria drew back the covers to get into the bed.

"Go away. I'm asleep."

Maria let out a snorting laugh as she clambered into the bed. "I wonder why I don't believe that?"

Harriet couldn't stay mad with her any more than she could with Harriet and let out a small laugh of her own.

"I'm sorry I was not nice to you tonight, Harriet." The apology came quickly. "No one is more important to me than you. Certainly no man. But Mr. Davenport is so wonderful. I think I might be a little in love with him already, and you have Luke Parker."

As Harriet turned, her eyes shone in the gloom to which Maria's had adjusted. "I am in love with him too, Maria. I don't want Luke Parker. I never have. No matter what he or his grandmother thinks of the matter. Mr. Davenport is so self-assured."

"I love Mr. Davenport's eyes. Those glints of green and amber seem to sparkle." Maria sighed.

"His hair is so thick and dark. I almost touched it once or twice tonight." Harriet put her hand to her mouth at the thought of doing something so inappropriate.

Maria giggled before adding sombrely, "His voice is like silk. It flows over me when he talks. I expect he will sing with Nathaniel tomorrow or at the ball."

Harriet smiled at that thought before her face turned more serious. "What should we do? We cannot decide for him who he should choose. That is if he likes either of us in that way."

"What if we make a pact?" Maria suggested.

"Like we used to do when we were younger?" Harriet nodded.

"We can each do our level best to make him fall in love with us," Maria began.

"No pretending to be each other." Harriet wagged a finger in front of Maria's face.

"I would never!" Maria protested, but at Harriet's stern look, she relented. "Not for something as important as this. No matter whom he falls in love with, the other will graciously concede so we can remain friends."

"The best of friends because we are sisters," Harriet confirmed, holding up a hand between them in the bed.

"The very best because we are twins," Maria finished, ceremoniously grasping Harriet's hand and kissing the back of it concurrently with Harriet upon hers.

Acknowledgements

I want to say an enormous thank you to some special people in my life:

Most importantly to my daughter, Emily. "Everything I do, I do it for you." It is fitting that I dedicate this book to you—my first book-baby, for my first real baby.

To my draft readers for your input, suggestions, encouragement and kind praise. Dorothy Beattie, Cheryl Duffy, Amy McCoy and my sister, Janine Westgate. You are incredible women, and I am lucky to know you.

To the fantastic author and editor Gretchen Jeannette. Thank you for all your help and inspiration, for pushing me to do better, and for bringing to life your own heroes, Niall, Ethan, and Dalton.

To Emily Wygod of Endeavor Therapeutic Horsemanship, Bedford, NY, for encouraging my girl's love of riding and checking my horse terms.

To Tracey Lusher-Chamberlain for butting in with your English degree when asked and helping me sort out my O Level mistakes. I will never tell you where to get off.

To my linguists, Maud Piquet, Jéssyca Santana, and Patricia Widmayer, for checking my French, Portuguese, and German translation, respectively.

To Barbara Baker, good friend and music therapist supreme. Thank you for asking after my book every week, listening patiently to me rambling about it, and forgiving me for not practising your music with my daughter.

To Adriana Tonello, thank you for the fabulous artwork on the front cover. "I think this is the beginning of a beautiful friendship."

A special thank you must go to Gordon Brooks, who reviewed some of my battle and fight scenes. His practical experience is so valuable, while mine is only from books, TV and movies.

To my Mum "Gal Junie" for *Eastease* and *Old Joe*, and for pointing me in the right direction in life, even if I didn't always follow it. See Old Joe and other songs and poems in my mum's book—'O'de June'. https://www.amazon.co.uk/Ode-June-Gal-Junie/dp/B0CPJ3P42T

To my Mother-in-law, Margaret Butler, thank you for listening to me talk endlessly about my book when you probably would have preferred to hear about your granddaughter.

To Luis Fernando Jiménez for suffering listening to my singing so he could set out the music for "Old Joe". When I was young, my mum wrote the song but never had it on music sheets.

To the extraordinary moms and mums I have met, many I call dear friends, whose courageousness in fighting for their children with disabilities has inspired me in my care of my own child. To all the excellent caregivers of children and adults with disabilities and special healthcare needs.

To women everywhere—I assure you that you all have a bit of Helena's spirit within you.

Thank you all.

Trish Henry~Green

I don't believe in God, but I believe in Good.
~ Gal Junie

Culture does not make people. People make culture. If it is true that the full humanity of women is not our culture, then we can and must make it our culture.
~ We Should All Be Feminists by Chimamanda Ngozi Adichie (2014)

Responsibility to yourself means refusing to let others do your thinking, talking, and naming for you; it means learning respect and use your own brains and instincts;
hence, grappling with hard work.
~ Adrienne Rich (1929-2012)

About the Author

Trish Henry Green is the author of the Historical Fiction saga Redway Acres (originally published under the name Trish Butler), set in the east of England. Also a contemporary detective series based in the fictional New Jersey town of Rockmond.

Born in Norwich, Norfolk, England, Trish moved to Connecticut in the USA in 1999. Her daughter was born there two years later and has an intellectual disability. In 2022, Trish returned to her home city of Norwich with her daughter and began using the penname of Trish Henry Green (previous titles published under 'Trish Butler' are being rereleased).

Redway Acres, which Trish calls Pride & Prejudice with horses and a healthy dollop of feminism, is set during the early 1800s in Lincolnshire, Cambridgeshire and Norfolk, UK, an area that she knows well. Over her twenty-plus years in Connecticut, Trish has gotten to know the tri-state area well, and hopefully, enough American English terms make her contemporary mystery book sound authentic.

Trish always wanted to write a book and finally realized that dream at the age of fifty. There are now six main books and one companion in the Redway series, and so far, one book of her Rockmond Mysteries has been published.

Read her blog about her process, The Road to Redway, the Redway Acres saga, Rockmond Mysteries, excerpts, poetry, and her characters on her website.

www.trishhenrygreen.com

Follow Trish
Twitter (X) @trishhenrygreen
Threads @trishhenrygreen
Instagram @trishhenrygreen
www.facebook.com/trishhenrygreen
https://www.facebook.com/groups/thereadingstable/

Redway Acres – Maria

Must a woman always be blamed for the mistake she made as an innocent sixteen-year-old girl?

Maria Wyndham is the younger, more vivacious twin sister of Harriet.

After their parents' deaths, she and her sister move to the grand estate of Eastease and become wards of its owner, Alexander Harker. and their cousin, Nathaniel Ackley.

Just in time for a ball for the twins' sixteenth Birthday, their guardians' friend, Robert Davenport, arrives to dance and lavish them with gifts. Captivated, Maria vies for his attention despite Harriet's interest in the man.

In this story of sisters, Maria's silliness and love of life often hide her intelligence and loyalty. As Maria's story unravels, it pushes the bonds of family and friendship to the limit. Finally, she finds the strength to survive and pursue her happiness.

Praise for Maria

"The twists and turns of this book easily captured my attention and made me feel even more deeply invested in the characters."

~

"Intrigue, heartbreak, characters you love and some you despise, fill this page-turner."

Redway Acres – Martha

How can a woman achieve love and success when an unseen enemy hounds her every move and men wish to claim her achievement as their own?

Martha Hopwood dreams of meeting a man who can make her feel as petite as her sisters, yet will encourage her determination to provide the best haberdashery shops in the country.

Mr Woodhead takes up residence at the nearby estate of Copperbeeches and pursues Martha at home and Eastease when her family visits there. His sudden departure from Eastease, when all were still asleep, prompts Martha to consider an independent future.

Martha pursues her ambition whilst recovering from heartbreak, overcoming disappointment and finally deciding what truly makes a man a gentleman.

In a time when a woman could not be married and independent, Martha Hopwood has to consider where her best future lies.

Praise for Martha

"Martha is definitely a woman ahead of her time!"

~

"Martha is a delightfully told story that unfolds at the perfect pace to reveal these beautifully crafted characters."

Redway Acres – Harriet

When being female limits a woman's desire to pursue her passion, Harriet must use everything at her disposal to prove herself as talented as a man.

As the last surviving Wyndham, Harriet inherits the enormous Wyndham estate on the outskirts of Bath in Somerset. After troubling times, Harriet can finally make a life for herself in her own home.

Navigating a tangled web of family history, Harriet runs Wyndham House with help from her uncle's long-time friend, Bertram Horncastle, and neighbour, Baroness Freyley.

Her passion for music comes to the fore, inspiring her to risk everything in its pursuit until she has to decide between fulfilling that passion and the man with whom she is in love.

Praise for Harriet

"This book clarifies that women, even in repressed English 1800s countryside settings, were remarkably intelligent and strong. Trish Henry-Green is much better and more inspiring for young women than Jane Austen!"

~

"The story unfolds beautifully as we experience the coming of age of a young woman
taking control of her life."

Redway Acres – Amelia

What a strength of mind an intelligent woman must possess to ignore detractors and follow her chosen profession.

Amelia Hopwood, encouraged in her love of books and discourse by her father, lives with Dowager Janine Alcott at Bernier House, home to injured soldiers and abused, destitute women.

Amelia aids the dowager in helping the women regain their self-respect and continues her education by learning all she can from Oliver Grosvenor, the doctor who tends to the occupants of Bernier.

In a time when a woman was not considered as intelligent as a man, Amelia proves herself worthy time and again. Her passion becomes her work, while those all around her, except one man, cannot understand her determination not to have a family of her own.

While she works through the twists and turns of her grief, can she make room in her heart and find love without losing the power to choose her own destiny?

Praise for Amelia

"In an age where women were allocated as possessions and lived in many ways via their husbands' choices/commands, Amelia defines her own life and fulfils her dreams as best she can within the confines of the era."

~

"She faces challenges with a level head, amazing courage & understanding."

Redway Acres – Emmalee

Can a woman weather the effects of an impossible choice and ensure the best outcome for everyone?

Emmalee lives with her controlling parents on the North Norfolk coast. In expectation of her marrying well, the family often travels to their London home for the social season. Emmalee has long believed in her destiny—an arranged marriage to David Ackley, the youngest son of the Earl of Aysthill. However, to Emmalee's horror, during their much-anticipated first meeting, she discovers that David desires someone else.

Despite a cloud of controversy, the couple find themselves forced into a marriage of convenience, and David's reaction to his perceived misfortune results in far-reaching consequences for his family and friends.

A pregnancy, an accident, and an unexpected death thrust Emmalee into the demanding role of Countess of Aysthill, to which she rises with a dauntless spirit. Emmalee dotes on her two sons, William and Nathaniel, who invoke differing affections from their father.

Emmalee continues to hope that time will heal the breach her marriage suffered even before she spoke her vows. But just as the wound finally begins to mend, a ghost from the past returns.

Praise for Emmalee

"Reading this book has got me re-reading & thoroughly enjoying all the first five books!"

~

"In Emmalee, we meet a heroine as resilient as she is spirited, who endures despite the trials and responsibilities laid at her feet."

A Redway Companion – Charlie

A man's worth is measured not only in his strength but also in overcoming brutality to be empathetic, selfless, and loving.

Young Charlie Mickleson from Colbourne near the Welsh border is indentured to farrier Doyle Brewster, but all is not as it should be in Charlie's world. Brewster and Justice Leland Cavell, who recruited Charlie, subject him to abuse, leading an adolescent Charlie to run away.

To escape Cavell's pursuit, Charlie finds employment in the stable at Thornbane Lodge in Cambridgeshire, working for the well-connected Hopwood family. In the course of his duties, Charlie meets Harriet Wyndham at Redway Acres, who offers him the job of stable manager at the larger Wyndham Estate near Bath. A grateful Charlie accepts, though his choice will bring him closer to home and the clutches of the one man he hopes never to see again.

Will Charlie evade Cavell's devious plans, or will his desire to seek justice cause him to lose everything?

Praise for Charlie

"An amazing book that I couldn't put down."

~

"A tale that Dickens or Trollope could have written."

Rockmond Mysteries

Ctrl+Alt+Deleted

Can love survive a painful separation and the discovery of secrets never meant to be uncovered?

Charlotte McBain, the tech consultant for Rockmond PD's missing person team, has disappeared.

She went missing after her boyfriend, Mateo Jaso, one of the team's detectives, left their bed in the middle of the night to console a friend whose worthless husband had left her again.

Sean Benson, who heads the investigation into Charlotte's disappearance, must explore the history of Matt's alcoholism, the unusual, straight-talking Charlotte, and their passionate and sensual relationship, leaving no stone unturned in his effort to find his teammate.

No one is above suspicion—ex-lovers, estranged family members, and those who disapprove of their interracial relationship. So, who has the most to gain by separating Charlotte from Matt?

Will they find Charlotte, and if so, will the incident and the secrets uncovered forever affect her relationship with Matt?

Find out in this character-driven, missing-person mystery.

Praise for Ctrl+Alt+Deleted

"A very clear, easy-to-follow story that kept a thrilling pace all the way to the end."

~

"Great book. Had me guessing the whole time."

Printed in Great Britain
by Amazon